VAE VICTIS

BOOK 3

VAE VICTIS

BOOK 3

Ivan Kal

Podium

This is a work of fiction. Names, characters, places, and incidents are either products of the author's imagination or used fictitiously. Any resemblance to actual events, locales, or persons, living, dead, or undead, is entirely coincidental.

Cover design by Kaion Luong

ISBN: 978-1-0394-5550-4

Published in 2025 by Podium Publishing
www.podiumentertainment.com

Podium

VAE
VICTIS

BOOK 3

Difficulties

"Goddammit!"

I ducked to avoid the screeching birdlike creature that dived at me and attempted to claw my head off my shoulders.

"Language!" Khalil yelled as he batted one of the birds away with his shield.

"Fuck you! I'm a vampire. God already hates me," I shot back as I whirled my serpent-tongue spear above my head, cutting two of the birds down.

The twins, Jiyun and Daehyun, stood back to back, holding their swords high and protecting each other. Seeing that they and Khalil were fine, I turned my attention to the shrinking form of the screaming Aurora in the distance as she was being carried away by one of the damn birds.

"I'm going after her," I yelled, hoping that the others heard me and would keep themselves safe. I could move faster on my own.

I dashed forward then focused all my attention on the form in the distance. With a flex of my will, I triggered [Overburn Skill—Track]. The sense of direction blossomed inside of my chest, pointing at Aurora.

I wasn't happy that I had to burn the skill, since I didn't have many utility skills on my shelf, but I didn't have the time to swap my skills right now, nor did I want to use my [Quick Swap Slot] in case I needed it later. For all the power that my Mask gave me, I had quite a few limitations, one of which was only being able to hold three of my blood-gained skills active at a time—well, six if I used [Swap Profile].

I dropped my serpent-tongue spear on the ground. It was too heavy and cumbersome for me to carry and run at the same time.

"Saia!" I yelled at the small dragon who was battling the birds in the air. "Keep them off me." Without checking whether she responded, I ran to the cliff's side then jumped and grabbed a ledge.

My nails, like claws, bit into the stone and allowed me a better grip. Even though it was daylight out, whatever was casting the light in this place wasn't a real sun, which meant that I didn't lose any of the advantages my vampire nature gave me. Though, at this point I had grown strong enough that I didn't even know how much sunlight would weaken me anymore.

My vampire nature had progressed into the realm of an Elder vampire. Something that shouldn't have been possible, except apparently it was, and almost no one else knew how vampires actually aged. I had been turned by a second-generation vampire. My sire was the firstborn son of the originator of my vampire bloodline. And apparently, the closer a vampire is to the original, the faster they grow—who knew.

That made me only two generations removed from an original, which accelerated my growth significantly. There was a lot I was still unsure of about my sire's revelations, but I was glad for this part.

With my first profile being active, I had [Lesser Strength], which boosted my already significant physical strength. I tore up the cliff at a speed that few things would be able to match.

I knew that I had to be quick. The bird had taken Aurora somewhere up ahead, probably to a nest, and I didn't want to think about what could be waiting up there.

The birds were the size of ponies, and looked reptilian, like dinosaurs covered in thick feathers.

I glanced back, to the clearing where the others were still fighting, and saw that a dozen birds were still there, fighting. I hoped that most of them had gone on the attack, and that I wasn't about to jump into a nest filled with twice that number.

I reached the top of a cliff, and pulled myself up over the top, then pulled out one of my daggers with my left hand and my revolver with my right. I scanned the nest, locating Aurora immediately. She was struggling with the large bird who had taken her. Broken spikes of stone pierced through the twig nest beneath her to spear through two baby birds. The mother bird was obviously pissed off as it tried to peck Aurora to death while avoiding her knife swings.

More baby birds were tottering toward Aurora, snapping at her with their sharp beaks and trying to eat her. I raised my gun, lined up a shot, then fired. A single bullet pierced the mother bird's head and blew its brains out. I holstered the gun, not wanting to waste any more ammo, and then jumped forward. I cut through the baby birds while Aurora moved back and slumped against a rock.

Once I was done with my bloody work, I stepped up to her. She was breathing heavily and holding her knife in a trembling hand. She was covered in cuts and claw marks on her forearms. Her long, padded jacket had protected most of her body from the attacks, leaving only her shins and lower arms unprotected, but it had been pierced on her shoulders where the mother bird had caught her when it picked her up.

"You okay?" I asked as I pulled off my backpack and pulled out my water flask.

Aurora blinked at me, obviously in shock. "I—I'm fine. Just peachy."

I didn't believe her. Aurora was the weakest of our group, though only because her Mask didn't lend itself well to the environments we found ourselves in more often. Her Mask allowed her to sense and shape stone, and it had some limited ability to shake the earth. It wasn't something that she could use when picked up by a bird. She was lucky that the nest had been built on top of a rocky cliff.

I grabbed her arm and started pouring water over her forearm, cleaning her wound. The scent of blood made the **thirst** ache inside of me, but I had more than enough control over it by now, and I easily pushed it aside.

"I'm fine, Marianna," Aurora complained as I fussed over her. She was a human, and therefore she was fragile.

"We need to get you to Khalil. He can purify your wounds and make sure they don't get infected."

"Mari," she said again, making me raise my head and meet her eyes.

I didn't let up, I kept working as I held her gaze. "Why didn't you use your knife before?"

She winced at that, but then she pouted and looked back at me defiantly. "I'm not a vampire, Marianna, I can't survive a drop from those heights."

I narrowed my eyes but didn't respond—she got me there. I've forgotten what it was like being human. If she had knifed the bird while in the air, she would've splattered against the ground.

I sighed. "You need to be more careful; you've gotten too used to being able to sense everything coming."

One of Aurora's new skills let her sense vibrations more clearly through earth and stone. It had been an invaluable skill for their group, but, as they had just learned, it didn't do shit to detect monsters flying through the air.

"Why didn't you detect them?" she asked. It wasn't an accusation. Aurora wasn't the kind of a person to do that; she was just genuinely curious.

I grimaced. "They were upwind, so I didn't smell them, and the howling gale around the mountain masked their approach."

That was my mistake. I, too, had gotten used to always being able to tell that danger was near. Between Aurora's skills and my innate senses, we had never run into something without knowing that it was there.

A rustle behind us made me whirl around, my hand going for my weapons, but I relaxed once I saw that it was just Saia.

"Is everyone else alright?" I asked.

"Feedback: All the foes are dead; there are no critical injuries."

I took a deep breath, then looked back at Aurora. "Let me get some blood, then we'll make our way back down."

Aurora at least gave me the courtesy of trying not to look disgusted. I turned and started gathering the dead birds. Maybe some of them would give me good skills.

We made camp at the base of the mountain. With the bird nest taken care of, there wasn't anything else around that could threaten us.

Khalil knelt next to Aurora, who sat next to their fire, and used his skills to treat her wounds. He had his [Lesser Blessing of Purification] to ensure that there would be no infection, then he used his newest skill [Lesser Cure Wound]. It wasn't a skill he had gained from his Mask, but rather his Ornament, which was **Medic**. He had picked it up back home as Constantinople was constantly in need of people to care for the wounded.

Having a city filled with rifts would probably do that.

The skill could barely heal scratches, but it did help somewhat. They were lucky that he had gotten that skill a few days ago, while helping care for Daehyun's wounds from their previous battle.

I tried not to look at the rest of her group, as I felt a bit guilty. They had been fighting and surviving this place for sixteen days, and all of them carried injuries and evidence of their struggles. I, on the other hand, was the picture of perfect health, and any injury I suffered was healed in seconds.

"That was something," Jiyun said as she walked over and sat down next to me.

"It was." I nodded. "We made a mistake, got too comfortable."

Jiyun inclined her head. "We won't make the same mistake again."

I managed to push back my retort. The only reason Aurora wasn't dead was because I was a vampire and was able to follow the bird that had carried her away fast enough to save her.

I glanced up at the sky, looking at the glowing ranking list that was displayed above. Earth—or Terra as the Grand Spell was calling it—was losing. It wasn't by much, a million points, which on the scale of what they were doing was only a dozen or so trials. But, there were a lot fewer Terrans still in the challenge. One hundred had been reduced to just over forty, while the Suul—the other race, from the second world—still had around sixty still alive.

My sire and I had made a big dent in the Suul challenger numbers by killing over twenty of them, but it didn't seem to faze them. The individual rankings had also changed in the last few days. The points my sire and I got from killing the Suul had pushed us to the top, as we had been granted all the points that they had previously. But the others had caught up, dropping us to the fourth and sixth place, respectively. The individual list also told the story of two different philosophies. Terran challengers were clearly pursuing individual power, as most of us held the top twenty list. The Suul had their points distributed among all of their people, and if the past was anything to go by, they worked in larger groups.

Once again, I was annoyed at the fact that people just couldn't see beyond their own personal gain.

"Thinking about leaving us behind?" Jiyun asked, her tone joking. I turned and looked at her, seeing that there was some truth in her question too.

"No, of course not."

"You could've done a lot better without us slowing you down." She looked back at the others. Her brother Daehyun, Khalil, and Aurora were on the other side of the fire, just far enough that they couldn't hear her whispered tone.

"I would never do that," I told her. Yes, she was right, they were slowing me down. But there was safety in numbers, strength too. We'd encountered several situations that would've been difficult for me alone, and while the others weren't vampires, their Masks did give them powerful skills. They weren't weak, not at all.

"We are only going to keep falling behind," Jiyun said, her head turned to the sky to look at the lists.

"I could try to scout more. I don't need sleep, and with Saia I can cover twice as much ground. We could try to focus on the trials. They give more points and better rewards."

Jiyun grimaced. "Yeah, but they also pit us against other people."

That was one of the issues with trials—there was a very real chance that any trial would put us in a position to fight against other people, Suul or Terran.

"Ultimately," I started. "They all made their choices, just as we made ours. We are here to gain power, to become stronger in order to help our people back home. I've . . . I think that today was a wake-up call. Aurora could've died; the rest of you could've died. We need to make a jump ahead. None of you have reached the Second Investment, and I think that you need to before this challenge comes to an end."

Jiyun met my eyes, her expression turning determined as she stood. "You're right. Let's talk with the others. We need to change up our tactics."

I took a deep breath, then followed her to the others.

Moving Forward

Jiyun's thoughts that the group was slowing me down were true. And my reasoning for staying was true too—there was safety in numbers. And yet, there was a different reason I wouldn't leave them: obligation and debts. The sacrifice I had chosen to give, to promise, to the Way, the world itself, for my school of being. The Heart of Azure and Scarlet was my guiding star now, and I had an obligation to my team.

They alone had remained with me when we first arrived in this challenge, when many others had turned away. They had put their trust in a vampire, a dangerous thing, without knowing me before.

That deserved a consideration on my part. But there were still things that we could do to improve and get more out of this challenge.

The conversation about what we were going to do went better than I had expected. It seemed that I had underestimated my new friends. In my defense, I've often been disappointed by others, and trust does not come easily to me.

"Then it's decided," Khalil Abd al-Nur said. He was my old friend from another life, from back before I was turned. It still surprised me to see just how much he had changed from the cheerful and pious man I had met at university. Though, perhaps, I simply didn't know him that well back then. It was hard to tell. We both had kept secrets from one another. He was a Knight Priest of the Order of the Dragon, a member of one of the oldest and most powerful organizations in the world, the Knights of Constantinople, vampire hunters. It was his job to hunt my kind, which made our relationship complicated.

We were close once, friends definitely, perhaps would've been something more, but life had separated us. I was recalled to the cartel, and then turned. We had no contact between us for years until the world ended. Now, here we were, on a halo that served as a battleground for a challenge issued by an intelligent spell with the power of a god. Life was crazier than fiction it seemed.

"Good," I added, looking over the rest of the group. The Korean twins, Kim Jiyun and Daehyun, sat next to Khalil—the two had proven to be capable fighters and good friends, or at least something close to that. On the other side of them, Aurora was snuggling up to Saia, with my now much larger cute-dragon-nightmare-nano-goo-murder-machine attempting to extricate herself from Aurora's embrace.

"I'll take up first watch, and Saia and I'll leave to search for trials once Daehyun takes over," I said as I turned back to Khalil.

He nodded. "I don't need to tell you to be careful, but please, try not to get pulled into any dangerous situations. If you encounter others, it would be best to avoid them altogether."

I inclined my head in agreement. I had no desire to fight other challengers. My name was near the top of the points list, displayed to everyone up above us, which gave me a sinking feeling that some might try to force the issue. Greed was a powerful emotion, and everyone here wanted power. I hoped that the fact that I was a vampire and probably one of the most powerful challengers in here might deter them, but I had lost faith in the intelligence of other people the moment I saw them separate and decide to work for themselves instead of together.

Khalil held my eyes for a long moment, then seemingly satisfied that I would listen to his words, he turned and started getting ready for sleep, the others following along.

I didn't know what the two of us were now. The last few weeks spent fighting and surviving together had done a lot to bridge the chasm that the years had carved in between us. Though, there were still things that stood in the middle, more secrets. I was a vampire; he was a vampire hunter. If that was all, we might've been able to get over it. Except, every time I looked at him, I was reminded of my sire's words and revelation. The Knights of Constantinople had attacked and sunk a ship carrying one of the original vampires, my . . . *Grandsire? Grandmother? It is so strange to think of the fact that I was only one removed from one of the originators of the vampire race . . .*

The attack by the knights had inadvertently caused the sinking of Japan, the death of millions. How did I even start that conversation? *"Hey Khalil, so, it turns out I'm actually a third-generation vampire, and my sire's sire is one of the three original vampires."*

I couldn't even imagine having that talk. Since then, every time I talked with him, I felt this thing between us, secrets. And he had noticed, though neither one of us was drawing any attention to it.

It was even more difficult to explain when my eyes were now completely emerald, the mark of an Elder vampire. I had led them to believe that it was a side effect of my Mask's growth. I had reached the Second Investment at the same time my eyes had changed; it was a plausible explanation. Now I knew that my growth would be far faster than what everyone knew about vampires.

My growth was linked to my heritage, and the quality of blood I consumed. And I was almost completely certain that the amount of Investment a being had made the blood richer. I didn't know if my sire had made that link yet, but I had spent a month on Ish Vimza, drinking blood from beasts that were in their Third or higher Investment. I could feel the difference in the blood.

A part of me was terrified of my growth, but another was excited, as I had seen the final destination that awaited me. My sire's obsidian feathered wings were always at the forefront of my mind. I imagined what it must feel like to have that much freedom, to be able to fly away anywhere one wanted.

I pushed all those thoughts aside as I focused on the task at hand, keeping watch, or rather taking care of some things that I didn't have the time to do before. Like dealing with my skills and talking with Shadow.

Saia trotted over to me and settled next to me on her haunches. She was growing just as fast as I was. She was now the size of a large dog, perhaps a greyhound, where before she was the size of a chihuahua. Her growth was fueled by the constant fighting we encountered, though most of it came from the Suul that my sire and I killed. I allowed her to consume everything, and I was starting to get a bit worried about the future. I knew that she was created to serve as a combat platform and personal armor for Ke Erzi, who basically looked like dragons from Earth's stories.

And from what I remembered encountering in my first rift where I found her, the remnant of the Ke Erzi homeworld, the dragons were the size of a school bus at least.

But she was approaching the size where she would be able to cover me completely in armor, though there was little need for that now. There were few things that could actually damage me enough to outright kill me. Having Saia as an independent drone, flying around and helping with both combat and scouting, was much more effective.

"You getting any closer to finishing the engram?" I asked as she settled in next to me. Saia had been built with hundreds of support, defensive, and offensive engrams—which were basically magic and technology combined systems. Most of those no longer functioned in the way that they were designed to as the result of the Grand Spell subsuming her reality into Kirios. The rules of magic had changed.

But Saia had started to slowly put those engrams back together, repairing them or altering them enough so that they could function again. So far, she'd been focusing on the ones that were more likely to work, and she was close to getting at least one of her engrams to work—[Manufacturing]. I was looking forward to that. Even though it wouldn't allow her to build anything that was magical, that contained Source-Weave components, mundane items would be within her capabilities. And seeing as one of my biggest issues right now was ammo, or rather the lack of it as I was down to my last four rounds, I was looking forward to turning the tiny dragon into my own personal ammo factory.

"Feedback: I'm getting close," Saia responded, her manner of speaking betraying her personal interest in the topic. She tended to refer to herself as *this Unit* when she talked about things that she didn't particularly care about.

"What does close mean exactly?" I asked.

"Feedback: Weeks."

I grimaced. That meant after the challenge was over. I sighed. Again I lamented my wasteful use of ammunition, but there wasn't anything that I could do about it.

"Can you show me my full Mask details, please?" I asked. One of the engrams that she possessed was [Mask Reader], gained when Shadow had gifted her an enchanted item called the Reader that could read and present the information about a person's Mask. I'd asked Saia to change the name to just [Inspect].

Saia didn't respond verbally, but she displayed my information over my vision, and I took a long look at it.

Marianna Rojas (The Star That Dances In Blood Beneath the Light of the Broken Moon)

Mask of the Blood Reaver (Physical, Weave, Esoteric) — Second Investment; First Carving
Ornament of the Revelator (Weave, Esoteric) — No Investment; Eighth Carving
Ornament of the Practical Student (Physical, Weave, Esoteric) — First Investment; No Carving

Attributes:
Physical: B
Weave: F
Esoteric: C

Skills:
P1-Beast Bonus
[Mist Step]
[Lesser Strength]
[Lesser Constitution]

P2-Beast Bonus
[Debilitating Wave]
[Sonic Screech]
[Dodge]

[Swap Profile]
[Overburn Skill]
[Blood Gout]
[Quick Swap Slot]

[One Truth Verified]

[A Lesson Remembered]
[Practical Learning]

|Potential Augmentation| trait

Wearing the Mask of the Blood Reaver grants a significant increase to all attributes. All cooldowns are greatly reduced. After the Mask is removed, all used skills are put on long cooldown.

Slotting skills of the same type grants bonuses.
Current bonuses available:

Beast: Slotting in skills that all contain <beast> type increases their effectiveness and reduces cooldowns. All physical senses are heightened.

Movement: Slotting in skills that all contain <movement> type increases their effectiveness and reduces cooldowns. Air resistance of your body is reduced.

Combat: Slotting in skills that contain <offensive>, <defensive>, or <martial> type increases their effectiveness and grant you an escalating damage bonus for every target killed in a short period of time.

The information was extensive, though the actual [Inspect] engram didn't provide all of that information, but Saia had displayed everything that I would think relevant as she had access to that information.

I'd gained another Carving since my fight with the Suul, but I'd gained no skill. Not that I expected one. Getting more than two or three skills per Investment tier was incredibly rare. My two newest skills were incredibly powerful.

[Blood Gout] allowed me to siphon blood from any source near me. It served to help me both feed and heal during battle while also weakening my foes. I imagine having one's wounds suddenly start drain of blood was not a good feeling.

[Quick Swap Slot] allowed me to switch any skill on my shelf with one that was already slotted in my [Empty Skill], allowing me to bypass the cooldown time that was required when changing skills. Useful, especially when I needed something in a pinch, and I didn't want to waste the skill by using my [Over-burn Skill], which consumed the skill from my shelf in the process.

My last boon was the improvement of my trait, and the **combat** type bonus. I hadn't had the time to experiment with that, but now was a good time for it, and I had some skills that had the tags required. Plus, I wanted to collect on the skills from the Suul. I had killed many in battle, but I had also drained blood from all the others that my sire killed. If my understanding of how my Mask worked was correct, the skills I gained drinking from those I didn't kill would be their weaker skills, and those from the ones I drained while personally killing would be their strongest.

I still didn't have quite enough data to be absolutely certain about how it worked, but this would be a good opportunity. I should have around twenty new skills waiting for me from the Suul alone, not counting the beasts I fought and killed since then.

Sometimes, I couldn't help but think how broken my Mask seemed to be. Though there were many limitations, having to drink blood to gain Investment seemed perfect for a vampire. But eventually I might hit a plateau, and I didn't know how I felt about always looking for more powerful blood to drink. If people figured out how it worked, it might give them ideas about stopping me before I turned into a blood-crazed lunatic. The way I had to gain the skills was annoying sometimes too. Having to defeat the source of the blood I drained within my soul, or pass a test in cases where the blood was freely given, was an additional hurdle.

I understood the reasoning though. If I didn't need to do any of that, it would almost seem too easy to gain new skills by conning someone powerful into giving me blood, assassinating someone, or even just procuring blood after their death.

There was a lot of thought behind the Masks and how they worked.

Not for the first time, I wondered what exactly the Grand Spell was doing and why. Was it even thinking things through, or was all of this just instinct, or some ancient set of instructions given by its creator?

By now, it was obvious to me that the Grand Spell was learning and changing. Some of the things that Shadow, the powerful Tsu-gi and my adoptive family member, had taught me on Ish Vimza were no longer correct.

There had been no challenges in the previous Expansion Intervals, where the Grand Spell had added other worlds to its own. Nor had it ever added more than one world during an interval, and this time there were two.

It was obvious to me that the Grand Spell had learned from Earth. Challenges and rifts were both something new, and they had a great resemblance to things present in the fiction and entertainment found on Earth. That suggested something more than a mindless intelligence, that most people of Kirios considered to be their god. Though, I knew better. I knew the truth, the reason why, and who had created it.

The message in a bottle I'd found in the ruins on Ish Vimza, made by the original people of Kirios, had made it clear that the Grand Spell was made to protect the world from a threat that they had encountered. I knew that the blight, the red haze and whispers that I had encountered before, were somehow linked to it, even if I didn't know exactly how.

I turned my thoughts back to the matter at hand.

"Can you keep watch over everyone for a while?" I asked Saia. "I want to go and speak with Shadow, change up my skills for tomorrow."

"Feedback: Of course, Mari."

I smiled and then focused inward. A moment later I was in my soul space.

Skill Farm

I manifested within my soul space, a large wooden room reminiscent of the Japanese-style hut that my sire used to live in. The walls held shelves with stone bowls placed on top of them, many of which also held glowing orbs that signified a skill. Simple plaques hung below each occupied bowl that described the skill that they held. There had been some changes in my soul space. Mainly, the ceiling had risen and a second level had appeared, more empty shelves had appeared on the walls above, and there was an entire floor that went around the walls with a gap in the middle that allowed me to see up. To the side there was a ladder that led up.

I turned my attention to the floor I was currently on, looking for any more changes.

In the center of the room were three pedestals. The center one held my Mask, while the other two were empty and signified my Ornaments that were incorporated into my Mask.

I approached and took a closer look. My Mask had changed again. The style was Mesoamerican, and it was made out of obsidian and jade, with gold speckled through it.

The Mask was obviously a monstrous depiction of a vampire, though as it changed it had become cleaner, predatory rather than just monstrous. The lower face resembled an Oni mask, and had teeth carved into the material, with long incisors. Two horns of polished obsidian stood on top of it, with gold lines and elaborate carved markings. Two more horns were placed lower and more to the side of the Mask. Golden and jade Ornaments were attached to those two horns, the actual Ornaments of my Mask, and they, too, had changed. They looked more like earrings now, but with detailed etchings pressed into them.

My Student Ornament had advanced to the First Investment, and was now the Ornament of the Practical Student, though I hadn't advanced it since then. There was little opportunity for me to progress it further, as the Investment it required was learning—well, practical learning now probably. I hoped that I would have the chance to gain some Investment for it now.

Behind the three pedestals stood another seven, my six [Empty Slot] skills, three on either side and separated by the seventh, the [Swap Profile] skill. There were more pedestals on the other three walls around me, pedestals holding my other skills just below the shelves. Though, I could see that one skill was missing.

I had a suspicion and walked over to the ladder and climbed to the next floor. I found my [Quick Swap Slot] skill up there against one of the walls. It made sense, given that it was my Second Investment skill.

The floor above was simple, the same as the bottom, only with the hole in the middle that allowed me to see down. I jumped over the railing and back down.

Then, I turned and headed for the corridor that led to my Hallway of Doors. The familiar doors welcomed me, though a few were missing, the ones whose skills I had used with [Overburn Skill]. The skill wording did suggest that I would be able to get that skill back if I found another source of it.

Either way, I continued down the corridor, pausing for a moment in front of Shadow's door. The elaborate wooden carving of a mountain rising from the mist and a giant tree growing over it greeted me. Shadow, or at least a copy of him made by the Grand Spell, was a guest in my soul space, and he could leave his room—probably because he was far more powerful than me, or as he had once postulated, because of my trust in him. I didn't know if any other powerful being would be able to do the same, which worried me. I had two doors that held powerful monsters within, the reaper and the sikiri that I had encountered on Ish Vimza. Both of which I had yet to test myself against.

The reaper was a Sixth Investment beast, and had been killed by Shadow. I've gotten its blood afterward from its corpse, and I wasn't sure if I would be able to kill it. It had nearly killed Shadow. And a fight in my soul space was a lot different than real life. For example, Shadow and I had killed the sikiri together by baiting it into a trap. I wouldn't be able to do the same here. Fights in my soul space were a more straightforward matter.

I wondered why Shadow hadn't left his room. He had to have noticed that I was here. I didn't dwell on it though. Even if he was a copy, he deserved some consideration. I didn't enter his room, though he was the person I had come to see. Instead, I continued down the corridor. I could see another change ahead.

After another dozen or so doors, the corridor split into two, one heading right and one left. I glanced both ways, and saw that only the right side held doors for now, so I walked down it. There were another three dozen doors here filling the corridor up for a few dozen meters until it ended in a corner that turned to the right. I walked down the empty corridor until it wrapped back to the original split. My Hallway of Doors was now a square loop. I wondered how it would change once I filled it with doors.

With my exploration finished, I decided to enter a few doors and collect new skills. I stepped in front of a simple door with a talon mark on it and with an effort of will manifested my weapons. It rose from the floor beneath me, along with my revolver. My soul space replicated any equipment that I carried on my person. That also meant that my revolver had only four rounds, the same as I had in the real world. The ammo would reset once I left the soul space.

Most of the doors were occupied by beasts that were easy for me to deal with, ones that we'd encountered in the wild or the rifts we finished.

I entered the first one and was met by one of the birdlike creatures that we had just fought. It was flying above me in lazy circles, and moved to swoop down and attack as soon as it noticed me. I waited for it to come close, then stepped to the side and swung my serpent-tongue spear, splitting it down the middle.

The two parts dissolved and left behind the glowing orb that was the skill. I picked it up and carried it over to one of my shelves and put the skill in.

> **[Dive]**
>
> Dive down from the sky executing a powerful attack.
> <beast><physical><movement><offense>

It was a simple skill, though I wondered how it would work for me as I had no wings, not yet at least. Perhaps it only required me to be airborne. I would have to test it out, but I didn't think that the skill was worthy enough to be put into one of my profiles. Which meant that it was destined to be used with my [Overburn Skill] if I ever had the need.

I returned back to the corridor, looking for the next target. There were no more doors for the bird monsters, despite me drinking blood from several different birds. That meant that all of them had the same skill, and I couldn't have copies. Perhaps if I lost the skill and I drank the blood that contained the skill I lost, I might be able to get it again, but I just didn't have the time to test that out.

I went through another few doors containing various beasts, getting a few more skills, none of which were anything special. I looked them over on the shelves:

[Lesser Charge], [Lesser Tough Skin], [Lesser Stab], [Lesser Screech], [Lesser Stalk].

All of them went into what I called my *burn* category, handy as one-use skills, but nothing more than that. Now, I was left with the doors that I held more hope for. I drank the blood of twenty Suul, and each of those had at least a few Carvings. The two of their greater form Suul were probably at least in their First Investment. I was missing some doors, which told me that a few of the Suul probably held the same skills, but I was still hoping to gain some powerful new tools.

I entered the first door, picking one of the less ornamental ones that I knew indicated the weaker of them. The Suul stood in front of me on top of a small plateau where I had fought and killed him before, during the Trial of the Summit.

The Suul were a reptilian, or perhaps avian-looking, race. My foe was tall, towering over me by a full head, standing proud at three meters in height despite being hunched over. His legs were thick and muscled, ending in three toes with curved talons. He walked on digitigrade legs, and had a long, muscular tail stretching behind him.

His skin was gray, but the edges of his body were covered in brown and yellowish scales, small in some parts like the torso and inner areas of his body. But there were also larger platelike scales that covered his shoulders, more like those of a crocodile.

A thin and narrow waist held up a wide torso with long, leanly muscled arms.

His long neck had dewlaps from the torso up to the jaw, with barbs sticking out the bottom edge. He had a flat elongated snout, with two nostrils that stood above sharp teeth that had no lips covering them. The snout seemed to be covered by thin skin, but that receded to bone along the jaw. The teeth looked like they protruded off a single piece rather than being individual teeth.

He had hornlike spikes growing from the top of his head, sticking backward and parallel to the ground. I remembered that the other Suul had a different number of spikes, but this one had four, two on each side.

His body was covered in paint: His chest had painted swirl patterns, and his thighs had yellow painted lines that curled in curious waves around his legs.

His eyes were circled by dark paint that made them stand out, their predatory glint clear, even in this place.

His clothes were slim, and the fabric pulled around his body like a wrap. Around his neck hung a strand of twined rope, adorned with colored stones. He had piercings all over his body, most of them bone, though some stone or metal.

His weapon was the type that most Suul seemed to prefer: a long and thin spearlike weapon that had crescent-shaped spurs sticking out from about one fourth way to the top, which could serve like hooks or spikes when the weapon was swung from side.

I had inspected the weapons after the fight, when I had the chance. They seemed to be made of some kind of incredibly tough wood, that I had verified was as strong as steel. I could break the weapons with my strength, but I was a vampire that could tear a person in half easily enough.

I approached the Suul with my weapon raised high, my elbows parallel with the ground and the tip of my serpent-tongue spear pointed at the sky. I settled into the Azure Moon Style's **Stalwart Mist**, the first Kata: *In the Mist, Await*. With bent knees and stable stance, I waited as the Suul charged.

It was a copy, one without any apparent intelligence, capable only of fighting. Only those whose blood was freely given seemed to retain something of themselves in here. That didn't mean that my foe wasn't dangerous—it held all the combat capability it held in life.

It just didn't matter. The Suul dashed in and stabbed forward, stabbing me through the heart. For most, that would've been a killing blow, but as a vampire, my heart didn't beat nearly as often, and the wound wasn't even enough to tickle me.

My weapon was a cross between a sword and a spear, as tall as I was, with one third of its length being the handle and the rest a long, sinuous blade as wide as my palm.

The **Stalwart Mist** technique was built on the principles of retaliation, on using my fear and instinct to react. Shadow's style was built on illusions of thick mist, of tricking an opponent to attack a mist clone then retaliating with a savage attack.

I had no illusions or mastery over the mists; instead I relied on my superior regeneration. The core principle of my style remained the same as that of Shadow's. Wait for the opponent to commit, then retaliate.

The moment the Suul went all in on his attack, the moment he trapped his weapon in my chest, I responded. My weapon came down from above my head, cleaving the air in a whistle as it carved through the Suul's head and split him from the top, down to the waist.

The Suul died, and the skill remained.

The wound in my chest healed in barely a second, and I left to deposit the skill in an empty bowl. The skill I gained was [Dash], which told me that the Suul I just defeated was probably one whose blood I drank after it had died. It was likely one of his lesser skills. I turned back to the corridor and started making my way through the doors. None of the Suul posed much of a challenge. They were a threat when in a group, but individually they couldn't match my advantages. A few of them had fought with different tactics, some even using the acid that they were able to spit out, but ultimately, I didn't have any issues with them.

Most of the skills I gained were lesser or not that useful, but I did get two stronger ones, probably from the Suul that I had drained in the fighting. The skills [Triple Thrust] and [Crescent Swipe] were both combat related and from their descriptions looked strong. I put them on my list of combat-tagged skills. I planned on making one of my profiles activate that trait, as it gave me some bonuses that I wanted to test out.

Next, I entered the room that was occupied by one of the greater Suul, one from their leader caste, of which I had encountered two. These were a lot stronger than the regular ones, taller and with darker gray skin and black scales. From my conversation with them, I assumed them to be religious leaders of some kind.

I also knew that they were as strong as an Adult vampire, at least, though I didn't know if my new status as an Elder vampire would impact our strength difference any. I had my [Lesser Strength] active, which did scale my physical strength and made me even stronger.

Either way, I knew that they would be a challenge, and I didn't want to risk it too much.

"Saia," I called, and the dragon manifested inside my soul space. The physical form she had in the real world wasn't really her. It was just a drone that she controlled from within my body. The actual Saia was bonded to my nervous system and my body in general. She lived inside of me, and this place considered her a part of me.

"Query: Yes, Mari?"

"I'm about to fight one of those big Suul. Can you give me some help?"

Saia immediately flowed over my body, her mass now great enough that she could cover parts of me in armor. We hadn't had much need to use it outside, but we had tried it. She covered my arms over my elbow and up to my mid upper arm, then my legs up to my thighs and then around my neck like a gorget and up to cover my jaw over my mouth.

Those were the areas that I considered the most important to cover: my limb joints and my neck. As a vampire, the only thing that could really impact my combat ability was an injury that needed longer to heal, like the joint bones, and losing my head—which was the reason for the placement of armor. A hit to the spine was a danger, but my reflexes were enough for me to move and avoid it the moment I felt something pierce my flesh.

Saia's surface was smooth, marked only by the hexagonal patterns that were familiar to me and faint bluish light that shone through the lines.

I rolled my shoulders, getting accustomed to the new weight, then stepped into the room. The Suul was alone in the forest where I had encountered him. Standing at least four meters tall, he towered over me. In his hands was a giant macelike weapon, a thick rod made from the same wooden material as the other Suul weapons, with a round ball attached on top.

It noticed me immediately, but didn't move to engage. Instead it waited for me to come to it.

I had no choice but to oblige it. For this one, I settled into the Scarlet Moon Style's second Kata: *Tempest in the Mist*. I ran forward, careless of any defense. I let my instinct guide me. I felt the **thirst** rise up from within, its hunger singing in my veins. The Suul reacted, moving to the side as it swiped its mace at my side. I jumped over it, swinging my serpent-tongue spear one handed, holding it by the end to extend my range. The tip of the blade caught the Suul across its snout, cleaving a large flap of flesh open.

I landed and whirled in a flurry of multiple attacks as I danced around the Suul. My speed was superior, even with Saia weighing me down. In seconds, the Suul's body was covered in wounds as it tried to step back and recover.

It used a skill, its mace suddenly enveloped in a faint light as it surged downward with a speed that I hadn't expected, intent on splattering me.

[Mist Step] turned me to mist, and the attack shattered the ground where I stood. I re-formed next to it, then stepped close.

[Swap Profile]
[Debilitating Wave]

My skill billowed out of me, staggering the Suul and giving me the opening I needed. I jumped on it, ramming my spear through its neck as I landed on its shoulder. I tightened my thighs on its body then caught the blade with my other hand on the other side of its neck where it was sticking out covered in blood. I flexed my arms and twisted, tearing its head off its body in a gruesome display of blood and gore.

Light red, almost pink blood gushed out of the wound for a second before it dissolved along with the body.

I fell to the ground and took a few quick breaths, and my heart beat a single powerful thump, pumping oxygen through my slow-moving blood.

I wasn't sure how that worked exactly. This place was in my soul; it wasn't real. Yet, I still had to follow rules, it seemed. My body tired the same as it would in the real world.

My muscles twitched from exhaustion, and I sat down next to the glowing skill orb. Vampires were strong, fast, nearly unkillable, but we were not the endurance hunters that humans were. A vampire conserved its strength by operating at less than their optimum constantly, so that they would be able to move at incredible speeds and use great strength in shorter bursts. I had just gone through dozens of rooms, fighting and gathering skills. Even if this place wasn't actually real, it seemed that I still needed to rest.

Thankfully, resting for a vampire meant just sitting still, without moving a muscle. The time dilation between this place and the real world allowed me some time to do that, but not too much.

Once I felt somewhat recovered, I stood and went over to deliver the skill to a shelf.

[Pulverizing Smash]

A powerful downward attack that amplifies your strength.
<physical><esoteric><martial><offense>

The skill was powerful, and finally something that I could consider using in one of my profiles. With that done, I walked back to the corridor, heading for the second greater Suul room.

The second fight was harder. This Suul had the chance to use more skills, but ultimately I prevailed and gained another skill.

[Harden Self]

Harden a part of your body.
<physical><source><defense>

A useful skill, though probably not essential for someone like me. It would be more useful as a burn candidate in an emergency, since the [Overburn Skill] actually improved the skill somewhat when used.

I went over to the shelves and picked up skills that I'd noted before. I swapped out three skills from my second profile for new ones, then stepped back.

P2-Combat bonus
[Dodge]
[Triple Thrust]
[Pulverizing Smash]

I left my first profile as is: the beast bonus with two passive skills [Lesser Strength] and [Lesser Constitution] with one movement in [Mist Step]. It was a powerful combination that I didn't want to change as I didn't think I had anything better yet.

I had chosen the new skills in order to activate my new trait bonus. I wanted to test it out.

With all of that finished, I turned and headed for Shadow's door. I had a lot to tell him.

Weave Among the Mists

I found Shadow sitting on the edge of the cliff on top of the plateau that overlooked the mountaintops piercing through the sea of mist. The setting sun cast everything in an orange glow.

His legs were crossed beneath him, and his nine tails were swaying behind him gently. I walked over and sat next to him, joining him in admiring the view.

A lot had happened since I last spoke with him, a lot that I was struggling to come to terms with. I realized just how much I had come to rely on his advice. We found each other on Ish Vimza, saved one another, and he had accepted me into his family. Had given me a name, which meant the world to me.

The family that I was born into sold me to the cartel, and my sire . . . he stood by and watched them hang me. I know the reasons why he acted as he had, but still, he had done it. Shadow was the first person who accepted me fully for me. Sometimes, I found it hard to identify with the person that was Marianna Rojas, the vampire cartel member. It was the other me, *The Star That Dances in Blood Beneath the Light of the Broken Moon*, that felt like the real me. In the moments when I danced among my enemies, while I drew blood and had it drawn from me, those were the moments when I felt myself the most.

The Star That Dances in Blood, it was an apt name that Shadow had given me. Only now did I realize just how true it was. He had seen through me, understood me better than I had ever understood myself.

I struggled to begin. His opinion, even that of his copy, meant a lot to me. I'd been stalling before, by clearing all the rooms before coming here.

Somehow, he could tell, so he broke the silence first.

"Tell me," he said simply, and I sagged in relief.

I started with everything that had happened since I'd last visited. When I reached the point in my story about the meeting with my sire, I had to pause and try to marshal my thoughts. For a moment I almost slipped into my sire's teachings, trying to suppress my emotions, but then I remembered.

I do not suppress my Emotion, I Embrace.

He taught me that, so that's what I did.

My nostrils flared. "He stood by and let them hang me because he had a debt. Me, his Fledgling. As far as the vampire kind is concerned, his daughter."

I clenched my fists, felt my nails bite deep into my palms, drawing blood. "A life debt, he said, as if he didn't have the same toward me. I didn't ask to be sold, I didn't ask to be turned. He made me who I am. His blood ran down my throat." I ran the fingers of my left hand down my right. "Through my veins."

I closed my eyes. The **thirst** had woken up. It whispered within me, reacting to my emotions. The voice was so faint, filled with gibberish that I couldn't understand yet still knew the meaning of. It wanted me to feed. It believed that blood would solve all of my problems, that it would make me feel better.

"And in the end, none of that meant enough for him to break his word. He was powerful enough that he could've interfered, and he decided not to."

I was growling by the end, my heart beating faster, blood surging through my body. I took a deep breath, grabbing hold of my anger with an effort of will.

It was okay to feel anger, but I wouldn't let it control me.

"We all make mistakes, Little Star," Shadow said softly. "My own life is filled with things that I regret greatly. I do not mean to make it seem that you must forgive and forget. I believe that I can offer some context, as someone who had lived a long life like your sire, though his age is . . . it is greater than even the oldest of those on Kirios. Regardless, when you live a life that is so long, change is difficult. Your word becomes much more important to you, as most other things become fleeting. He apologized to you, and that is an acknowledgment of his wrong. He spoke to you and offered the truth as recompense."

"As if that is enough to make things right," I whispered.

"If you had died, it wouldn't have been. Yet, the reality is that you lived. I will not tell you how to feel toward him, or what your future relationship with him should be. That is your decision to make. I would only ask that you give consideration to the whole."

I didn't respond. I didn't know what to say yet. Part of me was glad that it wasn't about me, that he was remorseful, even if I was so confused that I didn't even know how to feel anything other than anger. It was not lost on me that the part of me that wanted to forgive was the part that had been so starved for any type of familial affection since I was a child. It was probably why I had bonded with Shadow so quickly.

At least I wasn't in denial about that. Becoming a vampire put a lot of things in perspective. It cut through the bullshit that humans told themselves when they were trying to avoid things. A vampire's brain worked differently—a predator didn't have the need for defense mechanisms.

I shook my head. Those thoughts were for later. "Thank you for listening," I said and stood up.

Shadow turned, and the fox ears on top of his head twitched as he gazed up at me. "Of course."

I glanced to the side where a set of stairs led to the trial that this entire room was here for in the first place.

"I want to try the trial," I said.

Shadow stood and stepped next to me. He looked at the path leading to the trial and then, after a few seconds of contemplation, spoke.

"I don't pretend to understand your kind, your strengths and weaknesses. If what you say is true, and I have no reason to doubt it, perhaps you are strong enough now to attempt it. Your strength is certainly high enough. A B rank at Second Investment is a testament to your kind's power."

"I want to try it anyway." I steeled myself, making a decision. The challenge had just under two weeks left, and I wanted to win. "I need power."

My fight with the Suul had shown me clearly that even with all of my advantages, I could die, and I could be overwhelmed. If my sire hadn't arrived and saved me, I would be dead.

"You know that I will be gone if you complete it," Shadow said slowly.

I blinked. I had forgotten. "I . . ."

He grinned at me. "Don't worry. I'm not afraid of dying. I'm not real in the first place. I'm part memories, part imprint of the real Shadow, and part the Grand Spell. I won't really be gone. But you will lose access to my advice, my presence."

My face fell, but then I closed my eyes and straightened. "I can't keep relying on you. And besides, in less than five months the portals will open, then after that the protection around our continent will be lifted. You, the other you, will be able to come over then."

Shadow didn't comment on that. He just kept grinning at me. "Very well. Then you should attempt the trial on your own." He looked pointedly at Saia. "I know that she is part of you, considered so by the Grand Spell, but . . . I would ask that you honor the customs of my ancestors anyway."

I inclined my head, and Saia flowed from my body to retake her drone form.

"You don't need to stay here anymore," I told her. "No need to split your attention."

Like Shadow, this physical drone of Saia wasn't real. Perhaps nothing here was. Her connection to me allowed her to manifest inside here, but it meant taking away the processes that were even now watching over our camp in the real world.

"Statement: Acknowledged."

With that, she faded out of sight and out of my soul space. I turned to Shadow, but hesitated. He had already told me that he wouldn't share anything about the test, the Weave Among the Mists Trial. All that he had told me was that there were three parts to it.

I inclined my head to him then started walking. The path led away from the ledge and into a narrow chasm with stairs carved through it, leading deeper into the mountain.

It didn't take long for me to reach what I could only imagine was the start of the trial. A giant stone arch stood before me, contrasted against the open sky above me and flanked by the mountain on either side. The entrance was decorated with images. A figure with wings folded on its back stood in the center of a round arena, with wiggly lines drawn all around it. This would be a Tengu-gi, Shadow's father's kind, also confirmed by an elongated nose that was even longer than Shadow's.

There were six more images, all depicting the same arena. Only the figure changed. It was apparent to me that the images were depicting a movement set of some kind. It was like a dance, with whirls and gestures of the arms in some strange flowing movement. The last image had the figure standing with arms wide as the lines moved around it.

I frowned at it, then walked forward. I knew little about the trial. Only that Shadow used it to gain a skill, and that it was something used by his father's people to gain mastery of their **Way of the Mind**, a state that could sometimes be dangerous.

I expected danger, Shadow had said that I could die. He had believed it likely, even. His people didn't allow anyone below the Third Investment to even attempt it. But as a vampire, physically, I was probably stronger than any Tengu-gi without their Mask.

The stairs continued beyond the entrance, leading down into the arena, which was filled with thick mist. There was little sound, except the soft groaning of stone around me that probably no one else but a vampire would be able to hear.

I stepped down, entering the mist until it was a thick fog and I was submerged in it. Soon I could no longer see past my face. The world became dark gray, and I focused on my other senses to guide me. It didn't take me long to realize that the thick mist had a weight to it that made it hard to breathe in. Thankfully, I didn't need to breathe often.

I walked straight forward until I reached the end and a stone wall. I reached out and touched it, but felt no give or any clues to indicate where the exit was. As I walked along the wall, I detected holes at set intervals, every few meters. Finally, I made my way around the entire arena and realized that there was no exit.

I started walking every step of the arena, looking for any clues. I found nothing. Finally, around ten minutes later, I went back to the exit and stepped out of the mist. I took a single deep breath, then let it out slowly, before taking in another. A vampire needs a lot less oxygen than humans do. Our blood is slower, thicker, and conserves oxygen a lot better. We still breathe, of course. We wouldn't be able to talk without air in our lungs.

I could see why Shadow was worried. Anyone attempting this trial would need to be able to hold their breath for a long time. If I had attempted it before I reached the Elder stage I might've had some issues. I felt a lot stronger now. And I still didn't know what I had to do to pass it.

I turned to the images at the entrance, assuming that they were a clue of some kind.

The lines inside the depiction of the arena were obviously meant to be the fog. The figure was dancing, and at the last image the fog was moving around him. Now I noticed small notches all around the arena, and realized that the mist was moving around the figure and into those holes.

I crossed my arms and tapped my fingers against my elbow. If I was to take the images literally, the figure danced and then the mist moved. That . . . actually reminded me of something that Shadow had explained to me long ago. About the Esoteric attribute, the one that he had called the *perfection in all things*. It was supposed to be closely linked to the school of being; it was the truth between the person and the Way itself.

Shadow had shown me a skill like that once, one that he hadn't gained from his Mask, but through the perfection of an act. I remembered how I felt when he used it, the way that it had echoed in my mind and impacted the world itself.

Something about the movements of the figure on the images reminded me of that act.

Was that the test? Being able to perfectly execute these movements in such a way that the world would respond, that the mist would flow around me?

Shadow had implied that would happen eventually, once my school of being, my Heart of Azure and Scarlet, reached a point where my dedication to it and my sacrifice were recognized by the Way itself.

If the Source was the fuel for magic, the physical manifestation of that energy, the Weave was the patterns or the skills and spells that commanded it. The Way was then the reality put together, and according to Shadow it was the combination of immutable rules and laws that made it up.

I looked at the images and rolled my shoulders, I didn't have anything to lose by trying it. I settled into the first position, following the instructions on the wall. There were no movements depicted in between positions, so I had to fill those in myself. I opted for the shortest and most logical movements in between the two positions.

I practiced it for a few minutes, but I got it quickly enough. After all, near perfect coordination was my kind's thing.

I walked down into the arena again, then settled in its center. I assumed the first position, then started to move, following the dance that I had seen on the walls. I whirled through the thick mist, my hands spread wide and my footing certain. Every move was perfect, with barely any sound made—my steps were soft and my passage through the mist cutting. The only sound was that of my clothes rustling against me.

When I came to a stop in the final position, my hands thrown out wide and my head tilted to the sky, nothing happened. I rolled my shoulders and walked back to the center. I should've known that it wouldn't be that easy.

I grimaced, then started again. Three more times I danced, and three more times nothing happened, I felt nothing.

After my fifth attempt I walked out of the mist and took a deep breath. I studied the images again, to see if there was anything that I missed, then went back inside.

This time, I tried to empty my mind completely and focus only on the movements. A step to the side and a whirl, my right arm coming up above my head while left went low. I crouched then stood as I stepped out and threw my arms out at the mist.

Nothing.

Again and again I tried, and nothing happened each time.

Finally, I was interrupted. Saia manifested inside the mist.

"Statement: It is time for watch change," she told me.

I sighed and walked out of the mist. I had hoped that this would be an easy way to get power, I should've known better.

I walked down the stairs back to Shadow.

"What is the point of that thing?" I asked, knowing that he wouldn't answer.

He looked at me, his tails swaying gently behind him.

"It is a rite of passage for all Tengu-gi that want to descend below the sea of mist," he said, and I knew that I would get nothing more from him.

I already knew that the trial was something that Tengu-gi underwent when they wanted to master themselves, and that only those who passed it were allowed to come down their mountains.

I shook my head, then paused. Perhaps there was a hint in that too. The Asha Kai-ni continent was covered in mists all the time. The trial seemed to be about controlling the mist in some way, so it made sense to have the Tengu-gi equipped with the power to be able to do that if they wanted to venture down their mountains.

Still, I didn't have the time to think about that nor attempt the trial again. I waved at Shadow and turned to leave, then when I reached the doors, I paused and glanced back.

His glowing orange eyes stared right back at me.

"Hey," I started. "Do you think that I'd be able to beat the mature ferrorn?"

Shadow laughed.

I left my soul space without attempting to fight the beast. The mature ferrorn was a beast that Shadow had killed when he saved me on Ish Vimza, the one whose young I had killed when I arrived in the jungle. According to Shadow, it was in the Fourth Investment, perhaps even close to the Fifth. It was a dangerous beast, a hunter. My physical strength at this point should be enough to match it, or at least Shadow thought so.

But I didn't have the time for it. I would have to do it next time I entered my soul space. For now, I had exploring to do, and trials of the Grand Spell to find.

Scouting

Saia and I left in the same general direction, but not together. Or, rather, a part of Saia left, in her drone, while her core and a thin band around my wrist remained. We wanted to maximize the area we could cover, so we separated. She couldn't be too far away from me, as the core of her being was within me, but she could range out several kilometers away from me.

It was hard to get lost in this place. It was a halo after all, and there were only two directions that one could feasibly go. We picked a big landmark, a mountain sticking out in the distance on the curve of the halo, and decided that was our destination. Saia took the left side, while I decided to head to the right.

I was glad that the others had agreed with this plan. We all needed to get stronger. And looking up and seeing Terra falling behind Suul'dar every day had lit up a fire beneath our feet.

I ran through the forest, searching for any signs of trials, but I only encountered beasts, which I avoided, though I did make note of their locations. The team would need to make their way through here if I found something ahead.

For the first hour, I was surrounded by a forest, until I stepped out into a completely different biome. A lush grassland stretched in front of me. Plains and pastures speckled with lakes and rivers.

I didn't pause for long. I ran across the plains in the open. There wasn't much cover, which made me hypervigilant of my surroundings. I crested a hill and came to a stop. It looked like a good location to scout things out a bit.

I reached back and pulled out my serpent-tongue spear from the improvised sheath behind my backpack, then I slung the pack off too.

I pulled out my binoculars. It was one of the few items that I had managed to save. A couple of days ago I'd had an accident over a river, where I lost a lot of my supplies. My gemstones, my ammo boxes, ferro rods, and a few bandages all spilled out and were lost to the current.

Thankfully, I still had my grapple with paracord, binoculars, and gourds with blood and some bandages.

I looked through the binoculars, scanning the plains and looking for anything of interest to direct my heading. The mountain that was my destination still loomed in the distance on the upslope of the halo.

I noted a large herd of beasts that looked like a cross between a bison and a rhinoceros, as they had a horn growing from their foreheads. I would've called them unicorns if they weren't so wide and thickly built.

I decided to avoid them. Then, a glint of purple light caught my eye. It was a rift. We didn't know exactly what the colors of rifts meant, but from what we had gathered so far green rifts were the easiest, and were most often just puzzle themed. Blue were harder, and had a chance of being resource rifts—meaning once they were cleared they wouldn't be repopulated with beasts if there were any inside, but they would remain with any resources within. White, like the one that I had cleared on Ish Vimza, was still unknown as I hadn't encountered another like it since. Red were rifts that were close to breaking open and spilling monsters out. I didn't know if they started as any other color and then changed, or if there was a specific different shade of red rifts—what we knew about them was that they disappeared once cleared. Purple though, that I hadn't encountered before.

My task was to find trials, but . . . Rifts did provide Investment, and I was sure enough that I could clear any rift fast enough that it wouldn't be an issue.

I packed my stuff away and then rushed across the plains toward the rift.

"Did you find anything?" I asked once I got close to the rift.

Saia's voice answered from the thin band around my wrist. "Report: No trials or rifts, only a large group of animals."

"Can you get your drone somewhere safe? We never tested how the connection between it and you will behave if I'm inside a rift."

"Feedback: If rifts are wormholes that serve to transport those who enter to another place, then the distance between the drone and myself will be too large for me to continue operating it at a distance. I've left simple instructions and have hidden the drone as best as possible."

"Great, heading in." I tightened the grip on my weapon, then stepped close to the rift and felt it pull me in.

The moment of disorientation passed quickly, and my feet hit solid ground. Immediately I could tell that this was going to be a pain.

The rift behind me vanished, meaning that no one else could enter, and that I would have to accomplish something in order for the exit to appear. We still didn't know a lot about the rules of how many people could enter a rift; it seemed to vary. Some were apparently solo, while with others the entrance vanished after a set time frame after the first person entered. Others had a hard cap of three, of five, or even six.

Like all rifts that were on the surface, the sky here was filled with lights of nebulae and stars. It was a flat plain, like the one that was outside the rift. A few trees grew here and there, but I could see across the entire rift. Like all others, it was a chunk of ground, an island floating in space, perhaps two kilometers across.

And it was filled with kobolds, an army of them, hundreds. As I rolled my shoulders and prepared, I had a thought about what kind of a rift this was. There were few people that could survive this on their own, but the fact that the entrance vanished as soon as I entered meant that it was probably limited to one or at most a handful of people. That put purple rifts in the dangerous tier, unless this one was an aberrant one.

"Report: I lost contact with my drone."

"Expected," I said simply.

I dropped my backpack to the ground then started walking toward the kobolds, I pulled the helmet from where it hung on my belt and put it on, fastening the clasp below my chin. I still wore my vest, and after my fight with the Suul, I was down to my last spare plates, as the others had been ruined in the fighting.

My second profile was currently active, which meant that my Combat Bonus was active too. This seemed like a perfect opportunity to test things out.

I waited until they were relatively close. Their screams and roars of challenge assaulted my ears, and their charge shook the ground.

I dashed forward, straight into their first line, and swung, cutting down half a dozen of them with a single attack. I felt a shudder pass through the Way, the world around me, and knew that some of them were activating skills. I didn't try to evade them but pushed forward, settling into the third Kata of **Veiled Mist Assault**: *Advance, Whirling Mist.* I spun, wielding my weapon and carving up room for myself as they surrounded me.

I could feel my bonus activating, it pulsed within me. With every death at my hands, I felt stronger. It was as if every time my weapon connected with a foe, I got a burst of strength. I was tearing through them, armor, flesh, and bone.

Some of the kobolds were taller, more muscular, carrying larger weapons. One swung a double-headed axe at me, and I sidestepped just enough for it to avoid splitting my head in half. I bent my knees as the axe hit the ground, and then stabbed forward, activating [Triple Thrust].

My weapon was surrounded by a faint sheen, and then my muscles burned as it stabbed forward three times in the span I could finish one thrust. I punched two holes in the taller kobold's abdomen, and the last stab obliterated its head.

Something struck me in the back but didn't penetrate my armor. I twisted, acting on instinct as I let all the emotion I felt over the last few weeks flow through me. My anger at my sire, the feelings of inadequacy, even shame. It all rose through me, and the **thirst** sang with me. It wanted me to feed, but I directed it, guided it. I fought, time ceasing to have a meaning as I danced through blood and carnage.

Everything faded away but the slow pumping of my heart, the rage inside of me, and blood that splattered all over me.

From time to time, an errant thought would slip through. The same as I had before, wondering how and why these kobolds were attacking me. They were clearly intelligent, and they spoke, yet they only wanted to kill me. Were they another race that the Grand Spell found somewhere else? Or were they like Shadow inside of my soul space, copies of real people?

I didn't have the time nor the will to wonder. They wanted to kill me, and that allowed me to retaliate and kill them in turn. That was all that mattered.

Something smashed into my side, sending me flying into a group of kobolds, and I bowled through them and took them to the ground. Others jumped over me, piling on top of me and trying to smother me in a mountain of bodies. Stabs punched through my thighs, my side, my neck, one even through my cheek and into my mouth. I bit down and shattered the blade with my teeth, then roared and pushed, standing with a dozen kobolds clinging on to me and stabbing me with their short knives.

[Overburn Skill—Sonic Screech]

I took a breath that inflated my lungs past what was comfortable, then I opened my mouth and felt my throat tear open as my vocal cords vibrated with the air pushed by an Elder vampire's strength.

A screech blasted out, raw and high pitched. I felt it expand and saw the air shake. The kobolds closest to me twitched, their eyes exploding out of their sockets as blood rushed through every orifice in their head. They fell from my body, and every kobold near me followed. Most within a short distance were dead on the ground, while those farther away fell to their knees, stunned.

I jumped forward over them, my wounds healing as I swung my weapon and cut down everything in my way. I laughed as warm blood splattered over my face, my tongue sneaking out to get a taste. I could hear the **thirst** whispering.

It was frantic—the blood all around me was sending it into a frenzy. My vision darkened, turning red with a haze that was familiar to me. It was stoking the fire of my emotions, trying to make me lose control. But that wasn't who I was. I had an obligation, a debt to collect. I entered a rift, and kobolds charged me. Death was a suitable price.

My emotions were mine, not the **thirst's**. I was the only one that controlled it and myself. I embraced my emotions and used them as fuel. Silently, I offered the **thirst** a promise that there would be blood soon. My muscles burned, and the **thirst** calmed, almost as if it understood that it would get nothing if it tried to overtake me.

My movements were wild, erratic, but that was by design. I whirled, uncaring for any attacks coming my way. I let them hit me and draw blood—they were inconsequential. A dirk stabbed through my ankle, cutting through a tendon and making me stumble and fall to my knee. A kobold jumped at my face, its eyes filled with madness and its mouth foaming red.

I dropped my weapon and grabbed it midair. The kobold stabbed my arm, but before it could take its dirk out, I pulled it into a tight embrace that crushed its bones against me. My jaw opened, and I bit into the side of its neck, sucking blood like through a straw.

More attacked me from behind, stabbing me in the side, and one climbed on top of my back. I barely had the presence of mind to realize that that could be dangerous when I felt something flowing over my arm beneath my clothes. A strike impacted the back of my neck and bounced off. I realized that Saia had moved and covered me there. That was dangerous. It was incredibly hard to kill a vampire like me, but severing the spine at the neck . . . My bones were tougher, so perhaps I could've survived that strike, but I had to be more careful.

I dropped the dead body in my arms, felt the blood fill my stomach, and the **thirst** fed on it immediately. My wounds healed faster, my heart pumped, and I took a deep breath.

I switched from Scarlet Moon Style to Azure Moon. I drew the dagger from my hip with one arm then let my fear rise to the forefront. I almost died; it was easy to call up.

A sharp rise of panic alerted me. It was hard to explain what it felt like, like a sixth sense perhaps. One that was a combination of things. Through my perception of the Way, I could feel when skills were being activated, as my other senses were constantly assaulted by information. The vibration of the ground and air, the scents around me, the light and shadows on the ground, all of it together touched something primal in my altered brain. Perhaps it was the **thirst**, flowing through my veins, my brain, but the result was emotion—fear and panic. I whirled the moment a blade touched my back. Instead of a stabbing wound, it cut open a thin and shallow cut across my hip, and then my dagger was in the kobold's eye. Its head exploded from the force of the strike, my dagger and fist passing clean through.

Part of it was my Elder vampire strength, and part I knew came from my new bonus.

Another of the tall kobolds came at me, this one carrying a wooden shield and a spear. I let him stab me, guiding the strike to my abdomen just below my vest plates. I pushed myself forward along the shaft, until I was close enough to stab him in the head.

I twisted once I punched through his jaw with the dagger, breaking the spear in my stomach and with my leg reached for my own weapon on the ground. With a roll over the handle and a kick up, I threw the serpent-tongue spear up to my free hand.

I grabbed it and swung, cutting through the legs of nearby kobolds, giving myself more free room and time to rip what was left of the spear out of my guts.

A slight pain on the back of my thigh alerted me to an attack, and I moved, now fully aligned with the **Stalwart Mist** technique.

The first Kata of the technique, *In the Mist, Await,* was all about waiting before attacking. With Shadow, I modified and altered his techniques for my own use. **Veiled Mist Assault** was rooted in anger, in unrelenting attack regardless of any injury taken. Each Kata built up on that, with *From the Mist, Strike* being fueled by my anger for a devastating attack from ambush—where Shadow would do so from the mist, I used my natural vampire stealth to accomplish the same.

The second Kata, *Tempest in the Mist,* was the flurry of attacks from multiple angles, using my anger to fuel a torrent of devastating blows. The last Kata, *Advance, Whirling Mist,* served to chain both of those together, to advance through the carnage and create confusion through aggression, and create opportunities for ambush from the open.

But it was **Stalwart Mist** that I now called on. The technique that was rooted in an idea of fear, both my own and that of my enemy. Fear was a survival mechanism that all life had, and it told us many things. Most important, it told us when there was danger around.

I most often fell into the Scarlet Moon technique, as it came easier for me. But in moments like these, when I was surrounded with enemies, when I felt fear for my life, my connection to the Azure Moon technique came to the surface. I settled now in the second Kata: *Overwhelming Mist.*

As I turned to my attacker, turning a deadly strike into a scratch, I stepped close to him and raised my weapon. Every Kata was a set of movements that I incorporated in my fighting. The first Kata was retaliation, the swift turn and lashing out. The second was a follow-up, comprised of three moves.

My first came as a strike from above. My blade came down, and the kobold that had attacked me from behind was cut in half, from top of the head to groin.

My second came as a dash forward and a grab. I let my weapon go with one hand and grabbed one of the two halves of the dead kobold, raising it up above my head and letting the blood and gore pour all over me, turning me into a nightmare. Then I threw the body at the kobolds running at me. Their dead hit them and sent a handful stumbling to the ground.

My third came as I dashed forward behind the body, then swung my weapon.

[Quick Swap Slot—Dodge>Crescent Swipe]

[Dodge] wasn't as useful in this situation, so I quickly swapped it out before I activated the new skill.

[Crescent Swipe]

My weapon left a silver arc hanging in the air for a split moment, a line tracing its path. The dozen kobolds that had been close enough split apart, their heads sliding off from shoulders.

I looked around, seeing that the attackers had faltered. Whether that was because they actually felt fear didn't matter in the end. I created room, and that let me take control of the fighting again. I switched back to the Scarlet Moon technique and danced forward.

The dead were everywhere. Blood had soaked into the ground, and I was left watching the carnage that I had wrought. It was a battlefield of the kind and scale that I hadn't seen often. This was what humans feared when they spoke of my kind. Each of those kobolds was no weaker than an ordinary human. Some were even stronger. And yet it didn't matter. I was an Elder vampire, and before me they were nothing.

Yes, I was exhausted, my legs barely holding my weight, and I could see why vampires feared humans. It wouldn't take much to ambush me now and kill me. I resolved myself to being smarter, I couldn't keep putting myself in these situations. Thankfully, I had a lot of blood to drink and time to recover.

The exit to the rift had appeared in the center of the plain, with a chest right next to it. The exit was still closed, probably until I opened the chest, the same as my first rift had been.

But for now, I had a few hundred corpses to drain of blood.

"Saia, consume."

The small part of Saia that was with me flowed over my body and into the pile of corpses as I grabbed one and started to drink.

Rewards

Drinking blood from over a hundred kobolds turned out not to be that easy. Vampire metabolism is fast, at least where blood is concerned, but it still took me longer than I had planned on staying in the rift for.

The vampire body is completely different from that of the human that it originated from. The changes start with the Fledgling phase and continue until the Elder. I didn't have the chance, nor any way, of checking my own changes, though they were evident.

It starts slowly: Muscle and bone start getting denser, stronger. The digestive track of a human is unneeded for a vampire, and most of it gets cannibalized to create a new organ that stores energy. The stomach is enlarged and changed in order to be able to hold more fluid, and without bowels there is only a more straightforward and efficient waste removal system.

My body processed the blood almost as quickly as I could drink it. The **thirst** took whatever it needed from it, while the waste got prepared for removal. And after drinking so much, there was a lot to remove. Which was why I remained in the rift. It was already embarrassing enough; I didn't want to risk doing it outside of the rift.

I forced myself to drink as much as I could. My Mask gained Investment from the blood, and while the kobolds were lower Investment than me, there were still a lot of them.

Near the end, my effort was rewarded.

Mask of the Blood Reaver — Second Investment; Second Carving

No skill again, but it was still early in my Investment tier. I hoped to be able to raise at least my Revelator Ornament to the First Investment and see if I could consolidate it with my Mask along with my Practical Student Ornament.

I looked over the carnage, the bodies vanishing into dark smoke as Saia went behind me and consumed them, breaking them down for materials. The memories that the blood provided me with were disjointed, unclear. As if the kobolds were in some dark place, and then they were here.

It made me almost relieved, made me suspect that perhaps they weren't real like many others I drank from. It was a faint hope, I knew. Whatever the Grand Spell did with beasts it put into its rifts was messing with my ability to gain memories from blood.

Saia flew over and landed next to me, or rather a new drone that she had created with the material she had gotten from the rift. We'd discovered a while ago that the higher Investment the material she consumed was, the more of it she could actually use. While Saia might seem like a purely technological creation, she was not. Source-Weave, as her creators called it, was an integral part of her.

She needed materials that were infused with it, and while everything around us was somewhat infused with it now, the levels didn't compare to bio-logical life that had Investment. Though, Saia had told me that, on Ke Erzi at least, there were certain types of ores that held more Investment that she could use, and even needed in order to make some of her engrams functional again.

"All done?" I asked.

"Feedback: I have consumed and processed all that I was able to."

Her new drone was about the size she had been before entering the chal-lenge, the size of a dog, though not quite as large as her other drone.

"Could you do me a favor?" I gestured at myself, covered in blood and gore.

Her drone broke apart and surged over to engulf me, consuming the mat-ter. One of the benefits of having a dragon AI attached to your nervous system turned out to be a free cleaning service.

As she worked, I spoke.

"You can enter my soul space without me now, right?" As our bond advanced and the synchronization rate rose, her access to my body increased. The current benefits were that mostly that she leached less energy from me and her [Repair] engram could aid my natural regeneration more.

"Feedback: Yes." A part of the liquid puddle that was writhing over me vibrated and answered.

"Could you do me a favor and catalog all the skills I have on my shelves? The amount is starting to get out of hand, and I want to be able to look them over and come up with new profile pairings."

I didn't really need that; I was connected to them through my Mask and could kind of sense each and every skill that I had. But I was a visual person, and Saia was able to display anything in front of my eyes, which could help me plan ahead, without my needing to enter.

"Feedback: Of course, Mari."

"Thanks," I said, then turned and started walking toward the reward chest nearby as Saia finished up her work.

The chest was made from black wood, unlike any of the others I had seen before, and was a bit more ornamental, with a metal frame. And a lot smaller than the others.

I reached down, raised the cover, and looked at my rewards.

Two larger pouches were present. Opening them, I confirmed what I already suspected: gold coins in one and gemstones in the other. Though the gemstones seemed to have been the upgraded versions, about two dozen of the D-grade stones.

There were six elements with four each: fire, metal, earth, nature, air, and light. I set them aside for later. The team had gathered quite a few gemstones from rifts, but most were F or E grade, which weren't that useful. I was trading for the ones that I needed and looking to gather enough to upgrade them. To get one C-grade stone, I would need forty D-grade ones, which was a lot of E grade, seeing as how one D-grade stone equaled twenty E.

I put the two pouches in my backpack and looked at the rest of the rewards. There were three more items, all small.

Two rings and a fist-sized crystal that pulsed with orange light.

"Saia," I said as I reached down and grabbed one of the rings, "any idea what this is?"

It didn't feel like just a normal ring. It felt more like the items that Shadow had on Ish Vimza: his Reader and the rod that cast a field around it. Both of those had been gifted to Saia, and by consuming them she had integrated them as part of herself, turning them into engrams, [Inspect] and [Threat Reduction Field] respectively. It could be an enchanted item, something created by a Masked, or such a creation replicated by the Grand Spell. Or it could be a relic from the Ancient Ones, the Vim, or perhaps even some other long-gone and forgotten race. It didn't feel like an infused item like the ones that we had been getting as rewards from rifts, though those mostly gave skills, so one could always know what it did.

A part of Saia on my body flowed and turned into a tiny dragon version, standing on my wrist and looking up at the ring in my fingers. She had upgraded the [Inspect] engram on her own, and had studied each reward item we had gotten, and we had wondered if it would allow her to figure out what enchanted items did without having to consume them fully. She was a lot more sensitive to Source than I was. Weave was my lowest attribute, though my Esoteric was high, which allowed me to feel imprints of Source-fueled Weaves on the world around me, even if I couldn't always tell what they were.

"Report: The item is Source-Weave infused. The engram within is unfamiliar to me but I can postulate what it does."

I waited for a moment, then rolled my eyes. "Any chance you're going to share with me?"

Saia turned so that her blue eyes looked into mine. "Feedback: Yes, of course, Mari. The item seems to be able to create and release a scent. It is unclear as to what kind."

I blinked, then looked at the ring for a long minute. Now that she said it, the ring did look a bit like a flower with a pale gem set in its center. I turned it around then put it on my finger. I trusted Saia and her inspection of it. The ring didn't seem to be something too dangerous.

Nothing happened once I put it on, so I tried to focus and think of a scent. Nothing happened for a bit. Then I tried to tie in a memory of when I experienced a scent. Almost immediately I felt the ring activate, and the scent of roses started wafting out of it.

"Huh," I said as I looked at it.

"Statement: The ring has a Source reserve, at the current rate of consumption, it will work for approximately one hour."

That was interesting, and probably useful, especially for me. Vampires didn't have a scent, and I could use it when I wanted to confuse or trick others. I focused and tried to think about the effect ending, and it did.

"Hey, can you make a description of it and display it for me?"

Saia tilted her small head, her eyes flashing. "Feedback: I can, why?"

"Just humor me, please?"

A moment later, a text window opened in front of my eyes.

Scent Ring

Can emit any scent that the wearer wishes; the effect lasts for one hour.

I grinned, then wondered how people who didn't have Saia would be able to tell what items like these did. Shadow had mentioned that there were people that specialized in identifying the enchantments on relics. So perhaps there were people out there with Masks that could do the same. Others would probably take a risk and experiment with them.

Thankfully, I wouldn't need to do that. I picked up the second ring and offered it to Saia. "And what about this one?"

Saia didn't answer verbally this time. Instead, more text appeared in my vision.

Lesser Ring of Regeneration

Accelerates natural regeneration, approximately one day's worth of charge.

My eyes widened. Increasing my already monstrous regeneration would be useful.

"How much would this help me?"

"Feedback: Regeneration speed increase would equal to approximately one percent."

I blinked. "What? That's . . . nothing."

"Feedback: Your body requires a lot more energy to achieve regeneration at the rate it does. Your body stores this energy in your abdominal organ and spends it to fuel replication of thirst bacteria which then converts into whatever kind of cell is needed for the repair of the body."

I opened my mouth, then closed it. It seemed that with our connection improving, so did her understanding of my physiology. I knew some of that stuff. Mostly I had learned in school back before I was turned. My sire taught me precious little.

"Well, that sucks then," I said as I rolled the ring over my fingers.

"Statement: The ring would be much more effective for someone whose natural regeneration was much slower."

I glanced at her. "How much more effective? How would it affect a human?"

Saia had consumed human bodies before; perhaps she could estimate.

"Feedback: It would at least double the regeneration rate."

That was a lot, actually. If I gave it to the others it would speed up their recovery significantly, especially with Khalil's little healing skill. "But only for a day?" I asked.

"Feedback: That is how much charge is within. I believe that the Source within will replenish in time."

That made sense, I didn't think that these were supposed to be one and done items.

I put it in one of my pockets, planning to give it to the others later. I picked up the last item, a fist-sized rough-cut crystal that pulsed softly with orange light.

"Statement: I am detecting a significant amount of Source within that item."

"Like with the skill gemstones?"

"Feedback: Negative. The Source gemstones have within them an engram matrix; this one lacks it. I am detecting only pure elemental Source."

"Any ideas what it could be?"

"Report: At seventy-three percent, the highest likelihood is the possibility that it is a crafting reagent. Probably intended for use in enchantment."

"Huh, that's cool. Useless to me, but cool, I guess." I turned it over in my hand, trying not to be disappointed. I didn't have a crafter Mask, nor did anyone I knew. Maybe I could find someone at the camp back on Earth, but it wouldn't help me any now.

"Query: May I have it?"

I turned to find Saia looking at me. "Why?" I narrowed my eyes in suspicion. Her tone was one that I was familiar with.

"Feedback: I believe that I could use it. The Source within it might be able to serve as a suitable substitute to the elements missing or no longer operable in my [Plasma Shot] engram."

My eyebrows rose in tandem, and my jaw dropped. "Really?"

Saia didn't answer immediately.

"Feedback: I am uncertain. It is possible."

Well, I was willing to take the risk anyway. Having her repair one of her old engrams was never a wrong thing. The ones already active were incredibly useful.

"Have at it then." I offered her the crystal, and Saia flowed over it to envelop it fully, another section of gray goo separated from my body to cover the crystal more fully. Then it re-formed into a slightly larger drone.

"You're not consuming it?" I asked, I could tell that her drone's shape had shifted to accommodate the crystal's size inside of the drone's torso.

"Feedback: No, it is a required component that I cannot easily recreate. I could consume and take the collected Source, but that would destroy the container. I will not waste it."

I nodded. "You know best. How long will it take you to fix it?"

"Feedback: Unknown."

I didn't respond. I didn't pretend to know anything about what she was doing. After a bit, Saia spoke again, changing the topic.

"Input: I've also compiled the list of the skills on your shelf."

"Show me."

A moment later, a list of skills popped up in front of my eyes.

[Harden Self]
[Lesser Tough Skin]
[Lesser Camouflage]
[Lesser Stamina Recovery]
[Lesser Night Sight]

[Lesser Screech]
[Debilitating Wave]

[Dodge]
[Dash]
[Parry]
[Lesser Pounce]
[Lesser Leap]
[Lesser Stalk]
[Lesser Charge]

[Peck]
[Bite]
[Slash]
[Swipe]
[Stab]
[Smash]
[Quick Claw]
[Double Strike]
[Lesser Diseased Bite]
[Lesser Stab]
[Lesser Strike]
[Greater Stab]

[Sharp Eye]
[Hive Mind—ratkin]
[Lesser Command—ratkin]
[Lesser Call Wind]
[Lesser Intimidation]
[Lesser Acid Spit]
[Lesser Track]
[Lesser Imitate Prey]
[Lesser Encourage Growth]

I looked them over for a moment, then spoke.

"I see that you sorted them."

"Feedback: This Unit tried to. There are many ways to classify them, though it can get confusing, as many share the same tags. This seemed clear enough."

I rolled my eyes at her. "Thanks. I assume that the last group is miscellaneous?"

Saia simply inclined her head.

I shook mine and frowned. I had a lot of skills, even with the couple that I had burned out, and I would be getting more most likely. The kobolds would net me some, though I doubted that it would be many. They weren't that highly Invested, and chances were that those that did have skills would have the same ones, and I didn't get duplicates. It was also very clear to me that few of the Suul had any more magical Masks, as their skills seemed to be mostly physical in nature. That was the case for most of the beasts that I fought and drank from so far too.

According to Shadow, beasts either got infused with Source and turned into an offshoot of their race, or they developed an affinity later in life, when they reached higher Investment. I could expect to get more Esoteric and Weave related skills from higher Investment beasts or people.

I also took the time to enter my soul space and swap out my skills again, slotting [Dodge] back in. With that all done, I stood and stretched. Saia finished cleaning all the gore from my person, and I collected my weapon and backpack, while the rest of Saia formed two bracers on my wrists, and the drone settled on my shoulder.

With one last look at the rift, I headed for the exit.

Aggressive Diplomacy

The moment I left the rift, there was a pressure in my head.

Mask of the Blood Reaver — Second Investment; Third Carving

The Investment gain from finishing the rift was enough to push me to the next Carving, which either spoke to the Grand Spell's perceived difficulty of the rift, or perhaps the fact that I finished it solo.

Either way, that tiny moment of distraction allowed the welcoming committee the opportunity to ambush me.

"Don't move!" a voice yelled out and four guns were pointed my way. Two were hunting rifles, small caliber. One was a Glock of some kind or the other. The last one, though, was a fully automatic rifle. I didn't know that much about human guns to be able to tell their make at a glance, not beyond the more famous models. But I could recognize enough. These were weapons gained as rewards from the Grand Spell, replications made from materials that didn't degrade as Earth metals did. I hadn't had the chance to inspect any of them closely enough to see what changes the difference in materials, if any, caused.

Immediately, I took in the situation. They were human; their sweat clung to them and their heartbeats betrayed them. I didn't smell any silver, so their bullets wouldn't be that effective. Still, a bullet to the head was a bullet to the head, and I had four guns pointed my way. I had a helmet on, but there was only so much that it could do. True, I was likely to heal from such a head wound, but all it would take was for it to enter at a right enough angle to buy them some time.

These people were Masked, the guns wouldn't be their only weapons, not if they had been picked to enter this challenge. For all I knew they had skills that would make their bullets more powerful.

On the other hand, I was now an Elder vampire. They would need some powerful skills to slow me down.

All that combined meant two possibilities. They had seen me enter and decided to ambush me once I left, or they just stumbled on the rift by chance and decided to wait.

The more important question was whether they knew what I was. That would tell me a lot more about where this encounter was likely to go. If they knew and still decided to ambush me, I could expect some tricks. Only two vampires had entered the challenge, myself and my sire. Each of the one hundred challengers had been close enough to see our eyes. My sire's had been fully emerald, those of an Elder, and mine had been cracked pupils with emerald spilling into my iris—an Adult. Neither were something anyone with any sense of self-preservation would try to face.

And my eyes now mirrored those of my sire, no pupil or iris, just two emerald orbs surrounded by white.

I raised my head slowly, showing my eyes clearly.

The reaction was immediate.

"Fuck," one of them said.

I had a moment to study them. The man directly in front of me was tall, with dirty blond hair that was cut short. He, like his friends, wore simple clothes: a dark shirt and fatigues. They each also had different types of protective gear. Most of it looked to be skateboarding pads on their knees and elbows. One of them had a biking helmet on, and another a Kevlar vest. They had backpacks and utility belts on with different items slung through them.

To the blond man's left was a woman, shorter than me by a full head, with long black hair, brown eyes, and the helmet on her head. Her cheek had a nasty red cut that was probably infected.

To the right of the blond guy were two men, looking like brothers. They had brown hair and wide blue eyes that stared at me in horror.

Their reaction shifted what my response to the situation would have been.

I didn't remember them, though I'd only really paid attention to the top ten challengers. Still, I didn't underestimate them. They had advanced their Masks enough to be offered the chance to enter the challenge, and they'd probably advanced more while here. That they were still alive spoke much about their capabilities.

Seeing how they clearly had no idea who they were ambushing, I was of a mind to just let them go, and yet . . . They'd threatened me, and the core of my school of being had to do with debt and obligation. All actions had a reaction; all decisions carried with them a weight, a debt. I'd given no cause for them to threaten me, and they most certainly had—they could've lowered their weapons immediately, apologized, but they had not. And now I had to balance the scales.

"That is some welcome," I said slowly. I had to be careful with my words. I had realized just how little I'd paid attention to my promise to the Way.

The four barely reacted, shocked or frozen with fear.

"Would you be so kind to lower your weapons?" I asked slowly.

They exchanged looks, but the three of them looked to the blond man across from me for an answer—making him the leader of the bunch.

"If we lower them, you'll kill us," he said.

The corners of my mouth twitched upward. "It's so cute that you think *that*'s the only reason you aren't dead yet."

Their fear spiked, hearts beating faster, their palms sweating and hands trembling. The more this went on, the greater the chance that one of them would do something dumb, on purpose or on accident.

"Jason," one of the brothers whispered to the blond man—who was Jason apparently. "That's her, the one that was at the top of the list."

"I know that, Mark," Jason hissed back, his eyes never leaving mine.

They didn't move for a few seconds, so I spoke again.

"I believe that I've demonstrated my intentions well enough. If I wanted you dead, you already would be. So, weapons. Now."

The woman lowered hers first, followed by the two brothers, and finally the man in the middle—Jason.

"Ah," I said slowly, finally allowing myself to move more freely. I took a step to the side, while keeping them in my sight. "That's better. Now we can talk like civilized . . . people."

They grouped together, their weapons held tightly in their arms but not pointed in my direction.

"We didn't know that you were the one in there," Jason said.

I raised an arm and scratched the top of Saia's head on my shoulder. That drew their attention to her, and they blinked, unsure what they were looking at.

"Fly, Saia, keep watch," I whispered, too low for them to hear. I didn't think that there were more of them, but for all I knew this was all just a play, and more were preparing the real ambush.

Saia took to the sky, and the four flinched but were smart enough not to react any other way.

I walked in a circle around them, each step measured and light, I was gliding across the ground. It unnerved them, I could tell.

"Perhaps introductions are in order? I'm sure that you know my name already, but propriety is important. You can call me Star," I said, making a decision to use part of the name that Shadow had given me. It was a name that was supposed to be private, yet the Grand Spell had announced it to the world. It felt somehow fitting for me to use it, as if I had one name for friends and one for all others.

"My name is Jason," their leader said after a moment. Then he looked to the woman and introduced her. "This is Diana, and these two are Mark and Matt."

I didn't outwardly acknowledge them; instead I kept my eyes on the leader.

"So, what do we do now?" I asked, my tone just low enough that they had to strain to catch my words.

"We meant no insult. We didn't know," Jason answered. His voice was barely even shaking. I was impressed with his composure. Few humans would be able to stand before an Elder vampire and speak as if to an equal. There was a primal part of their brains that understood the reality, that they were prey and the vampire, the hunter.

"Yet, offense was given," I responded. "And it must be made right."

They exchanged looks, but it was the woman who mustered the enough courage to speak.

"What can we do to make it right?" Diana asked.

I smiled in her direction, and they recoiled. *Fangs, right.*

Her question had opened the floor for negotiation. She had admitted to a debt between us, and now I could extract the price.

"Well, that depends on what you have to offer," I answered, one finger tapping against my lips as I pretended to consider it. "I guess that I shouldn't be trying to take too much from you. We are all here for the same thing, and Earth will need as many of us as possible if we are to keep what we have when the portals open."

They blinked, obviously not expecting my words.

Jason was the one that spoke next. "This is about what you and the others spoke of before, the other continents and races and all that stuff?"

I tilted my head. "None of you are Exemplars?"

They exchanged looks then shook their heads.

I had expected as much. "What I said before was the truth. We are part of another world, and they will come to try and claim what is ours, land and resources."

I looked them over, studying them more in depth. The state of their clothes spoke of some hardship—like mine, theirs were filled with holes and covered in blood and dirt. They hadn't been just surviving.

"Tell me, why did you decide to ambush whoever left this rift?" I pointed over my shoulder at the purple light of the rift.

"We just stumbled onto it," Jason answered. "We were worried that some of those aliens were inside. We didn't want to leave any of them behind our backs."

"The Suul? You had encounters with them?"

"One," he answered. "We met with a group of them in a trial. They . . . they killed one of us, and we gunned them down."

Diana looked away at that, her lip trembling. The one that died was someone close to her perhaps. It seemed like these four, five counting the one that died, knew each other before the challenge. They seemed somewhat prepared. The fact that they still hadn't spent their ammo meant that they had a lot in reserve. The only way to get that was from rifts, or perhaps some skills, though I didn't think that they would get a skill that powerful just yet. To have been qualified for the challenge without being Exemplars, these four had to have started pushing the moment the Grand Spell arrived, adapting to the new world, clearing rifts and fighting to survive.

That spoke well of them.

I hummed to myself, again making a point of thinking. Then, I spoke. "As I said, we'll need strong people, so it's not in my or anyone's interest to take from you and make you weak. So, I will consider the matter of you threatening me settled if you provide me with information."

"Information?"

"Yes." I grinned. "I am looking for trials, and you've obviously explored some of this place. So, tell me, do you know of a location of any?"

After a short conversation with the four, I called back Saia and instructed her to send back her other drone to Khalil and the others. Then I made camp with my four new . . . friends. I wasn't sure if I wanted them to be part of our group, but there was safety in numbers, and while I didn't outright offer, I did imply it. Inviting them straight up might've carried with it an obligation from my side to keep them safe. I didn't want to do that.

Saia's smaller drone, the one that remained with me, informed her of the others' progress. It didn't take her long to find them as they'd been moving in this direction since I left.

And it only took a few hours for them to catch up.

"Mari!" Aurora yelled when she noticed me. She ran over to give me a hug. I sighed and patted her shoulder stiffly for a moment. "You're back, and you have new friends!"

She leaned and glanced at the awkward group of four people behind me who rose to their feet.

"Not friends, now go pester them." I shooed her in their direction, leaving her to handle the social parts that I hated, and I walked over to the others.

Daehyun had his sword out, ready for a fight, but sheathed it once he saw me, while Jiyun smiled at me hesitantly. Khalil walked over and gave me a quick hug.

"So, you found what we're looking for?" he asked.

I nodded. "They have, at least." I gestured at the four being swarmed by Aurora.

He looked over at them with narrowed eyes. "Think we can trust them?" he whispered.

I shrugged. "Don't know them well enough for that, but I don't think that they are going to try anything. They wouldn't live long after trying."

Khalil looked back at me then nodded.

"When do we leave?"

"As soon as you can get ready. They know the locations of two trials, and I want to do them both. One opens in six days, and the other requires twenty-one people to join, and some spots are already taken."

Khalil's expression turned determined, and he stood. "Very well then."

With that, we got ready and started back.

Interlude - Vampire

Khalil walked at the rear of their group as they made their way across the plains, his mind occupied by many difficult thoughts.

He cast his gaze at Marianna as she led them forward, then to the new group just behind her. Jason, Diana, Mark, and Matt were from the U.S., though from what they could figure out their land had been shifted to the middle of Africa. The people they encountered outside of their small town said that they were in Congo.

That they'd managed to survive was an achievement that he could respect. He'd heard stories of what happened during the first month in Constantinople, the sheer number of people that died, even with all the advantages that Constantinople had.

The vampires, the knights, but perhaps more importantly the beasts. The city had a massive population of stray cats, and when the world changed, they changed too. Source infused them, some mutated and grew larger, others changed in different ways. But few of them turned really feral. The cats had been part of the city's life and culture for centuries. They were used to people, they were fed by them, lived on their streets. When the beasts spilled out of the rifts, the people didn't fight alone. Many people, Khalil had learned, had gotten Masks related to rearing pets or combat animals.

But, even with all of that, Khalil knew that it was the vampires that had turned the tide. They'd broken through the hordes and closed the most powerful rifts.

Vampires. He still couldn't quite believe that his order was working with them, but the end of the world made strange allies. The city was now run by a council, with the various city officials sitting in alongside vampires, bishops, allamah, fāris of the Followers of Furūsiyya, and knights of the Order of the Dragon.

It was a strange reality, and one that Khalil had found himself in the thick of. As the city's only Exemplar, he had been relied on by the leaders for more than just information. He had one of the highest Investments in the city, and likewise in the world. The older vampires advanced their Masks slowly, apparently, as most of their Masks were related to crafts that they had once practiced and that were no longer relevant or easy to accomplish. It was a small mercy. He shuddered to think what would've happened if they gained Investment as fast as Marianna did.

The only reason the balance of the city worked as it did was because the knights had gained Investment at a faster rate. They might not be able to match an Adult or Elder vampire one-on-one, especially now that daylight was no longer the weapon it once was against them, but there were more of them.

He looked back at Marianna and the four that kept casting glances at her back. Did she realize just how terrifying she was? It didn't seem so to Khalil, and she terrified him too. More so, perhaps, than others, because at times he could see glimpses of the old her, the woman that he had met in America at school. The kind and shy girl that was quirky and funny, who was his friend.

Now, she spoke with that barely above a whisper tone that the vampires used, as if she constantly had to remind herself to speak louder so that the humans could hear. Her head moved every now and then, when she heard something that none of the rest of them could.

Now she sat perfectly still, unmoving and unchanging, and only a rare inhale of air betrayed the fact that she wasn't a statue. She moved silently, her every step taken with such care and grace that she seemed to almost glide across the ground, weighing less than air. Yet, when she fought it was clear that she weighed at least twice as much as he did.

Then there were her eyes, two small orbs of emerald, like the reflections of the calm sea. There was no sign of a pupil or an iris, just two emerald mirrors surrounded by white. The eyes of an Elder vampire. Khalil still couldn't quite believe it. When he had first seen her in this place, when he had convinced himself that it was her, her eyes had been those of an Adult vampire. Her explanation that her Mask had advanced her vampire condition had seemed ludicrous.

Yet, she went from Adult to Elder in mere days. Khalil had no idea how that was possible. He was certain that she was hiding things from him, but then again, he was hiding things from her too.

The moment the challenge had been announced, the Council of Constantinople had started debating whether to send him in or not. It was an opportunity to learn about the state of the world from others. But as soon as he had mentioned that the name Marianna was familiar to him, that it could be someone he knew, the choice was made.

Especially since she was at the top of the rankings and had a strange addition to her name. He still hadn't pressed her about it; she had simply said that she had gained that on Ish Vimza, the continent where she had been sent as an Exemplar.

The leaders of Constantinople were interested in everything about advancing Masks, and Khalil's job was to learn as much as he could about it, and how to best gain Investment.

As far as that mission was concerned, he'd already accomplished it. Marianna had shared freely what her mentor from Ish Vimza had taught her, how different types of Investment worked, and in far more detail than what the Elves had taught Khalil on Elvaros.

Now, he was in this strange place, unsure of what to even do. What Marianna had said was right. They had to push harder than they had so far. To gain more Investment and more points, to try to win this challenge. The others were shortsighted. This wasn't just a rush for personal power, this was about the survival of their entire civilization, humans, vampires, and shifters alike.

Working with a vampire was not something that he had expected that he would've even willingly done, not after what he had seen happen on Elvaros and the callous murderous rage that the vampire there had unleashed.

The sight of him never seemed to leave Khalil's dreams, the ghastly monstrous face, thin skin and wide fleshy wings. What he had seen was everything that his order had taught him the vampires truly were deep down inside.

When he had reported what he had witnessed to his order, he had been allowed in the inner circle, allowed access to information that wasn't widely known. He had learned what before being summoned as the Exemplar he had only believed to be a rumor, a fairytale. That the oldest and most powerful of vampire kind could transform into those hideous monsters.

Only twice had the order encountered vampires that old. The first time had been in the year 1453 during the last siege of the city by the Ottoman Empire. The counterattack by the Byzantine vampire was the reason the Ottoman Empire didn't push over the strait, and why Constantinople was both a Christian and Muslim city today.

The vampire had decimated the army but died when the Ottoman army managed to trap him in the Bosporus under a sunken ship, ensuring that he couldn't move until he drowned.

At least the records believe that the vampire died, as he didn't resurface again. For the longest time, they had believed the vampire to have been one of the originals, the creators of the vampire kind.

It was only later, in the 1600s, that they encountered another who could transform into the same form. The only reason they were certain it wasn't the same vampire as the one in Constantinople was that this vampire was a woman.

Now they knew that there was a stage after the Elder vampire, the one that they called Ancient vampire. It was a title used by the vampires too, and the order believed that they had started using it simply to muddy the waters. And yet, perhaps they were just hiding the truth in plain sight. Who knew with their kind.

Khalil looked at Marianna and tried to imagine what she would look like when transformed into such a monstrous being. A part of him worried that this was all a trick, a trap for some nefarious purpose. That Marianna had lied to him, that she wasn't as young as she claimed to be. And the more time passed, the more worried Khalil became. The speed at which her strength grew was too much.

He didn't know why she would trick him so, but if she was not in fact young, but actually an Ancient vampire capable of shifting her body into that monstrous form, then . . . What was the color of her eyes compared to that? They knew so little about vampires that old. For all he knew they could alter their appearance at will, appear to be whoever they wished, even human.

Perhaps she had always been a vampire, even when they met so long ago.

He shook his head, pushing those thoughts and fears far away from his mind. He couldn't allow fear to rule him. He would judge her based on her actions, and nothing he had seen now or before had given him cause to doubt. To condemn another with no cause would tarnish his soul under God's grace.

They drew closer to their destination, and soon they found a stone shrine with an altar within, the same as the last trial they had encountered.

The group spread around it, making sure that there was no one else around, though Marianna's little dragon—another thing that he was completely baffled about—had already scouted ahead.

Khalil walked up to stand next to Marianna as she looked down at the plaque.

Trial of the Forest—Gathering Point Seven

Join in the Trial of the Forest! Touch the scepter to reserve a spot. Up to three individuals can register at a single Gathering Point.

18/21 spots taken.

"Three people?" Khalil asked.

Marianna nodded. "Yeah, and it looks like we made it just in time. We'll need to choose who goes quickly."

"You, obviously," Khalil started. The trials were already dangerous enough, and sending anyone other than their strongest would be stupid. "It seems like it is taking place in a forest. That might influence who we choose."

Marianna glanced back at the others as they approached. Aurora leaned over her shoulder and took a look. "Only three?" She repeated Khalil's question.

"Khalil and I should go," Marianna said, surprising him.

"Why me?" he asked.

"You can heal," Marianna simply said.

Truthfully, his healing wasn't any good. It accelerated the natural healing process, and not very well. Though, it did help.

"We have your new ring," Khalil countered. "It's better than anything my skill can do."

Marianna waved her hand. "You're also good with your sword and shield."

"Jiyun is the best of us with the sword other than you."

Marianna glanced at the Korean woman and her brother.

"What do you think?"

Jiyun was the one that answered. "You should take one spot, obviously. The rest depends. If we knew more about the trial, it would make this far easier." She shook her head and looked at the others. "Aurora is situationally very powerful. Her ability to sense stone at a distance could be useful."

"It is called the Trial of the Forest," Marianna pointed out. "If we are dropped into a real forest, it will mean less stone in the ground. She won't be able to use her stone spikes as much as she'd like."

"Hey!" Aurora protested. "I can still shake the ground and open cracks in it! And you are underestimating just how much stone there is in the soil."

Marianna grinned at her antics, showing her fangs. If they hadn't spent so much time together since coming here, that would've been a far more threatening expression than what he knew Marianna meant it as.

"I'll stay."

Khalil turned to look at Daehyun who had a determined expression on his face.

"We should talk about it, brother," his sister Jiyun said.

"There isn't much to talk about. You are better than me with the sword, and besides, we aren't just making a decision on who goes but also who stays."

He glanced behind to the four newcomers who were setting up camp. Khalil grimaced as he realized what he meant.

"He's right. Two of us will need to stay with them, and . . . I want to believe in the good of the people, but we don't know them."

Marianna tilted her head. "So, what do you suggest?"

Khalil looked back at her. "You should go because you're the strongest of us, Jiyun because she's second strongest, and Aurora because, frankly, I don't trust her without you around to keep her in check."

"Hey!" Aurora complained.

"Anyways." Khalil ignored her. "Daehyun and I will stay and get to know the other group, maybe clear a few rifts in the area while we wait for you."

The four newcomers would stick around for a little while more, as they had agreed to show them the locations of one other trial, the one that would start in six days.

Everyone looked to Marianna. Clearly, the decision was hers to make. Finally, she sighed and agreed.

Forest Buffet

The trial started exactly ten minutes after the three of us registered, leaving me with barely any time to prepare. Jiyun wore her hanbok, slightly dirty from all the fighting, though not covered in blood, since Saia was able to consume any organic matter and cleaned the group's clothing fairly often. Her sword was sheathed and secured to her waist. She also had a small ring that gave her the [Lesser Stamina] skill, which allowed her to fight for longer. Her boots were also a reward from a rift and provided her with a tiny increase in her leg strength, which increased movement speed.

Aurora still wore the gambeson we got from the last trial, which looked more like a dress on her lithe and shorter body. In her hands she carried a staff we got as a reward that gave no skills but was sturdy enough to be a dangerous weapon. Daehyun had been teaching her how to use it properly, and she had gotten good enough that she only rarely hit herself on the head. At least it gave her something to protect herself with if attacked up close, though last time she panicked and a bird managed to pick her up, so perhaps it would be best if I made sure nothing ever came close to her.

Saia flowed over my body, forming the basic armor set, as we worried her drone wouldn't be transported if she wasn't on my person. The armor had grown somewhat as she had gathered more mass. Now she covered my upper torso and neck, shoulders, and arms, as well as my legs from my feet all the way up to the mid-thigh. Soon she'd be able to cover me whole. Though, the actual protection her current form provided wasn't near what a full armor could. She couldn't activate her protection engrams in this setup, nor was it structurally as solid as she would like, seeing as how I wore clothes beneath.

But armor wasn't high on my list of priorities. I didn't really need it.

The transport to the trial happened swiftly, dropping the three of us in a deep forest, surrounded by massively tall trees whose canopy prevented us from seeing the sky. Still, enough light filtered through to allow us to see, though we were in a deep shade.

"Look!" Aurora exclaimed and pointed at a small stone pedestal with a golden plaque on top of it.

"Saia, scout around, please," I said as I followed Aurora and Jiyun.

She flowed over my body and formed her drone, then flew off to circle our position.

The plaque was the same as the one we had encountered previously, giving information about what we had to do. Though, this one was a bit more informative.

Trial of the Forest—Entrance Seven

Goal of the Trial—The area is filled with beasts. Gather as many points as possible. Only points gained inside this trial will count toward the total. The trial will last for three days, and the top three challengers at the end will be granted a reward.

Beware! The Forest is home to four kings and an emperor, who rule over other beasts. Killing any of them will grant additional points.

Shadow Ferrorn King; Third Investment—30,000 points.

Golden Flame Angul King; Third Investment—30,000 points.

Stone Dragon Tortoise King; Third Investment—30,000 points.

Starry Sky Spirit Owl King; Third Investment—30,000 points.

Calm River Ungoir Emperor; Fourth Investment—90,000 points.

"Well," I started. "That's interesting. Two of these kings are animals from Earth."

"What do you think that means?" Jiyun asked.

"Who knows? It is already apparent that the Grand Spell is taking a bit more of an active role in all of this." I waved at the plaque. "Whether it has taken animals from Earth and improved them, then placed them here, or it just recreated them or whatever else, it doesn't really matter. What matters is that we have a good opportunity here."

"You aren't thinking about going after any of these, are you?" Aurora asked with a shocked expression.

I pointed my finger at the first beast king on the plaque. "I've faced a ferrorn before, on Ish Vimza, both a young one and a mature one that was in its Fourth Investment."

And that was back when I was just a Fledgling vampire with no Mask. I was far stronger now. But this also gave me a reference point. A Third Investment ferrorn was considered a powerful beast, and I was confident that I could take it.

A smile rose on my face. This was an amazing opportunity for me. The blood I drank on Ish Vimza gave me on average between one and two Carvings, and that was on Kirios. This place counted as Earth—or rather Terra— and Suul'dar, which meant that the increased Investment gain was active. I could push myself ahead just by going around and drinking blood. I didn't even need to kill the beasts myself. People would be leaving carcasses everywhere, I only needed to find them.

I felt almost giddy at the opportunity.

"Hey," Aurora started. "At least we don't need to fight other challengers."

I looked at her with a raised eyebrow. "Oh honey," I said slowly.

"What? It's a trial about killing beasts!"

Jiyun cleared her throat. "It's a trial about gathering points. Killing people gives you their points. And seeing as how Marianna is near the top of the list right now, killing her would probably guarantee someone the win."

Aurora's mouth hung open as she looked from one to the other. Then she threw her hands up in the air. "I hate this place."

I chuckled, but then sobered quickly. "I say we go for the kings. Beasts outside usually give between a few hundred to a few thousand. Split three ways that is going to be a lot of beasts if we want to take the top spot. Not that we should avoid any other beasts—we should kill anything in our way."

Jiyun and Aurora exchanged looks, then turned to look at me as Jiyun spoke. "And what about other people?"

I tilted my head before answering. "I'm not going to attack first, if that's what you're worried about. Though I don't have much confidence that others will leave us alone if we meet up with them. The Suul though, I'm not taking any chances with them."

Jiyun dipped her head. "I agree."

"That's the plan then," Aurora said, then turned to look back at the plaque. "You know, if these names are literal, I could probably track this Stone Dragon Tortoise King."

"Good thing we brought you then." I smiled at her.

She stuck her tongue out at me, but her eyes sparkled mischievously. Then she closed her eyes and with an expression of concentration used her skill. I'd grown more sensitive to her skill, so I felt it ripple across the Way. It was a strange sensation to describe, almost like I felt a sudden change of pressure in the air.

"I got a lot of big stone formations, but nothing that's moving, though I guess the beast could be resting. Maybe we should check some of those?"

I nodded. "The Grand Spell would've infused Source in the animal. Mutation usually comes with growth, from what Shadow told me at least."

"This way then." Aurora pointed, and we followed.

Saia would come back eventually with her report. Her drone always knew where I was, so it wasn't an issue. And then I could send her out to search for other kings, or this emperor.

Tracking down the king beasts proved a bit of a challenge. Saia's scouting had discovered a few beasts in the area, and without anything else to go on, we headed toward the closest one. It was a big brown bear, one that was obviously changed by the Source. It wasn't larger, but instead it had horns on top of its head that curled forward. It was unclear what other changes it could have, but I knew that it would have at least some skills.

I could scent it at a distance as we huddled behind a giant root of a tree and looked at the bear pushing its snout in a big bush, looking for something. By now, I was fairly adept at telling how powerful beasts or people were, at least roughly, by the smell of their blood. The more Investment the target had, the more appetizing their blood smelled.

I would put this one in between the First and Second Investment, give or take a few Carvings up or down.

"Okay," I started. "Aurora, you distract it with that ground wobbly thingy you do. I'll go ahead and smack it on the head, and Jiyun you go around and stab it in the back. Saia, you fly above and make sure that nothing comes and pounces on us while our backs are turned."

"Wobbly thingy?" Aurora nearly screeched.

I jumped on her and pulled her down as the bear raised its head. "Shhhh." I put my hand over her mouth, as her wide eyes looked back at me.

"Great," I said as I saw the bear turn in our direction. "Same plan, only faster. Aurora, go!"

The blond jumped to her feet and pointed a hand at the charging bear as Jiyun started sprinting away from us and Saia took to the sky. I felt the bear activate a skill, and its speed increased as it leveled its horns at us.

The ground beneath its feet shook, and a crack opened up. The bear slipped and toppled, skidding across the ground. I rushed forward, raising my serpent-tongue spear for an attack from above.

The bear noticed my approach and roared as it pushed with its legs and tried to skewer me. I danced aside and swung, opening a gash on its shoulder, spilling blood all over the ground.

Before it could recover, Jiyun blurred at its back and stabbed her sword through its stomach all the way to the hilt. The bear's cry of pain accompanied a quick attempt at turning around, and I took advantage. With a quick step, I got close and stabbed my weapon through its neck straight down into its body. The bear shook for a few seconds, refusing to die, and then slumped to the ground, as its last breath drew near.

I didn't wait for it to die, and instead got close and bit into its neck, drinking deeply.

"Uh, gross, Marianna, you couldn't have waited for like two minutes?" Aurora said from the side, but I ignored her.

Memories flooded my mind: the bear moving about the forest, encountering other beasts, the biome of the forest changing often. From a distance it heard a shrill call of an owl and ran, leaving a territory where the tree trunks were white and the leaves above black.

I shook my head and pulled out of the memories, then stood. Jiyun had her eyes averted while Aurora looked at me with morbid fascination in her eyes.

Saia landed next to me, her drone now almost coming up to my hip.

"Some help, please." I tapped my chin, and Saia's eyes flashed.

"Statement: I am not your personal cleaning service."

"Oh, please, you want to eat anything that has even a tiny bit of Source-infused biomass, and look." I pointed at the bear. "We got you a whole bear. The least you can do is help the girl out a bit."

Saia's eyes narrowed, then a tiny portion of her separated and swallowed up my face.

"Thash nosh—argh!—" I tried to speak, but my words came out all muffled as she spilled over my mouth and nose.

Aurora laughed nearby, and Jiyun cleared her throat.

"That got us eight hundred points each," Jiyun said as I pulled Saia away from my face enough that I could speak.

"How do you know?" I asked as Saia finished and flowed down my body and to the ground to rejoin the drone.

Jiyun just pointed above her head. A fading number 800 floated there. I blinked and looked at Aurora, who had the same number. I raised my head and saw that I had the number floating above me too. In a span of another two seconds it faded completely and was gone.

"Okay then," I said slowly. "Guess that's how we know. Wait, do we have to do the math or . . . Saia, you're on math duty."

The dragon gave me a look of utmost contempt, but didn't comment.

"Okay, I have some information. It looks like there are several different biomes of the forest around. The trees change colors. I'm going to make a guess and say that each king and emperor live in a different biome."

"What would this one be then?" Aurora asked as she looked around.

I followed her gaze. "Green leaves and tall trees, I don't think it matches any of the big beasts' names. Maybe the shadow ferrorn?"

"You said that you encountered that type of beast before. What was it like? How dangerous?" Jiyun asked.

"Very. It's like a cross between a big cat and a lizard. From what Shadow told me, the species living on Ish Vimza evolved through the Source so that it had increased strength and a kind of aura of terror. Seeing as how this one is called a shadow ferrorn we can assume that it has shadow skills. It shouldn't be as strong as the ones I fought on Ish Vimza, though. Well, the mature one at least. The bear did pass through a dark biome on its way here, so perhaps we can find the ferrorn."

"Let's go then," Jiyun said. "We don't have any time to waste."

We spent the entire day pushing forward, following the bear's memories in reverse. We encountered a few beasts along the way and dispatched them quickly enough. None were over the Second Investment, at least I didn't think so. Aurora gained two Carvings, bringing her up to Ninth Carving, just one away from advancing her Mask to the Second Investment. Her Investment was tied to utilizing the earth or stone. It didn't require combat, but it did require using her skills to achieve some goal. Mindless use of skills didn't do anything. That was what she told me, at least. I was sure that there was more to it; she was an Exemplar and had learned from the dwarves directly. That they had allowed her to take one of their respected Masks was incredible. Shadow had told me that that rarely happened.

Jiyun was close as well. She had been on her Ninth Carving before we entered, though her Investment was more related to her use of the blade and got less for just fighting and killing.

I, on the other hand, got another full Carving. Getting Investment from blood was really unfair, for everybody else at least.

We'd gotten close to 2,000 points each, which I thought was a nice haul for half a day. We rested for a while until Saia flew back from her scouting and landed next to me.

"Report: Humans ahead, a group of two."

We got to our feet and ready. "What gear do they have?"

"Feedback: Metal armor and weapons."

So, they had geared in the challenge or had primitive gear made before heading in. Not many had things like that.

"Aurora, Jiyun, you go ahead and meet them. I'll be nearby."

Aurora raised her eyebrows. "Why?"

"I want to see what they'll try to do without knowing that I'm around."

Jiyun nodded. "A vampire's presence will change how they'll act."

With that, Saia told them a more precise direction, and they were off, while I followed after them at a distance.

It didn't take them long to meet up with them, and I hurried forward so that I could hear more than a hushed murmur.

"We should continue together, there is strength in numbers," one of the two men said. He was tall, and carried a double-sided axe that had a larger head but a shorter handle than what such a weapon should have. It occurred to me that it could've been a dwarven weapon because of the handle length.

The other was just a handspan shorter than the first and carried a sword. Both had the same armor, a gambeson like Aurora's with an identical breast-plate secured over it. Obviously rewards from the rifts.

"We can take care of ourselves, thank you very much," Aurora huffed.

I blinked; I had missed the start of the conversation but this . . . *Oh, no.*

"Two little girls like you, all alone surrounded by beasts. We could help you out," the other one said.

Oh, no, no, no. I nearly stepped into a tree from shock. There was no way this was really happening, no way these people were for real, not here. Did they not realize where they were? No one was here if they were weak.

"Thank you, but we don't need any protection," Jiyun said stiffly, her hand gripping the handle of her sword tightly.

"C'mon," one of the men started. "We're just trying to help; you don't need to be a bitch about it."

I nearly gagged, and that was my cue.

I walked up behind them, in clear sight of Aurora and Jiyun, though the two men heard nothing.

"Yeah," the other man said. "We should team up. We could take down beasts faster, get more points, look after each other's backs. We're both a man short."

"How did that happen?" Jiyun asked, and I paused just behind the two men, interested in learning why they were just two. I didn't sense anyone else nearby, nor had Saia reported anyone either.

The taller of the two men seemed emboldened that Jiyun wanted to continue the conversation that he spilled immediately. "We partnered up with Jean Dubois, you know that guy that was in the top ten? But the fucker decided to abandon us once we read the trial rules. Well, screw him, we don't need him!"

Jean Dubois. I remembered the name. He was the only one among the challengers that had arrived with a full set of armor, and one that looked like it had been made from materials common on Kirios. I had a suspicion that he was one of the Exemplars that had made a deal with one of the Kirios factions and was equipped by them.

"What about you two?" the other man asked. "Someone left you, or did you lose someone? This place is dangerous after all."

Aurora tilted her head. "We never said that we're alone." She made it sound so innocent, the way she said it, but her eyes betrayed the mirth she attempted to keep in.

"What?" They stiffened, suddenly realizing that perhaps they didn't stumble upon two helpless women in the woods.

I was close enough now that I could touch them. I leaned forward and whispered.

"So, you're going to protect our helpless little selves?"

They yelped and turned, readying their weapons. I saw the moment they fully took in what they were looking at. I had Saia in her armor mode, but that left my face clear. They could see my eyes, and I saw the exact moment when they realized what I was.

I wrinkled my nose as one of them quite literally pissed himself.

"Ah, damn."

Hunting Kings

I t wasn't my fault!" I said, just a tad bit embarrassed.

Aurora snickered next to me, and Jiyun avoided looking at my face.

"I am not that scary," I mumbled. Granted, I did want to scare them a bit, but I did not intend to make them have an . . . accident.

Aurora laughed, then quickly sobered up. "Wait, you're serious?"

"What do you mean?" I asked.

"Marianna," Aurora said, her voice steady. "You're terrifying, you do know that, right?"

I blinked. I opened my mouth, then closed it. I wasn't really that dense. I knew that I was a vampire, and that people were afraid of me. It had been my reality for years, since I was turned. But, it had also been true before, when I worked for the cartel as a human. There was always an undercurrent of fear when I interacted with people.

Now though . . . I had seen it, of course. What the public, the people outside of those that I had grown up with, believed was much different. Vampires were monsters out of old stories.

But me? I wasn't all that. At least I hadn't really thought about it. I always found the fear of others amusing because I knew who I was inside, that I wasn't someone who would just snap and kill everyone in the room.

Yet perhaps I was wrong.

Seeing how I didn't respond to Aurora's question, Jiyun changed the topic.

"Was it really alright, letting them go like that?"

"You told them a lot about the area," Aurora added.

I grimaced. The truth was that I had incurred debt toward them. They hadn't really done anything other than say some stupid stuff. And I not only scared them but also caused a lot of humiliation to one of them. I didn't need to do that; I had no real cause to do it. I only realized it after it happened. I really needed to start acting with more thought.

I repaid my debt to them by giving them information that I had gained from the memories of the bear and other beasts we encountered. It had also netted me another Carving in my Revelator Ornament, bringing it up to nine.

I turned to look at Aurora and opened my mouth, then hesitated. I didn't want to reveal what the reason for my actions was. "They aren't important, and I don't think that you wanted to group up with them."

"Of course not," Aurora huffed. "At least they told us that there are Suul in the area."

I grimaced. That was an issue. Even the two other challengers had confirmed that the Suul did not respond to any attempts at diplomacy.

"We always expected to meet with them again," I said. "But with Saia scouting ahead we should be able to avoid them. It is best if we focus on killing beasts."

Both girls agreed, and we continued, following the memories of beasts that showed me a path to a part of the forest shrouded in shadows.

We had to hurry. We'd already been here for a day and had gathered around 10,000 points each killing beasts, but that wasn't going to be enough. The two humans were close to that number too. We only had two days left.

The shift from a normal forest—or rather relatively normal forest—to one filled with deep shadows wasn't subtle. One moment the trees were tall and brown with a green-leaved canopy, and then the bark was dark, the canopy thicker and the leaves a deeper green that almost looked black.

We continued on cautiously. We'd already encountered a few beasts that seemed to be more adept at stealth, enough so that neither Aurora nor Jiyun detected them before we got really close. My senses had become our only early warning, that and Saia's scouting ahead.

It was barely an hour into our trek through the dark forest when we came upon a corpse of a large beast, its wounds familiar to me. Big chunks of meat were gone as the beast fed on it. The blood was still warm.

"This was done by a ferrorn," I said as I inspected the wounds and the tracks nearby. What confused me was why the beast had left the carcass here. Something either spooked it, or perhaps it just didn't act in the same manner as such predators on Earth did. "This ferrorn is definitely not a young one, though by the size of these tracks and wounds, it is not quite the size of the mature one I encountered before. Though, this species might just be smaller."

"So, we are going after it?" Aurora asked nervously.

I nodded. "I can track it, I think." I had some tracking experience from when I learned the skill. I had lost the skill, but the knowledge taught to me by the remnant of Martin still remained.

I did have a [Lesser Track] skill, but it was on my shelf, and I didn't want to waste a slot in my profile for it. My senses should be more than enough to follow after the beast. In the worst case I could burn the skill. It wasn't that important.

We decided on a rough plan of attack once we found it, then set off. I was in the lead, with Aurora just behind me and Jiyun taking the rear. Saia was in her drone form and flew above us in the canopy, shrouded by the shadow.

I followed the tracks and the scent of blood that it left in its wake. We still didn't know if this was the king, or just another ferrorn, but we kept ready for anything.

It didn't take us long to reach a large cave entrance surrounded by bushes and vine growths. We came to a stop nearby, hiding behind a tree and looking inside.

"It's there, I can hear it," I whispered.

"How are we doing this?" Aurora asked.

"I think plan C should work," I said slowly as I glanced up at Saia who had grabbed hold of a low branch above us. "With the slight change of you going in and drawing it out."

Saia tilted her head, then nodded. I turned my attention to the girls. "Jiyun, you take that rock by the entrance. Aurora, you stay here and strike the moment it follows Saia out. I'll be above the entrance."

Without too much more talking, we scattered and got in position. I climbed to the top of the cave entrance, my weapon held firmly in my hands and ready. I verified that the girls were in position and motioned to Saia. She flew into the cave, and almost immediately a loud roar echoed from within. Saia blasted out with the ferrorn following behind her.

It looked generally the same as the ferrorn I had faced before, smaller than the mature one that I had faced on Ish Vimza, which made it come up to around my shoulder. Its color was different too. Instead of blue skin with purple stripes, this one had black skin with gray stripes. Its back was covered in the same growths that the other of its kind had, only these were sharper and looked more like spikes.

Its sinuous neck stretched forward as it looked up at Saia flying above it. Then the ground shook; its footing slipped, though it didn't fall. I leaped from above, stabbing my long-bladed weapon in an attempt to skewer it through the back. I triggered [Triple Thrust], and the air shimmered as my spear stabbed forward.

The ferrorn slid to the side, the shadows around it flickering. The attack that was meant to pierce it in the center of its back missed. One of my thrusts caught the back side of its body, opening a long but shallow gash on its thigh.

The ferrorn turned and pounced on me immediately, its jaw opening wide.

Shit. It was faster than I expected. [Dodge] let me twist out of the way, my muscles straining as the skill pushed them beyond their limits. As the ferrorn flew by me next to the cave entrance, Jiyun blurred from the side, her sword flashing in a crescent that cut its side. The ferrorn roared again and turned to attack when the wall of the entrance shifted, and a stone spike grew out, piercing its shoulder.

I dashed in, swinging my weapon from above, but the ferrorn fell into its shadow.

I cursed inwardly and turned, looking around for any sign of it. A faint noise and an imprint in the Way alerted me to the skill being used. I jumped next to Jiyun, pushing her out of the way as the shadow in front of her rippled and the ferrorn started to rise. I swung my weapon one handed at it.

Another imprint in the Way just behind me told me that I had fallen into a trap. The ferrorn rose from the shadow ahead of me, while something attacked from behind me.

I tried to evade, but didn't get away in time. A thin shadow spike rose from my own shadow and pierced through my forearm, making me drop my serpent-tongue spear, just as the ferrorn's wicked claws came down toward my head.

I didn't have the time to evade, so I stepped into the attack instead.

[Overburn Skill—Lesser Tough Skin]

I felt my skin harden, as I collided with the ferrorn. I wasn't light, but it out-massed me. It bowled over me, its claw raking across my back and getting stuck on the plate of my vest. As we were falling, I twisted and landed on top of it before rolling and getting my feet in between us and kicking as hard as I could.

I threw it off, but its claws caught and ripped my shoulder open from back to front. I bit back a scream and got to my knees as the ferrorn recovered and came back at me.

Saia dived from above, her claws scratching across its face and making it cry out in pain. I took the moment to recover; my hand hovered over my revolver, but then I decided against it. I only had four bullets left.

Instead, I yelled out.

"Saia, blade and chain!"

The dragon disengaged and flew toward me, changing midair. I caught the blade and chain, but not all of her turned into weapons. She had enough mass now that she could do more than a single thing. Her drone, slightly smaller, turned around and continued the attack on the beast.

The ferrorn dashed toward me, but a crack in the ground opened up, trapping one of its limbs inside. Jiyun attacked from behind, dancing around it, and attacked its hind legs, cutting deeply to slice through its tendons.

I whipped up my chain then let it fly from above, wrapping it around the ferrorn's head. With a groan, I pulled, dropping its head to the ground and immobilizing it. Jiyun saw the opportunity and got on top of it, stabbing the back of its neck. The ferrorn started thrashing as she sliced through and her blade came out through its throat. I kept a tight grip on it as it died. As it stilled and its breathing got labored, I stepped close and gripped its long neck with one hand to keep it steady while I leaned down and drank my fill, finishing it in the process.

The memories flowed through me, and I let them sink in.

Once I was done, I stepped back and sighed.

"Are you okay?" Aurora asked.

She and Jiyun stood nearby, having approached while I was drinking.

I frowned then saw that she was looking at my bloody shoulder. "Fine, it's already healed."

She shook her head. "I'm never going to get used to that. Also! I got another Carving, I'm Second Investment now!"

"Congratulations," both I and Jiyun said, though I could see the slightly envious look on Jiyun's face.

"I got another skill too. I'm going to be a lot more useful now," Aurora announced.

I raised my eyebrow. "Oh?"

As an answer Aurora's face scrunched up, and she focused. I felt the skill activate, and the ground beneath my feet rose up quickly enough that it launched me in the air. I twisted and landed on my feet, looking back at Aurora unamused.

"Aw, that's not fair," she complained.

"Don't worry, I'm sure it will be useful on things other than me."

Aurora stuck her tongue at me, and I chuckled.

I turned away and rolled my shoulder as I looked back to the cave. "Well, I know why it left that beast carcass behind," I said to the others.

They gave me a strange look as I walked toward it. Inside I found what I had seen in its memories. The ferrorn was attacked by a human, and it killed him. I found his corpse inside, mangled and half eaten. Still, I didn't look away.

Instead, I searched around and found things that had survived. I left the cave with a small dagger and a ring that gave the [Lesser Night Vision] skill.

The dagger went to Aurora while the ring found its way to Jiyun's finger, after a thorough cleaning.

With that done, we continued through the forest, Saia scouting and leading us toward more beasts as we searched for more kings.

"Stop, stop, stop!" Aurora called out as we walked through the woods.

We fought another three groups of beasts. We killed a predator that attempted to ambush us, that looked like a big lizard that lived up in the canopy. It had skin stretched between its legs that allowed it to glide like a flying squirrel. That manner of ambush didn't end well for it.

The other two were a staglike herd and a wild boar that had steel spines growing out of its back.

"What is it?" I asked, already looking around for any danger.

"I can feel a large piece of stone moving!" Aurora said.

"Stone Dragon Tortoise?" I asked.

"Probably." Aurora nodded excitedly.

"Lead the way!" I said.

We'd already walked through two different biomes, though we hadn't found another beast king or any sign of them.

With the last one that we killed we each got 10,000 points, and so far we were nearing 30,000 points each total. Which was great, as it was almost the end of day two. There wasn't really nighttime on this halo, nor was there a real sun. The light was generated somehow, but at least we could tell the time since the end of the day was announced in the trial.

Aurora led us forward, and we made good time.

Finally, we reached our destination.

"There it is." Aurora pointed as she whispered.

I looked to where she was pointing and saw a tortoise the size of a bus slowly trekking through the bushes, chomping the thick roots that grew out of the trees.

"And so it is," I said slowly. The tortoise's shell was solid rock, pale gray in color with a spiked surface covered in moss. Its limbs were tree trunks, and its head had a stone ridge on top of its forehead.

"How do we do this?" Jiyun asked.

Honestly, after the ferrorn I was pretty sure that I could take it myself. But we were here so that all of us could get stronger, so I had to get them somehow involved.

These king beasts were strong, but they were ultimately beasts. We had weapons and teamwork on our side.

We came up with a plan and then executed. We left our packs and gear we didn't need behind a tree and headed for the beast. Like before, attacking from an ambush was a huge advantage, something that could end a fight before it really started.

Aurora began our attack by opening up a crack in the ground beneath the tortoise's foot. It fell in, a surprised grunt leaving its throat. Saia landed on its head from above, intent on clawing its eyes out as I rushed it from one side and Jiyun from the other.

Saia's claws skidded off the stone on its forehead as it moved its head out of the way, then faster than I had expected, it pulled its body inside its shell.

My spear missed the neck and hit the ground, while Jiyun's bounced off stone. Then the ground started to shake. A moment later, a pulse of rolling dirt exploded out from beneath the tortoise's shell, sending all of us to the ground.

As I fell, I saw the beast peek out of its shell, then stand. It looked in my direction and opened its mouth. Orange light blossomed deep within its throat so fast that I could only stare in shock. The last thought that went through my head was a simple reminder—*right, Dragon Tortoise*—and then I was on fire.

My skin was burning, and I screamed. I dropped to the ground and rolled, but the fire didn't seem to be going out. I could hear fighting around me through the roaring of the flames. The sound and the stench of my burning flesh roared up. I was healing and burning in a loop, the pain became every-thing. The **thirst** raged inside of me, its whispers filling my head.

An idea occurred to me, and I quickly acted.

[Swap Profile]

The pain lessened by a little as [Lesser Constitution] activated, but I focused on getting my feet under me and taking a step.

[Mist Step]

It was agony; it was like in an instant I had combusted completely, and every single part of my body was submerged in lava. And then the pain lessened. I was lucky. I hadn't known if that would work. When I re-formed, the fire didn't fol-low me, but I was completely burned, my flesh melted and dripping off my body.

I grabbed the rags that the clothes on my body had become and ripped them apart. Then the cacophony of voices rose from within my veins.

Drain them all, kill, kill, kill, feed, take everything. Grow! More, more, more more more more . . . Take all the power, take everything. Join their blood to ours, let us sing together. Drink, drink, drink.

The chant was pounding inside my head, and my head turned, one still functioning eye seeing only red. The beast was on its back; a meatbag was standing next to it, stabbing into its exposed flesh.

Another meatbag was coming my way, waving its thin hands, its warm blood pumping through its veins. My tongue slipped out but found no lips to lick; instead it passed over my fangs, cutting a long line that made my blood drip into my mouth.

The meatbag paused, and I took a step forward. I needed to drink, to drain, to heal. The meatbag took a step back; it was yelling now, turning and looking at the other one. Something landed nearby, but it had no blood singing within. It smelled of metal and strange crystals, I ignored it.

The other meatbag looked over, its sword raised as it gestured. The second meatbag ran for the one with the sword, next to the beast.

I launched myself forward, my legs barely holding me upright.

The meatbag with the weapon in hand swung, but it didn't attack me. Instead, its blade cut into the neck of the beast, and blood sprayed forth.

I changed direction, smashing into the neck of the beast, my teeth sinking into the wound and tearing flesh, swallowing the bloody chunks as I tried to get more and more blood, faster and faster down my throat.

The **thirst** was chanting still, but its attention shifted, and my mind cleared. With an effort of will, I grabbed hold of the **thirst** and took control of my emotions.

As I calmed, I didn't stop drinking. Everything that went into my stomach was quickly pulled out and sent through my veins. My heart was pounding in my chest like that of a human. Pumping my thick blood through my body and sending new blood where it needed to go.

Memories were drowned by the thrumming of the **thirst** through my head, just flashes that I couldn't parse.

My sense of self was heightened. I could feel the **thirst** working to heal me, feel it eating the burned skin and growing new healthy flesh. I could also feel something else, something both foreign and not, helping the **thirst**. It was as if the **thirst** had an accord with this thing. It thought that it was part of it.

And then the sensations faded, and I continued to drink, not trusting myself to do anything else. Finally, after a long time I felt like I was finally coming back to myself.

"Uh," I heard Aurora say. "Mari? Are you good? We have a situation here."

I still felt hungry, my body felt drained, but I pulled myself from the dead tortoise and turned my head.

Saia stood near me, her back to me as if she was standing guard. Jiyun was next to her and Aurora closer to me, with her back to the tortoise's side.

Across from them stood three Suul, their long lancelike and spurred weapons held pointed straight at us.

"Faithless," one of the three Suul, one with blue paint over his lower jaw and long neck, said. "Your deaths will aid the cause of the Horde."

My anger rose, and I stood up, glaring at three assholes that were about to be dead.

Emperor

I was pissed.

No, I was beyond pissed. My skin was raw, barely healed, my throat hurt, and I didn't think that I could even speak if I wanted to. One of my eyes was all blurry, and it ached. The fucking tortoise had nearly killed me. A fucking *tortoise*! Me, an Elder vampire.

My emotions were so far beyond something simple like anger that I didn't even have the words to explain them. And here came three Suul, and their dumb, holier-than-thou attitudes and their stupid faithless shit. They were dumb stone-age cave people, stupid ignorant zealots that believed in the same nonsense that half of humanity believed in and used as an excuse to wage war for thousands of years on one another.

"Lie down on the ground, faithless," the Suul said, as if he was being merciful. "Bare your throat and take your place in the dirt."

Ignorant fucking *malparido* pieces of shit.

My sire's words echoed in my head. *Endeavor to never start anything. But if you have to, if your hand is forced, or matters of honor demand it, then end it quick; we do not play with our prey.*

"Mari, what are we—"

I didn't listen, I threw myself at them like the rabid fucking monster that I was. *Forced hand? Hah!* The fucking assholes threatened us, threatened me with death. It was a matter of debt; there was no honor in any part of their worthless bodies.

I didn't think; I just acted. The Suul were surprised but reacted quickly. A spear stabbed through my stomach, attempting to stop my reckless charge, and failed.

I kept going, breaking the weapon with my weight even as it impaled me straight through. I swiped with my hand, faster than it could even follow, and opened its throat up with my nails as sharp as claws.

The **thirst** sang its encouragement, but I was in control now. I just let loose. The Scarlet Moon Style sang in my mind. The other two Suul attacked, and I let them; their skills gave them speed that wasn't great enough to match mine. I still let them hit me. Not because I couldn't avoid them, but because it didn't matter.

A stab through my shoulder didn't even slow me down. I grabbed the spear and pulled, bringing the Suul close enough that I could grab its neck and pull it down to my level. I bit into its throat and drank as it thrashed against me, trying to stop me.

I heard a gurgle from behind, a yell of warning, but it didn't matter. Acid splashed against my back, but after the agony of the fire, it barely tickled. I threw the drained husk aside and turned.

The last Suul turned to run, but I didn't let him. [Mist Step] sent me through him and on the other side where I re-formed and turned, taking a spear straight through the heart. I swung my hand down, breaking the shaft, then in a single quick step got close enough that I punched straight through his torso.

I tsked to myself as I missed the heart. I could hear it pumping just next to my forearm, deep in the chest cavity. I pulled out my arm then caught the falling head and sat down with it in my lap, my teeth sinking into the throat. Then I started drinking.

I still felt drained, I still felt like I was burning. I was raw. The blood flowed down my throat, and I moaned in ecstasy of it. There was nothing better in the world than this feeling. It was life itself.

"Okaaay," I heard Aurora say nearby.

"Get away from her," I heard Jiyun add in a whisper. Fear made her voice trembly just a little bit.

"You don't think that she's going to, uh, attack us? Right?" Aurora added.

"Report: Marianna's biometrics are returning to normal."

I felt a tiny twinge of regret at the fact that they were afraid.

Mask of the Blood Reaver — Second Investment; Fifth Carving

My Carvings jumped ahead again, still no new skill though. I hoped that I would get something good soon.

I opened my eyes and looked at them over the corpse in my lap, still drinking blood.

They exchanged looks, but then continued watching in a kind of morbid fascination.

I sighed and pulled my teeth from the rapidly cooling flesh beneath me. I wiped my mouth with the back of my hand and threw the Suul off me, then stood up.

The way they took a step back made me wince inside.

"I'm not going to hurt you," I said slowly. "I was injured and hungry. I wasn't going to harm you." I didn't know if I was lying. At the time, they had been just bags filled with blood to me, and yet I wanted to believe that I would've gone for the tortoise whether Jiyun had opened its throat or not.

Aurora gave me a long look, then nodded to herself. "I trust you," she said and took a step forward.

Jiyun swallowed, then followed. "I do too. We are a team."

"Yeah," Aurora said, now smiling. "Team Sunny!"

I groaned but allowed a smile to blossom on my face.

Aurora got close to me, and looked me over, a faint blush on her face. "Uh . . . are you all right, your skin is kinda . . . pink? And I don't think that's because of all the blood."

I looked down. She was right. My skin was pink in places, freshly regrown, and it was still regenerating and regaining its darker tan. She was also right about the blood; it covered me. I was also topless. Looking around, I located my ruined vest and shirt.

"Ugh, that was my last shirt," I grumbled. I should've packed more, but I hadn't anticipated going through them that fast. I shouldn't have let my sire have one.

Aurora cleared her throat. "I can give you my gambeson if you—"

I waved my hand interrupting her. "Nah." I shook my head. "It's fine, you need it, and it's not like anyone will look at me and think about doing anything. I'm a vampire."

Aurora shifted and bit her lip. Her eyes were stuck on my chest. I narrowed my eyes at her, and somehow, she noticed my attention. She turned away, a blush spreading over her neck and cheeks.

I rolled my eyes. "Saia," I called to the dragon. "Can you help me clean up? And maybe cover me up a bit?"

"Feedback: Of course, because this Unit is your personal cleaning service."

"Don't be a baby," I chided as she flowed and spread all over my body, including my face, again.

"You killed it," I said a while later as Saia swarmed over the body of the tortoise, consuming it.

Jiyun and Aurora both looked at me with proud expressions on their faces. "Yeah!"

"Aurora flipped it over with her earth-moving skill, then I attacked its weak spots while it was immobilized," Jiyun added. "It tried to breathe fire at us again, but after what happened to you, we were more careful."

I nodded. I had to admit that I had underestimated the two of them. I thought that I had to protect them, to be the one to take the brunt of the effort in the challenge. I was wrong. They didn't need my protection; they were sufficiently capable by themselves. In fact, they'd protected me instead. I made a mistake that nearly cost me my life.

Being an Elder vampire gave me power, but even vampires had weaknesses. The sun used to be one big weakness, even for older vampires. But fire was one too. Not because we were somehow weak to it, no more than a human or a shifter was, but because it sent our system into a frenzy. Our bodies tried to regenerate the damage as soon as it happened, and burning was the worst kind of injury to suffer. Especially if we didn't quench the flames quickly. It drained us rapidly and prevented us from healing properly.

It was also agonizing, as I had just experienced.

"Thank you for helping me," I told them finally.

The girls gave me soft smiles.

"We are a team. It's what we do," Aurora added.

That we were.

"Report: This beast's Source-Weave infused biomass is familiar to me," Saia said once she finished consuming the tortoise's body.

I frowned from my spot nearby where I was finishing up drinking the Suul.

"What do you mean?"

"Feedback: Some elements seem to resemble of my [Plasma Shot] engram."

I narrowed my eyes. "You mean like the fucking fire blast that I took to the face?"

Saia's eyes flashed. "Feedback: Yes."

"Can you use it?"

"Feedback: It will prove beneficial in repairing my own engram."

At least getting nearly burned alive wasn't all for nothing.

"Okay, hop on and cover me up, please," I told her.

Since I'd lost my shirt and vest, Saia flowed over me and dressed me in a long-sleeved tunic-like garment. Like her surface, it was silver with tiny hexagons etched on the surface. It was also extremely skintight. Since I still wanted Saia to have a drone out, she couldn't use a lot of herself for my clothes. From what she shared, it was part of the undersuit that the Ke Erzi would wear beneath her full armor mode. Apparently, it was supposed to regulate heat, though that wasn't necessary for me.

I looked down and grimaced. It was form-fitting in the extreme, completely hugging each contour of my body. And it wasn't restrictive at all, meaning that I could move as freely as I wanted. It looked almost indecent on me, even more so somehow than if I was just nude.

"Couldn't you, like, make a plate and cover my chest or something?"

"Feedback: I could, but I would need mass from the drone."

I grimaced; the utility of her drone was too much. She still came up to my hip at her current size, which made her capable of being a bigger threat in combat. I decided that lowering her combat ability in return for my modesty wasn't that important.

I turned to where Jiyun and Aurora were taking a short but much needed little nap. They were humans, after all. The end of the second day was approaching, and tomorrow we would need to make the last push for points.

But, as much as I'd like to let them sleep, I needed them awake. I walked over and jostled them. Jiyun had advanced into the Second Investment, which put her on equal footing with Aurora now. But there was more for us to gain here. We gathered our things then headed out in search of more monsters.

We hunted monsters for several hours, each getting another Carving, and hitting high 40,000 points from just beasts. My points were far higher, as I had killed the three Suul. I realized that the winners of this trial were going to be the people that had killed the other challengers. It was inevitable. The three Suul had barely 200,000 points altogether, which was less than what I had total. Though, this trial boosted my points by a lot.

I knew that the main reason their numbers were that low was that the Suul probably worked together a lot more, so they split the gains.

Still, the only way someone was going to catch up to my numbers now was if they killed other challengers. Which made me a bit paranoid.

I had Saia watch out for any other challengers and help us avoid them as we focused on killing beasts. While that might not give us the win outright, the beasts in this trial gave more points, and those counted toward our main gain for the entire challenge. It also helped us gain more Investment. By now, I was fully healed and recovered, the blood from all the beasts working wonders.

"I think we should head that way." I pointed as we took a short break after killing a beast.

"Why?" Aurora asked.

"We haven't been able to find any other beast kings, despite heading to different biomes. Most likely others got to them before us. I think that we should go for the emperor."

"You think that it's that way?" Jiyun asked.

I nodded. "From the memories, I know that there is a river that way, and the emperor beast has 'River' in its name. It's our best shot at finding it."

"You really think that is necessary?" Aurora asked. "You killed the Suul and got their points. Unless someone else kills more than three other challengers, it's unlikely that they have more than you."

I waved my hand. "It's not about winning. I mean, sure, I'd like to win the trial, but it is more about the opportunity for growth. I'm sure that the Fourth Investment beast would push us ahead by a lot."

Jiyun tilted her head. "Isn't it too dangerous? You nearly died from the tortoise."

I grimaced. "That was my mistake, and if I'm being honest, I feel like that beast was at least mid-Third Investment. No way was it on the same level as the ferrorn. But it is your choice. We are a team, and we'll do it together or not at all."

For a moment I considered telling them that I needed its blood, that my Mask required it to advance, but I didn't.

"You think that we can handle it?" Aurora asked.

"I do." I nodded and smiled. "We might not know what it is, but I'm sure that we can rise to the challenge."

Aurora and Jiyun looked at each other and then agreed.

We found the river in a couple of hours, killing beasts along the way. I had Saia scout ahead down the river as we walked its banks searching for our target. We had to step away and hide among the trees when other groups came through as we didn't want to deal with them after what happened with the first one we encountered.

It turned out that assholes that didn't want to work together at the start of the challenge were still assholes. Thankfully, once I showed myself, their attempts at intimidation vanished, and they executed a hasty retreat.

We walked for hours, and I was starting to fear that we wouldn't find it in time as the trial slowly drew to a close.

Then Saia flew back.

"Report: I have found the Calm River Ungoir Emperor."

"You sure?"

"Feedback: As much as I can be. It is a powerful, large beast."

"Let's go."

We walked down the river, ready for anything, while Saia filled us in on what the beast looked like. It didn't take us long to find it. It was sitting on top of a rock next to a shallow ford.

The ungoir was a reptile, with blue scales and fins over its spine and on top of its head. It was large, about the size of a full-grown elephant, except it was lithe. Its head reminded me of an eel. It was long and curled up on itself in a weird way so I couldn't see all of its body, so it might be larger than it looked. The most important thing was that it was sleeping.

Which was the most perfect opportunity for us to ambush it.

"Okay," I whispered as we hid behind the tree. "I say we try this the quick way."

"And that is?" Aurora asked.

"The *stab it while it sleeps* way," I clarified.

"It has long claws," Jiyun commented, and I glanced back at the beast. She was right. It was curled up but I could see one of its limbs, which was tipped with wicked claws.

"Don't worry. We'll just drop from above kill it in one shot, and we won't ever need to see it use them," I said with a grin.

Aurora sighed; I cringed. "Why, Mari, just . . . why?"

I closed my eyes. "Fuck, I know."

Jiyun looked at Aurora and me like we'd grown an extra head. "What is happening?"

"She jinxed us," Aurora told her.

Jiyun blinked once, slowly. "Aha."

"Let's get to it. I don't want it to wake up," I continued, hoping that fate wasn't going to be laughing in my face soon.

We had a plan. Now it was all about executing it. I didn't want to mess up like with the tortoise, so I made a mental note to not be an arrogant vampire.

The fact that the beast was sleeping on a rock made Aurora a lot more dangerous to it, so her job was to stay hidden and deal the first blow.

Jiyun was near her; her job was to keep Aurora safe and help where needed—in case they fucked up royally, that was, as the plan was still to kill it in a single strike.

Fourth Investment beast meant that its skin was a lot more durable than the others. The fourth tier was a big leap ahead. Invested became more at that point, their bodies denser, more powerful. I remembered the powerful beasts that I faced on Ish Vimza.

I had the physical strength to injure them. I only hoped that it would be enough.

My job was to deal the killing blow, preferably in a single shot. I climbed the tree directly above it. My trusty serpent-tongue spear tied to my back, and I had already used [Quick Swap Slot] to replace [Dodge] with [Slash]. Saia was sitting on a nearby branch, waiting in case she was needed just like Jiyun.

I crawled along a branch until I was directly over the beast. Then I got ready.

I pulled my weapon from my back, and once I was in position I waved at Aurora.

She waved back, then pointed her hand at the beast and focused. I waited. There was the impression of the skill being used, as Aurora shaped and blasted out spikes made out of stone directly from the rock the beast was sleeping on. It yelped in pain, and I dropped down, triggering a skill.

[Slash]

My weapon blurred down and cut clean through the beast's neck just as it was attempting to rise. The head toppled to the ground, blood splashing out of the wound.

I grinned like a maniac and turned around to look at Aurora and Jiyun, who grinned right back at me.

"Ha! It worked."

Their expressions turned from mirth to panic as their eyes widened.

Instantly I turned around. The beast kept moving, uncoiling from the rock even as its head remained on the floor. Three stone spikes were clearly visible on the rock beneath, but only the tips were bloody; they hadn't penetrated deep.

I watched in total disbelief as from next to the cleanly cut neck that I had just slashed through, two more heads rose up to glare at me.

"Ah, fuck."

I was so shocked that I didn't react in time as one of the beast's two remaining heads lashed out and hit me across the chest, sending me flying into the ford. I landed in the water, hitting my back against the hard rocks.

The beast roared, and then the ground shook as the now two-headed beast charged at me.

Offer

So, the emperor beast turned out to be a hydra-like creature with three heads. Would I have liked to have known that information before? Of course! But there's little I could do about it now. Sure, I could curse myself for being impatient, for not waiting and watching the beast longer. But then again, we were on a time crunch and the trial was drawing to a close.

The ungoir was down a head, but that didn't seem to be slowing it down any. I sat up in the ford, water soaking through me, and grimaced at the sound of bones popping in my chest as my ribs settled back in place and healed. The beast had nearly caved in my chest with that strike, and now it was charging at me.

Before I could even try to think of a way out, the ground rumbled, and the beast slowed as it attempted to keep its footing. Jiyun charged from behind and leaped over its back; then her hands flashed as she swung her sword, and six crescent cuts appeared in its back.

I saw the blood gush out, and the beast roared in pain and anger. Its tail swung and swatted Jiyun from the air, sending her beyond my sight.

Saia dived and slammed into one of the heads, then started clawing at it. I got up and realized that I had lost my weapon, leaving only my daggers and my revolver.

I cursed then charged forward as the beast's second head grabbed hold of Saia with its maw and started shaking, attempting to rip her apart with the other head.

I drew one of my daggers then hurled it with as much strength as I had. It slammed into the second head's eye, and it let my dragon go.

"Saia, glaive!" I yelled.

[Overburn Skill—Lesser Leap]

The dragon collapsed into a pool of goo that flew at me, then re-formed into a glaive and bracers as I leaped. I swung with [Slash], intending to cut off another head, but instead my glaive opened a deep gash in the side of its neck as the beast retreated.

Both heads glared at me, each with one good eye. One still had my dagger stuck in it, and the other had been mauled by Saia.

As I dropped to the ground, the beast reared back, its heads rising high above me. Then the ground split open, and one of its legs fell in. The stone on the riverbank flowed and flashed upward as spikes formed and impaled it in the stomach. They didn't get deep before they broke, but they pierced the skin.

I took advantage. I ran forward, letting my anger rise and flow through me, I focused on the pain in my chest and the embarrassment of being wrong again, my worry for Jiyun, all of it rose to the surface.

The Scarlet Moon Style used those emotions to fuel me forward. *Advance, Whirling Mist.*

I flowed, spinning beneath and cutting open its chest, not stopping as it roared again. I danced to its side, my glaive twisting in my arms and opening up new wounds all along its stomach.

Its tail lashed out, and I ducked beneath it, my glaive swiping across its back leg. It leaped forward, getting away from me, but I went after it, moving so fast that it could barely follow me. We waded into the ford, and the ankle-deep water slowed me down some, but not enough.

It raised its limbs and pounded the ground, sending water and rock flying in all directions and forcing me to step back.

Its heads rose, their mouths opened, and the long necks bulged. Then, two fast-moving bolts of water smashed into me, sending me flying as the crack of them breaking the speed barrier echoed in my ears.

I smashed against the rocks on the riverbank, breaking bones and spraying blood out of my mouth as my bones were shattered and organs pulverized.

My mind got foggy, and my vision doubled as the beast hobbled toward me. The ground was shaking, and someone was yelling. Spikes of stone rose from the water, but the beast ignored them. I saw a sword fly through the air and strike its side, sinking in by perhaps a third of the blade.

The beast was close. It was bleeding so much from so many wounds that the river had turned red. Both its maws opened as it prepared to chomp down on me.

I raised my arm.

[Blood Gout]

Its wounds split open as blood rushed out of it like from a fountain. A dozen ropes of blood flew out of it, startling the beast and forcing it to retreat a step as all that blood flowed straight into my open mouth.

The **thirst** rejoiced; my body burned as it healed at a rate that nothing else on Earth but a vampire could. I rose, the pain just a distant throbbing—**the voices of the thirst wanted more.**

The skill ended, and I pounced on the unstable beast as it fell to its knees from the blood loss. I wrapped my limbs around one of its long necks, my claws digging in deep and clawing to get deeper.

Its hide was tough, covered in scales, though not everywhere. I opened up long gashes then slipped my hands inside, gouging flesh, using skills every time they came off cooldown.

[Triple Thrust]
[Slash]

The head started coughing, blood spouting out of the wounds I was making.

The other head struck before I even had the chance to respond. It bit my hip, serrated teeth gnawing on my bones. I screamed and bit into the neck in front of me, drinking.

Water rose all around me, attempting to drown me. Unfortunately for the beast, I didn't need to breathe.

The beast collapsed, the first head wheezing while the other weakly attempted to pull me off. Quickly, its bite lost its strength, and I turned my attention to it. I pulled out my second dagger and stabbed the other head straight through the top of its skull. Then I continued to drink blood and let the memories flow.

The beast was an emperor, the top of the food chain, yet its memories were unremarkable. Except that it had butchered a group of Suul on the first day.

***Mask of the Blood Reaver — Second Investment; Seventh Carving
[Blood Empowerment] skill gained.***

Finally, the second skill. I had a vague idea what it did, though no details. The name was suggestive enough.

Once I was done drinking, I stepped back, my leg giving out and forcing me down to my knees in the water. I glanced down and saw the damage it had done to my hip. Even with my stomach full with blood, I was aching all over.

I turned my eyes away from the beast, looking for Jiyun and Aurora, and found them immediately.

"Ah, fuck."

Jiyun was propped against a tree, holding her stomach, clearly injured—whether from that tail strike from the beast or something else, I didn't know.

A man stood over her, a hooked harpoon in his arms and pointed at her head. He wore full black plate armor, with dark blue and red strips of cloth hanging from his shoulder and waist like a cloak and skirt. His helmet completely sealed his face, leaving only a thin strip for him to look out of. A finlike crest topped his head, tilted backward.

Two more stood nearby, both burly men, wide and muscled, wearing rough-looking clothing that barely covered them. Just a simple set of loose pants that were tied with a rope and a fur vest. I had seen both of them before, though they had worn different clothes back then. One of them was holding Aurora, pinning her hands behind her back. Both shifters were bald, with full beards. The one holding Aurora was the older one, by the look of the lines on his face and the gray in his beard. Which put me on edge—shifters weren't as long lived as vampires, but they could live for a long time. That he even showed signs of age meant that he was very old. Their scents were those of nature, but the smell of blood clung to them. I recognized the scent of Suul blood.

I knew all three of them.

The armored man was Jean Dubois, and the other two were Guo Li and Guo Zhang, both shifters and, if I was correct, related. Three of the top ten Masked, four, if one counted me.

Aurora gave me a weak smile. "Sorry, Mari," she said, as if it was somehow her fault that we were ambushed.

The shifter pulled her back, and she winced. I nearly took a step forward but managed to restrain myself. I was still healing. Buying time was the priority.

"May I ask why you are holding my friends captive?"

"Hah, friends. Thralls maybe," the younger of the two shifters, Li, said.

I refused to rise to the provocation.

"What's all this about?" I said slowly.

The shifter that was holding Aurora, the older one, Zhang, spoke. "You know what this is about, vampire."

"No, I really don't. I've done nothing to you. We are all in this together, even if you want to pretend that we are not. What the fuck do you think this will accomplish? The only thing you are doing is trying to weaken Earth, which

I guess if you've switched sides and promised the other races something, is actually your plan." I looked pointedly at Dubois and his clearly too advanced armor and weapon. He didn't answer my provocation, choosing to remain silent instead, so I turned back to glare at the shifter holding Aurora.

"Grandfather," the other shifter, Li, whispered. "Her eyes."

Zhang's brow furrowed. "Your eyes weren't like that before," he said as he noticed. "You wore contacts, didn't you? You deceived us even at the start."

I bit my tongue to keep myself from speaking. There was no point trying to explain. What even could I say? My sire made it clear that people didn't know how vampire maturation really worked. Anything I said would be taken as another lie. He was a xenophobe; he hated my kind.

Scratch that, the original plan was to buy time, but unfortunately, I lost my shit immediately.

"So, your plan is what exactly? Because let me tell you right now, I'm not doing this dance, especially not with you *pecueca*." I narrowed my eyes at him. "I don't care what you imagine you are doing here. You'll let my friends go, or I'll come over there and rip your fucking heart out."

"Threats. I expected nothing less from your kind, leech," Zhang growled at me in a guttural tone that I felt in my bones.

"Stop your posturing, pup. You're quite literally threatening my friends. Get off your high fucking horse." If he thought that I was an Elder vampire, then calling him pup would probably fit. If only I could try to sound a bit more distinguished, it might sell it better. Though, if I was as old as he probably thought I was, I could get away with talking however I wanted.

"Pup, hah," Zhang bit out. "I've walked the land for three thousand years, leech. I've killed dozens of you *Elders*. You're not as untouchable as you think you are."

That made me pause. Three thousand years was insane for a shifter. I didn't even know that they could get that old.

"Oh, yeah? So, what are you waiting for? Let's dance." I rolled a shoulder.

Just as Zhang opened his mouth to respond, he was interrupted.

"Enough." The voice came from the armored figure of Jean Dubois. It was deep, sounding slightly muffled as it was coming from the helmet. "We're not here for your old racial feuds."

Zhang glanced at him and growled. "This is a mistake, but fine, say your piece. The leech will not listen. Her kind thinks only of themselves."

I frowned, turning to look at Dubois.

"Ms. Rojas," he started slowly. "Forgive my companions. We are here for a simple conversation."

"Aha," I said, glancing at Aurora and Jiyun. "And you thought that threatening my friends was a good way to get that conversation?"

Dubois glanced at Zhang before speaking. "I was . . . persuaded that you wouldn't listen otherwise."

I narrowed my eyes at the shifter, who raised his nose at me. Arrogant bastard.

"Why not let them go now. Then we can talk?"

"I fear that now it is too late; I would much rather say my piece while I have your attention," Dubois answered.

I debated just rushing across the distance and slaughtering them, but decided against it. "Go ahead then, I'm listening."

"We've come with a proposition. As you've correctly surmised, I have an arrangement with a patron from one of the Kirios nations."

It was obvious, but I was glad to have it confirmed at least.

"What kind of a proposition?" I asked, though I already knew the gist.

"The kind that will see us through the hard times ahead. You are an Exemplar," he said slowly. "You understand what is coming. We must have allies that can help us weather the storm."

I looked from him to Guo Li, the younger of the shifters. Both Dubois and Li were Exemplars, like me. "What happened to all of us are on our own? Didn't you say that we don't have to fear the other races? That the Elves won't come as conquerors?" I asked the younger shifter. It was his words that had swayed the rest of the challengers, that had convinced the others that working together was the wrong move.

"I still believe that. The Elves are custodians of nature. They will do what my kind has wanted to do for thousands of years. Let Earth recover without the greedy hands of humans and vampires taking from her. Dubois also has a point, Not all Kirios factions will have our best interests in mind," the shifter bit out. I didn't think that he fully agreed to be here, talking with me. Dubois seemed to be the one in charge, which was interesting. The two shifters were stronger. If Zhang really was as old as he said he was, then he should be a lot more powerful than a Masked human, even if he had reached Second Investment.

"You still haven't said what this offer is." I turned my attention back to Dubois. "Let's hear what you promised for that nice suit of armor."

Dubois didn't rise to the provocation. "My patron is from the Naga-shan Empire. They are the only race on Kirios that has not splintered into many different factions. And they've offered us aid in what is to come."

"In return for what?"

"The Naga-shan have no need for great stretches of land or resources," Dubois said. "They live in the oceans. All they require is a small piece of our coast where they can build cities."

"Aha, so they don't want land, but they want it?"

"These cities would be jointly controlled; they only wish for places where they can trade freely."

"And for such a small sacrifice they will help us fight off all the other factions that will try to make claim to our land?"

"Fighting off everyone is impossible; you must know that. We can preserve a small part with the help of the Naga-shan, ensure that we endure."

It was a smart play; it was my play. He wanted to do the same thing I wanted to do. Except I didn't trust any of the factions that wanted to come in, nor any deals that they offered. Shadow had warned me, had told me what would happen. The factions of Kirios had done this many times before, and the last time they did it they robbed an entire race of its land, turned them into nomads.

"What do you want from me then?" I asked finally. "As Li has already said, we are all separated back on Earth with little ways of connecting."

"All you would have to do is stand aside when the portals open. Not initiate any conflicts with any of the factions arriving. The Naga-shan will make arrangements to ensure that there will be no conflict, that the other factions will not wage war on us."

I looked at him for a long few seconds. Just stand aside, don't fight, so simple. It sounded a lot like what Shadow told me happened with the Harpiem last time. It sounded nice—we would get protection, maybe a little piece of land where we could survive and start again, under the guidance of other factions, of course. All in return for not fighting, because let's face it, the factions of Kirios didn't believe that we stood any chance. It was all about minimizing the effort required to take from us. Except, this time it was different. There were two continents, two races. The factions of Kirios would have to split their focus.

"So, they have you going around to others, getting their agreement not to fight once invaders come, and you think that they have no ulterior motives?" I asked finally.

"Everyone has ulterior motives. The Naga-shan just don't have the same goals as us. Allying with them makes sense."

Perhaps he was right. Shadow warned me against trusting any of them, Naga-shan included, but maybe we had to make tough choices. It might be the best option we had.

Except, I didn't want to. I was a vampire, sired by the firstborn son of the first vampire. Yeah, it was going to my head a little bit, but hell, I was actually special. And I made a promise to Shadow and to myself. I wasn't going to let them do what they had done so many times before.

"And if I refuse the offer?" I asked slowly.

Dubois didn't answer immediately. "When the portals open, there will be conflict, it is inevitable. My task is to ensure that the conflicts don't spiral out of hand into something . . . undesirable."

"That wasn't an answer," I said slowly, my eyes falling on the silent Aurora and Jiyun. I felt the tension of his body inside of the armor, the way that the shifters adjusted their positions.

"Some sacrifices have to be made." Dubois shrugged.

"Oh. My. Fucking. God." I closed my eyes. "You cannot be this idiotic. A literal alien god has invaded our world, turned it into its playground, and here you are playing hitman for people that want to take what belongs to us at the cheapest price."

"The Earth doesn't belong to anyone, vampire," Zhang growled.

"Oh, fuck off."

He narrowed his eyes at me. "You don't act like any Elder vampire I've ever met."

"Oh, you've never met anyone like me, shifter." I grinned, showing my fangs. It seemed like we'd come to an understanding. "My answer to your offer is no. I will not stand aside and let the invaders take what is ours."

"You act more like a Fledgling, wild and with no control. A vampire with no control is a danger to everything in its path."

Now he was finding excuses why our conflict was justified in his eyes. Not that he needed too much; his hate for vampires was obvious.

"That is unfortunate," Dubois said slowly. "The world is changed; I had hoped that your kind might see reason."

His hand tightened on his harpoon, and I knew that there would be no more talking.

My issue was that they had hostages. Zhang held Aurora, and while he might or not might be as old as he said, he was a shifter. Shifters, like vampires, grew stronger with age, though not at the same rate. I didn't know too much about them, except that they could reach the strength of an Adult vampire while in their human form. If they shifted into their true form, then they were stronger, though not quite as powerful as an Elder vampire, at least I didn't think that they were. Though their shifted form came with other advantages.

Aurora was actually the one I was worried for less. Zhang obviously didn't consider her a threat and was barely paying any attention to her. That was a mistake; they were standing on rocky ground, Aurora was a lot more dangerous than he probably suspected.

Jiyun was the one that I was worried about. She was sitting on the ground, Dubois above her with his harpoon pointed at her throat. Jiyun's finger held the regeneration ring that I had given them; Aurora had to have gotten it to her. So, she was probably in a better shape than she let on.

Li was the only one of the three that was completely free to act.

If I was going to ensure my friends' survival, I had to make myself the biggest threat as fast as possible, force them to focus on me and not them.

Saia was on the ground in front of them, she had remained in her glaive form for the entirety of the conversation, hidden in plain sight. I didn't know where my serpent-tongue spear was, so I only had my daggers and revolver as weapons.

There was going to be a fight. It was inevitable; they had incurred a debt by threatening Aurora and Jiyun with no cause. Their offer was made and refused, so there was no debt there, unless they decided to come after me as they implied.

I made eye contact with Jiyun then Aurora and saw resolve in their eyes. They were ready.

"The conversation is over, so, what now?" I asked. I had to have a confirmation, I had to have them cross the line to satisfy my obligation to the Way. "Are we just going to stare at each other, or are you going to let my friends go?"

"Sadly," Dubois started, "we can't do that. This trial is our best chance at ensuring that the people who think like you will not remain relevant to our future."

"*Saia*," I whispered, so low that no one could hear. I didn't need to speak out loud. Saia was part of me; she could detect the movements of my jaw and tongue. "*Protect Jiyun.*"

"So, you'll just kill us then." It was Aurora who asked the question.

Dubois shrugged. "It is better this way."

That was enough. I drew my revolver as I dashed forward. I fired from the hip once, hitting the younger shifter, Li, in the stomach with my first shot. Zhang's head snapped toward the direction of his grandson, his mouth open to say something, but he wasn't fast enough.

As I raised my arm and fired again, my next shot caught him in the chest, my third in the throat, and my last going through his cheek.

The four gunshots of the H-tech Rhino revolver thundered out in less than a second, startling everyone. Aurora had expected me to do something, and she reacted. While I shot, she shook the ground, and spikes made out of stone grew out behind her, forcing Zhang to let her go.

[Blood Empowerment]

I didn't know what exactly the skill did, but I needed all the help I could get. I holstered the revolver and crossed the distance to Dubois as he was stabbing his harpoon toward Jiyun's chest. She twisted away, but it wasn't going to be enough. Unfortunately for Dubois, he underestimated just how fast a vampire like me was. I arrived faster than even I expected.

I backhanded him across his breastplate with all the strength I had. I noticed the tips of my nails turning red like crystals, and the deep scarlet of my veins spread just beneath my skin as my skill fully activated. I felt stronger than I'd ever been. My strike dented his armor, and sent him hurtling through the forest.

Saia flew from my body, the parts of her that were bracers, and flowed to join the other part of her over Jiyun, keeping watch.

A massive roar grabbed my attention, and I saw Zhang barreling toward me, his body bulging and shifting. In a fraction of a second, he went from human to a monstrosity on two legs.

Humans called shifters werewolves, which was a derogatory term for them, as they had no connection to wolves at all. Zhang's skin turned pale, almost gray in color, and smooth as it shifted to tough and thick hide that was covered instantly by extremely fine brown fur. His neck burst into a short black mane, and his skull elongated into a wide and vaguely wolflike shape, if one squinted and it was dark.

The shifters were related to the animal called Andrewsarchus and had more in common with zebras and giraffes than they had wolves. A shifter in their transformed shape looked like a cross between a hippo and a wolf. And no matter how comical that image might sound, it was in fact incredibly terrifying.

Zhang didn't drop to four legs; he didn't shift into a full animal form. Instead, he remained upright, in a kind of a mutated hybrid transformation that I had never heard about. He roared, then charged.

Blood Feud

Humans love making lists about everything and anything. One of their favorite topics is about what the deadliest animals in the world were. I remembered reading those lists too. One animal that they often put on top of such lists was the hippopotamus, a common hippo. They were murder machines the size of a tank.

Shifters were the same. Their primal form came from the smaller but no less dangerous version of the animal that was supposed to be extinct for a long time. I had no idea where vampires found the animals to experiment on them, but I'd just learned that my sire was over forty thousand years old, so what did I know. The experiments with the **thirst** had changed it significantly in the shifters. The mutated hybrid form before me didn't quite look like the images of the Andrewsarchus that I had seen. His torso was still human shaped, only thick and muscled beyond anything I had ever seen.

His hand was larger than my head and tipped with thick, sharp, clawlike appendages.

His head was surrounded by a thick but short mane of black fur, and his massive snout opened to show wickedly sharp teeth in front, and thick molars in the back.

He roared as he charged, his vest and pants barely staying on his body. Every step he took shook the ground as if he had gained twice his mass in barely a span of seconds.

He moved faster than I expected.

I dashed to the side, evading the attack that ripped a massive chunk of the tree trunk that was behind me, sending debris flying everywhere. I could smell such a thick and rich scent of the **thirst** on him. His body was filled with it, the same way mine was. Only his was changed, different. I'd never encountered anything like this before, not with any other shifter I'd met.

His blood sang to me, and the **thirst** within me answered. It wanted a taste.

Zhang followed, attacking in a flurry of swipes, each meant to take my head clean off. He was obviously enraged because of what I did to his grandson, not that Li would die from that. There was no silver in those bullets, and he would heal quickly, even from the head wound.

The shifter came after me, trampling like a wild beast he accused me of being. And yet, his every movement seemed too precise, too strong. He wasn't as fast as me, but he was definitely just as strong, even with my new skill boosting me. His story about killing Elder vampires before suddenly seemed a lot more truthful.

If he was as old as he claimed, he had far more experience than me. I couldn't allow him to dictate the tempo of the battle.

I had one chance to turn the tide and end it before he could overwhelm me, and I knew just the thing. If there was one thing I knew about old people, it was that they were set in their ways; new things were harder for them to use.

He hadn't used any skills, perhaps forgetting that he even had them. My Mask was my advantage, my trump card.

I had learned the lesson from the emperor beast. I wasn't going to sit and wait to see what kind of a trump Zhang had. I wasn't going to give him the chance to use any of it.

[Quick Swap Slot—Slash>Debilitating Wave]

I lost my combat trait bonus, but it wasn't doing much for me here anyway.

[Debilitating Wave] blasted out of me, hitting the charging shifter head on. He faltered, fell to his knees, and caught himself on the ground with his arms.

I placed a hand over my chest and pulled. My Mask manifested, and I placed it over my face, then charged in. I raised a hand and swung down with my fist and [Pulverizing Smash]. I hit him across the back, heard bones break as he slammed against the ground and bounced off. My other hand came down, stabbing with my dagger and [Triple Thrust].

He managed to move out of the way somehow, just enough that my stabs caught him across the shoulder blade instead of his spine. He let himself fall and rolled, an arm lashing out and grabbing my legs, pulling me down before jumping at me, clawing across my thighs and rending flesh.

I screamed as I lashed out at him, cutting up his snout with my dagger and stabbing with my clawed fingers into his eye, squishing his eyeball in between my fingers. He opened his maw and came at my face.

[Overburn Skill—Lesser Screech]

I ruptured his eardrums and made him rear back. I got my feet in between us and kicked him off, sending him flying into a tree with enough power to break the trunk and send the tree falling.

[Swap Profile]
[Mist Step]

I re-formed next to him before he could recover, my dagger stabbing into the side of his head. It didn't put him down; he wasn't human. It dazed him, however, enough that I managed to get three good punches at his snout, cracking the bone and disfiguring him, before he retaliated.

A massive fist punched through my stomach and out my back. The pain was agonizing, but my anger drowned everything out. I pulled my dagger out of his head and stabbed into his arm, between bones then twisted, shattering them, and with a knee on his torso pushed myself off, tearing his arm apart, leaving his forearm and hand in my stomach.

He was healing. Not as fast as I was, but faster than I expected. Bones of his snout cracked and shifted in place; a new eye grew in an empty socket.

I had to end it.

[Blood Gout]

He retched as blood poured out of his wounds, out of his mouth from internal ones too, and into my waiting mouth. My jaw dislodged, my Mask split open, and a monstrous maw gulped down all of the shifter's blood. It was the most powerful blood I had ever tasted.

More than any of the beasts on Ish Vimza, more even than Shadow's blood. It was greater in a different way. This was not highly Invested blood, I could tell. But it was filled with the **thirst**, with the bacterium that turned me, that made me who I was.

The sensation threw me for a loop, so much so that I didn't realize that

Zhang had moved. He came at me, his body blurring faster than he had ever moved before, a charge skill of some kind.

He slammed into me with enough speed to blast all the air out of my lungs, to crack my ribs. He picked me up then slammed me against the ground, stunning me.

He opened his jaw and snapped down to bite my head off, and there was nothing that I could do to stop him. A spike of stone blasted out from next to my head, piercing the inside of his mouth.

It bought me enough time. With a roar I grabbed hold of him and rolled him off me, then came up on top of him, straddling him.

He tried to pull out the broken stone spike out of his mouth with his one remaining arm, but I didn't give him a chance.

I rained down strikes against his head, cracking bones and caving in his skull, then I stabbed my red-tipped fingers straight into his mouth. My nails looked more like claws as they pierced through the soft flesh inside. I grabbed a bone, then twisted his lower jaw clean off.

I clawed deeper, tearing his throat out, digging until I reached the spine. I crushed it in my hand, then stood, pulling the weakly twitching body with me. I grabbed the top of his snout with one hand and kept the other in the gaping hole in his throat, holding it by the collarbone. Then I pulled and tore his head clean off with a roar.

I raised the body above my head with a grunt—it was heavier than I had expected—and opened my mouth, letting blood drip down straight down my throat.

There was little thought in my mind, only the **thirst** singing, its voice so clear I could almost hear something coherent. I felt myself expanding, as if my skin was too tight for me, my muscles were burning, and my stomach felt like a bottomless hole.

There was a pressure in my head, and my Mask advanced again.

"No! Grandfather!"

The yell pulled me back, and I dropped the corpse aside as I saw the other shifter, now healed, changing. His bones cracked, and he dropped to all fours, the true shifter form.

I growled at him and got low, waiting for him.

A chime sounded, and light surrounded us just as he charged. It raised us from the ground and kept us from moving.

"No!" Guo Li yelled. "I'll kill you, you fucking leech!"

Before he had the chance to say anything else, the world vanished, and I was in the now familiar gray expanse. I took a few deep breaths, calming down, and found that I couldn't. My mind was whirling, my stomach was burning a hole in my body, and everything felt heavy. I didn't know what was happening.

I closed my eyes and chanted out loud. I didn't need to calm down; I needed to ride the wave, to guide.

"Ambition . . . is the drive to achieve Greatness. Emotion is the fuel that grants me Purpose. Calm is the surrender to the will of Others. Control is the shackle that robs me of Ambition." I felt whatever it was that happened to me subside, though I still felt like I was a size too big for my body. Everything felt . . . tight.

"I do not conceal my Ambition, I Relish. I do not suppress my Emotion, I Embrace."

And embrace, I did. I took the victory, the thrill of the fight. The knowledge that I had bested someone strong. Guo Zhang was a powerful shifter, and old, far older than shifters were supposed to get. His blood was . . . its taste rivaled that of my sire. And that spoke to his power more than anything.

I had no doubt now that he had done as he had said. That he had killed Elder vampires before.

I shook my head and tried to stand, but instead of standing I toppled to the ground, a groan escaping me unbidden.

I rolled and looked down. Right, I still had Zhang's arm stuck in my stomach. I pulled it out and stifled a cry. My chest felt like it was pulverized, and that was not even counting the agony of my body healing. Zhang's blood was accelerating it, but he had done so much damage that it was taking a while.

I was a wreck. I raised my head and saw a pedestal along with a chest nearby. The trial had ended, which was fortunate. I didn't know if I could've handled Guo Li in my state, and Dubois had probably recovered from my strike too.

Aurora had saved my life with her stone spike. I would need to thank her properly later. I hobbled over to the pedestal and read what it said on the plaque.

Congratulations for finishing the Trial of the Forest!

You've finished in the 1st spot and were rewarded 60,000 points. You will be transported back to the Trial entrance after collecting your reward.

I nodded. Killing the Suul, two kings, an emperor, and Zhang had given me enough points to finish first. I only hoped that the others were alright. Saia's drone wasn't with me, which was . . . I glanced down and realized that I wasn't wearing the tunic that she made. She had to have slipped during battle. My instructions were to protect Jiyun; she would've done that. If she needed more mass, then she would've left me undefended. I was more durable than her skinsuit was. Well, Saia was always with me. She was inside of me; she just couldn't communicate without extra outside mass.

I hoped that the Grand Spell didn't just leave her mass in the trial. That would be a pain to recover.

I walked over to the large silver chest and opened it up to see my rewards.

"Damn, no shirt?" I raised my head and glared at the gray mist that surrounded me. "You couldn't help a girl out, huh?"

There was no response from the Grand Spell, not that I expected one. I shook my head and turned my attention back to the rewards.

The first thing I grabbed was a pouch filled with gemstones, as had become standard reward. I glanced inside and saw that there were two dozen of the stones, most E-grade, and a handful D-grade gemstones. I put them aside, and checked the second pouch, this one filled with gold coins.

I really had to figure out what to do with all the coins I was getting. Earth didn't really have an economy right now; money was worthless, and we would probably be surviving on a barter system for a while . . . it occurred to me then that once the portals opened and the factions from the rest of Kirios arrived, they might actually want them.

"Huh." I shook my head and continued looking through my rewards.

One of the items was a pair of boots, leather by the look of them, though very simple. I looked them over, but there wasn't anything that would suggest what they did, so I put them aside. Next was a box of ammo, smaller caliber than what I needed but still welcome, especially as I'd just fired my last.

The third item was a golden lantern. Again, I had no idea what it did. I would have to wait until Saia could communicate to see if she could figure it out. The fourth item was a rolled-up scroll. I frowned at it. As soon as I touched it, I could feel something faint within, an imprint on the Way, only not quite like a skill. I didn't mess with it anymore, just put it next to the other stuff.

The last item was a wooden cube, and as I picked it up, I noticed that it had a paper tag attached to it. I blinked, then turned it over and realized that it had writing on it.

Simple Wooden Cabin

Press the lever on top and place in an open space to manifest a Simple Wooden Cabin, 50 square meters in rectangular size. Once placed, the cabin can't be moved.

"The fuck." I raised an eyebrow. Then glanced at the gray mist all around me. "If you could always put tags on items, why not do it for everything?"

The Grand Spell, unsurprisingly, didn't answer.

"Unless you don't want to mess with people who've made identifying such objects their life's work," I thought out loud. The Grand Spell was clearly learning, adapting on the go. According to Shadow, it was always introducing new stuff with every Expansion Interval. This time it had obviously taken inspiration from Earth's fiction. But it also had to juggle a lot of things that it had already put in place before.

The more I learned, the more amazed I became at what an achievement the Grand Spell was. I knew that its creator made it as a way to prepare and fight against the threat he saw beyond Kirios, and though I didn't yet understand how, I was sure that the Grand Spell was working toward that goal.

I took the cube, and as it was the last item, I prepared to be transported out as the plaque said. I gathered all the items, and soon enough I felt the familiar sensation of being transported.

I arrived back in the forest next to the registration pedestal. Immediately I noticed the others. They were gathered around Saia, or rather her drone, who upon my arrival immediately turned her head to look at me.

"Look! She moved her head!" Aurora jumped up excitedly. "That means Marianna is fine!"

I blinked, then quickly realized what was happening. The drone had probably been inactive, since it didn't have the connection to Saia's main body within me.

"Of course I'm fine," I said. The others were all there. The four humans, Jason, Mark, Matt, and Diana, sat at an improvised camp. Daehyun sat next to Jiyun as Khalil tended her wounds, his hand glowing with a yellow light.

Aurora whirled around and rushed to give me a hug.

"Mari!" She tried to squeeze me but failed miserably. "You're alright? You were pretty banged up in there."

"Healed, all better now, see." I pointed down, which prompted her to do the same.

We both realized it at the same time.

"I'm glad that you're good, Marianna," Khalil said as he started walking toward me.

"Stop!" Aurora yelled.

Khalil froze. "What's wrong?"

I rolled my eyes as Aurora stepped closer in front of me, blocking Khalil's sight of my topless chest. "Saia, could you give me some clothes, please?"

The dragon trotted over and a small piece of her detached and flowed over my body, creating a skintight makeshift tunic.

"You know," Aurora started. "That isn't that much better."

I chuckled and stepped aside. I walked over to Jiyun and knelt next to her. "How are you?" I asked.

"My ribs are bruised, but I'm doing better, Khalil and your ring are helping. I should be able to walk by tonight."

"Good. You did great." I turned to look at Aurora. "You both did."

They smiled at me. "I finished first," I told them.

"That's great." Aurora clapped her hands then gestured at Jiyun. "The two of us had the same amount of points, so we shared third."

I blinked. "Great. And I see that Saia was transported with you two?"

Jiyun nodded. "She was next to us when the trial ended, so we grabbed her. We didn't know if the Grand Spell would transport her with you. Though, she stopped moving once we were getting our rewards. Also"—she shifted and reached behind her to pull something forward—"we managed to grab this too."

I nearly squealed in joy but managed to control myself. I had an image to keep. I reached forward and picked up my serpent-tongue spear.

I had already made peace with the loss, but now I felt an immense relief.

"Thank you. It was a gift, and it means a lot to me."

"We noticed," Aurora added over my shoulder.

"Okay." I took a deep breath and looked around at everyone. "Let's debrief. There is a lot to say."

Everyone gathered around the fire, and Aurora, Jiyun, and I started recounting the events of the trial.

Purpose

Once we were finished telling the others what happened, there was a long silence. The four newest additions kept looking at each other, and I could almost taste their fear.

Their presence was a bit of an elephant in the room. I didn't want to send them away just so that the rest of us could talk, but they weren't really part of our group. We had an agreement with them. They had to lead us to another trial that started in six days. It might actually be the last one we could do. There was just about a week left in the challenge.

Our efforts in the trial had netted us a lot of points, pushing me to the top spot again, and giving Terra the lead, which meant that others had done well too.

This also made me a target. My points alone were nearing a million. If someone killed me, they would get all those points for themselves.

Our plan didn't change. We wanted to win, and we were on track to do just that. Both Jiyun and Aurora had risen in the ranks, getting in the top twenty. They hadn't killed any of the Suul, so their points lagged behind a bit.

"Was there no other way?" Khalil asked after a while.

I turned to look at him. "They decided to press us, to make us agree to their proposition. They threatened Aurora and Jiyun just so they could talk to me."

Khalil grimaced. "Dubois's offer does make some sense. If we can get through the next period without violence, we should explore that path."

"Without violence?" I asked. "He's obviously made a deal that requires him to take out people who are likely to oppose the other factions, people like me. That makes his deal with the Naga-shan inherently violent."

Khalil looked at me, then sighed. "You're right, of course. I just hate seeing conflict among our people at a time when we should be as united as we can be."

I opened my mouth to rebuke him, but then thought better of it. He'd always been an idealist. Yet, I did trust him to understand that sometimes there were no good choices.

"Before I left for this challenge," Khalil continued, "Constantinople was preparing to send out expeditions and gather survivors. We'd repaired a couple of boats and were going to head along the coast."

That reminded me. "You should have them head west, across the Mediterranean and into the new inland sea."

"You mean for us to meet up?" Khalil asked.

"After what just happened, I think that we need a more unified front. I doubt that we'll be close enough to help each other. But communication, even delayed, should be our priority. I will head north with my group," I said slowly, thinking about the survivors back at the military camp. I didn't know if they would follow me, but . . . I was done wasting time. Dubois's action had shown me that I had less time than I even thought.

"If what my sire told me is true, the coast is days away, I'll try to establish ourselves there. Having access to the sea and routes across and along it will be instrumental."

I'd been thinking about what kind of an area I could lay claim to for when the portals opened. Something defensible would probably work, but that would mean a lot less territory. But if I could gather more than one group, all along the coast, where we could use the sea to travel between us faster than on foot? That might work.

"I'll need to find some coastal towns, commandeer some boats." I smiled at him.

Khalil had a pensive look on his face. "Many of the modern ones survived; fiberglass and composite materials didn't seem to be as affected as metals are. You'll need to find boats with sails though."

"That's good. Then my plan could work."

I turned around and looked at the rest, my eyes settling on Aurora. "You're north of me, in the States?"

"Alabama," Aurora answered. "Monroeville."

"You should head east," I told her. "From what my sire told me, the entire US East Coast now comes out on the inland sea."

Aurora was the one that worried me the most out of our team. She was all alone back on Earth. Her town was abandoned by the time she returned from her term as an Exemplar.

"You think that's smart? I don't know if my home was shifted around. The coast used to be south of me," Aurora said.

"It's either that or you stay put, and I try to find you. Though that might be harder."

"You really mean to have us meet up?" Aurora asked, her voice low.

I blinked; I realized that somehow that had started being one of my goals without even consciously deciding on it. I looked over at the others.

"Yes," I said softly, my eyes finding Jiyun and Daehyun. "I don't know where Korea is. My sire wasn't that specific; he only said that part of Asia was missing from the northern part of our continent. But we know that there is a giant new inland sea in what he believed to be the center of our continent. Finding it might be a good orientation point, as Constantinople should be at the northeastern end of that sea."

"We can try," Jiyun said. "Though we are surrounded by rifts and beasts. Seoul is in between us and the coast, and we don't know what is behind us. We've been unable to explore the wild and see if we can reach the other coast."

I nodded; I had already expected as much. The two of them were potentially far away, unless Korea had been shifted someplace closer.

"You mean to come to Constantinople?" Khalil interrupted with a question, his tone surprised.

"If I can, or at least close enough that we can communicate. Honestly, what you said about how the city united to survive has me optimistic that they would be good allies. And it is a good fixed point that all of us should be able to locate. Find the inland sea and follow the coast until you reach the Mediterranean, and the city is on the other end."

"The vampires of the city are some of the oldest in the world. Do you owe them your allegiance?" Khalil asked, then tilted his head. "I know that the way it usually works is that a vampire owes fealty to their sire and that line. I don't know where your sire and the Colombian covens fall in that hierarchy. But from my understanding, the oldest vampires are generally accepted as leaders over others, regardless even of coven or bloodline."

The old stories that a vampire had to obey their sire, the supernatural control part, were just that, stories. But they came from truth. Vampires operated in covens, and usually when a new vampire was made, they became part of that coven, with fealty to their sire and their sire's sire all the way to the oldest and most powerful vampire in that coven. Only Elder vampires could make a new coven, and to do that they must leave their old one. Sometimes a group would leave together, though that was rare. They usually started by siring new vampires themselves. Though their new covens usually remain allied with their old covens, that wasn't always the case.

This was common knowledge. I learned it in school before I was turned, probably where Khalil learned it too. His order had probably sent him to learn from the vampires themselves, as many had been our teachers.

I opened my mouth, then closed it. I didn't know how much to tell him, how much I could trust him. On one hand, I trusted his words about what happened in Constantinople. And I trusted him as a person. The people in charge, the ones he served . . . that was another thing entirely. Once, my allegiance was to the Lágrima Sangrienta Cartel and its master, Pascual de Andagoya. Because I believed that my sire was part of his coven. Now I knew that wasn't the case. My sire was there because of a debt. And besides, they tried to hang me, so fuck them.

By vampire law, my allegiance was to my sire, though he hadn't expressed any desire to exercise that right. I didn't know if he even cared about those laws. He probably predated them by a significant margin. But even if he did, there were only two vampires that would have authority over me, my sire, Akatsuki Jin, and his sire, the first vampire, who was either asleep at the bottom of the ocean or had hidden herself and was doing who knew what.

I locked eyes with Khalil, thinking. Relationships were give and take. They were a net of debts owed and paid. Khalil had trusted me by staying with me in the challenge when many had left. He had stood by my side, and listened to my counsel, followed me, when he had no need to. And despite everything, he was still my friend.

But still, I wasn't ready to reveal everything just yet.

"There are only two vampires in the world that could assert themselves over me: the one who turned me, and his sire. In terms of hierarchy, they would be above any of the vampires in Constantinople."

Khalil looked surprised at that. "It was my understanding that one of the oldest living vampires is currently head of the Constantinople's coven."

I grimaced. My school of being, the philosophy that I lived my life in accordance with, was based on debts and obligation. On a balance in relationships. A lie, to me was an offense, and therefore it incurred debt. If I was to lie to him, I would shift the scale, increase my debt. Misleading him was the same, and I had already done that when I implied that I had reached the Elder vampire stage because I advanced my Mask.

He was going to figure out the truth eventually, when the other vampires advanced their Masks and didn't see the same results. Though, it wasn't really a complete lie. I was certain that my Mask did contribute to my maturing, but so had drinking the highly Invested blood of powerful beings and individuals.

I got more from them than most vampires did. My **thirst** was closer to the source, less diluted.

Still, I had to live in accordance with my school of being, my Oath.

"I'd rather not say," I told him finally.

He leaned back, and I saw his mind whirling behind his eyes. Finally, he nodded. "I understand," he said, but I did note a tiny twinge of hurt.

I sighed. At least he wasn't too offended.

I turned my attention to the four people who sat next to us and had been silent so far.

"I know that we've only just met," I started. "And obviously we have an agreement, but you are free to try to do the same as the rest of us once we leave this place. You said that you were in Congo, yes?"

"Uh." Jason blinked, surprised to be addressed. "Yeah. Honestly, we are just trying to survive."

"As we all are," Khalil told him.

"Right." Jason looked at his friends. Then at the rest of us. "We are nobodies, really. Not like you guys."

I leaned forward. "No, you aren't nobodies. The fact that you are here in the first place tells me a lot. None of you are Exemplars, yet you still managed to advance your Masks to the top one hundred list from among all of our people. You are strong, and you are survivors. You are exactly the kind of people that we need if we are to survive and keep what we have."

The four straightened up at my words, flattered.

"I'm not going to ask you to join the rest of us. I doubt that even we will be able to really gather again on Earth. But if we try to work toward the same goal, ensure that there are people, survivors, and establish a presence that can defend what we have? Then we'll be in a lot better position."

"You really think so?" Diana asked.

I nodded. "Yes, my plan is to set up on the coast of the new inland sea. I'll make sure to build ways of signaling to others that there are survivors, that there is civilization. And I'll try to gather as many as I can, spread across the coast and establish a territory that can protect itself."

"That is ambitious," Jiyun said.

I nodded. "It is, and I will do it. It's the only way for us to weather the storm. I won't be making any deals with invaders that include them taking our land and resources. Though dealing with them is inevitable, we must become big enough of a threat that we can stand up to them."

"I do agree, and perhaps we have a chance," Khalil said. "Though I've seen some of the power that the high Investment Masked have. It equals and perhaps exceeds that of Elder vampires."

"It does," I added. "From what I've been told, high Investment Masked are like Elder vampires on steroids that also have magic. But, that is why this is our chance. The Grand Spell gives us opportunities, even as it destroys our world. We are growing faster now, gaining Investment at an accelerated rate. That is another thing that the other factions will come here to exploit. They will send people that can benefit from the Investment gain on Earth while we are under the Grand Spell's protection. We need to reach high enough that by the time the portals open we can fight back."

"This challenge has pushed us ahead significantly," Jiyun said. "We've all stepped into our Second Investment."

"And we need to do more," I told them. "The moment our year is up, we will lose the accelerated gain and be on even footing with the rest of Kirios. That will slow us down significantly."

It occurred to me at that moment that perhaps these challenges were introduced to allow the new races more avenues to grow and catch up to the races already on Kirios. The Grand Spell had to be aware of what happened in the past with other races. The Harpiem, from what Shadow had told me, had a very small number of high Investment people, and every race before them had less than the one before them. The Elves and Dwarves were the ones that had the most.

"You are almost to your third," Aurora said. "You really are advancing faster than the rest of us." It wasn't an accusation, more a curiosity.

"The type of Investment that I need is easier to gain here."

"Type of Investment?" Jason asked. "Khalil and Daehyun told us some of it, but, uh, we didn't quite understand fully."

"Each Mask requires a certain type of Investment. Think of it like this: You grow by doing things that are in line with your Mask. Someone with the Mask of a Fighter needs to fight. My Mask requires blood to advance."

"Oh," Jason said, his tone betraying his nervousness. "I guess that makes sense."

I looked over everyone as the conversation died down. We had a rough plan. At least I thought that we did, for when we left the challenge. Now, all that was left was to survive until the end of it.

* * *

I took the first watch as the humans went to sleep, so I sat with Saia next to me.

"Feedback: The boots have a sound muffling engram," Saia said as she finished inspecting my rewards.

"Useful for sneaking around, though not really for me. I'll give them to one of the others. Next?"

"Feedback: The lantern gives off light but can be recharged with light-related Source. Leaving it in direct sunlight would be the easiest way."

I looked the golden lantern over, just a tad bit disappointed in it. "What about the scroll?"

"Feedback: It possesses an engram, and an infusion of Source-Weave. This Unit sees no way for it to be recharged, so it is my belief that it is a single-use item."

I blinked. "Really? How do I use it, and what does it do?"

"Feedback: Opening the scroll will activate the engram. It will launch a concentrated fire Source-Weave from its front facing side."

"It's a fireball," I said slowly, my jaw just about to hit the floor.

"Feedback: That term is technically correct."

"Hah, I got a scroll of fireball. Sick. Wait, can you replicate the engram?"

"Feedback: Possibly, but why? The engrams this Unit already possesses are of a far higher quality and destructive level."

"Can you use your other engrams?"

"Feedback: I'm getting close to repairing [Plasma Shot]."

"You've been getting close for a while. Could you replicate and make this Fireball Scroll reusable?"

Saia hesitated for a while. "Feedback: Yes. Though there really is no point. I shall have the [Plasma Shot] engram operational soon."

I opened my mouth to ask her to do it anyway but paused. It really seemed like she didn't want to do it. I got the sense that she was proud of what she was, what she could do. Perhaps she felt like the scroll was beneath her? Either way, I knew that she would do as I asked. She couldn't really disobey my orders. So, I decided not to press her about it.

"Okay," I said and stashed the scroll away. Then I pulled out the ammo box. "Could you make me some new rounds for my revolver?"

"Feedback: Yes, but I've actually come up with a way to improve on resupply."

I tilted my head. "How?"

"Feedback: My work on incorporating the Source crystal into my [Plasma Shot] has given me an idea."

"Oh?" I raised an eyebrow, then furrowed my brow at her. "Wait, where is that crystal? You were keeping it whole. Is it inside the drone?"

"Feedback: I've cut it up into smaller pieces to make it more manageable to carry."

As she said that a dozen small crystal shards rose to the surface of her dragon head. I blinked. "That didn't destroy it?"

"Feedback: No," she answered simply.

Well, she did know better than me after all.

"So, what's this new idea?"

"Feedback: I've made progress in the repair of my [Manufacturing] engram. Enough that I believe that I can utilize the Source generated by these crystals to make a substitute propellant and craft new bullets from my mass."

"Really? How would you do it?"

"Feedback: The substitute would be a variation of a small fire explosion engram. The firing mechanism of your weapon would, of course, be useless. I would need to trigger the engram remotely for every round, but it would still load the next round as well as give me a sign to trigger the engram in the first place."

I got, or at least I thought I did, what she was saying. Though I had some concerns. "Would there be any lag?"

"Feedback: Mari, I'm a sentient artificial life form designed for intense asymmetrical warfare. No, there will be no lag. In fact, my design will fire the bullet before the pin even strikes the primer."

"Right, of course." I nodded, then something occurred to me. "So, this fire explosion engram, would it resemble something like this scroll by any chance?" I tapped the Fireball Scroll at my waist.

She paused for a few seconds. "Feedback: Its design has contributed to my idea, yes."

I shook my head. "Well, let's test it out."

Interlude - Sire

Akatsuki Jin, or rather, the man who currently answered to that name, stood on a branch high above the ground. He kept his presence obscured. His heart didn't beat, nor did he take a breath. There was no scent coming off his body that was not from the environment, as vampires didn't produce such things, and the shirt he had borrowed from his daughter had some camouflage patterns on it that added to his intent of not being noticed.

This realm where he found himself was strange. He had hardly ever seen its like in all his long years of life. It was artificial, that much he was certain about. He even had a word to describe it: halo. Despite being ancient, Jin had made a point of keeping up with the human advancements and ideas. Being old, contrary to what some would believe, did not make one all-knowing, or particularly smarter than the rest. Jin had learned much, that was certain, but he never knew more than the collective knowledge of his world. He was not some great thinker, though he had met many. He did not advance the sciences, though he had inadvertently helped some make such advancements.

He was an Ancient vampire, one of the first of his kind. Second only to the originals in age, and one of the strongest beings that had ever walked the planet. Once, he had been arrogant enough to believe that there was little that could threaten him. That he had all the time in the world to achieve his goals.

It was one of the most common traps that young vampires fell into, thinking that the world was as unchanging as they were.

Jin had made a mistake, proving that even one as ancient and experienced as he could fall prey to such simple traps. Jin had failed; he had failed his sire, and he had failed his spawn, his daughter. But while he did feel guilt, he was also tens of thousands of years old. He understood that such emotions weren't helpful to be dwelled on. Guilt had its purpose, as all emotion did, for vampires especially, and once that purpose was met, it was far more important to act and clear the debt that guilt had inflicted.

His debt was why Jin had entered this challenge, why he was now in this strange place. To watch over and aid his daughter in the ways that he should've when he had first given her the gift of the thirst. Or to cut her life short if she had fallen to the temptations of her baser nature. He'd had many fears and many hopes before entering this place, but none of them proved true.

His daughter was far more than he could've ever hoped her to be. Emotional, strong, dangerous, all of that and more. So much more, terrifyingly so.

He sat in the tree and watched her as she conversed with her growing dragon companion. He was unsure whether what he was watching was even reality. Marianna's growth had accelerated again.

He had misled her before, when he said that she hadn't matured because of her Mask. He was certain that it was a factor, as she probably also suspected. And when he told her that it would take her a decade to reach full maturity, the Ascension phase.

What he was feeling from her now was astounding. Her **thirst** had expanded. It had grown and had started the final changes. He had almost not recognized her when she returned from the trial; that was how much she had changed in mere days.

He had overheard her talking about what she encountered within the trial. That gave him context to what he was seeing and sensing. If the shifter she killed and drank the blood from was indeed three thousand years old, then his blood would've accelerated her growth significantly.

Shifters were different from vampires; the version of the **thirst** within them was richer and calmer, and it developed faster, relatively. It was one of the reasons vampires and shifters hated one another, because vampires used to hunt them and enslave them so that they could feed on them and accelerate their growth. Vampires used to hold them as pets and slaves.

That practice ended with the shifter and human rebellion some eleven thousand years ago. When they rose up and killed one of the three original vampires and, in the aftermath, caused the fall of Atlantis and the loss of most of the early generations of vampires.

After that, Jin's sire put a stop to the practice everywhere. She eradicated all records of shifter blood's effects on vampires and tasked Jin with making sure that the practice never returned again.

Thankfully, only truly old shifters would give any kind of real benefit to the current older vampires, as their strain of the **thirst** was diluted.

Every once in a while, a vampire would realize the benefit, and Jin would usually come along and execute them before they could get any foolish ideas.

Shifters weren't as long lived as vampires. The oldest of them that Jin knew of reached five thousand years before dying of old age. Three thousand was unheard of in the age since the fall of Atlantis. Their culture had become too driven by strength. They tended to kill each other off in pursuit of power. And they'd lost parts of their diets that had kept them healthy for longer.

That Marianna had managed to kill a shifter that old was a miracle already. She was young, untrained, and yet she had managed it. She was . . . raw, in the most primal way possible. And her Mask had to be making her stronger.

She had obviously adapted to it with far greater ease than Jin had. His was the Mask of the Explorer, as had once been his life's work. To walk and explore the world, and he had done it. Was perhaps the first person to walk it all.

His Mask had advanced quickly as he made his way across what Earth had become, though he didn't understand much about it. Now, he knew that his travels had been gathering Investment.

Marianna's Mask was obviously related to her growth. Even Jin could feel himself getting stronger as his Mask advanced.

And yet . . . from what he was sensing from her, she was right at the edge. She could make the transition tomorrow, or in a week, a month. She was so close that it was insane.

She was the fastest growing vampire he had ever seen. Even his siblings that had gorged themselves on rivers of blood had only managed to advance so far in a handful of years. Marianna had done it in three months.

True, she had been a Fledgling for years, and even then, she had reached the Adult stage fairly quickly. But this was unprecedented.

Part of Jin was worried that this was going to affect the other vampires too, though even if their Masks halved the time it took them to fully mature it would still take them hundreds of years as there were not many vampires left that were of earlier generations. And those that remained stopped making Fledglings a long time ago, so perhaps it wasn't too bad.

He was trying to decide whether he should go down there and talk with her, prepare her for what was about to happen to her. The jump from an Elder to a fully mature vampire was significant.

Only, he was worried that his presence would be unwelcome. His guilt had infected him. He should've done better by her, done more. He had become too lethargic, too lost in his own world, unaccustomed to change. As many of his kind did when they became truly old.

He knew that such emotions were unhelpful, so he pushed them aside, suppressing them with great skill.

He decided against meddling with Marianna. Anything he said or did could color her expectations and hinder her growth. She had done well on her own, better than he could've hoped for. She was a monster, in all the ways humans called their kind. And she reminded him of his sire, his mother.

Jin closed his eyes for a moment, gave an old prayer to the stars, the gods of his people, then turned and left.

He shouldn't have remained close for so long. He had already confirmed that Marianna wasn't feral; there was no need to linger. Only his sense of obligation had kept him nearby, in case she needed help.

His daughter had grown, without him there, but such was life. They were vampires. There was time for their relationship to be mended. She was too young for the harm he had done her to be anything but fresh in her mind. Time was needed, and he would give it to her.

But that didn't mean that he wouldn't help her in other ways. He had overheard her goals. The young fools in Constantinople would probably try some schemes with her if she ever reached the city, but she would be far more powerful by then. He hadn't visited since the early 500s, but he remembered the whelp that ruled the vampires there. He wasn't even seven thousand years old. Though few older vampires remained. Jin had taught the whelp a lesson once before, and perhaps Marianna would see if he had learned it well. He didn't worry about her; for all intents and purposes she was a queen of vampire kind, even if she didn't know it. Her blood would sing to them, and the older ones would know her lineage. The rest would be too weak to threaten her.

She wouldn't need his help there. Though, perhaps he could see about finding this Dubois. Humans were a far greater threat to her than any vampire. There was a reason vampires hid in the shadows in this age. Lessons of the past had been well learned.

The halo was large, but Jin was fast enough that he might have the chance at finding a single human. Though, perhaps a challenge was what Marianna needed more.

He didn't rush his decision. For now, he would just explore. Take life as it came. It had been a long time since he was free to enjoy it. And this would probably be the last such opportunity in a while. Once he was back on Earth, he would need to focus on finding his sire.

She would be needed for once the protections surrounding them fell and the vultures came. If there was one thing he knew about his mother, it was that she was very territorial about her home. The races of Kirios hadn't seen anything yet.

Scarlet Moon

We spent the next few days clearing rifts and hunting beasts. Sadly, the number of beasts in the halo was nothing like that in the trial, nor were they as highly Invested. Which meant that my advancement stalled again. I got only one Carving. Though that pushed me to the Eighth Carving, which put me even closer to Third Investment.

I was, obviously, ecstatic about that. I hoped that I would get another skill, though since I already got two, I might not get another.

I still felt weird, as if my body was one size too small for me. I didn't know how exactly to describe the sensation, but it got worse every time I drank blood. When I say worse, I don't mean that it was bad. It was just . . . strange. It subsided quickly, though, after each time I fed, so I assumed that it had something to do with my Mask approaching the next tier so fast. I knew from Shadow that such advancement was rare on Kirios. The only reason we here could do it was because the Grand Spell accelerated our growth.

"Hey, it's time," Jiyun said as she came over.

I glanced at her and stood from my watch post. "Good. I need to take a look around my soul space for a little bit."

Jiyun relieved me of the watch, but as I was about to walk away, I saw the expression on her face.

"What is it?" I asked.

She hesitated, then seemed to make a decision, and her expression turned determined. "How do you have any hope left?"

I blinked, surprised by her question. "What do you mean?"

"Hope about the future, that we'll be able to survive, that we'll be able to find each other outside of this trial, that we'll manage to hold against the other factions. It all seems so hopeless. Outside of here, we are surrounded by rifts and monsters, by survivors that all just want to look after themselves. We can barely survive that, yet you want us to stand against an invasion in barely a few months. I know that you went to Ish Vimza, so you didn't see them, not really. I've seen the Oni-yi. They are warmongering brutes the size of giants and with the strength of an Adult vampire. All they want is to fight. Their clans constantly war against one another. The only time they don't is when there is a new Expansion Interval, when new land is added to Kirios. They will gather all the clans and cross the oceans in a crusade, to make new clans and take land."

"You underestimate what we can do. We aren't some primitive people dropped into the depths. The Source might've messed with our technology, but we'll recover it quickly. It is what we do. We'll figure out new ways of making things work. It is they that don't understand. They've never met anyone like us before."

"You really think so?" Jiyun asked.

"I do." I nodded. "I don't think that even Shadow understood all that I explained to him. He'd given me many warnings, told me what to expect, but I could tell that he, too, was looking down on us. It is understandable. Masks are the only thing that matters to them, and we'll be limited there. Perhaps if we're lucky we'll take advantage of the time the Grand Spell gives us and get a few people over the Fourth Investment tier, but if that is all that we'll have then what you fear would be true."

I looked away from her eyes and up at the sky, at the names and lists displayed there.

"But we aren't just that. We are vampires, and shifters, and humans. And I . . . I won't let what happened to other Harpiem happen to us."

Jiyun didn't comment right away. When she did, her voice was low. "You really believe that, don't you?"

"What? You think that I'm arrogant to think like that?"

"No." She shook her head. "I wish that I had that conviction. And if I'm being honest, I believe it of you. You are the first vampire that I've met, but . . . I somehow doubt that others are like you. I . . . I know there are things you're not telling us. I mean, it's obvious." She smiled at me, and I tried not to wince.

"But," she continued, "I trust you. And I know that you'll do what you say you will. I wish that I could be like you. Would—would you ever consider making me like you? Turning me?"

I froze, my brain shutting down completely. I hadn't expected that question from her. My first instinct was to refuse her, and I opened my mouth to do that, but then I paused. "I . . . I've never done it," I admitted to her.

She blinked. "I thought that the process was straightforward."

It was; I had my blood drained while being fed my sire's. It was a lengthy process, something that I didn't quite remember. The issue was what happened after.

"It's dangerous. Few vampires survive the transition. The Fledglings lose themselves in the blood thirst, and they require constant attention. And a high percentage of them just never get enough control to be able to function normally. They are put down."

"Oh," Jiyun said.

Now that she'd asked, I started thinking about it. Turning people would be a way that we might be able to get more power to defend ourselves. Though, it would also pose a danger, if the new Fledglings turned feral.

I glanced at Jiyun. "I'm not completely opposed."

"You're not?" Jiyun looked taken aback.

"No, there are just . . . factors that I am not sure of. I . . . can you keep a secret?" I asked.

Trust wasn't easy for me, but . . . Jiyun had stood by my side, had fought and bled with me. I considered us friends, more than that, even if we'd only known each other for a short time.

"Of course, Marianna," Jiyun answered.

"There is a reason my vampirism progressed so fast, I . . . It has to do with who my sire is. Most people think that vampires grow with age, and they do. But diet matters too, and one more thing. Their generation. How far away they are from the originator of our race. And I . . . my sire was the firstborn son of one of the original vampires. That's why I'm as strong as I am, why I grew so fast. Blood does more for me. I think that Investment in the blood contributed significantly, but I can't know for sure. All the vampires alive today are separated from the original by hundreds of generations. That's why it takes them so long to grow."

"Wow," Jiyun just said, clearly shocked.

"I wish that I could tell everyone." I shook my head. "But Khalil . . . His people have been opposed to mine for a long time. I don't think that they know the real reasons behind how vampires grow. I wish that the world ending could make us more united, but I just don't know. It's one of the reasons I want to go to Constantinople, to see for myself."

"I understand. I'll keep it a secret."

"So, I am not opposed, but I would need time to speak with my sire again. According to him, a Fledgling made by us would have a harder time of it. More of them turned feral. It would be a great risk."

I met her eyes. "What made you ask?"

Jiyun shrugged. "I'm falling behind."

I pulled back. "What? You're in your Second Investment."

"Daehyun is catching up to me. My Mask . . . it is harder to advance, and I feel like I've been stalling in my craft."

"It's barely been a month in here. You can't judge your progress like that. You gain most Investment through introspection and through mastery of the blade. You didn't have the time to do it here."

She nodded, but I could tell that she wasn't quite convinced. I put a hand on her shoulder, and she looked up at me.

"I know that you want to protect your ancestral home, so if you don't want to search and meet up with the rest of us, that's fine. Dig in, survive. I'll find you. And then we'll see about making you a vampire, if I can be sure to do it safely."

She gave me a shaky smile and stepped away. "I will, I promise."

Ornament of the Revelator (Weave, Esoteric) — No Investment; Tenth Carving > Ornament of the Revelator of Secrets — First Investment; No Carving

Once I finished the conversation with Jiyun, I retreated back to camp. I didn't need much rest, so I entered my soul space. I'd only had the time to go in and take a few new skills from the beasts whose blood I drank in the trial. None of them were anything of note, mostly lesser mundane skills that I probably wouldn't ever use. And more than half of the beasts were missing, meaning that I already had the skills that they would've given me, or they didn't have any skills at all. Some were fairly low Investment, so that was possible.

Only two of the Suul granted me skills, the [Lesser Stomp] and the [Lesser Strike]. The lesser skills were all underwhelming for the most part. When used they gave a slightly increased power to an act, but in general the best use for them that I'd discovered was to rapidly change one's flow. Depending on how and when a skill was used, it could completely shift my momentum, redirecting me in ways that I couldn't ordinarily move.

The kings had given me better skills. The shadow ferrorn had given me the [Shadow Spike] skill, which let me manifest a spike out of a shadow. It wasn't particularly tough, probably because my Weave attribute was so low, but it could be a good distraction. The dragon tortoise, sadly, hadn't given me its dragon breath; instead I got [Stone Skin], which as it implied turned my skin to stone for a few seconds.

It was a good skill; it just made it harder for me to move, so I didn't like using it that much.

I hadn't entered the room with the ungoir emperor. It was a Fourth Investment beast, and powerful. I defeated it before with Aurora's and Jiyun's help, which was significant as I'd come to realize. Both of the kings had been tougher fights in my soul's space than they had been outside of it.

I was strong enough to kill them, but I still didn't want to risk it, which was why I hadn't yet gone after other of the more powerful beasts or Guo Zhang in my Hallway of Doors. The shifter had been a strong opponent, and again Aurora had interfered and saved me.

Another worry I had was just how he was going to act as a copy in my soul space. The real person had underutilized his skills, probably because they were a foreign concept to him. He had learned to rely on his own power. He hadn't even manifested his Mask. The copy, on the other, hand was made by the Grand Spell, and it would fight like the real thing, at least it was supposed to. I worried that it would utilize its skill a lot more. So, I left him for later, once I was stronger.

For now, I finally had the time to attempt Shadow's test again. I walked up to his plateau to find him in his usual spot. He stirred at my arrival, and turned around.

"You are different."

I tilted my head. "In what way?"

"You are close to the Third Investment, aren't you?"

"Yes."

"Good, you don't have much time. Passing the Fourth Investment barrier is the least that you must do in order to stand a chance when the portals open."

"You've mentioned that before, about the Fourth Investment being special."

Shadow nodded. "Most people take their entire lives to reach the Fourth Investment. It is the culmination of all their efforts. It is a leap forward, a greater change. It is the point where Mask and person become more intricately linked. You become the embodiment of your Mask."

"Well, I plan on reaching that point soon," I said. "Now, I have a test to pass."

Shadow grinned. "Go for it."

I walked up the steps and to the first arena. The mist welcomed me once more, and I stepped into it.

I took a few deep breaths and then started the dance. The movements came to me easily. I'd practiced them a lot, not in here but by using my [A Lesson Remembered] skill to relive the first time I learned them.

I could feel the mist on my skin, feel it in the air around me. I was . . . it was more intense now than it was before. I could smell it. I could feel the changes around me with every movement I made, as I displaced the mist or caused currents to send it into a spin.

I'd noticed that my senses had been slightly elevated ever since I drank Zhang's blood. The sensation of tightness inside was constantly present; it was only greater when I drank more blood. I realized that I should've asked Shadow if that was because of me being close to the Third Investment.

I finished the dance, and nothing happened, again. I dropped my head, the mist settled, the energy my movements created dissipated, and it stilled once more.

This wasn't working. I was somehow supposed to resonate with the world, to make the mist move by my will alone. That was ludicrous. I had no skill that could do that.

I paused, then switched my profiles.

[Mist Step]

I stepped forward. My body turned to mist and flowed through the lake already present. For a split moment, I became mist, my momentum carried me forward and pulled the mist around me along.

I re-formed and felt the lake of the mist still again. Somehow, I felt closer to the mist. Not in any magical way, except that I understood it more, somehow. It wasn't a logical thing, more instinctual.

I started the dance again, following the movements I'd learned. Now, I could put my finger on what I'd been feeling since the beginning. The movements were somehow wrong. They didn't fit. Something was missing.

I finished the set and paused again, thinking.

The only way that I would be able to pass this test was if I moved the mist out of the arena and through the gaps in the walls. The only way to achieve this, that I knew of, was via a skill, or magic.

I sat down with my legs crossed and used my skill [A Lesson Remembered] to look back on Shadow's instructions back on Ish Vimza.

Esoteric is . . . you could call it the perfection in all things. *A farmer after a lifetime of work, every action done with purpose and understanding. Imagine a blade master that had spent his entire life trying to master a cut. The moment he achieved it, he would gain a waybound skill that would tap into that perfection."* *He raised his hand then dropped it fast toward the ground.*

*[**Azure Moon Style**; Ruthless Palm]*

The skill echoed in my mind. I felt it impact the world around me. And just how he said, there was a perfection there. His palm stopped just shy of hitting the ground, but a ripple of air surged around it, blasting the dirt and dust away in a perfect expanding circle.

"There is greatness in the perfectly executed actions that resonates with the world around us, beyond just bending the Source to your will."

I came out of the memory. What I'd felt there, that skill, I didn't realize it then, but it didn't feel anything like the other skills I've felt before or since then.

When he used that skill, it didn't feel like he was triggering something and having the Grand Spell help him channel power. It was . . . it was just a movement, a perfectly executed action. It echoed with the world around us; it drew on the power that was at the core of everything, the Way.

That got me thinking more about the nature of this test. It was intended for the Tengu-gi, and it was old, a remnant from the time before the Grand Spell collected their world. It was a remnant from a time before Masks.

The Tengu-gi didn't have spells, they didn't have magic in the way the Ancient Ones—the Vim of Kirios—did before Valair Ankah made the Grand Spell. No, they were a people in touch with the world around them; they had no skills to move the mist.

The skill that Shadow showed me wasn't something that he had gained from his Mask, from the Grand Spell. In fact, the Grand Spell was just a medium to allow for growth of personal magical ability, a system to allow advancement regardless of talent, a framework for easier channeling of power.

It wasn't needed, magic existed anyway. Shadow's movement was acknowledged by the Grand Spell, but it wasn't tied to it.

He had called it a waybound skill. An action that resonated with the Way to create an effect. A perfectly executed action that held power.

Shadow had told me that his Mask had changed after he completed these tests, that it had gained the name Mistweaver of the Old Ways.

For a moment, I thought that perhaps this test was impossible to accomplish here in this place. Everything here was fake. Yet, I had to trust that the Grand Spell knew what it was doing. I pushed that thought away and focused.

I returned back to the center, settling in the first position. The different positions were shown for a reason, but something was wrong. So far, I'd been trying to make the most efficient and direct movements in between the two positions.

Now, I focused inward, I drew on my emotions and on my school of being. On my oaths, and the techniques I was taught, that I adapted into something that was mine alone. *Scarlet Moon Style* was rooted in survival, in fervor and fury. It channeled my emotions into a wild movement set, one that was not based in control but in relentless aggression. There was no defense in *Scarlet Moon Style*; there was only advancing, only going forward.

I moved through the mist, not in calm, direct, and efficient movements as before, but in a wild uncontrolled dance that resembled a battle with the world itself. I filled in the gaps in between the positions with the move set of my own.

I danced, and the mist whirled around me. My mind was filled with the thrum of blood crawling through my body. Anger at the world rose, things that I'd tried to ignore, so many injustices done to me. So many things that were unfair. My inability to say my piece, to yell and rage and just let my emotions out.

I killed so many things, people and beasts alike, since I returned from Ish Vimza. I had more power now than I'd ever had. My Mask advanced, and my nature grew. I learned the secrets of this new world, I learned the secrets of my old one, about my sire, my bloodline.

And still I felt powerless to convince people to follow me, to fight. Even those that were by my side were uncertain; I could see it in them.

I realized that this was never about saving the world for me. About ensuring that we as the children of the Earth retain something of what was ours. It wasn't even about our survival. I was robbed of everything that my life should've been. I was sold, I had no childhood, no mother's love. I had nothing. All that was inside me was a holy wrath, my everything, my whole world, my pain, my sins.

It was all about me. I wanted more. I wanted everything that I never had and more. I wanted to look my old Master in the eye and smile down on him as I pulled his spine out through his throat. I wanted to bathe in a river of blood and have everyone fear me and love me in the same measure.

I wanted the things that I was never destined to have.

Now, I had the power, and I was going to take it all.

I reached the final position, and I poured everything I had inside of me out into the world as I came to a stop, opening my body and throwing my hands wide.

All my emotion, thoughts, desires, and intent flowed out of me.

The world around me trembled, a pressure built.

[**Scarlet Moon Style**; Dance of the Shifting Mist]

The mist moved.

The Mistweaver

I fell to my knees, feeling drained. My muscles were burning as if I had just run at top speed for half a day straight. The mist cleared, drained through the holes in the arena. A grinding noise drew my attention to the wall just ahead of me, where a door lowered to reveal another set of stairs leading deeper into the mountain.

I stood on shaky legs and took a step forward. A part of me wished to go back to Shadow and tell him that I'd passed the first test, that I even managed to get a waybound skill, though I suspected that he already knew. The reason I continued was that I felt it was right. I had taken the first step on this test, and it felt like I had to walk it all to the end. Besides, Shadow was unable to discuss anything about the test.

I stopped next to the steps and gathered my breath for a few minutes before climbing up. On top I found another arch, leading into another arena submerged in mist. On the walls around the entrance were images, the same as before.

They showed a similar movement set, with small alterations, and with the addition of small, short lines shown flying toward the figure, with the mist whirling around them as if it was catching them.

I frowned, not quite understanding what it was meant to represent. I remembered that Shadow said that there was danger, that I could die during this test. I still thought that he underestimated what being a vampire meant, but I took his warning seriously.

I studied the images, trying to figure out what they represented, and realizing that the last image was also different. Instead of the mist getting pushed into the walls, it was moving in a circle around the figure, with the new lines carried by the mist.

There wasn't much else to do but try it. I was confident that I would be able to use the skill again. I could already tell that it wasn't like my other skills, not something to be triggered with a mental command. I had to be in the same mindspace, to execute the same movement set. I realized that it was about the alignment of a movement and my intent, a resonance with the world.

I could see why this was hard to achieve by most. It required a fine control of every muscle in one's body, a great coordination and timing. All things that vampires excelled at.

I stepped down the stairs and into the mist. I walked to the center and assumed the first position.

A dozen tiny clicks sounded all around me, startling me. I moved on instinct, following the movements I had created before. Things flew by me, flying almost as fast as bullets. Something nicked my ear and made me lose a step, then something pierced my right hip. I grimaced and ignored the wound, focusing on avoiding the rest. My movements became wild. I missed the steps I was supposed to take.

I realized now what the images were showing me. There were some kind of launchers all around me in the walls, and they were firing through the mist. The way that sound echoed in the arena, muffled by the mist, made it hard to hear the sources, but I could still hear and feel the bolts as they flew through the mist and displaced it.

There were dozens of bolts coming every second, accelerating, more and more being fired at shorter intervals. For every dozen I evaded, another found its mark. I stepped out of the way of one and another pierced my cheek, getting stuck in the bone of my jaw. If I had less dense bones, that would've pierced straight through.

I turned, and another stabbed through my chest, in between two ribs. I let instinct guide me as I focused on the core tenet of Scarlet Moon Style. I ignored the bolts, ignored the wounds I was sustaining. They were immaterial. I was a vampire, and I didn't die easily.

I remembered what the images showed, what the goal of the test was. I focused solely on the aggression of my movements. I whirled through the mist, focusing on it, and willing it to move.

[**Scarlet Moon Style;** Dance of the Shifting Mist]

The world answered. The mist moved as if it was part of my body, shifting in tandem with my movements. I spun and it spun; the mist churned and started sending the bolts off target. Then, as I continued through the positions, it started to move around me, creating a large half-sphere of fast-moving mist that acted like a shield—catching the bolts and keeping them trapped in its spin.

I reached the end of the dance, and the bolts stopped firing. I heard a click, and another door started to open on the other end of the arena.

As I stopped, the sphere of mist slowed, then collapsed, letting all the bolts clatter across the stone. The mist rushed back into its position, and I took a deep breath.

I was covered in blood. Bolts had pierced me over my whole body, dozens of them, a few of them piercing deep. I grimaced as my heart beat with a wooden bolt through it, sending an agonizing dull hurt through my chest. I started pulling the bolts out, one at a time, my wounds healing in seconds.

This wasn't the real world, yet in moments like these it felt like it was. I knew the consequences of dying in this place, Shadow had told me that some Invokers had been found brain dead after failing their ways of getting skills.

I pulled a bolt from my eye socket, throwing it to the ground along with what was left of my eye. The itching of it regrowing started immediately. Once, it would've taken me days, weeks even, to regenerate that. Now it happened in less than a minute.

I'd noticed in the trial just how much stronger I was, more durable. But it was the tortoise's fire that had really driven that point home. That flame was so hot that it melted the skin off my bones, and I'd survived it. That would've killed the Fledgling me in an instant, even the Adult me. I could heal from pretty much anything, but do enough damage in a short enough period of time, and even a vampire could die. Fire, aside from silver, was the greatest danger to us.

There was a reason humans had stories about vampires, pitchforks, and torches. Set a fire to a vampire's home, especially during the day, and you could be reasonably sure that you killed them.

It took me a few minutes to pull out all the wooden bolts and another few to heal fully. Once I was done, I continued on, heading out of the mist and up the stairs to the last test.

I felt like I understood it more now. The test was meant as a sign of passage, of maturity and capability for the Tengu-gi that wanted to venture down the mountains, into the mists of Asha Kai-ni. It made sense that their people would want to equip those who wished to go with the tools to survive in what Shadow had described to me as a brutal world.

I didn't know how useful what I learned here would be to me. Asha Kai-ni was the land of never-ending mist. Earth not so much.

Still, I continued, reaching the next arch. There were no images, nothing to indicate what I should do. I frowned. After the dangerous nature of the last test, I was a lot more wary of what this one could be. But no instruction at all . . . I sat down in front of the arch with my legs crossed, and thought.

The Tengu-gi were a solitary, introspective race. They lived above the rest, focusing on mastering themselves. Being in touch with the world, and contemplating its nature. They didn't interfere with the world below their mountains. This test was for those who wished to go into the mists, so there had to be some logic behind it.

The first test was to move the mist, a useful thing in the world where they were a constant presence. The second was to teach the person how to use the mist to protect themselves. I didn't know what capabilities the Tengu-gi had. Shadow only mentioned something called the **Way of the Mind**, but they had to be capable of surviving the second test. I doubted that the way I survived it was as intended. Few things could survive taking so many wounds.

The last test then had to be another lesson, something to help those going down to survive.

I stood and walked into the arena. As I reached the center, I heard soft clicks, too low for anyone but someone with my level of hearing to notice. An equally low hissing sound started surrounding me as something was released into the mist.

Poison? I wondered. I didn't move as it filled the arena and mingled with the mist. I grimaced. This did feel like cheating, as I was a vampire and didn't need to breathe that often. Especially not if I wasn't moving at my top speed.

I walked through the mist slowly, studying the arena. The walls around me were smooth, with no openings anywhere for me to push the mist into. I started to think what the goal of this test could be.

To simply survive the poison seemed too simple. There was only one thing that I could think about, and that was to remove the poison, or at least its threat.

The mist surrounding me was thick enough that I couldn't really see anything, and it was dark, as the arena was in the shadow of the mountain—surrounded on all sides. I couldn't see the poison, if it even had color. But, it wasn't mist, so I settled in the first position and started my dance.

I focused on the mist and my intent. Slowly, it started to move, swirling around me in a half-sphere that I'd learned to do in the previous test.

I focused on pulling only the mist, and pushing everything else out. Quickly I stood in a swirling mass of mist, and somehow I knew that the poison was pushed out to the outskirts of the arena.

Suddenly, the floor at the corners opened, and the poison and mist were sucked down. I remained in the arena waiting. I'd passed the final test, a bit anticlimactically perhaps. I had earned a waybound skill for myself, and now I had earned Shadow's skill.

I knew that I had to return to him, so I took a deep breath and turned, walking back through the other arenas and down the mountain, heading to find my much older adoptive brother.

Shadow waited for me on the plateau below, sitting on the edge and holding a glowing sphere in his hand—the skill. He stood as I approached, his expression blank but his eyes glinting with mirth. He bowed, his nine tails spreading behind him like a fan. Then he raised his hands and offered me the skill.

I straightened, then mirrored his bow and took the skill in my hands.

"Congratulations on finishing the test," Shadow said.

"Thank you," I said slowly.

"I see that I was worried for no reason." Shadow grinned.

"Not with no reason. The second test would've been hard if I had attempted it earlier," I told him.

He inclined his head in agreement.

"I got a waybound skill," I told him. "It seems almost like I cheated. I get two skills from you."

Shadow shook his head. "No, you did not get the waybound skill from me, though I suspected you would. There were other ways to accomplish the tests, ways that you could've achieved with different skills. The goal was not to follow the instructions; it was for a young Tengu-gi to demonstrate that they could survive in the mists of Asha Kai-ni."

I blinked, opened my mouth, then closed it and shook my head. "Well, I guess that it doesn't matter now."

I looked down at the skill in my hand. "This skill, what is it?"

Shadow just smiled at me.

"Can't tell me, or won't?"

He didn't answer. I sighed, then looked away.

"Once I leave this place, you'll be gone."

"Yes," Shadow said.

"I shouldn't have done this now, I should've waited. I—"

"Do not need me. And besides, the real me is still out there."

I grimaced. Saying goodbye wasn't something I was good at. And I wasn't ready just yet.

"Saia," I said, and the dragon manifested next to me in her drone. Her head almost reached to the middle of my chest now. She had been gathering a lot of mass in the challenge.

"Can you go and put this skill on one of my empty shelves?" I asked her.

The dragon looked at the sphere in my hands, then back at me and nodded. She took the sphere and flew out of the room.

"What are you doing?" Shadow asked, the ears on top of his head twitching.

"I don't want you to be gone before seeing me using your skill. I want you to see it."

"Little Star," he said with a kind smile. "I am just a copy."

"That doesn't matter to me."

Shadow looked at me for a long moment, his tails swaying behind him.

He was important to me, even this version of him, a copy. He had been there for me when I needed him, and while I always knew that I would lose him I still felt sad.

I felt it when Saia placed the skill on the shelf, and focused.

[Quick Swap Slot—Debilitating Wave>Mistshroud]

I activated the skill and felt a sensation similar to the one that I felt when I connected to the mist in the arena. Something poured out of me, and covered me whole. I felt stronger, I felt tougher, and my senses felt sharpened.

I looked down at my hands and saw them covered in black mist. I raised my head and saw Shadow looking behind me with a warm smile on his face.

I glanced over my shoulder and saw tails, nine of them to be exact. They were shaped out of black mist, almost looking like smoke, shifting around constantly.

"Tails?" I asked, surprised.

"It is my skill. It makes you look how it looks for me. You even have ears on top of your head." His eyes glinted mischievously. "It looks good on you."

"Oh," I said. Then I recognized the skill. "This is the skill that you used on Ish Vimza."

Shadow blinked, his eyes narrowing. "I don't remember showing it to you. I was too injured to try it."

I frowned. "It was when we fought the sikiri monster, back when the blight attacked my mind. When you helped me fight it off."

"Uh." Shadow tilted his head. "Little Star, I don't think that happened."

"What? You must remember! The blight was invading my mind, then you arrived, with this skill. You stopped it and it called you *Khanum*."

Shadow shook his head. "I—" He froze. Then his entire being twitched, as if he had just glitched out. I took a step back on instinct. I watched as his features returned back to normal, and a mischievous grin spread on his face.

"It looks good on you," he said.

I just stared at him for a long while.

He tilted his head. "Little Star, is something wrong?"

"Are you alright?" I asked.

He frowned, but answered. "I am glad that you've gotten this skill. It is my favorite, the one I love the most. It will protect you and give you strength when you need it."

I couldn't listen to his words. All I could think about was what had just happened. That had to have been the Grand Spell interfering. There was something that it didn't want me to know, but . . . there wasn't anything that I could do about that.

What just happened confused me, but it also convinced me that the copy in front of me wasn't the real Shadow. I had always held a little bit of hope that it was some part of him. And though in a way it was, it was also a puppet created by the Grand Spell.

I closed my eyes, and then put a fake smile on my face.

"Before I go, and you vanish. Tell me about the skill and what it can do."

There were mysteries that I wasn't yet equipped to delve into. But one day, I would.

I stood at the entrance to Shadow's room, looking back at the stairs leading to the plateau. He was back there, waiting to . . . disappear, I guess. I didn't know if he felt any fear. He didn't show any when we said goodbye, but he was a trickster. I was sure that he could hide it.

I took a deep breath, then left through the door and closed it behind me. I waited for a moment, my eyes closed, then I turned around.

The door was still there. I waited for a few seconds for it to start fading away—it didn't. I frowned, I had gained the skill. The purpose of the door was done. The other doors that I got from people had dissipated once I got the skill. I walked back in and up to the plateau, finding Shadow in his usual spot.

He raised an eyebrow. "Back already?"

"You're not gone," I just said.

"Guess not."

"How? Why?"

"It is your Mask, your rules, Little Star."

"I . . . your blood was freely offered, but I had others who did the same."

"You did, only they did not know what exactly they were giving, did they?"

"Uh, no, you think that matters?"

"Masks have strange rules. Yours is one that I have not encountered before. Even if its principles draw from Invoker type Masks."

I didn't have an answer, but instead I allowed a smile to blossom on my face. "Whatever it is, I'm glad. I enjoy our talks."

Shadow tilted his head. "As do I. We shall see how long this lasts."

With that, I turned and left, feeling slightly lighter, knowing that I wouldn't lose his counsel. I made my way to the central room and swapped out my profile skills again; I had to be prepared.

The Last Trial

We stood before the stone shrine, the entrance for a trial. There was less than a week left in the challenge overall. Terra had overtaken Suul'dar, though the difference wasn't too high. This next challenge could be the one that decided the victor of the challenge.

"Huh." Aurora bobbed her head. "That's interesting."

"Really?" I turned on her with narrowed eyes. "Interesting is what you're going with?"

Aurora chuckled. "I mean . . ."

I shook my head and turned my attention to the trial plaque.

Trial of the Tower—Gathering Point Sixteen

Join in the Trial of the Tower! Touch the scepter to reserve a spot.

Trial starts in: 17 hours

"There is no limit, it seems," Khalil said.

"It doesn't mention anything about teams either," Daehyun chimed in.

I grimaced at him. "You think that it is a solo trial."

"It could be," Daehyun continued. "There are no mentions of teams, or of a limit for this gathering point."

"He's right," Khalil said. "It could be a problem if it doesn't drop us in together. It would be a lot more dangerous."

I knew that he was right. If they were separated from me, then the likelihood of them getting hurt or even killed would be high.

"Guys," Aurora interjected. "We don't even know what kind of a trial it is. For all we know it isn't a violent one."

The rest of us exchanged looks. Every trial so far had been a violent one that pitted us against other challengers. True, in the end, the violence was a choice that was made, not implicitly required by the trial itself.

Which did make me feel somewhat better. The chances that we would be forced to fight one another, or other challengers was low, though I knew that if we did meet others, it was likely to come to blows—especially with the Suul.

"If we are not sent together, it will be dangerous. I can't protect you," I told them.

Aurora rolled her eyes. "Please, Mari. I mean, you're strong and all that, but we aren't that weak either."

"I didn't mean to imply—"

Aurora interrupted me. "Of course you did," she said, but her tone wasn't angry. "I don't begrudge you for thinking like that. You are a vampire, after all, and very powerful in comparison with us. But I think that you're underestimating us."

I bowed my head in apology. I knew that she was right, even though I was trying to make a conscious effort to give them the credit that they were due. I knew intellectually that they were strong, and that they weren't weaklings. It was just hard to keep that belief in mind when I was so aware of my own power. It was no wonder that vampires constantly looked down on everyone. It was almost impossible to do anything but be condescending when you could kill everything around you in less time than it took them to blink.

"So." I looked around at the others. "Are we all going in then?"

"I'm going to stay out," Jiyun answered. "I'm still not fully healed from the last trial. And besides, I'm unlikely to progress unless I start focusing on the blade and not just the violence."

I understood, especially after our talk, and I was glad that she knew her limitations. She had mostly recovered, but if they faced other challengers inside, her being even slightly injured could prove fatal.

"We'll stay too," Jason said, speaking for his entire group. "There are some rifts around here that we can clear instead."

I nodded, then turned to the others.

"I'm going," Aurora said, almost as if challenging me.

"I shall as well," Khalil added.

Daehyun just nodded.

I looked them over, then sighed. "I guess the four of us are going. We should probably plan on what to do if the trial separates us."

They all agreed, and we approached the pedestal, each registering for entrance in turn.

The light of the trial transport faded from my eyes as I was deposited into a small stone room along with Saia wrapped around me. The moment we entered, she flowed down my body and into her drone form, leaving me with only the parts of her that were the suit covering my torso. There was a single gemstone embedded in the ceiling serving as the light source, casting a pale blue light across the smooth walls of the room.

I looked around but saw only one thing of interest. Across from me was a pedestal with a plaque, and I approached it.

Trial of the Tower

Goal of the Trial—Climb the tower! The Tower is a personal trial, adjusted for your Mask and Ornaments. Each room will hold a test. The higher you climb, the greater the reward. At every point you may leave the trial, leaving with the rewards accumulated. The winner is the challenger that climbs the highest at the end of a five-day period.

Five days. That was just one day before the entire challenge ended. It was a long trial, and I relaxed, as it seemed like it wasn't going to be a trial that pitted us against others. At least the others wouldn't be in too much danger.

A sound made me turn and see a part of the wall slide open and reveal a set of stairs leading up. Next to it was a round plate with a plaque beneath it saying that placing a hand on it would end the challenge.

With a last glance around the room, I hefted my weapon and glanced at Saia.

"Ready?"

She trotted alongside me as we climbed up to the first room.

It was the same size as the last one, except that this one had a beast inside of it. It was the size of a wolf, standing on four legs with an elongated snout tipped with a wide, curled beak. It was covered in feathers, and its front limbs had wings. It didn't wait at all before it lunged at me. I stepped aside and raised my serpent-tongue spear, cutting its head clean off.

It fell to the ground with a thud. I blinked.

"Huh."

The door on the other side of the room opened, along with a section of wall that revealed a compartment with a small chest placed within.

"I guess that it starts easy."

"Statement: It would appear so."

I knelt and drank the blood of the beast. No use wasting it. Then I walked over to see what the reward was. It was just five fire gemstones, F-grade, almost useless.

I gathered them then continued on, climbing to the next floor.

The first five floors held beasts, none that were any real threat, but they were getting more dangerous, even if it was a steady increase in the danger.

The sixth floor was different. It was a larger room, and instead of a beast, I was presented with a series of tablets, with instructions written on them, and ahead of them was a weird obstacle course. I frowned as I studied them.

"This is a martial art, a movement technique," I said slowly. Saia didn't comment. "Why would it give me this?"

"Feedback: The plaque said that the tests were aligned based on your Mask and Ornaments. You hold the Ornament of the Practical Student."

I narrowed my eyes, then stood and went to check on the course. It was a series of disjointed platforms attached to a middle pillar, leading up to a final platform a few meters above.

I jumped on one, and immediately it tipped to the side, sending me slipping to the ground. I landed with ease, then jumped right back. With relative ease I moved swiftly, jumping higher and higher before the platforms could tip, and reached the top.

Once I did, nothing happened.

"Input: I believe that the intent behind the test is to follow the instructions on the tablets."

I rolled my eyes. "Of course it is."

I jumped down and approached the tablets again. They were obviously not made for a vampire, or a human for that matter—the pointed ears on the figures drawn was a dead giveaway.

Still, I started studying it, and the more I did, the more I realized that it was making sense to me. The technique seemed to be designed to aid in quickly shifting balance. I read it through a few times and then turned to the obstacle course, deciding to try to make it work in practice.

My [Practical Learning] made it easier for me to learn while doing, and it seemed that was what the test was designed for in the first place.

It didn't take me long to understand the concepts and incorporate them in my movement set. I could actually see how the technique could work with my combat techniques.

The quick steps and the way it utilized arms to shift balance was very reminiscent of some movements that Shadow had shown me. His hadn't worked with me fully as they relied on principles that required the added weight provided by his nine tails. I obviously had none of those. But these movements were much easier for me to use.

I experimented on the platforms, jumping on them and quickly adjusting my footing and center of gravity, then constantly shifting it until I reached an equilibrium with the platform.

Once it stabilized, I jumped to the next, doing the same. I fell from the second to last platform and grimaced, then immediately got back at it and reached the final platform on the second try.

As soon as I landed, the door to the next floor opened, along with the reward. So far, the rewards had all been F-grade gemstones, and this time it wasn't any different.

"Well, that was . . . easy."

"Input: Which suggests that we are still in the early levels of the trial."

"It would seem that this is more of an endurance race. I could see how some of the others would have issues. Getting through the rooms as fast as possible, but also conserving their energy."

"Input: The nature of this test offers a unique insight into the Grand Spell."

"Noticed that, huh?" I asked with a grin.

"Feedback: I have. This test is a net gain for you, no matter how you look at it."

"When you know the nature of the Grand Spell, it isn't that strange. Its task is to protect Kirios. We are its tools. Its purpose is to make us stronger. I've been looking at the trials and the rifts wrong. They are dangerous, they kill—too many perhaps—but they also allow the lucky or the capable to rise faster and higher."

"Statement: It would seem so."

"What I'm worried is that it had decided to implement all these changes now, in this Expansion Interval. That it had brought over two worlds is already a big deviation. It almost makes me think that it believes it will need more people."

"Query: You believe that the threat of its enemy, the blight, is rising?"

"I don't know." I shook my head. Maybe I was just imagining things. The message that I recovered on Ish Vimza was beyond ancient. The blight and what lurked beyond this world's skies had been there for a long time. It was almost arrogant to think that now that we were here things would change.

I shook my head and walked over to gather my reward, another handful of gemstones, then I continued to the stairs, climbing up to the next floor.

* * *

I climbed ten more floors before I reached anything that was even slightly challenging, and even then, it was just a ferrorn I dispatched with just a small bite on my thigh, which healed quickly enough.

"If the difficulty curve continues as it has so far, it will be a while before we get anything really dangerous."

"Statement: The trial is supposed to last for days. It's only been a few hours."

"Yeah, yeah." I waved my hand in agreement. "I've just been expecting something a bit more challenging."

As if my words insulted the world, it decided in that moment to prove me wrong.

"You hear that?" I said as a loud rumbling noise came from behind me and the door I entered the room through.

"Feedback: Yes."

It was faint, which meant that it was far away, but it sounded a lot like moving water. I rushed down the stairs, heading down the rooms that I'd cleared. I made it through seven rooms before I found the source. Water was rising through the entrance on the other side, bubbling up and flooding the floor.

"Right," I said. "Of course it wouldn't be that easy."

Now it became a race. I had to clear the rooms fast enough to stay ahead of the water.

I rushed back up and continued.

I increased my pace, clearing the rooms faster and faster. The rewards hadn't changed much from the start, being mostly gemstones, though now they'd changed to E-grade and then to D. I'd also gotten a small rucksack, which let me carry them all easier. My backpack was borrowed from Jiyun, who stayed behind, since I lost mine in the previous trial.

It was a day later that the rooms started getting harder. The ones where I had to learn something were the most time consuming, though my Ornament of the Practical Student had gained five Carvings putting it at First Investment; Fifth Carving, and though I didn't get any new skills, my Esoteric rating changed from C to B.

I'd also gotten a couple rooms with puzzles, like one that had three exits each with the writing above it saying that a different one was the real exit. I'd been able to use my [One Truth Verified] skill on those, but I lost a lot of time there when I had to use it more than once, The cooldown wasn't short.

That was when the water nearly caught up to me, which prompted me to blast through the next rooms as fast as possible.

I spent another day just cutting my way through beasts, simple puzzles, and learning different things. One room had instructions to teach me sewing—it was almost nonsensical. Yet, it did follow certain patterns, and the rooms were getting more and more difficult as I went up.

By the time the third day came I'd lost count of rooms. The rush of water behind me was a low thrum that was constantly assaulting my senses. My ears were far too sensitive and could pick it up even when I was dozens of rooms ahead. It was starting to gnaw at my thoughts.

So, irritated, I stepped onto another floor and paused. This one was a lot larger, with a taller ceiling. But what drew my attention was what awaited me inside.

A being stood across from me, wearing dark gray metal armor elaborately adorned with dark blue motifs in shapes of clouds and lightning. It covered the being whole and was a lot more form-fitting than ancient human armor.

He, and I was pretty sure that it was a he, had no helmet on his face. The weapon in his right hand was swordlike, about as long as my entire arm, and incredibly thin, a slightly curved blade that wasn't even as wide as two of my fingers put together.

He was just slightly shorter than me and had long white hair pulled back into a braid. His eyes were stormy, dark blue, and crackled with faint light as if lightning was flashing deep within. His ears were elongated and his skin light gray, making him an elf.

"You've come, foe. I've been waiting. You resemble an elf, though I see you are not."

I took a step closer, one hand tightly gripping my weapon as I dropped my supplies and rewards to the floor behind me.

"You've been waiting?" I asked, confused. *Did the floors intersect somehow?*

"Yes," the elf said simply.

"How are you here? We're supposed to have a grace period. Elves aren't supposed to be able to interfere yet."

The elf tilted his head. "Ah, this is an Expansion Interval then. So, another has come after the dwarves. It is as the seers have foretold."

I blinked. There was a lot of information in his answer. Dwarves? They were the second race added to Kirios, just after the Elves. If that was the last Expansion Interval he remembered then . . . "You—who are you? How are you here?"

"I do not know how I came to this place. One moment I was on the field of battle, and in the next I was here, all my wounds no more. I only know that I am supposed to wait for a foe, and fight with all the strength I have."

My eyes widened as I realized the truth. There were two options. Either the Grand Spell had kidnapped someone, or this man was a copy, the same as Shadow. Someone that had lived a long time ago, who the Grand Spell had recreated just to test me.

I didn't know how to react. Was I just supposed to fight this person? I could sense the power in his blood, could smell it. He was definitely in his Fourth Investment, and according to Shadow that was a moment when people became truly powerful, a tier that made a qualitative change in a person's being.

"Must we fight?" I asked as I got ready.

"I have no choice in the matter. And you and your companion seem powerful. It will be an honor to cross blades."

The same as Shadow, he had to be an amalgamation of memories and Grand Spell's own designs. I rolled my shoulders and glanced at Saia, who had grown significantly in the last two days, enough that she could offer me some protection now.

"Saia, armor," I said, and she flowed over me, changing and shaping a suit of silver armor. The first thing she created was a skintight suit over my body; then came the thicker plate. Then another layer rippled over me, looking like corded ropes of muscle, with solid lines of metal wrapping around muscle groups and important areas like my spine. Another layer rippled out over my upper torso and neck, protecting it.

She didn't make me a helmet, as she still hadn't figured out how to filter for my senses fully, so having it would reduce my natural advantages significantly.

"That is amazing. I've fought a dragon once, to see—ah."

I tilted my head. "What?"

"That is all I may say, it seems."

Like Shadow, he, too, was limited in what he could reveal.

"How long ago did your kind arrive on Kirios?" I asked instead, wondering if he would be able to reveal that.

The elf furrowed his brow, then answered. "Three thousand years."

I nearly whistled. He was ancient. It'd been tens of thousands of years since then. I realized that I was looking forward to this.

"I don't really want to fight you, but I need to keep climbing. What are the rules of the fight?"

"You give up, die, or you kill me."

I glanced behind him to the round plate next to the closed exit. I could walk up to it and place my hand on it to leave the challenge at any time.

"You can't submit?" I asked.

He shook his head. "I must fight with all that I have, to the death."

I smiled at him, showing fangs. If that was how it was going to be, well, I had no choice. "It's going to be an honor to fight you. My name is . . . The Star That Dances in Blood Beneath the Light of the Broken Moon."

The elf blinked then inclined his head. "I am Knight Lord Saevel of the Stormhome. May you always weather the storms."

He took a single step back, and took a sideways stance, his blade pointed at the ground.

With that the fight was on.

I leaned forward, then kicked off the ground so hard that the stone cracked. I lunged across the distance, stabbing forward with my serpent-tongue spear.

I surprised the elf, I could see it in his eyes. He hadn't expected my speed. Just as the tip of my blade was about to hit, he moved out of the way.

I felt skills being activated, but only barely. His skill use didn't ripple into the Way like others, I couldn't get any sense of what they were.

Before I could even react, his blade parried my spear sending the tip upward, and then he kicked me in the stomach. I grunted and took a few steps back before catching myself.

"You're heavier than you look," Saevel commented as he looked at me from above the blade of his sword. "And faster, stronger. You didn't use skills. Your kind are naturally that strong or you have an incredible assortment of passive skills."

He attacked immediately after, his form blurring forward and his blade singing through the air. I swung to block, but his blade shimmered as if it was made out of light and passed through my block.

I wrenched to the side; two strikes hit my torso and shoulder, nicking Saia's armor, but failing to punch through. The last nearly took my eye, but I twisted my head out of the way and only got a cut on my cheek. I dashed back, putting some distance between us.

"You didn't use your skills," he commented as he kept his blade pointed at me, his eyes peeking just above it.

He had dismantled me in that exchange. I was faster and stronger, and it didn't matter. He wove his skills through his movements in a way that I hadn't seen before.

This was a man who had fully mastered his Mask and his fighting style. I might be a vampire, physically superior to him, but I would have to do a lot better if I was going to win.

"Didn't think I needed them," I spat, wiping the blood from my cheek with no trace of the wound. It was a lie, but I didn't want him to know that I just didn't think of it in the moment. He raised an eyebrow at that, his eyes looking at my cheek.

Saevel smiled, a cold, predatory grin that made my heart pound. "Well, let's see them then."

He vanished. Not in a blur, but literally blinked out of existence as a bright light filled my vision and made me turn away. My blood ran cold. I spun just as the crack of thunder nearly shattered my eardrums. My spear was ready, my senses straining. The light was assaulting my eyes still, but now I saw the lines of movement. I whirled, thrusting blindly.

Nothing.

Then a searing pain in my back. I stumbled forward, choking on a cry. Saevel reappeared in front of me, stepping out of the lightning, his blade dripping crimson. He looked at his blade with a strange look on his face. "Less blood than I expected."

Fear rose up inside of me. And not the usual instinctual fear that told me when danger was coming. This was something else, a deep fear that I was just not good enough. That I wouldn't be able to win because he was just more skilled than me.

I roared, fury eclipsing pain, and drowning the fear. I lunged, abandoning all thoughts of defense, settling in the Scarlet Moon Style. I wasn't going to be defeated, no matter what. He met me head-on, his movements a symphony of deadly grace. Each parry, each feint, a calculated dance designed to break me. His technique was flawless, his every movement precise. It put my technique to shame. My movements were perfectly coordinated, my control was flawless, and yet before him I appeared as a child attempting to dance.

His skills pulsed across the Way, but I couldn't grasp them. At best I got a moment's notice before he used them.

With every exchange I came out the loser. I was bleeding from a dozen wounds, but I refused to yield, to stop. Every time he struck, I struck back harder. A single blow would kill him, and I could tell that he knew that. He couldn't win in a conflict of might, but he evaded, deflected, parried. It was . . . annoying, and it only served to fuel my fear. Every time he vanished, I anticipated his return, learning his rhythm. He dealt me a dozen strikes that would've crippled anybody else, but not a vampire.

He was learning, realizing that putting me down wasn't going to be that easy. With every next strike he tested a different target, almost as if he was timing how long each wound took me to heal.

I attacked, and he slipped away, his body moving as fast as lightning, and I knew that I couldn't let this continue. I reacted.

[Mist Step]

I jumped backward, turning to mist and passing through his attack and flowing over his body. I re-formed behind him, my blade ready for the attack.

[Blood Empowerment]
[Overburn Skill—Greater Stab]

The attack that was supposed to pierce him straight through the center of his back instead found his shoulder as he twisted aside. I pushed my blade in, intent on cutting deeper, but he suddenly got faster and dashed forward faster than I pushed. He slid himself off the blade in a feat of precision that I envied.

He jumped away, twisted in the air, and while flying touched a hand to his chest. He pulled out a smooth Mask, gray with blue lightning bolts painted on its surface, and slid it over his face. I reached for my own chest, but lightning struck me, sending me flying back until I hit the wall behind.

He was in front of me, his blade flashing with speed and accuracy that made my own look clumsy. I protected my head, letting him carve up my body instead.

I knew that I couldn't let his attacks keep coming, and the **thirst** sang inside of my mind.

I roared and pushed forward, swinging widely with speed that eclipsed his. My veins bulged as my blood burned inside of my veins, making me stronger. He danced to the side, twisting and attacking behind himself blindly. I let him hit me, his blade cutting into my side. I dropped my elbow, trapping his sword in my body.

A tiny ripple in the Way betrayed him activating a skill. I didn't hesitate.

[Swap Profile]
[Slash]

I cut from above, my weapon's long reach catching the elf as he dropped his weapon and tried to evade my strike. I channeled every ounce of vampire strength I had, and my armor, Saia, tightened as the coils of artificial muscle augmented me further. Saevel's eyes widened in disbelief behind his Mask as my blade cut through his collarbone and down into his chest.

Time seemed to slow; the lightning flashed in his eyes then winked out. His eyes met mine, and his Mask slipped from his face to reveal his lips turned up in a smile.

"Well . . . fought," he whispered. Then, the life drained from his eyes. He fell, his body dissolving in light and vanishing along with the weapon still stuck in my body.

Silence.

I fell to my knees, blood seeping out of my wounds. I took in a deep breath and closed my eyes. I won.

Hammer of the Earth

I sat in the room for a while after the fight. My wounds had long since healed, but I felt their presence as if they were still fresh. The battle, too, was fresh in my mind, every moment of it replaying as if I was watching a movie. As a vampire, physically, I was always the most powerful being in the room. I'd always felt that way, since the day I was turned. With what I now knew of my bloodline, it was more true today than it had ever been before.

Yet, I had nearly lost. If Saevel had held a Mask that gave him command over fire, if he had been able to prepare and know how to fight a vampire, I wouldn't have won. The way he fought with his skills was unlike anything I had seen before. It was seamless; his Mask was part of his entire being.

I was approaching the Third Investment, and with my vampire heritage I was used to punching above my Investment. Beasts were one thing—they might be equal or even stronger than me, but ultimately an animal was still an animal, no matter how cunning. But a person utilized their Mask in ways that I hadn't imagined.

A Fourth Investment elf nearly killed an Elder vampire at the Third Investment. I hadn't really understood how Investment improved people. I knew that based on the Mask they became faster, stronger, and Saevel's Mask was clearly combat based, and had improved his speed significantly—enough to be able to match a vampire. My Mask didn't improve my physical attributes to the same degree because it was spread out across all three—Physical, Weave, and Esoteric.

I had always won battles because I was a vampire, not because I was better—this battle made that clear to me. Now that it was over, I had so many different thoughts about things that I could've done. I hadn't even used the skill I got from Shadow, which was probably my most powerful one right now.

I had to start practicing with my skills a lot more. I had a lot of versatility, and my meta skills like [Overburn Skill] and [Swap Profile] helped my limitations a lot, but I still didn't have a concrete path.

Still, it was frustrating to realize that I wouldn't have been able to win if I wasn't a vampire.

"Query: Are you alright, Mari?" Saia asked. "Your vitals are outside the normal range."

I closed my eyes and took a deep breath, then let my heart beat. It calmed me down. There was no reason to dwell on what I couldn't change right now.

"I'm fine." I shook my head and stood, looking around. "He didn't leave a body," I commented. "Wonder why that is. The beasts did."

"Input: It could be because of the nature of what he was. A copy of a real person would not possess the essence that your Mask requires in order to create a copy within your soul space."

"So, you think that he was a copy too."

"Feedback: It seems the most plausible, based on his words and the nature of this trial."

I nodded, glad that we agreed. "Yeah, you're right. The beasts could probably be real. The Grand Spell could've just transported them or had them in storage somewhere. I guess that it didn't transport real living people because it would go against its desire to see people get stronger. Copies of the dead are apparently on the table."

Saia didn't respond to that. She was slowly repairing the damage to the armor I was wearing, Saevel had done a number on it. It wasn't the final version of Saia's armor, the thing that Ke Erzi would wear in battle. It was just the part that would augment their physical attributes, which I figured would be better. This was our first battle where I had the opportunity to really use it.

"How did the armor handle?"

"Report: I've been able to augment your physical strength by 5% on a constant base, and boost that to 15% in crucial moments, though the energy drain on your body increased by 80%."

I grimaced; I did feel a bit hungry. I walked back to my supplies and pulled out a gourd filled with blood. I took the opportunity as I drank my fill to think. Having Saia in armor mode during this fight wasn't at all the right move. It slowed me down, not because it was restrictive but because I wasn't used to fighting with it.

"You should change back into your drone form, for now. I think that you'll be more useful that way."

Saia flowed from my body and back into her dragon form. She was getting bigger, though not large enough to ride just yet, unfortunately.

"Statement: I agree. Numerical advantage will prove more beneficial in the near future."

With that, we moved over to the rewards. The usual gemstones were there, though this time there were two extra utility gemstones, one black with a white dot in the middle, and the other white with a black one—both were D-grade by their shape. The white one would change a skill from passive to active, while the black one would change the skill entirely.

I put them aside for now and looked at the extra reward I'd gained.

I picked up a dark blue crystal and showed it to Saia. "It's the same as the fire one. Want to bet this one is lightning based?"

"Feedback: That would be a poor bet." She touched it, her eyes flashing. "You're correct."

"Any chance you can use it for an engram?"

Saia tilted her head. "Feedback: Yes. The alterations I'm doing to [Plasma Shot] will allow for change of Source-Weave type."

I blinked. "Lightning Shot?"

"Feedback: Potentially."

"Have at it then." I offered her the crystal and watched as she swallowed it whole.

Then, I glanced back at the entrance. I couldn't hear the water climbing up behind us. We'd gotten quite a lead on it. We still had over a day in the trial, so I decided to take a short break and figure out my profiles and skills. I also had a big supply of gemstones. I rummaged through and counted them up, realizing that I had enough to merge the lower ones and have enough D-grade stones to push one to C. I swiftly started pushing them together, until the pile became a lot smaller, with a few dozen random D-grade stones and a single C-grade metal gemstone.

I looked it over, thinking about which skills I could put it in. Currently, my [Lesser Constitution] held an E-grade gemstone, making my skin just slightly tougher than it ordinarily was. I didn't know how much of an upgrade a C-rank would be, but out of all my skills, that one seemed to be the most compatible with the stone. [Blood Empowerment] might work too, but it didn't feel quite right.

I pulled my Mask out, then focused and pulled the old stone out of the skill. It shattered once removed, but I had expected that—the stones were single use. Slowly I pushed the new C-grade stone and focused on my [Lesser Constitution] skill.

Once that was done, I replaced my other stones with D-grade ones. For [Mist Step] I merged air and water stones, turning them into a single mist stone. I pushed it in and then tested the skill out.

I turned to mist, a larger volume than before, and then re-formed after a step. But a mist remained, not too thick, but clearly there. I narrowed my eyes as something occurred to me, and I started running around. The new cooldown for [Mist Step] was five steps, and as soon as it ticked down, I stepped as mist again. I repeated it five times before there was enough mist around me that it was slightly harder to see.

Then I changed my movements and danced.

[**Scarlet Moon Style;** Dance of the Shifting Mist]

The mist responded, far easier than the one in the test. This one felt even more a part of me. It shifted, following my movements, gathering and thickening around me, obscuring me. Then as I changed my pace, so did it, following my will. It swirled around me, quickly, with powerful momentum in a protective sphere.

Then my skill ran out as I took a wrong step, and the mist slowed and spread out, returning to being just normal mist.

I stepped out of the mist and smiled; this was a good thing. I could work with this. With [Quick Swap Slot] I replaced my [Lesser Strength] for [Mistshroud], then activated it.

Black mist rose from my body, completely enveloping me. It felt like a second skin, one that was fully under my control. Shadow had told me a bit about how it worked, and what it was. The skill was a versatile, high-tiered one.

The Mistshroud could protect me, though its defense wasn't equal to even Saia's armor. It could hide me, though that was more useful in an area like Asha Kai-ni, which was always misty. Here it would make me slightly stronger, but I could also send it away from my body, have it act like a double made out of mist. Which was how Shadow used it most, as an improved version of his mist clone illusions. His Mistshroud was more powerful, of course, as he had many more skills that tied into it which I lacked. His had a physical weight if he wanted it to. It could injure, and act more like a double instead of an illusion.

I would have to settle for a distraction. But, as I activated it within the mist created by my [Mist Step], I felt connected to the mist. It felt as if it was a part of my body, and I could feel sensations within it. Saia, for example, was standing at the edge of the mist, tendrils of it touching her side, and I could tell that.

As I realized what it meant, I grinned. Saevel had shown me how to combine and utilize skills, even though I had never felt anything or been able to recognize what he was doing—it was obvious in the results.

Now, I was taking the first step toward figuring out how to weave my skills together too.

I climbed ten more floors, each occupied by a beast or containing a learning puzzle of some kind. They were more difficult, but while beasts were more powerful than me, they were not Saevel. I did lose hours on them, however, and the water caught up to me.

It felt like it was accelerating, so I knew that I wouldn't have much more time. I used the beast fights to refine my current profiles and put in gemstones in skills.

As I rested after a fight with a Fourth Investment beast, drinking its blood and healing, I glanced at Saia.

"Can you show me my Mask stats?"

Marianna Rojas (The Star That Dances In Blood Beneath the Light of the Broken Moon)

Mask of the Blood Reaver (Physical, Weave, Esoteric) — Second Investment; Ninth Carving
Ornament of the Revelator of Secrets (Weave, Esoteric) — First Investment; No Carving
Ornament of the Practical Student (Physical, Weave, Esoteric) — First Investment; Fifth Carving

Attributes:
Physical: B
Weave: E
Esoteric: B

Skills:
P1-No Bonus
[Mist Step] - Mist (D)
[Mistshroud] - Mist (D)
[Lesser Constitution] - Metal (C)

P2-Combat Bonus
[Double Strike] - Primal (D)
[Triple Thrust] - Lightning (D)
[Pulverizing Smash] - Primal (D)

[Swap Profile]
[Overburn Skill]
[Blood Gout] - Nature (D)
[Quick Swap Slot]
[Blood Empowerment] - Primal (D)

[One Truth Verified]

[A Lesson Remembered]
[Practical Learning]

[*Scarlet Moon Style;* Dance of the Shifting Mist]

Not all of my skills were compatible with the stones that I had, and I didn't want to use the two utility ones to change them. Not when I wouldn't have the time to get accustomed to those changes. I'd used the beast floors to get comfortable with the improvements that the stones made, and they were significant enough to be noticed. I'd also gotten another Carving, which was a lot slower than before. But I was approaching the next Investment, so I guess it made sense. I was drinking a lot of blood, but not nearly as much as I had in the last trial.

Some stones changed the way skills worked slightly. [Triple Thrust] became something more akin to what Saevel's attacks had looked like, tinged with lightning, while [Blood Gout] seemed to provide me an initial burst of healing when I drank the stolen blood, before my natural healing kicked in.

My waybound skill, though, was not compatible with any of the stones, not even the utility ones. It meant that such skills couldn't be augmented in any way, which did make sense. It wasn't a skill given by the Grand Spell, but by the Way itself.

I finished drinking and healing from my last fight and glanced at Saia as she completed repairs on her drone and the consumption of the beast's biomass. I felt the sensation of my skin being spread tightly over my body, and the pressure inside. It was getting worse, but I hoped that advancing to the next Investment tier would banish it. It felt like I was about to burst. But as the **thirst** consumed and fed on the blood, the sensation dissipated and settled in the background. Not gone, but dormant.

Once I felt well enough, we gathered our things and headed up to the next floor. As soon as I entered, I knew that this room would be difficult. On the other side, once again, stood a person. He stood straight, his hands folded over the head of a large two-handed warhammer as it rested on the ground with its pommel against the ground. The top of the hammer came up to his chest, which already would've made it a tall weapon, except that the person was close to three meters tall. He towered over me and was at least twice as wide. He was bulky, muscled, and wearing combat robes with armored pieces over his shoulders and upper chest. On his hips was a plated skirt that came down to his knees. Elaborate markings swirled over the pale green metal pieces, the same vibrant orange color as his robes.

I recognized his race from Shadow's retelling. His skin was dark green, with vibrant red hair, both on top of his head and on his face. He had two horns that rose from his temples and curved straight upward.

The man was an Oni-yi, one of the three races of YoKai-ni, along with Tengu-gi and Kitsu-oi. The Oni-yi were the people that Jiyun had stayed with when she had been sent to Asha Kai-ni as Exemplar.

Both she and Shadow had called the Oni-yi a brutish people that cared only for war. Nothing that I saw now screamed that. Instead, I felt danger on a level I hadn't felt from anyone but Shadow and my sire, perhaps not quite as intense, but enough that I knew that he was better than me.

I took a step into the room, Saia following behind me in dragon form.

"Foe."

His voice rumbled as if the earth itself was moving. It echoed against the walls of the room and made my bones shake.

I swallowed. He was stronger than Saevel was, a lot stronger. He had to be in his Fifth Investment, and looking at him gave me a sense that I was looking at an indomitable pillar of the earth.

"Greetings," I said respectfully. This man frightened me, and I was not used to that.

"Gratitude," the giant rumbled. "Even in death, the Last Intent grants me a challenge."

I blinked. The Last Intent was one of the names used for the Grand Spell, but it was one that was used by the Vim, the Ancient Ones who had died long before the YoKai-ni arrived on Kirios.

"You know you are dead?" I asked slowly.

The Oni-yi inclined his head. "I am an echo, but it matters not. I am here, and you will not pass beyond me. Your climb ends here, stranger."

I tilted my head. If there was one thing that could anger me, it was someone telling me what I couldn't do.

"Confident, are you?" I asked.

He shrugged. "I trust that the Last Intent would've offered me a suitable challenge, but you are not highly Invested. You do not know yourself, and your Mask does not touch upon a truth. You are a child, but even children can offer lessons. I look forward to learning whatever it is you have to offer, before I defeat you."

I narrowed my eyes. That was such a mess of a compliment wrapped around in an insult, but that was fine. He didn't know about vampires; he didn't know about me.

The rumbling of water behind me told me that I had little time. "Well then." I gripped my serpent-tongue spear tightly and settled into the first Kata of the **Veiled Mist Assault:** *From the Mist, Strike.*

"That is a Tengu-gi style," he rumbled, his eyes narrowed. "You are not of YoKai-ni. You are not Tengu-gi nor are you Kitsu-oi or Oni-yi. Their kind does not share their teachings with those not of their blood."

I didn't expect him to recognize my style just from a single stance. That was . . . bad, actually. But I had no choice. I almost rushed him with no notice, but at the last moment decided against it.

I pulled back from my stance, then I put one leg a step behind, bent my knees slightly, and bowed at the hip while keeping my eyes on his.

"I have the honor of being known as The Star That Dances in Blood Beneath the Light of the Broken Moon."

The Oni-yi's eyes widened in surprise and shock. For a long while, he didn't react at all. I waited, keeping my position. Then, he moved, mirroring my stance and bowing to me.

"I have the honor of being known as The Pride of Hasha Who Breaks the Earth Under the Shade of Hearth Home."

We both raised from our bows at the same time, and his eyes narrowed. "I did not expect this, but I see now. You are of her line."

"Her line?"

He opened his mouth, then paused, and I knew that he couldn't speak about it. I assumed he meant Shadow's mother, my mother too, I guess. He'd told me that she was infamous. I didn't realize that someone like this would've known her. I had no way of knowing how long ago Pride died, but then again Shadow had said that his mother had been alive before the Grand Spell took their world.

"We are here for a purpose, to fight," Pride said. "But customs must be followed. Do you exercise your rights under the Old Tree's Hearth?"

I paused, remembering that part of the name giving ceremony. I was afforded a day of peace, to talk and find common ground.

Sadly, the rumble of water behind me told me that I wouldn't have even an hour. I shook my head. "No," I answered him. "Let's do this."

I returned to my stance and glanced at Saia. "Stay out of this."

I wanted to test myself, to see if I could match him. I had entered the fight with Saevel unprepared, was too arrogant. This was going to be a lot different.

The air crackled with anticipation. Pride nodded, his grip on the hammer tightening. "Then let us begin." He flipped it over and put it in both hands.

With that, the world exploded into motion.

Pride slammed his hammer into the ground, and the earth surged upward, a jagged wall of stone erupting between us. I leaped back, barely avoiding the earthen spikes that shot from the floor. The arena was no longer a neutral space—it was his domain, and he was its master.

I darted forward, taking a step, and mist swirled around me. Pride's hammer crashed down, but I was already gone, a trail of mist left in my wake. I reappeared behind him, my serpent-tongue spear flashing toward his exposed back.

But Pride was faster than he looked. He spun, hammer deflecting my blow with a thunderous clang. The impact sent shockwaves through my arm, numbing my fingers. He pressed his advantage, a flurry of blows that forced me back, each strike shaking the ground.

With every attack, he grew closer to splattering me across the ground. And with each step, I grew closer to escape. As soon as my cooldown was up, I stepped, turning to mist.

I leaped around him, weaving in and out of his reach. Each strike I landed was met with a counter that rattled my bones. I was fast, but he was somehow just as fast. It was infuriating, the fact that somehow, he could match an Elder vampire's speed. I was strong, but he was unyielding.

The room started to fill with mist as I kept at my hit and run tactics. Then once there was enough that he couldn't quite see me perfectly, I executed my plan.

First, [Mistshroud], the black mist rose from my body, mingling with the mist all around me, letting me know exactly where he was.

Then, I started to dance.

[**Scarlet Moon Style;** Dance of the Shifting Mist]

I moved, and the mist moved with me. It gathered around him, and I sent the black mist flowing from my body, charging straight through holding a copy of my weapon, attacking straight at Pride. Meanwhile, I stepped to the side, then from his blind spot I attacked.

[Swap Profile]
[Overburn Skill—Lesser Pounce]
[Triple Thrust]

My serpent-tongue spear flashed with lightning; it stabbed forward at the Oni-yi's large back.

[Earthform Shockwave]

The mist was blown back, along with me. The ground shattered, cracking and breaking into pieces that were blasted in all directions around him, pelting me and breaking bones.

I crashed on the ground, rolling and groaning in pain.

"I see now how you know that style. But I am a son of Asha Kai-ni. I've lived in the mists for all of my life."

Right. I cursed myself for forgetting. I literally tried to use a combination attack on a person that had probably spent their entire life fighting in similar conditions. Stupid.

I pushed myself to my knees slowly, as Pride hadn't moved from his position. My painstakingly gathered mist had been banished, but at least I'd kept my grip on my weapon.

I narrowed my eyes on Pride.

"You won't triumph," he told me. "You show promise, but you lack the tools to win against me. You have great physical strength, greater than even mine, despite being on such a lower Investment. That is impressive, but even the strength of a Sixth Investment is nothing if you don't know how to use it properly."

I tried, very hard, to take his words as advice in the spirit it was intended. At least I had a rough estimate of my physical strength now. He said that it was equal to a Sixth Investment Masked, probably a physically focused one. That was good to know. It gave me a ranking of vampires against the Masked of Kirios.

"I'm not giving up." I spat a glob of blood. My wounds healed, bones cracked back into place and mended.

Pride inclined his head and readied his hammer.

I looked at him, then grabbed my revolver. A part, a very small part though, felt like this was cheating, dishonorable. But then I realized that the man could literally crack the earth with a tap, so I said fuck it. My gun was part of my power in the same way my Mask was.

I aimed and fired. The trigger presses were no longer necessary to fire; they were there just to tell Saia to trigger her mechanism in the rounds, and to turn the drum. I pressed four times in quick succession, half the drum gone in a second. The first two bullets hit him in the chest and penetrated into his chest. He grunted, surprised, then he reacted. A wall of earth rose faster than the bullets could fly, catching the rest.

I dashed to the side, opening my line of sight. I aimed and fired again, but he was ready now; his wall turned into a sphere around him, protecting him from all sides. I clicked the last time, emptying the entire drum and only getting two shots in. I tsked but decided that it would have to be enough.

Just as I was trying to decide how to break the wall, it shattered on its own. His spherical wall of stone broke in all directions, and I used [Overburn Skill— Lesser Charge] to get closer, swinging my weapon to shatter the projectiles, getting pelted by smaller debris. But I didn't care. I was in the middle of the fight; there was no defense.

As I reached him, the ground beneath Pride erupted, a geyser of stone and earth flinging him into the air. He roared, his hammer flashing above me as he prepared to swing down.

I pointed my arm at him, made a sign that I had prepared with Saia, and then leaped up to meet him.

Inside of his body, the two pieces of Saia, the bullets, reacted as she activated the simple instruction. When we made the new bullets, I got an idea. They were part of her, and she could control them. Sadly, such small pieces of her couldn't contain enough mass to hold processing units, which meant that they could only receive simple instructions from the control unit. Namely, return to the whole.

The bullets ripped free of Pride's wounds, making him grunt, his attack halted. I grinned as I met him in midair, my spear a blur. He managed to block one blow, two, but the third found its mark. It pierced his shoulder, a fountain of blood erupting

[Blood Gout]

The blood flowed into my open mouth, and my spear stabbed forward with [Double Strike].

Pride's roar turned into a choked gasp. The Way shuddered. My weapon found his body, and bounced off.

[Flesh is Metal]

His skin darkened, and his hammer fell, smashing across my shoulder and sending me into the ground. I hit hard, bouncing off, my shoulder shattered, my weapon lost somewhere else. As Pride landed near, I reached for my chest with my good hand and pulled out my Mask.

I placed it on my head and roared.

[Blood Empowerment]

I rose to my feet, drawing my dagger, and charged at him. His blood in my stomach burned, and healed me in equal measure. The shattered pieces of my shoulder ground against my flesh beneath the skin, sending agony lancing through that side, but I ignored it all.

[Overburn Skill—Lesser Acid Spit]

I spat at him, the hissing and the pain immediately assaulting my mouth. The spit in my mouth left it, but what remained burned a hole through my tongue. *Fuuuck!*

I hadn't thought that the skill would work like that, but I didn't have the time to even think about it. My blood bubbled up in my mouth, healing the hole that it had made in my tongue and cheek.

My spit landed on Pride's chest, sizzling and making him curse. He stepped back, and I followed, swinging my weapon.

He blocked with a forearm, my dagger barely scratching his obsidian skin.

Then he moved; he kicked my legs from under me and dropped his hammer on my chest, pinning me to the ground. I felt a skill activate, and suddenly the weight of the hammer might as well have been that of a mountain.

I tried to move, but it was too heavy. I raged, waving my hand and trying to cut his legs, but he had too much reach on me.

"It's over," he said calmly as he wiped off my acid spit from his chest with one hand while he gripped his hammer with the other. "You fought well, surprised me even, but you can't win."

My cooldowns went down. I could swap my profiles. I had enough room to kick off the ground and turn to mist. I could . . . I sighed. I knew that he had won.

I should be glad that he didn't smash me to paste when he had the chance. I looked up into his eyes and saw something that I hadn't expected to see—respect.

"I yield," I said as my mouth healed enough for me to talk.

He inclined his head, then stepped back. I got to my feet and bowed my head to him.

"It was a good fight," he only said.

And it was. I learned a lot. I glanced around and found Saia walking over with my serpent-tongue spear in her mouth and my backpack on her shoulders. Water was bubbling up from the entrance.

It was time to go.

"Thank you for the lesson," I told him and bowed again, deeper.

"May you walk in the shade of the Old Tree," he said.

I didn't know if his words were part of any customs, so I elected not to say anything. Saia and I walked to the other side of the room and the plate on the wall. She wrapped herself around me, and with one last look at Pride, an Oni-yi warrior, I put my hand on the plate, and left the trial.

Enough

was back in the gray world, a plaque with words written on it in front of me, alongside a chest. I approached, taking a look.

> **Congratulations for finishing the Trial of the Tower! You've conquered floor 79!**
>
> You've finished in the 1st spot and were rewarded 60,000 points. You will be transported back to the Trial entrance after collecting your reward.

Well, I was glad that I was in the first spot. The points, along with what I gathered on my climb, should be enough to cement me as the first spot on the challenge list. Now, we only had to ensure that Earth won too, especially since we didn't have much more time. If my count was correct, we had less than a day left until the challenge ended.

The ranking did make sense though. Especially if others had to fight with copies of Masked from Kirios, I doubted that any would've been able to get past the Fourth Investment one. If their climb was similar to mine, that is.

I walked over to the chest and slid it open. From what I understood the rewards were based on how high I climbed and what position I attained, so I was hoping for something good.

The first thing I saw was a folded clothing item. I pulled it out and frowned when I realized that it was a shirt, black with a low cut and long sleeves. I turned it around, but saw nothing that would indicate anything about its purpose. The fabric was soft to the touch, but didn't feel particularly tough.

Saia flowed from my body, leaving only the thin suit covering my torso, and shaping her drone form with the rest. "Statement: I don't detect any Source-Weave from that item."

My frown deepened. "So, it's a . . . shirt?"

Then I remembered the last time I was in this place getting a reward. I was topless and joked out loud about the Grand Spell not giving me a shirt. *Did you hear me?* I didn't know the limits of the Grand Spell's gaze, but here was a proof that it did monitor us. Or this was just a complete coincidence.

I tapped the parts of Saia that covered me. "Can you take this off?"

The rest of her flowed and joined the drone, and I pulled the shirt over my head. "Thanks," I murmured to the nothingness around us. I got no answer.

Before I rummaged through the rest of the chest, I pulled my revolver out and pushed the cylinder open then offered it to Saia.

"Can you reload?"

"Feedback: Of course."

I turned back to the chest as she manufactured more bullets. There were two items next to the usual pouches of gemstones and coins. The first was a sheathed dagger, with the hilt wrapped in orange cloth. I pulled it out, and as soon as it was out the blade caught fire. I blinked, leaning back and looking at the crimson blade and the wavy patterns I could discern on it through the fire. The heat wasn't too intense, but it was still on fire. I pushed it back into its sheath, and it went out.

The second item was a twin of the other dagger, except this one had a white hilt. I pulled it out of its sheath and immediately noticed the cold.

"How long do you think these daggers can use their effects?" I asked Saia.

"Feedback: Indefinitely."

"Really? How do you know?"

"Feedback: They are drawing Source from around us."

"Huh, I guess that they are going to be useful then."

I slid them through my belt, replacing the ones Shadow had gifted me and my own, putting them in my backpack.

With that, I recovered my gun from Saia and had her flow over me so that I was sure the Grand Spell would transport her with me.

As soon as I had taken all the rewards from the chest, the teleport happened. I was deposited back into the forest, next to the shrine that I used to register for the trial.

I turned, expecting to see my friends, but instead I was assaulted by the sound of battle in the distance. I frowned, gripping my weapon as I scanned the surroundings.

The remains of our camp were nearby, the fire still burning, but supplies were left abandoned, and signs of a struggle were present.

I saw a form in the distance with the corner of my eye and turned, recognizing Aurora running toward the battle. She had to have come out just before me and heard the battle just as I had, then started heading that way. It was foolish. She didn't know anything about what was going on. I nearly cursed, but knew that I had to follow after her as I lost sight of her behind a tree.

"Saia, drone," I said, and she flowed from my body completely. "Go."

She flew ahead, faster than me. I ran after. I focused my senses on trying to piece things together. I heard a lot of feet moving, clangs of many weapons, sounds of bullets flying.

I arrived in the clearing just in time to see Aurora coming up on the side of it. My party members were on one side, clearly in the process of running. The four newcomers, Jason, Diana, Matt, and Mark, were firing their guns as Daehyun, Jiyun, and Khalil stood behind them.

A group of eight humans were rushing at them with a large beast running ahead of the group and soaking up all the bullets. I recognized a shifter's true form, and the scent identified him for me—Li Guo, Zhang's grandson. The group of ragtag humans were behind him, and an armored form led the charge, holding a hand up and a glowing medallion that cast a protective barrier around them. I recognized Dubois immediately. Anger rose up from deep within. They had decided to try to hunt us down. I didn't even know how they managed to find us, though Li was a shifter, and his senses were capable of it—I should've thought of that.

But what turned my anger to wrath was the presence of a third group. Six Suul charged with the humans, obviously working together. One of them was taller, darker in color—one of their greater variants.

How Dubois managed to convince them was beyond me at the moment. All I could see was them attacking.

Before I could reach them, Aurora raised her staff then slammed it against the ground. The earth was sundered in between the two groups, opening up into a chasm and forcing the attackers to stop. The shifter didn't, though. He leaped over it, and despite bullets ripping through him, he slammed into Jason, his jaw closed around his head.

He snapped it off then leaped toward Diana, intent on killing the now screaming woman too. Mid-leap, Saia dived, a silver shape that smashed into him and sent both tumbling.

I reached Aurora, grabbed her around the waist, and ignored her yelp and attempt to elbow me in the face, then leaped toward our group.

I landed next to Khalil, and dropped Aurora.

"Mari!" Khalil exclaimed as he ducked behind a boulder along with the rest of my team, hiding from the flying bullets. Some on the other side had guns too.

I saw Matt take a bullet in the side and fall as Diana emptied her magazine into Guo Li, who wrestled with Saia on the ground, both of them biting and tearing at each other.

Diana and Mark dropped their weapons as they spent their ammo and ran toward our hiding place. On the other side of the chasm, the Suul rushed around, heading toward us, while the humans took shots from across.

Khalil stepped close. "We need to—" I pushed Aurora behind the rock then turned, cutting him off.

They had incurred a debt toward me, and now it had risen. They had killed a piece in my sphere of influence. Jason was not a particularly important one, true, but he was still mine. He had traveled with my team and held his end of the bargain with me. A price had to be paid for his death. And more than that, they stood in my way, and I was done being the reasonable one. There was no room in this new world for it, not anymore.

I stepped out of cover. A bullet found my chest, but it had no trace of silver. My body pushed the slug out in the span of a single step.

The shifter threw Saia from his body, her claws ripping long gouges in his shoulder and snout. Saia for her trouble lost a wing—but that was fine, it was only her drone.

The shifter turned his attention on me. It would seem that I was being underestimated. Masks, magic, skills, and an alliance with the Suul had to have gone to the people's heads. One look at my eyes should've told them everything they had to know, but still they came at me. They should've remembered the old stories better. I might not be as experienced as most other vampires with my power, but there was a reason Elder vampires were feared.

My muscles burned, bulging beneath my skin. The sensation of tautness across my whole body was rising again as **thirst** woke from the scent of blood in the air and my anticipation.

For a moment, it was as if I could feel alien emotions in addition to the whispers. Somehow even though I couldn't quite parse them, I knew that they aligned with my own.

Blood of lost kin sings, feed, drain, rejoin.

The shifter, Guo Li, stood and glared at me with red eyes. His true form was massive, as tall as any human and twice as wide. He stood on four limbs, his skin covered in short and fine gray hair. His body looked more like that of a bull than a wolf, or perhaps one on steroids, wider, appearing more stocky than lean, bearing powerful limbs that ended in spread out fingers with thick and imposing claws. They didn't cut through flesh, they rent it apart.

His head was wide, surrounded by a brownish mane. Elongated snout with a wide jaw, filled with thick sharp teeth, looking like a cross between an alligator, a wolf, and a bear. He was a monstrous beast, powerful and terrible.

He growled as I stepped forward. Suul ran toward us, but paused. They spoke, then half went around me, heading for the boulder where the others were taking cover. The rest spread out, watching me and Guo Li. Humans were crossing around the other side of the ravine Aurora made, heading our way too.

The near-ton of muscle and flesh trampled the ground as it came toward me. I pulled out my revolver, and fired, emptying the drum. Eight bullets found their mark: One hit his head, flattening against his thick skull; three found his shoulders, and the rest his limbs. He didn't even falter; the bullets might as well have been bee stings. I dropped the gun and extended my hand making a gesture.

Saia responded. The command was instant, this time pushing the bullets further in. Li stumbled as he flinched.

[Mist Step]

I re-formed next to him, at the side of his head, I swiped my weapon up, slicing open the side of his neck. He crashed to the ground, the wound already closing, but I followed up with more attacks, stabbing, slicing, cutting. He rolled swiping with his claws, but he was slow.

A shifter he might be, but he was not his grandfather. Zhang was stronger. He lashed out, attempting to bite me, but I danced out of the way, then I jumped on his back.

I rammed my serpent-tongue spear through his neck, slicing through the spine. He fell to the ground, twitching. I left the blade in, preventing him from healing, and reached down, biting through flesh and drinking.

Blood flowed through me, and the **thirst** rejoiced. The taste was divine, the same as Zhang had been, though less intense. My body spasmed, and memories flowed through my mind.

Dubois and Li tracking me by scent, finding the Suul and negotiating with them. Dubois offered them a win in the entire challenge, a chance to kill the person on the top of Earth's list—me, and get all of my points, enough to give them the win.

The **thirst** rumbled inside of me; my skin felt like it was about to burst.

Mask of the Blood Reaver — Second Investment; Tenth Carving

<u>**Mask Consolidation**</u>
Ornament of the Revelator of Secrets — removed
Ornament of the Practical Student — removed

Mask of the Blood Reaver > Mask of the Sanguine Reaper; Revelator Seeker

Mask of the Sanguine Reaper; Revelator Seeker — Third Investment; No Carving

|Potential Augmentation| trait — Evolve Skill gained.

[One Truth Verified] > [Smell Lie]

[A Lesson Remembered] > [Memory Like Blood]

[Practical Learning] > [Learning Through Blood]

[Channeled Blood—Essence Door] skill gained.

I rose up, sitting on top of the corpse of the shifter. I took a deep breath, agony spreading through my body. The pressure built and didn't abate. It felt like it was going to swallow me whole.

A sharp pain made me look down at a new wound in my chest. My eyes found a human with a gun pointed at me, firing again. The next bullet hit me in the cheek, I felt it flatten against the bone of my jaw.

I tensed, about to jump and rip him in half, but something pressed on the Way. A sphere of water hit him in the chest.

[Binding of the Ocean]

My muscles seized up as the skill hit me. I felt like every part of my body had just suddenly cramped up. As if I was under an ocean of pressure. The skill held me in its grip, and I didn't even know its source. From the corner of my eye I saw the Suul running up, their weapons leveled with my chest. Three of their thin spears pierced straight through me.

Then a golden light shone down on me from above.

[Act of Faith]

It filled me with warmth, and the binding on me shattered. The sensation within me reached a crescendo, and for a moment the world froze, time stopping entirely around me, and while my mind whirled, the **thirst** spoke.

The world is a feast laid bare before us, ripe for the taking. We shall drain it dry, leaving nothing but husks in our wake. Our hunger knows no bounds, our thirst no end. Wake.

Everything crashed down on me. I rippled and grew as I started to shift.

Khalil bashed away the Suul's attack, then dashed in, using his skill. A disk of yellow light appeared above the Suul then came crashing down on top of his head. It bowed the Suul, straight into Khalil's sword.

He cut out his foe's throat, then stepped back, taking stock of the situation around him. He saw the Suul attacking the rest of his team. Jiyun and Daehyun were being pushed back by three Suul; Saia had her jaws around one of their calves; and Aurora had one of them trapped in a small fissure of earth, crushing his legs as spikes of stone pierced through his body.

On the other side, Marianna sat on top of the shifter, her eyes closed and looking almost in bliss as blood trailed down her chin. Then he heard gunshots, and they hit Marianna, but she barely seemed to notice. The rest of the Suul went at her from the side, and Khalil started running, knowing that he wouldn't reach her in time.

He saw Dubois point his harpoon at her and launch something at her. It hit her in the chest, and she seized up, then the Suul reached her.

They pierced her with their lances, and behind them he saw one of their leaders, the dark colored Suul, towering over everyone else on the field. He charged and raised a massive wooden cudgel tipped with sharpened bone like a pick, preparing to strike Marianna and finish her.

They were a human and a vampire, friends, but with a chasm of secrets and worry between them. Still, he believed that their friendship was genuine, despite everything.

Khalil raised his arm.

[Act of Faith]

His skill rippled out into the world, manifesting what was needed. A golden light fell onto Marianna and broke the skill's hold on her.

Marianna's shirt ripped open on the back as two limbs pierced out. Khalil froze, memory assaulting him. He could smell the smoke, feel the heat of the flames. He could taste the blood on his tongue, and the scent of death.

Images flashed through his head. Dead bodies in the streets, men, women, children—Elves. Limbs torn from bodies, corpses drained of all blood. The beat of fleshy wings and a monster in the sky.

He snapped to reality as Marianna straightened. She roared in a deep voice that reverberated through the world in an absolute tone.

Khalil's heart froze in his chest, preparing himself to see the same kind of monstrosity he had watched burn an entire city in its wake.

Then, instead of fleshy bat wings, the two that grew from her back erupted in black feathers. Her skin changed tone. Instead of a ghastly and pale tone of the monster in his memories, it turned azure, a deep blue. Her brown hair turned pitch black.

The Suul reached her, his weapon coming down. Her wings beat down, shooting straight up into the air, sending everyone around her to the ground.

Khalil raised his shield to cover his eyes as wind nearly bowled him over. Then he recovered, his head turning up, searching.

She floated above them, her hair billowing around her, black wings spread wide. Her eyes glowed with an emerald light, and her blue skin contrasted against the sky. She looked like an avenging angel, lances still piercing her body, blood staining her visage, and no less beautiful for it. In a blur, she pulled the lances out of her body, glaring down at their foes.

Then she moved, a sonic boom following her descent, and he was reminded of the horrors and the monster he watched commit them.

Bloodline of Asza

I descended on my enemies, those who had put themselves in my path. I was death, I was hunger, I was power. My mind sharpened, the **thirst** calmed, I was an instrument of death.

They were nothing before me, so slow and so weak. I dove on the Suul leader, my hand grabbing hold of his head and pulling him down, ramming it into the ground and squeezing. His skull burst in my hands.

My wings beat, instinct guiding me, and I flew into the other Suul. The tips of my fingers had elongated; everything above the top joint grew out of my skin and hardened into clawlike extensions—similar to the shifter hoof-claws, only far more elegant.

I dropped next to a Suul and backhanded him, obliterating his head. I moved to the next before the others even had the chance to realize what had happened. The next one I caught by the shoulder, my claws biting deeply, and with a beat of my wings I lifted him up in the air above the battlefield.

He struggled, but it was no use. With my free arm, I grabbed his hip, claws digging into bone. Then, I pulled him apart in two above my head. Pink blood dripped over me, and I threw the two parts down at my enemies. They stared up at me, as I beat my wings and hovered above them. They looked upon their death, and they knew it.

Screaming started. I tasted their fear on my lips, heard their hearts attempting to escape their chests. They ran, and I followed. My vision had changed, sharpened, and I could see things around them, like heat, pulsing in beat with their hearts. I could see their blood beneath their skin, flowing rapidly.

I was faster than a bullet as I dove into the closest humans, and I ripped them apart. I tore their limbs off, carved their bodies apart, ripped their spines out, and crushed their hearts inside their ribcages.

[Blood Gout] erupted, pulling all the blood around me into my mouth.

The world became just the sound of tearing flesh and cracking bone. I ripped and tore, and I drank, and blood flowed down my throat and nourished me. They weren't even able to touch me.

When all the warm ones were dead, my attention was drawn to another in the distance, wrapped in metal, who hid his heat and the scent of his blood. I flew after him, reaching him quickly.

I slammed into his back, intending to rip through his metal shell. My claws bit into his back, tearing metal apart. Then his armor glowed, and a flash of light burned my eyes out. Something smashed into me and sent me flying back. I hit a tree and crashed through it, then hit another that sent me into a spin. I fell on my wing and shattered its bone as I rolled over it, until I finally came to a stop.

I growled, my head killing me, and my eyes itching as they regenerated, filling with tears and leaving my vision blurry.

I rose to my feet and looked at the form in the distance. The armored human was on his knees, rummaging through a sack at his waist. I rolled my shoulder as my wing healed, and rushed at him again.

I couldn't see well, but I didn't need detail to know that Dubois was in front of me. As I reached him, he pulled something out of his sack, then crushed it in his hand. A blue light wrapped around him, and I swung my arm at him.

It passed through, finding only air. The light washed out, and Dubois was gone. I took three quick breaths, then I roared with all that I had, shaking everything around me with the force of it.

With the roar went my frustration. There was no need to let myself get consumed by it. Emotion was not the enemy, but I guided it, not it me.

I stood up, blinking rapidly to clear my vision, then I turned and started walking back toward the clearing. As I walked, I felt both calm and not calm. It was a strange sensation to describe. I could feel the **thirst**; I could actually sense its attention. As if it was looking through my eyes. Its words were a low rumble, but the blood I had just consumed seemed to have calmed it.

There was a pressure in my head, and what I had unconsciously suppressed made itself known.

Mask of the Sanguine Reaper; Revelator Seeker — Third Investment; First Carving

I'd advanced my Mask. I'd entered the Third Investment. I would have to take a look at all the changes once I had the time.

I walked out of the forest and into the clearing. The rest of my group was standing next to the boulder. I saw Diana, Matt, and Mark next to Jason's body, mourning him. Khalil was helping Matt, tending to his wound.

Jiyun was leaning on her sword as Aurora bandaged a wound on her leg, while Daehyun sat on the ground, half of his face covered in blood from a long gash on his head.

Saia was nearby. Her drone had been damaged, but she had repaired herself.

The clearing was a scene of horror. Corpses, or rather what remained of them, lay scattered across the ravaged ground like worthless playthings discarded by a bored god. Limbs, twisted at unnatural angles, jutted from the crimson-soaked earth. Torsos, ripped open and emptied of their contents—it was a grotesque painting. Heads, some still bearing expressions of terror, stared blankly at the indifferent heavens. I had given them no choice, no mercy.

The once verdant grass was now a matted carpet of red and brown, each blade slick with gore. The earth beneath it, cracked, trampled, and churned, had become thick with viscous scarlet mud that clung to everything it touched. The air was heavy with the coppery scent of blood that teased my nostrils, making them flare.

It was a scene of violence, of brutality and indifference.

I didn't feel sorry. I felt no sadness or regret. I had made my decision, and this was just the first such field I would walk. There would be no more second guessing.

They noticed my approach and froze. I came to a stop next to them. Saia trotted over to stand at my side, then spoke.

"Query: May I consume biomass?"

I glanced at her, at the dead, then nodded. She walked behind me, heading toward the dead. For a moment I paused, realizing that I was topless, again, but then I shook my head. It didn't matter to me.

I looked at the others, their expressions a wide range of emotions. Fear and awe were mingled together. Aurora was the first to approach me. She walked up to me, her eyes reserved.

"Uh, Marianna?"

I tilted my head. "Yes?"

She nodded, then looked me over, her throat moved up and down as she swallowed. She opened her mouth, then closed it. She took a deep breath, seemingly steeling herself, then raised her head and looked me in the eyes without flinching.

"Are you alright?" she asked.

I leaned back. I knew that this had to be strange for her, not just the way I looked but the rest too. The result of my rampage was behind me. We had fought for a month together, seen a lot of death and blood, but most of it were beasts, and none had been this violent.

Yet I saw no fear in her eyes, no disgust. There was trepidation, sure, but I would've been more worried if she was completely fine with it.

"I'm fine, Aurora," I answered her.

She smiled. "I'm glad."

"You're not afraid?" I asked.

She shook her head, perhaps a bit too hastily. "No, of course not."

A strange scent filled my nostrils, and I realized it was my new skill. Somehow, I knew that she had lied. She was afraid.

"You don't need to lie to me, Aurora," I told her gently.

She looked up at me, her smile shaky. "I . . . okay, I am afraid, but not that you'll hurt me or anything like that. It's just, well, you are terrifying."

The scent of the lie didn't return, so I knew that she spoke the truth. That made me feel better. I didn't want her to be afraid of me, not in that way at least.

My wings twitched, and her eyes slid over to them. She took a step closer, then paused, her eyes finding mine again. "Can I . . . can I touch them?"

I blinked, not expecting her question. "Uh, sure."

She reached out with her hands, tentatively, and touched my feathers.

"Wow, they're beautiful, and soft."

I just stared at her, unsure how to react. I could feel her touch, and it was . . . pleasant. My worry that she would look at me like I was a monster vanished. I was a monster, but it didn't seem to matter to her, or the rest of my friends. I saw them approaching. The twins were propping each other up, and Khalil walked a step behind them, his eyes looking everywhere but at me.

"So." Aurora stepped back as the others got close, shuffling her feet and avoiding my eyes. "Is this a Mask thing, or a vampire thing?"

I looked at Jiyun. She was the only one that knew more about my parentage. Then my eyes slid to Khalil. He was my friend. I trusted him; I just didn't trust his people. Some wounds were too deep. I couldn't trust in his judgment, not without meeting his superiors first.

"It's a vampire thing," I said slowly.

"Marianna," Khalil started, his eyes taking me in with an intensity that made me frown.

"You are not surprised," I said finally as the little micro-expressions on his face slid into place.

"You're like him, only he didn't look like this." Khalil was speaking in a whisper. His eyes had a faraway look to them, his hands clenched into fists. But then they relaxed. One of his hands reached up and grabbed the cross around his neck, and his eyes passed over me again. "You look like an angel," he whispered, almost as if he didn't even realize he had spoken out loud.

There was something in his voice and gaze that made me look away. It was the same look he got when he spoke about God, about his faith. I pushed that aside, and spoke quickly.

"The vampire on Elvaros," I said, putting it together. He had to have encountered an Ancient vampire. His reluctance, his thoughts about vampires, it all made sense. If he had seen a vampire who had fully matured, who had Ascended, and seen it attacking indiscriminately, I understood. "That's where you've seen this."

My words seemed to get him out of his trance, and his gaze hardened.

"Did you lie to me?" Khalil asked finally, though I could tell that he was afraid of the answer. "Only Ancient vampires can do that."

"I—no, I didn't lie to you," I said simply.

We looked at each other for a long while. He opened his mouth to speak, but I turned sharply as I heard someone approaching.

Soon, he walked out of cover of trees and into the clearing, heading our way. My friends tensed, their hands going for their weapons.

I raised my hand to stop them. "It's okay. That's my sire."

That didn't seem to calm them down, I heard their hearts speed up.

I stepped in front of them and waited for him to approach. He stopped a few steps away, then bowed.

"Marianna, may we speak?" he asked, his eyes going behind me to look at the others. "Alone, preferably."

I waited for the onslaught of emotion, for my anger and resentment to bubble up. They were there, but I felt a lot more in control. The **thirst** was the weirdest thing; it was almost as if it was submissive.

I nodded, then glanced at the others over my shoulder. "I'll be right back."

I walked over, and we headed into the forest. We didn't go far, just far enough that we wouldn't be overheard.

"Ten years, huh?" I looked at him.

He met my eyes, his expression the same picture of calm serenity it always was. He still wore the shirt he borrowed from me; it was surprisingly clean.

"It was not a lie. It was an educated guess," my sire said after a moment. "I simply did not properly account for the quality of blood available to you now, nor your Mask's effect on you."

I narrowed my eyes, then nodded. I didn't smell the lie in his words.

"So, you were watching me still," I said.

He shook his head. "I explored a bit, but returned to find you today, as it is the last day in this place. There are things I wished you to know. It was a good thing I did, as is evident."

I tilted my head and raised my eyebrows. "Evident in what way?"

"I did not expect, initially, for you to reach this stage so soon. You don't know how to turn back, do you?"

I blinked, then realized that he was right. "Uh, yeah." I looked down on myself, covered in blood, my skin the color of the deepest sapphire. "That might be a problem."

The corner of his mouth raised up. "Sit, let us speak, and I shall guide you through it."

It took me an hour to relax enough and force the **thirst** to turn me back. And that was what it entailed in gist, communicating with the **thirst**. It was a strange, almost meditative trance. The **thirst** was alien. It wanted to feed and grow, or at least the **thirst** within me wanted that. I could feel it influencing my emotions, trying to force me to do what it wanted. I realized why vampires learned to suppress it.

Though my way seemed to work too. For my sire, he had to force the **thirst** to submit, make it do what he wanted. I didn't do that. I guided it, almost reasoned with it. My emotions and its were tools. I didn't suppress them—its emotions were as valid as my own. The transformation back came as an agreement: I would feed it more blood, and it would do as I wanted. A simple deal between us.

"Good," my sire, Akatsuki Jin, said as I shifted back. "I was worried that you would be unable to do it without knowing how to suppress your and the **thirst's** emotions. I am glad to have been proven wrong."

I sighed and rolled my shoulders.

"That was unpleasant," I said. Feeling your bones shifting around, your flesh molding and reshaping as your mass moved around, was not a nice sensation.

"It will get better and faster with time," my sire added.

"I hope so," I said. "I don't want to have to spend an hour every time I want to shift back."

He didn't respond, and a silence settled over us. Then, I broke it. "Was that all you wanted to speak about?"

He shook his head. "No, I wanted to speak more of our bloodline, your parentage. As you are now, you are one of the very few vampires in the world who can assume an Ascended form. As far as I know, there are, besides the two of us and the two remaining originals, only another five vampires able to do the same."

Another five? Nine total. That was a small number. "I think that one of those might be dead."

My sire tilted his head. "How so?"

"Khalil, my friend, he told me that he encountered a vampire who could change like me, only he didn't look like I did."

"Another bloodline, Desert probably, if he didn't mention a swarm of creatures."

I inclined my head. "The Elves killed him."

He bowed his head. "I see. The danger you spoke of is seemingly greater than I realized, if they managed to kill a vampire of such power."

He paused for a few seconds, then straightened. "Eight then. There used to be rules, made by younger vampires in times when they ruled from the shadows. Not to show such transformation to the humans. They tended to believe us demons, or angels depending, and crusades and pogroms were the usual results."

I grimaced. "I broke the rules?"

He waved his hand. "Rules made by your lessers. You are of the Bloodline of Asza, second in line. They don't make rules for you, my daughter."

Okay, that was a lot to unwrap. It was the first time he had ever referred to me as his daughter. I was not equipped to deal with that, not now, maybe not ever. So, I ignored it and steered the conversation away from the minefield of a topic.

"Asza?"

"The name of my sire, my mother," he said slowly.

"Grandma, got it." I tried to make a joke of it. I regretted it even before he winced.

"She . . . perhaps do not call her that in person. Grandsire would be proper."

I shifted uncomfortably. "Yeah, I doubt I will ever get the chance, not that I would even be able to tell if I ever met her."

"You will. All vampires of our bloodline know her; you will see in time. And she will know you and that you came from me."

"Oh. Well, good, I guess."

"There are a few more things you should know, if you are to interact with the other vampires of this age. The oldest of the current generation reside in Constantinople. One of them is Ascended. He is a child, but then all are to me. He knows some of our history, twisted and half-forgotten remnants. He will know the truth about how vampires grow, though your case is unique."

"Should I keep you a secret?"

"You are closer to Asza than any of the other still living other than me. You may do as you wish, in all matters. I do not care. The young like to believe that such truths matter, but they do not, not in the face of time. They will know her name, all Elders and older know, though to them she is a figure out of legend. A god to some. Your parentage has a clear line, a link to hers. The rest have lost their history; they do not know how close to her they are. Some will consider you a threat, others a messiah. It is always such. You do as you wish."

I swallowed. That was a lot of authority he was putting in my hands.

"I did plan on visiting Constantinople. I need allies if I am to give us a chance to resist. How will I compare to him, to other vampires?"

"You will be stronger than all but the oldest of the Ancient Ones. Though, you should not dismiss the Elders. They will have lived longer than you, have more experience. But, ultimately you will eclipse them all in time, perhaps even by the time you meet them. There is still room for you to grow. The whelp in Constantinople is the weakest of the Ascended. Three others usually dwell in Asia, mostly asleep, though they will most certainly be awake now. One moves around, traveling. I do not know which one is dead, so it could be any one of them."

I nodded. I would have to prepare to meet other vampires. "What about the other original?"

"Kark," my sire said. "He moved to the frozen waste during the last ice age. I do not believe he has left since."

"Frozen waste?" I asked.

"Antarctica is what it is called now."

I blinked. "Huh, anything I should know about him?"

"He is of the Desert bloodline, a loner. He and Asza were brother and sister, though such relations weren't that important in their time or mine. I do not know what he will do now that the world is changed. I believe that this event will draw the oldest of our kind out, and there could be more than I know. Some could've just gone to ground and not made any waves to be noticed. The same can be said of shifters. Many of their kind had moved into the wild unex-plored areas of our world, living away from civilization in the recent years."

I nodded in understanding. He was telling me that his knowledge might not be complete, which did make sense. The communication age was a recent thing. He had to be relying on actually running into other people over a great period of time.

"One more thing," he started. "Before I left the cartel, I spoke with them. It was Pascual's intent to return to Europe. He was exiled to the new world, and he believes that now is his chance to return and rise in ranks. With the state of the world as it is, Constantinople is a likely destination for him."

I struggled not to react, but anger surged within me. My old Master, the leader of the cartel that took me as a child and had my sire turn me. The man that ordered my hanging. A hand reached up to my throat—the scar around my neck had faded further, but it was still there. A silver-inflicted wound, a permanent reminder of how close to death I came.

"I see," I said slowly. "Your debt to him is settled?"

My sire inclined his head. "It is."

"So I may do as I want?"

"Yes."

I nodded. There was a lot that I wanted to do.

"If you meet with others of our kind, and they challenge you, though your power should be apparent to them all, tell them that you are blood of Asza, and blood of Ji."

"Ji?" I asked.

"My name, Akatsuki Jin, is a recent one, most will not know it. Ji is my first name, and one that most will know."

"Just Ji?"

He smiled. "We had no surnames in my time. That is a recent thing."

"Right." Sometimes I forgot just how old he was.

We lapsed into silence again, but it wasn't exactly uncomfortable. I was glad that I had someone to talk with about what I was, about all the changes I was going through. Being lonely was not something anyone enjoyed. Despite everything that happened between us, I did care for him, somehow. He gave me the gift of the life I now had, even if he had failed me.

I turned my eyes to the sky. I was on top of the list, my points pulling ahead of everyone else by a large margin. I gained all the points of everyone I killed, human, shifter, and Suul alike.

Earth was in the lead, by a lot too. We were going to win this, I was sure of it. There wasn't much time left.

My sire stood, and I followed him.

"Once this challenge ends, I shall return to the search for my sire. Asza will need me to understand the changes to our world and all the things that have happened during her slumber. Assuming that she hadn't been walking among the humans for the last few centuries."

"That's a possibility?" I asked, wondering what the original vampire was like.

My sire nodded. "I do not know if she went back to sleep after what happened, or if she stayed awake. We shall see."

I took a deep breath. "And after you find her?"

My sire looked away, his eyes going unfocused. "I will find you, and help you with what you wish to do."

"You don't want to do it yourself?" I asked.

"I am less equipped to adapt to this new world. You are young; you were an Exemplar, sent to other continents. And besides, I can see it in you, the desire, the need. Neither I nor my sire crave to rule. We had a long time to do all the things we wished. It is your turn now."

I didn't know how to respond to that, but a part of me was excited. I did want to rule, I did want to be the one that stood at the top of the world. For myself, yes, but also because I didn't trust anybody else to do it. There was danger out there, something that all of this shit was created to fight against. I didn't trust anyone else to take it seriously enough.

It had to be me.

"You should return to your friends. The challenge will end soon."

I nodded. "I . . ."

"Until we see each other again, daughter."

"Wait!" I said, and he paused.

"Could you do me a favor?" I asked, and he raised an eyebrow.

I told him, and he inclined his head.

"If it is on my way, I shall do as you ask."

"Thank you." I bowed my head. He returned my bow, and then turned.

My sire, Akatsuki Jin, Ji, then walked away. Leaving me alone.

After a moment, I turned and walked back into the clearing.

"I'll come for you." I looked at Aurora. We were sitting in a makeshift camp, waiting for the end. Saia, or rather her drone, sat next to me, close enough for me to keep my hand on top of her back for when the challenge ended.

"What if my town was shifted around? If I'm not—"

"If you are, then it will be on you to find your way to Khalil at Constantinople. I'll make my way there eventually."

"You'll come?" Khalil asked, almost as if he couldn't believe it.

I nodded. "I will, eventually. I have people around me that I want to take care of. And I don't plan on just saving myself. We need organization, and if I have to threaten and bully every group of survivors I find, then that is what I'll do."

"You sound more like a conqueror than a savior," Khalil said.

I shrugged. "We are at the edge of extinction, the end of our way of life already. The time for diplomacy and good intentions is over."

"Your way or no way?" Khalil asked.

"What do you want me to say, Khalil? You saw what happened earlier today. They came to kill us because I refused their offer. They gathered others, and they followed, even the Suul. Just because of greed, and because of their fear of my nature. I'm not going to let that happen again."

Khalil looked conflicted, but nodded. "I'll speak with the council, let them know that you'll be coming, and . . . I'll be asked to tell them about you."

I had already assumed as much. "Then tell them the truth. I'll explain the rest once I'm there."

He nodded, looking relieved that I didn't ask him to keep secrets from his order. I knew better than to do that. Loyalty was more than just blind obedience, but there was more to it. I trusted Khalil, but I understood his obligations, I wasn't going to ask him to choose between me and an order that had raised him, that had been his home.

I turned to Jiyun and Daehyun. "I've asked my sire to look in on you two if he is in the area, help you if he's able."

They blinked, then exchanged looks. "He's . . . like you?" Daehyun asked.

I knew what he was referring to. "Yes," I answered. "But older, and stronger."

They bowed their heads. "Thank you," Jiyun said. "You didn't need to do that."

I waved my hand. "We are friends, and I promise that in time, we will see each other again. Soon, if you join the next challenge." I grinned at them, showing my fangs.

Jiyun chuckled. "I don't know if I want a repeat of this. We were not prepared. If not for you, we would most likely be dead."

"We'll have to see how the situation back home is," Daehyun interjected. "It's been a month here, but only five days back there. Still, five days is a long time in this new world. Especially when rifts can break at any moment."

I nodded. I was a bit worried about the military camp back on Earth, but I would be back there soon enough.

I glanced behind at the other group. Diana, Matt, and Mark sat a bit away. They had lost one of their own, for which I was sorry. Jason wasn't involved in Dubois's beef with me.

"If you can, make your way to the inland sea. Head north and find Constantinople and Khalil," I told them. "I'm sure that the city will provide shelter to any you choose to bring with you."

At my words, Khalil nodded. "I can promise that. We've been looking for survivors; you'll be welcome."

They nodded, but didn't say anything. I didn't press.

Then it happened. The light shone, gathering around us.

I looked at my friends and smiled.

"See you soon."

Then I was gone.

The Return

Challengers!

The Grand Challenge is over!

The victor of the continental competition is: Terra.
Reward: 10% increase in all Investment gains until the end of acclimation period for the entire continent of Terra.

Top ten challengers:
Marianna Rojas (The Star That Dances in Blood Beneath the Light of the Broken Moon)
Akatsuki Jin
Khashul Ukh
Jean Dubois
Ervauk Hshak
Loshul Ku
Kim Jiyun
Aurora Everheart
Lester Black
Khalil Abd al-Nur

Rewards: Private

The Challenge concludes.

I read through the plaque in front of me as I stood in the gray void. Earth won the overall challenge, and I won the personal one. It seemed that the top ten all got some kind of reward.

"What do you think we got?" I asked.

"Feedback: It is impossible for me to speculate. Rewards vary."

I rolled my eyes. A chest stood before me, and I moved to see what it held. I slid it open and looked inside.

The usual pouches filled with gemstones and coins. I perused them and found three gemstones that were larger and differently shaped than the others, meaning that they were probably higher grade. I looked at them, wondering if they were B-grade. I stashed the pouches in my backpack for later, then looked at the rest of the rewards.

There was a stack of six scrolls, three pairs. One of them was familiar to me. The markings and the color was the same as the one in my backpack—a Fireball Scroll.

"Any idea what these two do?" I asked Saia, offering her one of each remaining pair.

She looked them over, placing one paw on top of the first, her eyes flashing blue. Then she moved to the next one.

"Feedback: The first one is an enhancement, I believe that it would increase a person's speed for a time. Like the Fireball one, it will target whatever is in front of it when it is unfurled. The second one launches a piece of ice-formed Source."

"So a Speed Scroll and an Icebolt Scroll?"

"Feedback: Affirmative."

I put them in my backpack. They were interesting items, but kinda not that useful as single-use items, to me at least. Based on what Saia had said, the Source levels within the scrolls were minimal. If I was hit with that Fireball, it would barely singe me. Though, I guessed they were Investment level appropriate as a reward. It was my fault for being a monster.

I was probably going to give them away to others. They might help people who wanted to study them, or perhaps it might help steer their Masks in a more magical direction.

The next reward was a circlet. I picked it up, then offered it to Saia.

"Feedback: This item appears to amplify any sound coming from the source wearing it."

I tilted my head. "Huh, I guess that might be useful if you're speaking to a lot of people. Especially since we don't have microphones and sound systems anymore."

I put it on my head and spoke, then frowned. I didn't sense any change in my voice. Then, I realized that there was a strange sensation coming from the circlet, almost like a skill, though somewhat distant. I focused on it, and immediately knew that I had activated the circlet.

I spoke again, and could hear a visible change in the loudness of my voice. Though, it was perhaps a twenty percent increase at most.

I took it off, and was about to put it away, when something occurred to me.

"Hey." I turned to the dragon. "What are the chances that this thing works with other skills? Like let's say [Screech]?"

"Feedback: Highly likely."

That might actually be good. I didn't have any skills like that at the moment, I'd burned them out, but I could always get another. I stashed the circlet and moved to the next item. So far, the rewards felt more in line with the trials that I'd already finished, not really something worthy of an entire challenge. The last two items, though, were different. I could tell.

It had taken all of my resolve not to immediately pick up the item in front of me. The scent of blood clung tightly to it.

I picked up the golden ring with a blood-red gemstone set in it. I could feel the Source woven through it. The item had a weight on the Way, like a skill, only it was constant.

I offered it to Saia, and she touched it.

"Report: This is an Invested item."

I blinked. So far, all the items we got were enchanted at best. Things that Masked could and did make. Shadow had told me that there were three types of items on Kirios. The Enchanted ones, made by enchanters or inscribers and related Masked. Then there were Artifacts, which were relics and remnants of items created by the Vim that had survived to this day. They were usually powerful, but their effects didn't always work properly as the nature of the Source was changed with the coming of the Grand Spell. They were still powerful, usually far more so than anything else around, even when they didn't work as intended. The last were Invested items. Items that had grown and changed over time, by getting Investment, the same way a Mask did.

"How do you know?"

"Feedback: Because when I use [Inspect] it gives me a lot more information."

Suddenly, a window opened up in front of my eyes, projected by Saia.

Ring of Bloodcast

Store a skill and use it by sacrificing your own blood. The power of the skill will depend on the amount and quality of lifeforce used.

"Huh." That was interesting. "It's basically my [Overburn Skill] but without the burn part. I think."

"Statement: Your blood is of a greater quality than most, so yes, a skill used through this means will be empowered."

Plus, I regenerated, and could easily recover any lifeforce spent.

"Any chance it says how to put a skill in it?"

"Feedback: No."

I had an idea, but that was for later. I turned to the last item, a cube with a notecard attached, just like the one that created a cabin.

I picked it up and read the notecard.

Simple Town

Press the lever on top and place to build a town around you with simple wooden cabins and palisade surrounding it, along with simple additions. Location determines benefits.

I stared at the card. "A town, my reward is a town."

I was pretty sure that this would've been the reward for anyone who took the first place. It was unbelievable, but I already got one that could build a cabin so . . . And it was a good reward, especially since it would provide what most didn't have right now—shelter.

"I guess this might make things easier," I said, thinking out loud. I had already planned on moving to the coast with any survivors willing to come with me. My initial thought was to find a coastal town and retake it from the monster and the wilderness. Now I wouldn't have to.

This was good. A great reward actually.

I put it in my backpack, then turned to Saia, ready to go.

The Grand Spell didn't let me wait for long.

I was consumed by light and transported out.

I arrived back in the same place I had left from, in the desert, away from camp. Two moons shone above me through a crimson sky. Immediately, I was assaulted with distant noise.

No, it was a roar, the trembling of the earth, the scent of smoke and waste. I turned my head. The orange night sky, I knew that meant fire. It was in the direction of the camp.

"Follow, Saia," I said as I quickly dropped my backpack where I was and had tapped the suit she made for me twice, indicating that I wanted it off.

The part of her flowed from my body and rejoined the drone, which was now large enough that she was the size of a horse. I focused and sent my intent and feelings toward the **thirst**.

There was food ahead, blood waiting to be spilled. It didn't take any convincing. My body shifted, wings sprung from my back, and my skin and hair changed color.

I took to the air and flew, heading toward the military camp. It didn't take me long to reach it. Smoke filled the air above, but it didn't bother me. I didn't need to take a breath. Through smoke, I saw fighting, I saw beasts, an entire horde of them. I heard gunfire and screams. The gate was broken, and beasts were spilling in, but not in the amount that I would expect.

Someone had set the field around the camp on fire. They had to have done it on purpose. I took a small breath, just enough to smell. Scent of burnt flesh and hair filled my nostrils. They had set the horde of beasts on fire, but there were too many of them. More were coming from the forest ahead, thousands. Packs of wild, mutated dogs. I saw a massive bear tearing down a tent near the entrance. And rats, they were everywhere, entire swarms of them. People were firing rifles at the beasts, others shooting arrows, or stabbing with spears and anything else they managed to get ahold of. There was chaos everywhere in all forms. People dying, running, fighting for their lives.

My pause took barely a second as I took the situation in, and then I descended, falling down through the smoke.

Interlude - Wrath of God

Father Sergio Rodriguez hid in his small tent, clutching a club in his hands as children from the camp hid behind him. They were supposed to send them away, but the monsters arrived sooner than expected, before they had the chance.

The children were afraid, and his attempts at calming them were not going anywhere.

"It'll be alright," he said, knowing that he was lying. "God will protect us."

His faith had been tested, but he still had hope. Three days ago, their scouts had detected the horde from the city. The rifts had ruptured, spilling out monsters that had pushed everything in the surrounding out of the city and north. Straight for them.

The sounds of battle were loud, and the cloth of his tent offered no protection against it. The children were crying, sniffling, and clutching each other. He didn't know what to do.

The fighting was getting closer and closer. He looked at the children. Something rustled just outside the tent. He couldn't let it enter; he had to keep the children safe. "It'll be alright," he repeated. He clutched his club tighter, then stepped through the thin divider, and out into the night.

The air was thick with the smoke from their trap. They'd burned half of the fuel they had left, soaked the ground in it and set it on fire. They had dug holes and made traps. None of it seemed to have mattered in the end.

A pack of dogs was in front of the tent, and Sergio knew he wouldn't survive for long.

He would buy as much time as possible; it was all that he could do. With one last prayer to God, he raised his club. The dogs growled at him, their mutated forms grotesque and twisted. Then they charged at him.

A crack filled the air, turning his eyes toward the sky. Something came down from the heavens, smashing into the ground in front of him, right on top of the monsters.

Sergio fell back from the force of the impact, and dust rushed into his eyes. Sounds of flesh tearing and bones breaking filled his ears, and then it was over. Sergio wiped at his face, then with blurry eyes looked ahead. He saw a tall shape walk up to stand in front of him through the smoke. He couldn't see much; they held a long weapon in one hand; long hair cascaded off their head; their skin was dark. But what he could see was glowing green eyes.

Is it one of the fighters? he wondered. Some of them had powerful Masks.

He blinked rapidly, his vision clearing. Then he noticed more. It was a woman, and her skin wasn't just dark, it was blue. She was topless, black hair falling over her chest to protect her modesty. The bodies of dead dogs were splattered everywhere around her.

His eyes caught movement behind, then his eyes widened as wings spread from her back. Long and black, feathered and impressive.

"Get back inside, Father," she said, a tone of voice that was both low and high, that reverberated with a holy tone that touched the soul. The voice was alien, but it was also familiar.

Sergio opened his mouth, but couldn't get any words out.

A sound caught his attention, and he looked up. A silver dragon the size of a bull flew above them, diving at something somewhere else in camp.

There was only one dragon that he had ever seen. He looked back at the winged figure in front of him. She grinned at him, and he saw her fangs.

"Now, Father," she said, snapping him out of his trance.

Then she beat her wings and was gone in a storm of wind and dust.

Sergio turned back as soon as he could, his heart filled to bursting. His prayers had been answered. God sent him an angel.

Angelo Serrano pulled his dagger out of the corpse of a dog that had nearly bit his face off. He pushed it off his body, the blood spilling over him and covering him whole. The beasts had gotten through the walls. The eastern quadrant was going to be overrun soon. The other scouts around him were fighting too, as did the non-combatants. It was chaos. They were all going to die.

His skill showed him danger everywhere; there was nowhere left to run. A loud roar came from the side, and a massive bear charged out of a tent, destroying it in the process.

He watched his death approaching, and was too tired to do anything about it. The bear came, long bone spines growing out of its back crackling with blue sparks.

Then a rush of wind, and wings. A silver shape smashed into the bear, jaws biting and claws tearing. The bear gurgled, its throat open, and it fell as a dragon ripped it apart.

Angelo almost laughed. The bear was dead, but death still loomed over him.

Then the dragon stood up from the corpse, and Angelo frowned—he recognized it. Only, it was a lot bigger.

There was a beat of wings somewhere in the smoke; then screams of beasts filled the air.

The dragon looked around and started attacking the beasts nearby, leaving people alone.

Somehow, it looked like Angelo would live.

Kai danced to the side, avoiding the jaws of a wolflike creature. She pulled her arm back.

[Power Strike]

Her fist flowed, a faint shimmer surrounding it. Her brass knuckles hit the strange creature straight in the side of the head. Bones cracked beneath her fist. The creature whimpered, and Kai advanced. She raised her hand, then stabbed the blade at the bottom of her brass knuckles straight in the beast's head.

She was next to the walls, protecting the gate along with the other fighters. A gunshot rang out from one of the towers, a sniper covering her. Beasts had attacked the gate, but they had barricaded it, as best as they could anyway. It didn't matter. Some of the beasts could climb over or even jump across the walls; they were just concrete and sand blocks. They didn't have room on the walls themselves to have people protect them, so they had to protect from within.

The beast that tried to attack her back fell, and Kai stomped on its head, making sure that it was dead.

The heat from the flames beyond the walls was scorching, and the smoke was strangling her lungs, but she still fought. She had to. She had started up on one of the platforms next to the gate. She had watched the big beasts coming out of the flames, some even on fire themselves.

They were a problem, but the rats were the worst of it. They were everywhere, and they could swarm and take down a person in seconds. They made holes in the walls to get through.

The beasts had gotten inside. She heard people yelling but couldn't understand anything.

Someone next to her fell, and a dog jumped on top of them, biting through their neck before Kai could even react.

Death was everywhere. She was going to die, she knew it deep in her bones. Still, she didn't run like some others. She stood and she fought.

"Gather close!" she yelled, hoping that others would hear her. They had spread too far. They couldn't cover each other like this.

Some heard her, and tried to listen. Not all managed to follow her command. In the distance, through the smoke, she saw a pair that had ended up too far away from the rest of them in the fighting, near a part of the wall that had nearly collapsed and had beasts getting in. They were trying to get back, one leaning on the other.

A large beast was charging at them. Kai grimaced and stepped forward, then started running, using [Burst of Stamina] to keep herself on her feet.

She reached the two and grabbed the one that was injured as the person in the tower fired at the charging beast. She sent a silent thanks—the man in the tower was surrounded by beasts, but still he fought, covering the rest of them, firing even as beasts attempted to climb.

"Oh, God, thank—" the other started, but she cut him off by picking the man up and throwing him on her back and running back.

They got to the gate, and she dropped him, his blood soaking her shoulder. She leaned him over the gate and yelled for their medic. A woman ran up from the small defensive area next to the wall, and started treating the man.

A roar made Kai turn around, as a large catlike beast jumped out of a tent, its claws covered in blood. It had gotten in somehow. That's where they had hidden some of their injured. She pushed her thoughts aside and bent her knees as it saw her and charged.

A loud rush of wind flew by her, and the beast was torn into two pieces, blood splattering everywhere. Kai blinked as a dark shape with wings floated above her for a moment, and then it beat its wings. It rushed among the tents, and beasts died faster than she could even see.

Then it shot up into the sky and was gone.

Silence stretched, only distant sounds of fighting remaining. Kai fell to a knee, trying to get air in her lungs. She didn't know what happened, but that they had a moment to rest, and that she would take it.

Carlito crouched behind a large wooden crate as a group of beasts ran through the street. His two daggers held firmly in his hands, dripping with blood. He was near the command tent—they had tried to move all of their non-combatants there, but in the chaos of the attack people got separated.

There was no real command structure, not that there was really any before. Gunfire sounded from his left, from the training yards. Carlito saw a lone beast sniffing around tents. It was large, and wounded—cuts on its side were bleeding lightly.

He got out of his cover and headed toward it, sneaking behind its back. It heard him, of course it did, because nothing could ever go according to plan for Carlito. His whole life had been a series of shit fucking constantly falling on top of him.

He raised his daggers and activated a skill.

[Bleeding Cuts]

The wounds on its body started bleeding profusely, but it didn't slow the beast.

Carlito waited until it was close, then dashed out of the way with his movement skill. It smashed into the crates, breaking the wood in the process.

Carlito jumped on its back, stabbing in a flurry. Every stab he made bled more than it usually should.

"Fucking. Puta. Die already!"

The beast twisted and turned, trying to throw him off. It rolled and nearly crushed him beneath its body. Carlito fell off, and the beast got to its feet, claws biting into the ground as it got ready to pounce.

"Fuck."

It growled, and then a rustle of a hundred little feet rushed out of a tent. A rat swarm flowed out, and Carlito cursed.

"Ah, shit."

Dying by being eaten alive by rats was really not the way he imagined going out.

Then, before he could even attempt to run, the rats swarmed the beast and started eating it. Carlito blinked, but took advantage, he got to his feet and started running as the rats killed and ate the beast behind him.

The beasts weren't united; that much was apparent to anyone looking from the outside. They were pushed together by necessity, running, driven into a frenzy by something worse coming behind them. The beasts had come out of the rifts, had taken control of the city and even now fought for supremacy within it.

But while the horde of beasts wasn't united, it didn't in-fight. It had come together, and it was moving forward and attacking everything in its wake.

So, when suddenly, across the entire camp and beyond, the rats turned on the other beasts, it was unexpected, and it changed the dynamic among the beasts. No longer was it them against everything—now they all started fighting for themselves.

Giving the people in the camp a chance.

Angel

I flew around the camp, killing beasts wherever I saw them. A few of the people took shots at me, but I didn't hold it against them. I didn't look human at all, and I was flying around through smoke with very low visibility, at least for humans.

I could see that there were too many of the beasts; the horde outside of the walls was still coming, despite the fire that kept most of them away. Even if I could kill them all, I couldn't be everywhere at once. People would die. Many more than had already died.

Saia and my intervention had given the people a chance, but it wasn't enough.

I flew up in the air, overlooking the field. Packs of dogs and wolves, bears, and strange creatures that had escaped the rifts were everywhere, as were rats milling beneath their feet. Then, something occurred to me.

I didn't know if it would work, but I knew that I had to do something.

[Quick Swap Slot—Mist Step>Hive Mind—ratkin]

The skill triggered.

My mind was suddenly filled with a thousand voices, with a thousand sights, a thousand smells. It overwhelmed me for a moment, and I fell out of the sky, crashing through a tent and hitting the ground hard. A burning spike was pushed through my head, but then the **thirst** woke up. Another thousand voices drowned out the minds of the rats, and I could think again. I had all of their thoughts in my head, could hear the commands given by the evolved rats, the need to feed, so similar to the **thirst** yet so much simpler, far more basic.

I focused, getting hold of myself, then triggered another skill.

[Overburn Skill—Lesser Command—ratkin]

The rats didn't think like how I did; they knew no words or complex emotions. But I had dealt with the **thirst**, and my mind was greater. I rammed a command, a bundle of emotion and intent, straight through the heads of every rat around. And in an instant they turned, following my absolute command.

In the radius ranging for a hundred kilometers around us, the rats started tearing every beast around them apart, and where they lacked targets, they turned on each other, eating their own.

I couldn't tell them to stop attacking the humans; that was too complex, but that was also no change at all. The rats were already attacking them.

I shook my head and stood, then quickly focused and used [Swap Profile].

The hive mind vanished, and I groaned as I stumbled out of the broken tent. I looked around, then took to the skies once more, looking for more beasts to kill.

Hours later, the dawn arrived. The sun caressed my skin as I broke through the clouds, exhausted, but also filled to the brim with blood.

Mask of the Sanguine Reaper; Revelator Seeker — Third Investment; Third Carving

I lost count of how many I killed, how much blood I drank. Everything blurred together.

The sun's touch weakened me, but not as much as before. At least I felt that way. The power that coursed through my veins felt slightly lethargic, but not fully weakened.

I beat my wings, enjoying the feel of the wind on my face. Here above the smoke and the clouds, it was peaceful. I had spent the night hunting, killing, tearing, and drinking. I'd ranged away from the camp, making sure that no big beast was near or that no remnant of the horde was headed their way.

The people in the camp had eventually realized that I was on their side, so the potshots dropped significantly.

Saia remained at camp, keeping it safe as I flew around. I was tired. For the first time in a long time, I felt like I could sleep. Like I needed it.

I knew that old vampires, the ones that I had joined now in power if not in age, slept at times. Their bodies required a lot of power, and blood gotten from humans wasn't enough to satiate them.

I understood that now. I didn't think that I would ever need to sleep like that, nor did I think the other vampires would, not anymore. The sun's effect on us was diminished, and the quality of blood was about to increase significantly. Investment was a tangible thing that I could feel: The blood I drank nourished more.

I still felt like I needed to rest.

I took a deep breath, expanding my lungs with clean air, then headed back down toward the camp.

I flew slowly, taking the time to learn how my wings worked. They moved on instinct; I knew how to use them the same way I knew how to move my arms or legs, an extension of me. But I was fairly certain I could use them better. In time, I would learn how, I was sure.

I made a slow circle around the camp, making sure that everything was alright. I could see people moving around down below, cleaning up after the battle.

Some noticed me. I saw a rush, fingers pointing. I decided against taking more time and making them panic.

I turned toward the big tent in the center, their command where I could see the biggest crowd of people, and more importantly, Saia.

I came in slowly, people taking steps back as I spread my wings wide and floated for a few seconds as I focused on landing lightly and not embarrassing myself.

Once I touched down, the rush of wind and the beating of my wings vanished, letting me hear better. I tried not to react as people whispered, but I heard the word "angel" from more than one mouth. A strange sensation washed over me, but I pushed it aside. I was still not that familiar with this form or the way that the **thirst** behaved now.

I walked up to stand in front of a group of three people: Catalina Flor, Diego Murillo, and Maximilian Dawson. Saia stood near them, and as I approached she trotted over to me. I looked them over, saw them looking at me with wide and shocked expressions. They had bags under their eyes, were covered in grime and clearly exhausted.

I closed my eyes for a moment, focusing inward and asking the **thirst** to help me change. I didn't need to convince it. I had held up my side of the bargain. My stomach was filled with blood.

My wings pulled back, and my skin turned back to its usual tan color as I changed back. I rolled my shoulders and opened my eyes, glancing around at the awed expressions on everyone's face.

I put my hand out to Saia and whispered.

"Shirt."

A part of her flowed over my arm to cover my torso, serving as a shirt. That made more of them whisper. Few of them had seen what Saia could do.

Before I could speak, two people walked out of the crowd that was now surrounding me. I recognized them immediately, of course.

The amazonian blond that towered even over me, along with the shorter brown-skinned man with a shaved head and a long scar over his cheek. Tattoos on the side of his neck were covered in blood, and new wounds marred his already rough face, but he had a wide grin.

Carlito whistled as he looked me over. "You were holding out on us, boss lady, eh?"

I rolled my eyes. Kai just nodded at me, and I gave her a short nod in return. They took positions behind me, as if that was their place, and I didn't dissuade them.

I turned my attention to the three in front of me, the leaders.

"You're short a person," I commented.

Max was the one that answered me. He smiled sadly as he faced me. "Carlos died in the fighting last night."

I bowed my head. "I didn't know him well, but I am sorry for your loss. The challenge is over," I told them. "I'm glad I arrived back in time."

The others didn't react too much. I doubted that they were capable of it. I could see that they didn't really know what to say. They had just survived what they had probably thought was going to be their last night. They needed time, I understood.

"I've cleared the horde in the near vicinity," I told them. "We should be safe for now."

Max shook his head. "Thank you, Marianna, we . . . we wouldn't have survived without you, and Saia." He nodded at the dragon next to me.

"It's what we agreed to. I'm sure that there is much to be done." I looked around at everyone gathered around, staring at me. "And I'd like to rest for a bit, if my tent is still in one piece."

"Right," Max said, glancing at the other two next to him.

Catalina shook herself out of whatever trance she was in. "I'll make sure you have a place." She looked out at the rest. "Go back to work. We need to clear out the carcasses and bodies before we can get some rest."

That seemed to snap people out of their trance, and they started moving. Catalina motioned at me, and I followed, heading to find a tent and get some rest. Later, there would be a lot to do.

* * *

I woke up in my old tent. It was small, barely large enough that I could fit inside. I was alone. Saia could no longer fit, so she had stayed outside—I'd sent her along with Kai and Carlito to help clear things out and consume as many corpses as she could. Hopefully she hadn't attempted to consume human corpses; they could get testy about that. Daylight still peered through the gaps in the entrance, so I assumed that I hadn't slept for long.

My sleep resembled the trance I used to fall into during the day. Though, it seemed a lot deeper, and I didn't dream.

I sat up and stretched my arms above my head. I felt completely rejuvenated; the sleep had left me in perfect condition.

I could hear conversations around my tent, so I knew that there wasn't anything pressing that required my attention. I had some time, so I decided to take a quick look at my Mask.

I focused and pulled myself into my soul space.

I appeared in the central hub and noticed the changes immediately. Everything was more detailed: the walls, the shelves, even the skill bowls. Before, the shelves had all been made out of simple wood. Now, it looked lacquered, and the bowls were more ornate.

I walked up to the center and the pedestal with my Mask, it had changed again, though the difference wasn't great. It was smoother, looked like it was better quality obsidian and jade. On the sides, where the two Ornaments used to hang from, now two bands wrapped up around the lower horns, one on each side, both gold.

The two side pedestals were empty, and lists of Ornaments were available for me to pick again. I wanted to look through it and see what I could take, but first I had something else to look at.

I walked to the back, where the information about my |**Potential Augmentation**| trait was written up. I didn't get any new bonuses this time around, but rather something called **Evolve Skill**.

I saw the physical change first: There was now a pedestal with eleven bowls on top of it, ten arranged in a circle with one in the middle.

One of the ones at the edge closest to me was golden.

I glanced below and read the new information.

<u>Evolve Skill</u>: Sacrifice ten skills to evolve them into a single more powerful skill. One skill serves as a base for the evolution, the choice of the rest guide and shape it.

That was . . . interesting. Really interesting. The golden bowl was probably to designate the base skill.

I had a lot of skills that I didn't really have much use for. I glanced around, wondering if I could experiment. I didn't want to spend too much time in here now; I still had to talk with people at camp. In the end, my curiosity won out.

I walked over to the shelves and started gathering skills. For the first test, I picked skills that I had less use of. I knew that there was probably a lot better way to do this, but I tried to at least keep to a team, but added something in as a bit of spice.

For the base skill I picked [Slash], the more physical attack skills added a bit to my strength when I attacked, but they weren't that necessary. Next I put in a few other attack skills: [Swipe], [Lesser Strike], [Lesser Stab], [Stab], [Smash], and [Quick Claw]. I wondered if I could make a more complicated attack skill from all of those attacks, but I didn't have that many attacks that I felt would be compatible. [Quick Claw] was already different, but I wanted to see what would happen. The last three I put in more versatility with [Lesser Strength]—because I didn't really feel a need for it anymore, I had [Blood Empowerment], and my own physical strength was already far above anything I was likely to meet. Then I put in [Dash] and [Lesser Intimidation].

As soon as I put in the last skill, all the bowls lit up. Then the skill orbs lit up and were pulled into the center bowl. It was done in moments: A new orb was created, and I reached out to take it. Then walked over to one of the shelves and placed it to see what it was.

[Rending Whirlwind]

Dash forward and attack in a whirlwind of your primary weapon, moving with incredible speed and strength, striking from multiple angles in rapid succession, exuding an aura of intimidation.

<esoteric><physical><beast><offense><movement><martial>

I was pleasantly surprised. It was a good skill. At least I thought so. I itched to test it out, and I did have a lot of new doors and skills to collect, but I didn't want to take too long in here. I put the skill on the shelf, deciding to test it out later.

Then something occurred to me. What would've happened if I had put gemstones in all of those skills? I cursed myself for not doing it, but if that could work . . . I could create more elementally charged skills. Next time. I shook my head and turned away.

With that done, I moved to check out my other skills, the ones that had changed with my Investment tier and Ornament consolidation.

[Smell Lie]

Detect spoken lies.

<weave><physical><sensory><communication>

[Memory Like Blood]

Relive any memory taken through blood.

<weave><physical><sensory><memory>

[Learning Through Blood]

Gain small insights into the experiences and capabilities of those whose blood you drink.

<weave><physical><esoteric><sensory><memory><learning>

[Channeled Blood—Essence Door]

Invoke the experience and abilities of any person whose essence you possess. The door and the essence along with the skill gained are destroyed in the process.

<weave><physical><esoteric><memory><invoke>

I knew that the skill descriptions weren't perfect, and that skills would encompass more than the words indicated, but what I read was impressive.

The loss of [A Lesson Remembered] wasn't perfect, as it was more versatile. The new skill allowed me to remember memories I took through blood, which were more immediate. Though, I had been suppressing and pushing them aside in the recent times, as I had drunk a lot of blood while in combat.

The last skill was the most interesting, and I didn't know how exactly it would work. I would have to experiment. So much to do, and so little time.

I took a look at my Hallway of Doors then turned away. I wanted to speak with Shadow again, to collect more skills, but I knew that if I went I would get stuck in there for a long time. And while time did pass differently in here than it did outside, I didn't have a lot of it to spare. I left the Ornaments aside for now too. I wanted to talk with Max and perhaps Shadow—though he was limited in what he could tell me—before doing anything.

I got out of my soul space and back to the real world.

I stood, looked at my weapons and pack in the corner of the tent. I debated gearing up, but decided against it. I took only my revolver, holstered around my thigh.

I stepped out, and the weird sensation from before returned. I frowned; the attention of people around me was like a physical thing. This didn't feel like it was coming from the **thirst**.

I pushed it aside and stopped next to Saia who was sitting in front of my tent, too big to enter. All the mass she consumed in the trial and from last night's horde had turned her drone from a tiny dragon that could fit in the palm of my hand to a dragon the size of a minivan.

She had gotten better at processing Invested mass.

"How long was I asleep?"

"Five hours," Saia answered.

That wasn't so bad.

"How big do you think you can get?" I asked her.

"Feedback: Uncertain. My control systems have been damaged over time. Some blocks had been put into places to prevent systems like me from going out of control in the same way the Biosource Autonomous Self-Replicating Swarm had."

I remembered her telling me the reason she had been created. To combat a swarm that had gotten out of control. She was similar to that swarm, except that her systems were controlled by a lot more restricted and advanced AI. Saia—or Self-Replicating Autonomous Interface Armor—couldn't be used without a host.

I also remembered what Shadow had said about dragons on Kirios and their size. Both Saia and I were interested in finding out if they were remnants of Ke Erzi or prototype units such as her.

"What are we going to do once you get too large?"

"Feedback: I am designed to provide protection and complete support in combat. Our synchronization has already risen enough that I can operate several independent drones. Though I have lost many of the engrams that such drone platforms would operate."

I nodded. "We'll have to talk and figure out things, but for now you can stay like that. You're a menace in a fight."

"Statement: I have enough mass now to provide personal protection in addition to a drone."

I grimaced. "Armor doesn't do much for me other than slow me down."

"Statement: That is true, and my current capabilities are far from what I was intended to operate with. This is my failing. I need to become more familiar with your physiology and find ways to augment you."

I tapped her on the head. "Don't worry about it. You provide enough support as it is. Speaking of, how is the [Plasma Shot] engram coming along?"

"Feedback: Success is imminent."

I raised my eyebrow, but didn't say anything. "Hey, how long does it take to craft a round for my revolver?"

"Feedback: Ten seconds per round."

"So, I had this idea. Can you set aside enough mass for, let's say sixteen rounds, that's two extra drums, and shape it like a bracer or something like that so that you can reload my revolver while in combat?"

Saia's eyes flashed. "Feedback: Not possible. My [Manufacturing] engram requires a certain amount of mass. The smallest amount of mass I would need to fit it in is a full chest plate."

"Not worth it then." I really didn't like being that restricted. Having her masquerade as a shirt was the most I was willing to take. At least it was easier to grow wings when she could just replace the clothing for me.

I was going to need to take the time and work with her to figure out more and better ways to utilize her capabilities.

Two figures approached, and I shifted my attention to them. Most people kept away, just staring from the distance, or throwing looks as they worked on things.

Kai and Carlito walked up, a big grin on the bald man.

"Heya, boss lady," Carlito said with a wide grin. The former gang soldier looked tired, and had a few scratches on his face.

"Glad to see you're back," the Nordic woman added a moment after.

I raised an eyebrow, and returned Carlito's grin. "Someone had to come save you all."

Carlito laughed. "True that."

Kai just nodded. I felt slightly strange, being here, talking with them. For me, it had been thirty days since we last saw each other; for them it had only been five days.

"So." Carlito pierced the growing silence, his eyes looking Saia up and down. "She grew up to be a big girl."

"Feedback: I increased my mass, technically growing, but if I am under-standing your underlying meaning right, you are implying that I was a 'small' girl before, a child. That is an incorrect statement, as I am approximately twenty-five thousand of your years old."

Both Carlito and Kai gaped at her with open mouths, then glanced at me.

"Are you that old too, boss?" Carlito asked, looking me askance.

I blinked at him. "Of course not." I scoffed.

"Ah." Carlito nodded slowly.

I looked at the two of them. They had found my tent awfully quick after I woke up. Meaning someone had told them that I was up. The two of them had kind of become my entourage before I left for the challenge. That they were here now sent a certain kind of message. And I wasn't really opposed; they knew how to handle themselves and I trusted them. And with what I had planned to do now, I was going to need people.

I focused on Carlito and spoke. "I need to speak with the camp leaders. Can you go out and find and gather them at the big tent for me?"

"Which ones?"

"Whoever is still alive, but Catalina and Max for sure," I told him.

Carlito gave me a mock salute then ran off.

I glanced at Kai, but she had her stoic mask on, her hands folded behind her back as if she was standing at attention.

I figured that now was the right time to start.

"So, how do you guys think that conquerors are born?"

Saia tilted her head, and Kai blinked in confusion. It was a pretty abrupt change of topic, true. But I had a lot to do, and little time to do it.

"Do you think that they just wake up one day and decide, hey, I'm going to go find a kingdom and put a crown on my head, demand people to follow me? And if anyone opposes me, I'll just kill them? Actually, I don't mean how they take power, but how does one decide to do it?"

I turned pensive for a moment, a part of me curious. History books never really went that deep into it.

"What makes one want to rule, to go around telling other people what to do?"

Neither Kai nor Saia answered initially. Saia probably didn't have much of an opinion; it wouldn't matter to her.

Kai, though, seemed to be thinking. Finally, she looked at me and spoke.

"Is that what you are going to do?" she asked me.

I tapped a finger against my chin. "How do you think people would react to something like that? If I started telling them what to do?"

Kai looked at me with a strange expression on her face, then glanced at the people around us. "You really haven't paid much attention."

That made me frown. "What do you mean?"

"You've kind of already been doing that since you arrived. And . . ."

Kai looked as if she wanted to say something more, but instead glanced to the side, where two kids were hiding behind a large wooden crate. I had, of course, noticed them.

I looked there, and the two yelped and hid behind the crate. A furious whispering erupted, and finally they decided to come out and approach.

I recognized them as the two orphan kids I had saved from the church, Lea and Juan. Seeing them again reminded me of Felix, and I felt a pang in my heart. I had failed him, but seeing the two, here and safe, made me feel slightly better. They survived. At least I didn't fail them.

They stood in front of me, looking up with their wide eyes. I raised an eyebrow, and Juan nudged Lea. She seemed to gather her courage and took a deep breath.

"You lied to us!" She pointed a finger at me as she accused me.

I blinked. "I did?" I asked.

She moved her small head in a nod that bore no argument.

"What did I lie about?"

Lea glanced at Juan, then back at me. "You told us that you can't fly!"

I opened my mouth, then closed it. She was, of course, right. I did say that. It was true at that time, but I didn't know how I was going to explain that to the little kid.

Kai looking on with interest made it even more awkward to try and explain now. So I just knelt next to her and leaned in and whispered.

"It was a secret."

Lea's eyes widened.

"You couldn't let anybody know that you were the Dark Angel." She nodded with an understanding expression on her face.

I narrowed my eyes. "That I'm what?"

Kai shifted uncomfortably, which told me that this wasn't just a kid thing. I had overheard some similar things from the people around us.

"Dark Angel, it's what Father Sergio calls you."

"Aha," I said slowly, then glanced at Kai. "Maybe we should make a visit to the father."

"Oh," Juan jumped in. "He's at the church tent with a bunch of other grown ups."

"Well, let's go." I stood up, intent on seeing what exactly had been happening.

* * *

It didn't take us long to reach our destination, though walking through camp had been an experience. People kept bowing to me, some whispering the words "Angel" and "Star Angel" as they made the sign of the cross at my passage. I didn't know how to react, so I just didn't.

The strange sensation that had been present since I woke up was present still, like an uncomfortable thorn in my side. Worse, I was pretty sure that it was coming from the people around me. I didn't know what it was, though. My sire didn't mention anything like this. Was it the **thirst** feeling their blood? I didn't know, and that worried me.

As we approached the tent that doubled as Father Sergio's church, I could hear his words.

"Lift your weary hearts! Despair not, for even in this darkness, salvation has arrived!"

Father Sergio Rodriguez stood on top of a crate, his voice thundering as he spoke. And the gathered people listened, kneeling before his tent. They were all tired, dirty, and many had bandages around their wounds. The scent of blood was thick around them.

"We have witnessed the abyss, the horrors that stalk our broken lands. We have known fear, the gnawing dread that chills us to the bone. The end of our world and the birth of a new one. But I say to you, fear no more! For the Lord, in his infinite mercy, has sent us a deliverer."

Oh no, I thought to myself as I saw the fervor in his eyes.

"From the smoke, she emerged, wings like midnight spread against the burning sky. A creature of blood, yes, but one standing against the encroaching night. She is the predator who stalks the predators, the terror that strikes fear into the hearts of monsters."

I was frozen. The sensation I felt before seemed to be intensifying, gripping me.

"Some may recoil at her form, at the power she wields. But I say to you, judge not by appearances, but by deeds! She is the Star Angel, the warrior of God, sent as his warrior to fight for us all. No longer does the sun's gaze burn her, a sign of God's will! Embrace her, my flock! Give her your trust, your loyalty, your prayers. For she is the beacon in the night, the hope that guides us toward a new dawn."

He noticed me then, his eyes meeting my own. There was an intensity there that I could feel like a physical touch.

"In her darkness, we find the light. In her strength, we find salvation. In her blood, we find the promise of a future free from fear. Praise be to God, and praise be to his warrior, our Dark Angel!"

He pointed, and the people saw me. They bowed.

"Go now, my children, there is still much to be done. But know in your hearts that even though the night is dark, we are not alone."

Some of the people crossed themselves; others clutched the crosses around their necks and kissed them, but all kept their eyes on me. I didn't say anything. I didn't know what to say. I kept my face impassive as they walked by, some even reaching with their hands to touch me.

I didn't know how to react, so I just kept my mask. Once they were gone, I moved.

The rush of displaced air washed behind me as I came to a stop in front of Father Sergio.

"What. Was. That?" I struggled to speak in a tone loud enough for humans to hear. My entire being was charged with anger. He had done something like this before, I brushed it off then. This . . . this was . . . I didn't know what this was.

He didn't seem frightened by my tone, by my visage of anger. Instead, he answered me calmly. "I asked you once if you would take away people's hope, simply because you didn't believe. We've been surrounded by nightmares and despair, and at the moment when we stared death in the eye, you arrived. You cannot stand here and not see it as providence."

"God didn't send me. I told you that before," I said slowly, every word dripping with barely contained anger. "The only one that sent me here was the Grand Spell, the Last Intent."

"And who's to say that the Grand Spell is not acting on God's plan? Even faith and religion must evolve and grow as we learn more. What we believed about the world is wrong. We can only be open to learning more and keeping our faith."

I closed my eyes. He was a priest, a man of faith. I had experience with them. Khalil was the same. I never understood that, the need to believe in something other than, something greater.

I had always been surrounded by religion. One didn't live in this corner of the world without having their life impacted by it. As a child, I'd attended church often, sat in the stone halls with the scent of incense burning in my nostrils. And as a soldier in the cartel I had dealt with priests and their flock.

I didn't have a problem with religion personally, but this felt . . . I stopped. I realized that I didn't know why I was angry.

These people were just looking for something to give them hope, as Father Sergio had said. I had come and saved them, as he had told them. He spoke through the lens of religion; that was what he understood and what these people believed in. Their gratitude toward me wasn't misplaced. In fact, they owed me a debt, and I owed one to them. I had decided to save them, to involve myself. There was a link between us.

As I looked closer inward, I realized that the strange sensation I was feeling was familiar. It felt like how I felt when I used my waybound skill.

I opened my eyes and looked at the priest in front of me. He was looking at me calmly, but I could . . . sense something coming from him. An imprint on the Way, a skill.

"You've advanced your Mask," I said.

He smiled and inclined his head. "Yes. It is called Mask of the Faithful Believer."

I opened my mouth, then closed it. I reached for his hand and turned to Saia.

"Inspect," I told her.

Kai and Father Sergio looked confused, but I didn't care.

Sergio Rodriguez

Mask of the Faithful Believer (Esoteric) — First Investment; Second Carving

---

Attributes:
Physical: F
Weave: F
Esoteric: D

Skills:
[Hear Truth]
[Calm Flock]
[Gather Faith]
[Imbue Faith—Dark Angel]

The Grand Spell was granting faith-based Masks and skills. What did that mean? I didn't even know they existed. But what was more concerning was his last skill.

"You used this on me," I said, recognizing what I was feeling since I arrived.

He had a bit of a sheepish expression. "I apologize if it affected you adversely. I didn't use it; it appears to be always active."

A passive skill, one that I didn't know how it affected me. I had to talk with Shadow, and quick, hope that he could reveal things about this.

I was feeling the people's faith in me. That was . . . actually something that I could use.

I had plans, and the reverence they held toward me could help that.

I opened my mouth to speak, but Carlito chose that moment to walk up.

"Heya, boss lady, I gathered everyone at the big tent. They're waiting for you."

I looked at Father Sergio for a long moment. "We're not done."

Too many things, and too little time.

I turned and headed to the big tent.

Plans

I entered the big tent, the command center of the camp, with Kai and Carlito in tow. Saia remained outside, too big to get through the entrance. Not that it really mattered since she was always inside of me and aware of everything that I was aware of. Today, she also doubled as my shirt, so she was included either way.

Inside, I was greeted by a visibly tired group of three people. Maximilian Dawson was sitting at the table, his head leaned on his hand. The young man looked like he had aged a decade in the time since I'd seen him.

Catalina Flor looked a little bit better, her appearance a bit more put together. I didn't know if that was because she had the time to rest or if her Mask of the Caretaker was helping her.

The last person was Diego Murillo, who was looking over reports with eyes that flashed around at rapid speed that even a Fledgling vampire would envy. Probably a skill gained from his Mask of the Supervisor.

At my entrance Catalina nudged Max and looked at me with a strange expression on her face.

"You've asked for us, Master?"

I frowned. I had spoken to them about this before.

"You don't need to call me that," I said.

Catalina looked uncomfortable. "Of course, lady."

I narrowed my eyes, then looked at Max. I'd spent the most time with him. "What is this about?"

"Nothing." He avoided my eyes. "We, uh, saw you yesterday."

"And?"

They didn't answer.

I guess that my form made a bigger impression than I realized. I should've seen it coming, especially with the way the rest of the people in the camp looked at me.

Once, I might've dealt with this differently, I might've talked and tried to appear more nonthreatening. But the challenge had opened my eyes to what we faced, so I let it be. I was not who I was before I entered the challenge. I knew who and what I was now. I was a vampire of the line of Asza.

"Well, let me first tell you what happened in the challenge."

I filled them in on everything. Well, most things. But more importantly what my sire said about the world. During our discussion, Max called in a man named Sebastian, who drew a rough map of the world based on the things I told them.

We were all gathered around it, looking down. It didn't have much detail, nor was it at all to scale. We knew that my sire reached the northern coast of the continent within a month, but not much detail aside from that.

"You want us to move to this coast?" Catalina asked, pointing at the map.

I nodded. "If I hadn't arrived yesterday, you all would've been dead."

They winced at that, but it was only the truth.

I looked her straight in the eye. "Staying here is equal to death."

"The trip will kill us. We don't know what we'll encounter, and we know that the wild is dangerous. This place is defensible," Diego added. "Now that you're here we can fortify it. We can—"

"No," I interrupted him. "This place is a deathtrap. The city rifts have broken, and beasts spilled out. Yesterday was just the first wave. You are not staying here."

Diego opened his mouth, clearly intent on arguing, but the look in my eyes made him stop. He remembered who and what I was.

I'd been acting like a human would before I left. What came back had finally let go of who I once was.

"He has a point," Max said, making me turn my head to glare at him, slowly. He raised his arms as if in surrender. "I mean about this being a defensible position. We are unlikely to find something like this out there, and there are hundreds of us—"

I interrupted him by placing a smooth wooden box on the table. They all frowned at it, then Max reached out and pulled it closer.

I waited until they read the notecard.

Their faces took on incredulous expressions. "This . . . what is this?"

"My reward for winning the challenge," I answered. "I don't mean to have you undefended. We will go north, and gather any survivors on the way. Then we'll use this on the coast. I plan on gathering more people, and claiming the coast of the inland sea."

They looked up at me, but didn't say anything. There wasn't really much that they could say, I wasn't asking, and I knew that they understood that.

They were relieved. I could see it in their eyes, in the way their muscles relaxed the more I spoke, the way their hearts beat and their lungs expanded. They had been at the end of the rope, struggling to keep people alive, struggling to make the right decisions. Now, they no longer needed to do that. They could finally rest, step back and let someone else make the decisions.

"The people I've made contact with in the challenge will be attempting the same thing. And we must be on the lookout for other Exemplars. Some will have sold out to the other factions."

"Is that really such a concern?" Catalina asked. "We're already barely surviving."

"Realistically, no," I said. "The world is too large for us to end up meeting any of the other Exemplars outside of challenges. But, in time, the portals will open, and then years from now the actions taken now will snowball into something more. We are not just surviving today; we are laying the foundations for future survival."

Max nodded, agreeing. The other two looked unsure, but didn't say anything.

There wasn't much else to say. I had told them what I wanted, and that was that. Strength was an integral part of my school of being, and that extended beyond just the physical. I wanted to rule; I knew that I could do better than them, I believed that. And besides, my connection with these people had been forged the moment I returned from Ish Vimza and decided to help them the first time.

The debt was tilted heavily in my favor, and I needed them to pay the price. Servitude was the only way I could get that from them without draining them all of blood.

"Start preparing for the trip," I told them. "I'll go scouting tomorrow morning. I should be able to fly ahead and find the coast relatively easy. And I'll deal with any visible threat in our way. That should give us an idea of how far the coast is, and let you prepare appropriately."

They nodded, and I turned to Max.

"I want to talk to you and your team."

He winced. "Leto and Joe died last night," he told me.

"I'm sorry for your loss," I told him, and I did mean it. "Anna?" I asked about the last member of his team.

"She's good." Max gave me a sad smile.

"Then get her and meet me in your tent in a little bit."

He nodded and walked out. I looked at Catalina and Diego and waved my hand. "Get to work. Organize the people and let them know what will be happening so that they can prepare."

With that, I followed Max out, Kai and Carlito walking behind me.

Once we were out of the tent, Carlito whistled under his breath. "Damn, boss lady."

I glanced at him and saw his grin. "What?"

He didn't respond, just kept his little gremlin grin on.

I sighed, then gave both of them a good look. "You two have been following me around an awful lot. I gather that you understand what that will mean now?"

"What, with you going all big boss on everyone?" Carlito asked. "Of course we know. People will try stabbing you in the back, and we'll be right there to stab them first."

I blinked. That wasn't exactly what I meant, but I'd take it. "I meant more that it'll be dangerous. I'm not going to sugarcoat this. Any survivor group we find that is established, that has resources and means, I'm going to press into service. Whether they want to or not."

Carlito glanced at the tall blond, then looked back at me. "The biggest dog on the street is the one in control, that's the rules."

I should've known. He was a criminal, a gang member. I turned my eyes on Kai.

She shrugged. "Whatever rules existed before, they're gone now," she said slowly. "I'd much rather follow a vampire that can kill a thousand monsters in an hour than someone like Catalina that can barely protect herself."

I nodded, satisfied.

"The two of you need to gain Investment, fast," I told them. "The challenge pushed me far ahead, and if I'm going to keep the two of you around, you need to be stronger."

"We've both reached the First Investment after last night," Kai said.

"Good. Now you need to get to the second, and fast."

"How do we do that?" Carlito asked.

"Earth's win in the challenge gave us an additional increase in Investment gain, so we focus on the type of Investment the two of you need. What're your Masks called now?"

Carlito answered first. "Mask of the Blood Butcher! I got two new skills since the last time we saw each other, Crimson Cleave, and Exsanguinate."

Kai grimaced at him. "Mine is now the Mask of Ironclad Fighter. I got Shattering Blow and Iron Skin."

Those were good upgrades, though it was almost expected. They had been through a lot, but then again, everyone had.

"Okay, those both seem like combat related Masks, so fighting beasts will give you enough Investment to advance. We'll see about getting you through rifts, and you'll have enough chances of fighting as we move everyone north."

"Whatever you say, boss lady! Wait, can I still call you that, or? Maybe Dark Angel? Dark Lady? Master?"

I rolled my eyes at him. "Boss is fine for now."

His crooked grin returned, and I could tell that he was having fun with me. I was indulging him a bit. I was glad that I had someone who felt free enough to talk with me like that. After spending a month with Aurora and her insanity, coming back to worship and bowing had started to grate on me unusually fast.

I flew through the air at speeds that I could once only dream of. It was an exhilarating experience, and something that I'd instantly fallen in love with. Already I couldn't imagine my life without being able to fly, to feel the wind on my skin and watch the land disappear beneath me.

At my top speed, I was so fast that the ground blurred by me. It took me around half an hour to find the coast. I slowed and settled down on the sand, exhausted from the effort of flying that fast. The sea stretched before me in endless emerald waves.

It would appear that our part of the continent hadn't shifted around too much. Medellín was between 200 and 250 km away from the coast. Assuming that the distance was around the same, and considering the time it took me to get here, I was probably moving at around 500 km/h. I had to estimate as Saia's systems that could measure it relied on satellites that didn't exist here. But I thought that we were right in our estimates.

That was a couple of hours long trip by car. But we didn't have that. On foot, at human walking speed, that was a day- or two-day-long trip. Assuming perfect conditions. We didn't have that. What we had was supplies, old people, and children. And a wilderness in between us and the coast, one filled with beasts.

It was not going to be two days. Still, it wasn't going to be as bad as I had feared. Now that I had taken the quick way here, I was going to take the slower route back, scouting out the terrain and any threats.

I'd left Saia's drone behind. Our range had increased with my gain in Investment level, and we wanted to test out the max range.

"Still in contact?" I asked as I sat on the beach, enjoying the breeze and resting.

My shirt vibrated, answering my question. "Feedback: Yes, though the signal is degraded, and the lag is rising."

That meant we were about close to max range. That was good. It meant that I could do more with Saia.

"So, any ideas about what the best location for a town would be?"

"Feedback: Access to fresh water is paramount."

I nodded. "Right," I said. Which meant looking for a clean spring, unless we wanted to boil river water all the time.

I took another half an hour rest, then I started flying along the coast looking for a good place to use my town item. I didn't plan to do it now. I didn't want to leave it without anyone present to hold it.

I still felt tired from my flight, despite resting, so I made sure to keep my eyes open for any threats. I had left my weapon back at the camp. I was new to flying, and carrying around a spear that was taller than me wasn't smart. And it wasn't like I wasn't dangerous without it.

I was worried about rifts. Colombia's northern coast didn't have many big towns that would've generated them, as apparently rifts manifested more in places with high population. Which I had somewhat confirmed on my trip. I had slowed down over abandoned and ruined towns and seen very few rifts.

What I was worried about was Cartagena and Barranquilla. Though, I also didn't know if I was north or south of Panama, which could be an issue too. But, if what my sire said was true, and our orientation was as I thought it was, then if I headed east, I should find the two coastal cities.

I didn't want to get us away from Medellín just for us to get hit by a horde of monsters from another city. Though, on the other hand, the two cities would be the best places for me to find boats that were still serviceable.

I made my way along the coast, seeing little danger. There wasn't much life, aside from birds, but those didn't seem to have been mutated in ways that made them any real danger.

I didn't push to my top speed. Rather, I felt like I couldn't. I had overextended myself without realizing it. After a few minutes of flying I was forced to land, and pull out a gourd with blood as I started feeling hungry.

It would appear that this form required more blood to sustain me. I sat alone, feeling a bit strange. I had spent a lot of time alone before all of this happened. But my recent time had been spent in the company of others. I found that I did miss people.

I missed my friends, Aurora, Khalil, Jiyun, and Daehyun. I looked at the sea, wondering where they were. I had promised to try to find Aurora, and I fully intended to focus on that once I got the survivors to the coast.

A part of me wanted to abandon everything and go look for her. But, I had a responsibility here, and I had to start making moves that would give me a foundation to stand against what was coming.

I knew that Aurora was strong enough to survive. I trusted her.

I got back into the air and continued along the coast. It took me around half an hour to reach the city. I saw it in the distance, and paused.

What I had seen of Earth since I returned so far had been nature slowly reclaiming civilization. Animals that had been changed by the Source into more dangerous versions, others that had changed their patterns and behaviors. The towns and villages I had seen on the way were abandoned, and while nature had reasserted itself, they were clearly recognizable.

What I saw ahead was not at all like what I had seen before. The entire city was covered in plants. Giant plants: A tree the size of a skyscraper grew in the middle, and the other buildings were covered in green. Watching from the distance, I saw no movement, no animals at all. There were also no signs of rifts.

"Input: I'm detecting an incredibly dense and powerful Source-Weave signature from ahead," Saia interjected, startling me.

"What kind?"

"Feedback: Nature based, similar in kind to a Masked, I estimate that it covers the entire city."

I blinked. "Invested plants?"

Everything was Invested to one degree or another. It just meant that it had Source within it. But plants . . .

"Feedback: The signature is coming from a singular source."

I narrowed my eyes, then landed at the edge of the city, on the beach far away from the trees. I walked toward it, noting that there was a particularly odd scent in the air. I paused, detecting a hint of sweetness in it.

The **thirst** woke up, and I knew immediately that whatever I was smelling was hazardous. I didn't retreat, though. I was a vampire, and the **thirst** was a jealous mistress. Only silver based poisons would work on me.

I kept going, getting closer, and keeping my attention on my surroundings. I noticed no signs of life, of anything moving at least. Which was weird—the city was supposed to have a lot of rifts, which should've broken open, spilling out beasts. I saw no signs of that either.

On the bright side, I saw a lot of wooden boats on the beach, and they seemed to be in a good condition. Finally, I entered the city proper, walking down the streets.

All my questions were quickly answered. The scent intensified, but didn't do anything against me. I saw flowers moving, twitching across the walls, opening up and spraying more of the same pheromone, or whatever it was, into the air.

I noticed the bones immediately. The stench of blood was thick enough here that I could detect it over the scent that the plants were giving off. Bones of animals were everywhere, vines curled around them.

The entire city was a graveyard of thousands. Not all of the bones were animals. I saw human skulls too, and many of the bones were unfamiliar to me. Strangely shaped skulls that I could only assume were from beasts not native to our world.

There were rifts here too, and they had broken open. And the plants had slaughtered everything that came out.

I grinned. This was perfect. This city was the reason why I saw few beasts around, it was the most dangerous thing around.

"Can you detect this thing in the air? I want to know how far it is spread."

"Feedback: I've taken a sample. With it I will be able to detect it anywhere."

I continued walking, now searching and looking for any supplies that might help my people. I would have to retrieve them for them, of course, but there could be a lot here that survived.

Saia would need to help me establish a perimeter, but I had decided that putting down a town close to the city would be the best course of action. Its presence would protect the people from anything dangerous coming in from the east.

It had probably already driven off anything smart enough to notice what was happening.

As I walked over a particularly grassy part of the road, I felt something rise up and wrap around my legs. I felt the thorns attempting to cut through my skin and failing. I looked down, saw the plants moving, trying to restrain me, vines climbing up my leg.

I tugged on my leg and ripped the vine apart. It was strong, I felt some resistance. If I was still a Fledgling, I probably wouldn't have been able to escape it with ease. Now, I felt like a serious punch from me could bring down a building. That thought did remind me that I'd never really tested the limits of my new strength. My speed was apparent. In bursts, I could move at speeds that the eye couldn't follow. Fast enough to displace air and cause shockwaves. I couldn't keep it up for long, but prolonged exertion wasn't a vampire's strong suit. Though what I now considered a prolonged period had changed. A full hour of fighting at top speed was something that I could do, but, as I had found out yesterday, it would wipe me out. And that hadn't even been a particularly difficult fight. It had still sapped my stamina and made me very hungry.

My strength, though. I hadn't had a chance to test its limits yet. I glanced to the side of a building covered in vines. I walked over, pulled my fist back, then punched it.

My fist went clear through the concrete wall. I barely even felt it.

I grinned, and started punching.

I sat on top of what was once a car of some kind. It had degraded to the point that it wasn't even recognizable, as most things had in the city.

I drank the blood from my gourds as I rested from my little testing session. I took down two buildings, with relative ease if I was being honest. They weren't that strong, so in the end I didn't learn much. Only that I was strong enough to do that. I hadn't found my upper limit.

The story my sire told me about his sire cracking a tectonic plate had sounded ridiculous before. Now, though . . .

I shook my head. I couldn't even imagine that I was that strong now. Realistically, I was probably not. Even if I had matured, my sire had said that I would only continue to grow in power. The other, older vampires at the same stage as me were probably stronger.

After about an hour of rest, I took to the skies again and flew around the city. It didn't take me long to find what I was looking for. I entered a hospital that was completely overgrown, and after tearing through a few vines attempting to restrain me, I started rummaging through the floors.

Plants had penetrated deep into the building too, but not as much as they had outside. A lot of the hospital was ransacked, which I had expected. Some people had obviously tried to hold out in here, as I found human bones wrapped in vines. But eventually I found locked cabinets and safes.

Breaking into them was easy for me, and I managed to find a lot of medicine. I didn't know anything about it, but just confirming that it was there was enough. Someone at camp would know more. And eventually I would come back and bring everything that was still here back.

With that done I headed out in search of other resources.

I'd managed to find food, water, and other supplies—a lot more than I had expected. Whatever happened to the city and the people living here happened fast.

If Saia was correct, all the plants around me were actually part of the same organism. I wondered what happened. Did some plant in the city just mutate in a strange way? Or was it something from one of the rifts?

Ultimately, it didn't matter.

There were a lot of resources here that we could use. Though, only I would be able to enter. The plant had blanketed the entire city area with its pheromones. I was making an assumption that the pheromones helped it catch and kill, as I hadn't seen much else that was dangerous. It had to have a way to disable that would allow its vines to do their work.

I finished my exploration, and took to the sky. It was time for me to return back to the camp.

Ornaments

By the time I returned to camp, the sun had started its descent beyond the horizon. The camp was busy, people moving around, preparing for the trip as I had ordered.

As I came in for a landing, there was a lot of finger pointing and yelling, but it calmed down quickly as they realized who the winged creature flying toward them was.

Once I was on the ground, the people around bowed as I walked by. I soaked it in. My whole life I had been the one on the ground, bowing to others. No more.

I checked myself, though. I had seen enough bad leaders to know what to avoid. I didn't want to turn into what I hated.

I saw Saia in the distance, helping carry supplies with her drone. People had grown used to her, even though she had gotten ten times bigger in a span of days for them. I left her to it.

It didn't take long after I landed for Kai and Carlito to come find me. They matched my pace, one on each side. Then Kai spoke.

"The first group returned from the rift an hour ago," she reported. I had put Kai in charge of the survivor fighters, seeing as how their previous leader, Carlos Cabrera, died fighting the horde.

The camp had been using a nearby arena rift as a resource mine, using the beasts within for food and gathering weapons that the kobolds used. I had them organize a few groups to clear it as much as they could before we left, looting weapons and meat for the trip.

"Good," I said, then turned to look at Carlito. "How's the camp been? Anyone looking to stab me in the back?"

"Nah." Carlito waved his hand as we made way toward my tent. "You're a vampire that can transform into a Dark Angel and tear monsters in half with your bare hands. No one's that dumb."

I suppressed a smile. He would be surprised how many people were actually that dumb.

"People are actually hopeful," Carlito added.

"They are?"

He nodded. "Father Rodriguez's people worship the ground you walk on, and the rest feel better knowing you're in charge now. Hell, most had expected it since the moment you arrived, even if they were afraid of you."

"And they aren't afraid of me anymore?"

"Oh, they're afraid, but you haven't started killing and feeding on people like a crazy vampire would. And between you and the shit that's beyond these walls, they'd rather throw in with you."

I was glad. That made things easier for me.

"Keep an ear out for anyone trying to gather some silver and stab me in the back again."

"Sure thing, boss lady."

We reached my tent, and I recovered my weapon and backpack with my gear. Then we headed to Max's tent.

He was at his table, and Anna stood with her back turned to the entrance, sorting through some crates. Everything in the tent was in some state of being packed up, at least the things that we'd be bringing with us.

Max looked up from the table when we entered, and gave me a smile.

"You're back," he said as Anna turned and greeted us too.

"Yes, you have the things ready for me?" I asked.

Max nodded and stood then fetched a large crate from the other side of the tent and put it on the table.

"We merged as many gemstones as we could, as you asked. There are still some F and E-grade left over, but we managed to get eight D-grade and one C-grade out of it."

I nodded. It wasn't as much as I had expected, but then again they didn't really have that much time to farm rifts.

"Okay, keep those for later. Give me all the E-grade ones," I said. I wanted to experiment with evolving skills that I put gems into.

He pulled a small box from within the crate and put it on the table. I rummaged through it, finding a nice spread of different elements. I picked one up and pulled my Mask out, then I focused on a skill that was currently on my shelf. I hoped that I could slot the gemstones in now. Immediately, I knew that I could do it, though I had to focus more intently than with the skills that I had access to.

"This is good," I said. "Did you do any work on the other thing?"

Max pulled out a sheet of paper. "Yes, based on the things you told us, and the research we did with the people at camp, I have a tentative proposal for you."

He pushed the paper over to me and I looked it over.

"A ruler Ornament?"

Max shrugged. "That's what you are, aren't you? It would be an easy source of Investment. If things work in the way that we think they do, then you should be offered that as an option."

I nodded. His logic was sound. I had spoken with Shadow, but he could only advise in general terms. Max had been working on Masks and trying to figure out how Investment actually worked.

"And for my second Ornament?" I asked.

"Something combat related," he said. "Your Mask needs blood, and you often get it by fighting beasts. If what you've told us is true, then you only need to decide if you want to specialize in killing beasts or take something more general."

I looked through what he had written, which was a more detailed explanation of what he said. It was mostly conjecture, but it was good work. "Okay, I'll need a private space to experiment for a little bit. Kai"—I turned to the taller woman—"I'm going to need you to watch over me. I'll be going in and out as I try to figure things out."

She nodded, and I turned to Carlito. "I also have some things for the two of you." I reached into my backpack and pulled out the two daggers I got as a reward, the fire and ice ones. I offered them to Carlito.

"For me?" he asked, then pulled the fire dagger out of its sheath. "Oh, hell yeah. Thanks, boss."

He grinned at me, and I pulled a pair of boots and the lantern and offered it to Kai. "I don't have any more weapons, but the boots muffle your steps, which can be useful, and the lantern is a light source."

Which was actually useful in a world where we no longer had electricity. She thanked me and then Max led me to a side room inside the tent.

I settled in and entered my soul space.

I looked through the list of Ornaments available to me. As Max had suspected, I had a lot of them offered to me. They were supplemental to a Mask, and as

I had learned, they could consolidate and evolve the Mask in different directions. From some things that Shadow had said, I knew that my Mask had been altered in ways that made how I got Investment different. Revelator remained, meaning that Investment revolving around truth would advance my Mask. Seeker had come from my Student Ornament, so I had to assume that it was related to learning, or seeking to learn. Since it was joined with the Revelator, perhaps I had to seek to learn the truth? Since it had consolidated into my Mask, perhaps doing so through blood.

I did get memories when I drank blood, so perhaps that was all there was to it. I would figure it out in time.

My choices of two new Ornaments would need to reflect what I wanted to do, and how I wanted to alter my Mask in the future. This wouldn't be something that most people on Kirios would have to worry about. They rarely advanced beyond the Fourth Investment, but I planned to reach as high as one possibly could, which meant that every ten Carvings I would have a chance of consolidating my Ornaments.

True, it could happen before going up an Investment tier, but according to Shadow, that was rare. It required gaining a significant Carving, one that came at a moment that was heavy with Investment from both the Mask and Ornaments.

The choices that I had before when I was picking my Mask were still there, Thug and Servant, and now, I'd gotten what I believed to be an improvement to Student—Scholar. But, I also had new ones, unlocked through my deeds since the Grand Spell arrived. Most of my choices were simple things like Fighter, Hunter, or Leader. The most basic of options as far as I knew. But there were a few new and more unique ones.

Blood Warrior, for example, seemed like something very useful and geared toward me. I could see how that could synergize and eventually consolidate well into my Mask. There were a couple more combat related ones that were interesting: Beast Hunter, Rift Hunter, Beast Slayer. But, if I was being honest, none of them really caught my eye.

My main issue was deciding what I wanted my Mask to be. To the people of Kirios, Masks were part of them, their life path. For me and people of Earth, they were something external, an added power.

I struggled with using my skills in the moments when I was lost in battle. I had to remind myself. It didn't come naturally as it would to someone for whom the reality of Masks and skills was known since birth.

Still, my Mask did reflect who I was, and my two Ornaments did too. Revelator meant someone who revealed truths, and it did resonate with me. I didn't like to lie. I felt like the truth was a both a weapon and a shield. Heart of Azure and Scarlet had that built into the core of it: A lie was a debt in my eyes.

From my Student Ornament I got the desire to learn, which was also a part of me. I knew that I was lacking in areas, and I wanted to improve.

I had seen glimpses of what Masks could do, the power that they could grant. Shadow felt like a mountain that I couldn't even dream of approaching. Even as injured as he was, I had felt his power. Even now, with as much power as I had, I doubted that I could be his equal. I didn't know what Investment his Mask was, but it was definitely higher than Fifth. And in the challenge I had faced a Fifth Investment Masked, and lost.

The choice now was about the future. My Mask was a part of me that grew in power as I fed on blood. It offered me ways to take the power of others for myself. It revolved around taking power. Choosing my Ornaments was about in what ways I wanted to augment that.

Max had suggested I take combat and leadership Ornaments. But combat for me was not a priority, I could take skills from others for that. I had already taken many.

I needed different types of power.

Leadership, I agreed with. And the only Ornament that fit that was Leader, something simple. Which was fine. Ornaments could reach Second Investment, so there was room for growth.

There was one Ornament that didn't fit within any of the other types.

It was called Blood Heir, which if I was being honest, I had no idea what to do with. How was that even a thing? Did the Grand Spell devise new Ornaments? It had to have. My Mask was based on vampires, and I didn't think Kirios had anything like us before.

And I didn't even know what this Ornament meant. What it would do. Shadow wouldn't be able to tell me anything about it, I already knew. But the Grand Spell had patterns. One could read in between the lines. It was something related to my vampire nature. It had to be.

If I was being honest, there wasn't much that appealed to me among the choices. Leader was a certainty. I wanted to lead, and I needed the skills that the Ornament would give me.

I shook my head, pushing all doubts away. If I was being honest, a lot of my decisions had come from within, done on instinct. I stopped trying to figure out what the best course of action was and picked the two Ornaments, Leader and Blood Heir. No Investment; No Carving, but it was a start.

There, it was done. I rolled my shoulder and turned toward the Hallway of Doors. It was time for me to get some skills.

* * *

I spent a while killing beasts and lower Investment humans and Suul. With my current strength, dealing with them was easy even without my weapons and skills. None of them were over Second Investment, aside from a couple of beasts that were higher. None of it was much of a challenge, but it was a good warm up.

I went back into the hallway after depositing the latest of a dozen skills on a shelf. I walked and looked at the doors, trying to decide which one I would enter next. I was ready for more of a challenge.

I stopped in front of an old door, the one leading to the mature ferrorn. The first creature I met on Ish Vimza that was stronger than me.

That was . . . a long time ago. I was without weapons, without skills, with just my Fledgling vampire strength, and even that was weakened by the sun.

Today, I was a different person.

I entered the room fully equipped to fight it. In one hand I carried my serpent-tongue spear, and in the other I had drawn my revolver. The Fourth Investment beast stood across from me, as intimidating as it was the first time I encountered it.

This time though, I recognized the effect of a skill. It had an aura of terror around it that wormed its way into my mind. I shrugged it off with ease.

It roared and charged.

I raised my arm and aimed, then pulled the trigger eight times. The beast obviously had no idea what the gun was, and the bullets found their targets. I put all eight of them in its head.

The mature ferrorn stumbled, fell, slid, and came to a stop just in front of me. I looked at the dead beast as its body fell away, and a skill remained. How much easier my time on Ish Vimza would've been if I had been transported with my gun? If I hadn't been nearly dead and with no weapons?

Perhaps it wouldn't have changed much. But I knew that weapons like the gun in my hand would've made things easier. Powerful Invested had tougher skin, were just stronger, had more skills. But, as I had just seen, not every Mask could stop a bullet. Granted, my bullets were made out of an alien biomass that I didn't fully understand. Saia had made them to ensure penetration against the toughest materials we had encountered.

Perhaps an ordinary gun wouldn't have helped at all.

I gathered the skill and walked it back to the shelf, then read through the plaque.

[Terror Grasp]

Exude an aura of terror.

<esoteric><physical><beast><offense><mental>

A good skill to have. I turned back to the hallway and went back to gathering skills.

My toughest fights of the day were the ungoir emperor, a beast from the challenge trial, and Guo Zhang, the shifter. And even they weren't truly dangerous. I had struggled the first time in part because of lack of information about their capabilities. Fighting them a second time, fully prepared, with time to plan, and having all of my weapons ready, was another thing entirely.

My revolver was, as before, almost unfair. My opponents in the rooms within my soul were as they had been the moment I had drank their blood. Frozen in a moment. It made them far less of a threat.

The two skills I got were [Water Burst] from the ungoir and [Nature's Rest] from Zhang. Which didn't really fit with my mental image of the shifter, but I guess that his Mask had to have been tied to nature. It did fit with the shifter culture. The skill helped him recover more from the rest while surrounded by nature. I didn't know how useful it would be to me, but I could always use it to evolve another skill.

Which was what I was in the process of doing. I decided on my ten skills, then jumped out of my soul space to slot in the gemstones in them. Then, once I was done, I returned and gathered them in preparation for evolving them.

The ten skills I'd chosen were mostly new ones, and almost all lesser or simple skills. I wasn't looking to make anything complicated. Instead, I wanted to see how gemstones would impact the newly formed skill.

The base for the evolved skill was a newly earned one and one that I used to have before. A few of them were skills that I had overburned before and had now found a new source of.

Base — [Strike]
—[Lesser Swipe]
—[Lesser Lash]
—[Lesser Thrust]
—[Jab]

—[Lesser Rend]
—[Rend]
—[Pierce]
—[Lesser Impale]
—[Impale]

Most of the skills came from the humans and Suul, with only a couple from beasts. I didn't know if that mattered. The tags seemed to only be relevant to my |**Potential Augmentation**| bonuses.

I'd put an E-grade fire gemstone in each of the skills, hoping that would influence the skill somehow.

I moved to the pedestal and placed all the skills in.

The evolution was quick. The skill orbs glowed then collapsed to the center into a new skill. I carried it over to the shelf and checked what I got.

[Cinder Strike]

A fiery strike that leaves behind a trail of cinders.

<weave><physical><offense><fire>

I smiled at my success. The effect wasn't that huge—cinder didn't sound too powerful—but the gemstones were only E grade, so I hadn't expected anything more. What did surprise me was that the result was just a simple strike. Perhaps the gemstones tilted the result into a more fire Source related result. More testing was required.

Unfortunately I didn't have enough skills for all of that, so I left it aside. For now, knowing that gemstones could impact the result was enough.

Ten skills for one was a lot, though. I would need to be more careful in what I chose.

With the skill done, I turned to my profiles. Having [Mist Step], [Mistshroud], and [Lesser Constitution] together meant that I didn't activate any of my trait bonuses—the only shared ones were <defense> for [Mistshroud] and [Lesser Constitution]. If I wanted to activate my combat trait bonus, it would require me to remove [Mist Step]. Though, the combat trait wasn't really that impactful with those skills, as it gave an escalating damage bonus. A movement trait bonus might be better, but I needed the two mist related skills together to use my waybound skill properly.

I left it alone and switched to my second profile; there I swapped out [Pulverizing Smash] for [Rending Whirlwind] in which I slotted a D-grade air gemstone. And I also replaced [Double Strike] for [Cinder Strike]. Attacking twice at the same time was good, but not necessary with how fast I already was.

With everything done I left my soul space and asked Saia to display my information for me.

Marianna Rojas (The Star That Dances in Blood Beneath the Light of the Broken Moon)

Mask of the Sanguine Reaper; Revelator Seeker — Third Investment; Third Carving (Physical, Weave, Esoteric)
Leader (Esoteric) — No Investment; No Carving
Blood Heir (Physical, Esoteric) — No Investment; No Carving

Attributes:
Physical: A
Weave: E
Esoteric: A

Skills:
P1-No Bonus
[Mist Step] - Mist (D)
[Mistshroud] - Mist (D)
[Lesser Constitution] - Metal (C)

P2-Combat Bonus
[Cinder Strike] - Fire (D)
[Triple Thrust] - Lightning (D)
[Rending Whirlwind] - Air (D)

[Swap Profile]
[Overburn Skill]
[Blood Gout] - Nature (D)
[Quick Swap Slot]

[Blood Empowerment] - Primal (D)
[Smell Lie]
[Memory Like Blood]
[Learning Through Blood]
[Channeled Blood—Essence Door]

[**Scarlet Moon Style**; Dance of the Shifting Mist]

Once I finished the overview of everything, I stood. I was ready for things to start moving again.

March

flew above the convoy of people and animals, heading north through the desert. The area surrounding our camp had once belonged to some other place on Earth, but had been shuffled around along with the military base we had claimed.

Now, we were abandoning it, heading north to seek a better place to make our home. Or at least the people here would make it a home. I wasn't sure what I wanted to do long term, and where I would settle. I had to look for more survivors.

We only had a couple of wagons that were still useful, that had been repaired after their metal parts rusted. They were annoying to use in this terrain, but they were better than nothing. Especially since we had Saia and a few cows to drag them.

We still left a lot of resources behind. Salva, the old mechanic who had the skill that allowed him to repair anything technological for a short time, had died in the horde attack, rendering the trucks into scrap. No one else had any skill that could do the same.

We were barely an hour into the march, and I could already tell that we weren't going to be making anywhere near the progress I had expected.

A shout drew my attention, and I swerved in the air. There was a commotion near the back of the convoy, and I dived down just as a massive centipede-looking creature burst out of the sand.

"Glaive," I said, and the two bracers on my arms flowed into my hands, transforming into a weapon. Since I didn't carry my large and cumbersome serpent-tongue spear around when I was flying, I had Saia add a bit more mass to the suit she covered me with in shape of bracers—just enough that she could change into weapons for me as needed.

I crashed into the giant creature, swinging my glaive through its head and cutting it clean off. The people on the ground cheered, lowering their weapons. They'd been shooting at it and doing little damage to the large creature with their small caliber bullets.

Their cheering died as the ground rumbled and more animals broke through the sand. I moved immediately, taking to the air and flying at the closest one.

A group of warriors approached from the side, arriving to help, with Kai at their head. I left one of the centipedes alone for them and focused on killing the rest.

Once I was done, I turned my attention to Kai and her group, watching how she gave them orders and organized the fight. She was at the front, dashing in at the centipede as the others took shots at it from the side, distracting it.

One of the hunters took aim, his hunting rifle glowing faintly, then fired a bullet that exploded on impact against the side of the centipede's head, stunning it. He was one of the few that had advanced his Mask. It was his First Investment skill, a powerful one at that.

Kai took advantage and rushed the creature. She jumped and punched with her brass knuckles. The strike shattered the creature's carapace, her [Shattering Blow] skill powerful enough to do a lot of damage.

The centipede fell to the ground, dead.

I was impressed. Kai met my eyes over the dead creature, and I gave her a nod, then flew off, looking for more threats.

It had been a week, and we were barely a third of the way to the coast. I had underestimated the difficulty of the journey. We tried to use roads as much as possible, but many had been reclaimed by nature, with plants growing from cracks in the asphalt.

The pace we moved at was impacted by various factors. The terrain, for sure. We had to cut our way through so much nature. The roads were not just broken—pieces of them were shifted. We could be following a highway and then suddenly end up in a desert that stretched for a kilometer ahead, or a lake that we had to go around, or a forest that we had to trek through. The wagons could barely go over what was left of the roads, let alone places where there were none.

Then there were the people. Most that were at camp were capable; no one infirm survived for long after the Grand Spell arrived. But, we still had older people, who couldn't keep up the pace most of the others could.

And . . . we'd had injuries, simple accidents. Kids rode in the wagons, but adding the injured on there slowed us down further.

Then there were the attacks from beasts, and the need to hunt for food as our supplies dwindled, having to go on water runs. All of it compounded together to make our trip a lot longer than I had intended it to be.

I was exhausted too. I was constantly flying around the group, looking for threats, searching for food and water. I'd started to sleep again, once every two or three days, and never more than a couple of hours, but it was draining.

I was hungry, and the beast blood was no longer as effective as staving off hunger as it once was. The Investment difference was too low, and . . . it lacked something that human blood didn't.

Which was why I gathered the leaders in one of the tents that were set up for the night.

Catalina, Diego, Max, Kai, and Carlito, with Father Rodriguez, stood around a table as I looked at them, trying to figure out how to say what I had to say.

"I need blood," I said finally, deciding that directness and honesty were most in line with the Heart of Azure and Scarlet. Lies and deceptions incurred a debt.

Catalina and Diego paled, while the rest looked at me quizzically.

It was Max who spoke. "Human blood, I assume?"

I nodded.

"I thought that you could live on animal blood?" Catalina asked, one hand clasped shakily around her throat.

"I can survive on it, but not for long term, and . . ." I paused, trying to figure out how to frame it without revealing things I didn't want to share yet. "Ever since I grew in power, the difference between my Investment and theirs makes what I take less effective. Human blood is still my primary source of sustenance. I could usually survive without it for longer, but I've been exhausting myself. Vampires aren't good at such prolonged exertion."

Catalina swallowed, and I looked around.

"I wouldn't need much, a few glasses worth a day."

It was Father Sergio who spoke up next.

"I can take care of this."

I turned and met his eyes. "You can?"

He nodded. "Of course. People would be happy to donate blood if you need it, especially as you don't need much. You saved our lives, and they can see you flying above us as a guardian angel day in and day out. I shall organize it, and ask for donations. I have no doubt that we'll have plenty of people offer their lifeblood for you."

I opened my mouth, then closed it. I didn't know what to say to that. I was aware how some people among the survivors saw me, and I didn't really do much to dissuade them. I felt uncomfortable next to them. I could feel their faith, their worship. It was doing something that I didn't understand, so I'd tried to keep my distance.

I nodded. No matter what, in the end I still needed blood. "Do that. Gather, let's say, three cups worth every day, and keep the donated blood in separate containers. I'll collect them at the end of the day."

"It shall be so," Father Sergio said with far more deference than I expected, but I didn't say anything.

"Do you have any concerns?" I asked the rest.

They shook their heads.

"We always knew what you are," Max said. "We trust you enough by now. To do anything else would be ludicrous. And if people want to donate, I see no issue with it."

"Good," I said, then dismissed them. They had to get their rest, and I had some more patrolling to do.

I walked over to the small tent that the priest raised alone every day we stopped to rest. There were people around it, hands joined in prayer. I didn't intrude on their ritual. I understood that it was what made them feel safe. I walked through them without making a sound.

I entered the tent and found the priest with three people inside. I had heard their breathing, of course, but I didn't expect them to actually be present. Two of them were women, one a middle-aged matron with a kind smile, and the other that looked like a younger version of her. The man was the same age as the older woman, and I could see that the younger woman and he shared the same eyes. A family then.

I gave Father Sergio a long look, trying to figure out what his plan was, because there was definitely something.

"Welcome," he said with a smile on his face. On the table were gourds, I could smell the blood inside of them already, as well as the scent clinging to the three people. They all had their arms bandaged, and I'd noticed that the cuts they made to drain the blood were all on the outside of their forearms. That was smart. I always hated the movies where the characters cut open their palms. It was stupid beyond compare; making a wound there would only make using that hand far harder while it healed.

"I've done as you asked," Father Sergio continued. "The offerings are separated in their own vessels."

I narrowed my eyes at his verbiage, but didn't say anything.

He picked up the first one and offered it to me. I walked up, glancing at the three.

"What are your names?" I asked.

It was the young woman who answered. "I'm Mona Sanchez, these are my parents, Alba and Martin Sanchez."

"Thank you for your gift," I told them and inclined my head.

"Of course," she said with a small shaky smile on her face. "You've been our guardian angel. You saved my family when you arrived during the . . . that night," she said slowly.

I'd saved them all, but I could tell that she meant something more. She or someone from her family had to have been more directly saved by my actions. I didn't remember, but I had moved around camp a lot, killing beasts that had gotten in.

I didn't say that, or ask what happened. I didn't want to make them feel like I didn't care.

"You should not feel obligated—" I started, but was almost immediately interrupted by the girl's mother.

"We didn't, we don't, feel obligated, that is," she said in a raspy voice, impacted by all the smoke that night probably. "When the father asked for volunteers to help you, we stepped forward first. We are a community, and we help each other. You've given much of yourself to help us, to keep us safe. We, everyone, sees that. We see you flying above us every day, and we know your effort. You're our Dark Angel. We'll always help you."

I didn't quite know how to respond, so I didn't. I just inclined my head then walked over and took the first gourd. I looked at the three of them and the priest. They didn't seem to be planning on leaving. Initially I planned on taking the blood and drinking it in the privacy of my own tent, but now . . . I felt like there was an expectation, a debt, despite their words.

I opened the first gourd and drank. As I had asked, there wasn't a lot of blood. I downed it in three gulps. It quenched my thirst, but it wasn't enough, I knew it immediately. I moved to the next, drinking it in the same manner, and then the last. Once I was done, I closed my eyes, feeling the **thirst** feeding. The tiredness that had seemed to cling to my bones slowly started to fade. I hadn't realized how much I needed human blood until now.

There was something within that made it just greater, more nourishing for a vampire.

"Once more, thank you for the gift of your blood," I said, then turned and left as they bowed. With my last glance I saw the priest's smile, and didn't like it at all.

* * *

The next few days were a blur of travel and vigilance. The terrain continued to be challenging, the landscape a patchwork of terrains and remnants of civilization. Some towns were completely overgrown, while others remained pristine, yet empty. We found no survivors. The only thing we encountered was more beasts. Some familiar, some terrifyingly new. Myself and the fighters led by Kai fought them all, protecting the convoy.

The donated blood helped. It wasn't the same as feeding directly, but it was enough to keep the hunger at bay and my strength replenished. I felt a strange connection to the people who offered their blood, a sense of responsibility that went beyond mere protection. Their faith. Father Sergio had made the donation of the blood into a ritual.

The way he spoke to me and about me was uncomfortable, as if I was a literal angel. I had thought that it was just hyperbole, a way to connect and give the people hope, but it was spreading and becoming more than that. I could see it in the people's eyes.

A part of me liked it.

It felt empowering to have people look at you and see something greater than themselves. I wondered if this was what old vampires felt like, back in the ages when they were venerated as gods. It took me a while, but I realized that there was a good reason for that.

I also had a lot of uncomfortable questions now, about religion and history and what was myth, legend, or truth. Vampires had been around for tens of thousands of years. And stories evolved, changed over time. The old gods could've just been others of my kind or shifters.

I didn't dwell on such thoughts too much. I didn't have the time. Getting the people to the coast was my only goal.

What was supposed to be a trip of several days at most ended up being three weeks. The weather grew colder, and the sea breeze chilled the nights. We encountered fewer beasts, but those we did encounter were larger, more powerful. Anything lesser had been driven out by Cartagena's plant organism.

The convoy adapted. Hunters honed their skills; fighters trained their bodies and minds and got better at keeping the rest safe. Children learned to scavenge and fight alongside their parents. Father Sergio's sermons became a source of strength and unity, his words weaving a tapestry of faith and resilience.

We had some deaths too. Some of the older ones, the injured who couldn't recover, and others who fell in combat.

I, too, adapted. I learned to conserve my energy better, to fight smarter, not harder. I explored my powers, discovering my limits and practiced using my Mask. It was, in many ways, a calmer period of time than the challenge. I had more time to think, to plan.

Max and Anna continued to work on Masks, trying to help others gain more Investment. And it seemed like it was working; a lot of people started approaching the First Investment, with many of them getting over it. A few even reached close to the Second Investment, like Kai and Carlito.

The people continued to offer their blood daily, and Father Sergio encouraged a ritual that had become a symbol of sorts. I accepted it gratefully, though I did feel my debt increase with every drop of blood I took. I'd asked it of them for nourishment, but it was also true that I gained more from it. Every day, more doors were added to my soul space. More potential power.

I was aware of the debt, even if they were not, but protecting them and intending on giving them a new home felt like enough that I didn't feel guilt.

I guided them across what had become a wild land, unlike anything that they were used to from their life before.

I gained a single Carving in my Leader Ornament, but no skill. The gain at least told me that I was on the right track.

I led the convoy to the location I'd chosen, which was near Cartagena, just twenty kilometers away. We had to pass close to the city to get to it, but Saia had assured me that the plant's influence didn't extend that far from the city. I chose a small peninsula just south of the city. Well, just west now, as the land had moved.

It was right on the coast, a resort town called Porto Nao. I had already scouted it out during my first trip, but also when we were a day out. It was abandoned; nothing lived there. Nature had reclaimed it, but the core of the buildings remained. Eventually, we would probably be able to reclaim it ourselves.

I was going to place the town on the coast. The reasons for it were many. First, the coast was now on a different sea, one that was in the center of the continent, not close to any ocean, and unlikely to have large storms. With it being a peninsula, the only avenue of attack by land could come from a single direction, and that led right to Cartagena, which I was counting on to act as a deterrent. And since I hadn't seen anything other than small birds next to the city I felt it was the safest place.

I'd flown over the peninsula and located several smaller rifts, even entered and found that one could easily be farmed for food and resources.

We cut through the foliage and finally reached the water. The convoy settled nearby, and I gathered the leaders on the beach, then pulled out my town creation item.

"How does this work exactly? It's just going to magic up a town for us?" Carlito asked.

I shrugged. "I have no idea, buddy." I was honestly quite excited to see what would happen.

"Uh," Max chimed in. "Should we all just be standing here? Is it dangerous?"

I didn't know, though I didn't think that the Grand Spell wanted to kill us.

"I don't even know the range of it, but I doubt it will be dangerous for us."

I'd picked a heavily wooded area along the coast. The item mentioned wooden structures, but I didn't know if it would use resources on hand or just magic everything up. I figured that it couldn't hurt to have materials on hand, to make it easier for the Grand Spell.

"Don't be a baby." Carlito nudged Max, who grimaced.

"It will be as God wills," Father Sergio said, and both Catalina and Diego nodded. I had seen them attending his sermons, and their fear toward me had slightly abated.

I guess that being exposed to me in my winged form had done wonders, even if it was not in the way I had expected. My hearing was good enough to hear the whispers. I knew what they called me.

Kai stood next to me, stoic and alert, the only one who didn't seem bothered at all about what was about to happen.

I decided not to prolong this any longer. I pressed the lever and placed the item on the ground.

It unraveled, and then a light fell on top of us from the sky. I heard exclamations of surprise, even a scream, but it was all drowned out by a thunderous roar like a mountain falling down.

I couldn't see, nor could I hear anything but that loud noise.

It didn't last long, and it vanished almost as fast as it arrived. I blinked, my eyes recovering faster than those of the humans around me.

What was before just a forested area had been transformed.

I took to the air and observed it from above. The town clung to the rugged coastline like a barnacle to a ship's hull. Encircled by a sturdy palisade of sharpened logs, the town was a patchwork of around a few hundred buildings, all constructed from deep brown timber. The structures leaned against each other, in a charmingly haphazard fashion, the roofs a tapestry of mossy greens.

Narrow cobbled stone streets wound between them, leading to four small squares where I could see buildings surrounding them with open front areas and counters, with raised solid wood screens that could be dropped. Like small shops.

The heart of the town, though, was the harbor. A long, wooden pier jutted out into the sea, lined with six fishing boats, four smaller and two mid-sized. Nets hung stretched along the dock, ready to be picked up and used.

The dominating feature was a sturdy keep, a three-story structure of thick timber and stone foundation that was near the center of the town. Its windows, small and deeply set, offered a panoramic view of the harbor and the sea, but also looked out over the town and the wild, beyond the walls.

Another building caught my attention by its shape, as it clearly resembled a human church. Most of the other buildings were made in a strange style, with single-sided slanted roofs and more rounded and taller doors. This building though, was clearly influenced by human architecture.

There were wells scattered around the town, a bit farther away from the coast.

Farther inland, at the edge of the town, near one corner of the walls, was a cluster of outhouses. I had seen only a few in the city, behind a couple of the larger buildings. It occurred to me just then that I hadn't given much thought to all the things that we'd come to take for granted in our world.

Another large building nearby drew my attention, and I flew down to investigate. It turned out that the large tiled roof building was a bathhouse, filled with pools of water and simple hand-operated pumps.

I walked out, noticing the others exploring the town on foot. I took to the air again, and saw that the convoy had started their approach, a few of them heading toward a large gate that led into the town.

I saw something sprawled beyond the palisade, and flew over to discover what looked like a simple lumber yard. Open storage areas, with just simple roof coverings were arranged on one side, while a large area was cleared out for work. There were even axes and other tools in one of the open shacks.

Despite its modest size, the town was more than I had expected. This was going to be a good home base.

The first few days were filled with Saia and me flying to Cartagena on supply runs. Medicine, food, and even simple things like pillows and mattresses were ferried to the town.

It had, of course, come empty of anything but the barest things necessary. There was no furniture, no decorations, nothing.

I put Catalina and Diego in charge of settling the people in, deciding who would get which building and so on. The keep was used as the central hub, and I'd also claimed the top floor as my home. Not that I had much need of it, but the symbolism mattered.

Few people among the survivors had knowledge about fishing, so boats had started heading out and catching fish.

I put Kai and a few other warriors to work exploring the rest of the small peninsula and clearing rifts.

Father Sergio occupied the church, of course, and started holding daily service. I had yet to attend, partly because I was busy and partly because I was afraid of what I would hear.

Soon the end of the month approached, and I sat, worried about the next challenge. I had been itching to go north and try to find Aurora, but since the trip to the coast with the survivors took too long I decided to wait and see if we could meet in the challenge. Perhaps she had moved already, and I didn't want to waste time looking for her.

Today though, I was flying across the sea, as I wanted to see what there was on the other side. Perhaps there were more survivors over there. From what my sire said, the other coast was occupied by the Sahara.

It was a harsh environment, but not densely populated. Which meant that fewer rifts had probably opened up, perhaps less danger too. There weren't a lot of big predators in the desert that could mutate.

I flew across in about the same time it had taken me to reach the coast from the military camp. Which meant that the sea was about 200 km across.

I flew over the coast, looking for any signs of . . . well, anything. It didn't take me long to see a large city in the distance. As I approached, I found what I had come to expect. Rifts, and beasts fighting for supremacy over the city. I flew above; a few mutated birds that I didn't recognize attempted to fly at me, but quickly learned that I wasn't prey.

I found writing that had survived the catastrophe that had hit the city, and learned that the city was named Dakar, and if my knowledge of world flags was correct, it was in Senegal.

I didn't stay too long. It was unlikely that there were any humans still alive in the city. I continued on, flying along the coast.

Then I decided to head a bit more inland, as there was nothing on the coast but depressing remnants of civilization torn down by beasts.

I was over the desert now, a sea of sand for as far as the eyes could see. I saw no signs of anything of interest, and was about to turn away when I noticed something in the distance. It looked like an oasis, with a road leading to it and a few buildings, but if I wasn't mistaken, I could also see movement.

I slowed down and headed for the oasis.

Once I arrived, I saw a battle taking place. A large shifter with sandy fur was fighting beasts that looked like mutated hyenas, an entire pack of them.

The beasts were larger, had spikes growing out of their backs, but the shifter was stronger and faster than them, I could tell immediately.

Yet, somehow, he was losing. It didn't take long for me to realize that he was standing in place and fighting the beasts instead of moving around, taking advantage of his speed and strength. He left himself open for the beasts to snip at his back.

I frowned. Then his actions became clear to me. He was protecting something in the rundown building.

I debated flying down and helping. My track record with the shifters wasn't great, but I didn't have any issues with them. Hell, some of my best trainers were shifters, and I had grown up around them. Granted, the ones I knew had served a vampire and because of that were shunned by the rest of their kind, but still.

I took a deep breath and made a decision.

Interlude - Survivors

Aurora dashed to the side, evading a sword about to stab her through the chest.

"Can't y'all just, like, stop coming after me!" she yelled as she retreated and unleashed her [Earth Quake] skill.

The four men wobbled, trying to catch their balance. One fell to his knees, losing his sword in the process.

"You're coming with us," one of them, their leader, presumably, said.

"Hah, nope," Aurora said as she set her feet and glared at them, gripping her staff tightly.

"We can help you," he said, trying the nice guy routine again. "We have a safe place with many other survivors. You'll have a home and be surrounded by other people. It's better than a rundown and abandoned town."

Aurora rolled her eyes. "Again, I don't need your help, buddy. I'm doing great on my own."

They managed to get back to their feet as the ground settled, and they glared at her. She didn't shy away from their glares. She had gone through too much to be afraid of them. They were barely in their First Investment, while she was approaching her Third. She was confident.

They'd come into town a day before, and both she and they had been surprised when they ran into each other. At first, she was happy to find more survivors. They all had to stick together. But then they started talking about their group, far north, a "kingdom."

They asked her to come back with them. They had apparently been sent out to search for other survivors and bring them back to safety. Aurora declined their offer, of course. She was waiting for Marianna to come get her. Aurora had tried to head to the coast, but the wilds were too dangerous for her. Not the beasts as much as the lack of supplies. In town she had a rift that she could get meat from, and the house she had settled in had a well of its own so she had water.

She wasn't like Marianna, who could survive in the wild all by herself. She had barely even hiked before the world went to crap. She hoped that Mari could find her, or at least that she made it to the next challenge as they had agreed.

These "Warriors of the Kingdom" that she had met didn't take her answer kindly. They started trying to persuade her, and once they realized that she wouldn't go, to force her. Unfortunately for them, she was a lot stronger than they were.

"I'm not going with you," Aurora stressed again. "And you cannot force me."

The leader, Rick, and the others exchanged looks. They had been surprised when she demonstrated her skills. They hadn't seen anything like it. That was when they had decided to take her no matter what.

"King Proximus has decreed that every survivor with a unique Mask must be brought before him," Rick said.

"I don't know what kind of a fantasy roleplay you guys are all playing, but try to pay attention this time. I. AM. NOT. GOING. ANYWHERE."

"These lands are claimed for the Sun Kingdom. Anyone living on our land is required to offer fealty to the king."

Aurora blinked at the clearly insane man. "I know that the world fell apart and that there are no real countries and stuff anymore, but man. Do you hear yourself? It's been barely three months, and you are already claiming land? Making kingdoms? Who do you think you are?"

Rick shrugged. "We need order. It is just how we're built, and King Proximus gave us that. He helped us survive and gave us the tools to retake our world. He was one of the chosen ones, given knowledge and gifts by the New Gods."

Aurora blinked. What he was saying made her suspect that whoever this king was might have also been an Exemplar. She didn't remember anyone like that in the challenge, but then again, not everyone had probably accepted to go in the challenge. And it wasn't like she had made many friends in there with the rest of the one hundred.

She hadn't revealed her Exemplar status to these four, and in fact, she had kept a lot back. They just knew that she was the only survivor of her town, not much more than that. She hadn't even told them about her Mask.

"I don't care," Aurora said, her face turning determined. She had tried to argue with them, then to run, but they pursued her. They weren't giving her much choice. "I'm not going anywhere with you."

"Regretful," he said and pulled out a vial from a pouch at his waist.

She frowned. "What is that supposed to be?"

The others did the same, all pulling out identical vials, with the same purplish liquid inside. Then they downed it.

Her eyes widened as she saw their veins turn violet and a cobweb of them spread beneath their skin. Their eyes darkened and turned the same color, their muscles bulged, and then they launched themselves at her.

Aurora barely reacted fast enough.

[Stone Wall]

The concrete beneath her feet shifted then rose as a barrier between her and the four charging men.

They were fast! Not Mari fast, but definitely faster than humans, even Invested ones. Unless they were like Third or Fourth Investment, which she knew they were not.

Aurora dashed backward as they came around. She saw the mad looks in their eyes. Whatever they just took, she knew it was bad.

They roared, spittle flying out of their mouths like they were some mad dogs.

Aurora stopped holding back.

[Sunder Earth]

The ground opened beneath them, cracking the concrete in half and widening into a chasm between them and Aurora. One of the men didn't stop in time and fell in, tumbling through the hole that was several meters deep. He hit the ground with a sickening crunch.

Aurora focused on the other three. She raised a hand and used [Shape Stone] with her newest skill [Stoneform Proficiency]. Hands made out of concrete rose and grabbed the three, trapping their arms against their torsos.

The struggled, but even their improved strength wasn't enough to break free.

Aurora closed the ground back up, their dead friend buried beneath forever. She felt guilty about that. She didn't mean to kill him. But she wasn't going to let it show.

She approached the others, who looked at her with violet eyes.

"I'm not going anywhere, and if you come back and bother me again, you'll end up the same as your friend. Understand?" she asked, trying to channel her best Marianna, and failing spectacularly.

Aurora just didn't have that same intensity a vampire had.

The three finally nodded, and their leader, Rick, spoke.

"I'll inform the king that this town is off limits."

Aurora sighed. She didn't know if she trusted them, but she wasn't ruthless enough to just kill them. A part of her whispered that Marianna would've done it, but . . .

Aurora wasn't like that.

She sighed, and released her skill, hoping that she wasn't making a mistake.

The pack of hyenas had tracked them across the desert. Even when Oluwatobi hunted them in the dark or tried to scare them away. He could've, and should've, killed them before, but he was fearful. The pack was large, and every predator knew that a pack of hyenas was dangerous. They took down lions with their numbers, and Oluwatobi couldn't risk death.

He had children to protect.

He looked behind him at the little den they had found in the oasis. His son and daughter slept, exhausted from months of constant wandering through the desert. Adanna and Ade were in their true forms, just like he was, so it was easier on them, but they were still only children.

Oluwatobi pushed his large head through the door, then looked at the pack circling around. They had approached while he slept. A stupid mistake to make, but he had been tired too.

Their roars, barks, yips, and growls rose in intensity, waking his children up. They yelped, their bodies and eyes showing clear fear. He nuzzled them, then barked softly, telling them to stay inside and hidden.

He stepped outside, surrounded. He took a deep breath, then roared, his voice drowning out the hyenas. For a moment after, there was silence, and he hoped that they would be frightened enough to decide this wasn't worth it.

Only they didn't. They had been tracking them for days. He could see it in their red eyes. They wanted his flesh, and they wanted his children.

Oluwatobi prayed to the Mother Earth, hoping for a miracle. The world had become a hellscape, ever since that night when his wife had vanished before his eyes. And now it felt like the nightmare was drawing to the end.

But he wasn't going to go quietly. He was not going to lie down and show them his belly. He was a child of the Earth, and he didn't give up.

He bared his teeth, clawed at the ground, and waited.

The hyenas attacked first, their twisted and hellish forms rippling with muscle as they charged.

He pounced, cutting the distance and grabbing the closest hyena in his powerful jaws. With a single bite, he crushed its skull in his mouth.

Pain lanced through his thigh as another hyena bit his hind leg. Oluwatobi whirled around and smacked the hyena down with a paw, rending flesh apart and smashing it against the ground.

Another hyena jumped on his back, biting. He roared, and bit and clawed and threw himself against the hyenas, but no matter how many he killed, another was there to take its place. He was healing from his wounds. He was faster, stronger, but he couldn't leave the small shack where his children were hiding.

If he had more room, if he could run against them . . . if, if. The world was mad. And as his blood soaked the floor he prayed again.

As if to answer his prayer, a loud crack shook the air, and something landed on top a hyena like a star falling from the sky, like the wrath of God.

The animal exploded in a shower of blood and gore, bits of flesh, organs, and bone scattering in all directions. Everything froze, and all eyes turned toward the small crater.

The first thing Oluwatobi saw were wings, as black as night, beautiful, the kind one saw on a falcon. Then the thing that had fallen from the sky straightened, pulling the wings back.

Oluwatobi saw a humanoid with blue skin, with glowing emerald eyes. The clothes she wore were skintight on her torso, hugging every curve perfectly. Long black hair fell over her shoulders, and strange bracers covered her arms.

She met his eyes, and then moved. The air cracked again, and another hyena exploded.

Oluwatobi could barely follow the movements, but he retreated, putting his back against the entrance to the shack and his children.

He didn't do anything but watch the strange creature as it slaughtered the hyenas with ease.

The Second Challenge

I finished the hyenas quickly, though not as quickly as I could've. Flying for so long had tired me out, and I could already feel the hunger rearing up its head.

Once I was done crushing the skull of the last beast, I turned to look at the shifter. He was a big one, the top of his head easily as tall as I was, and I was not a short person, not by human standards.

I could hear his lungs filling up and deflating, hear his heart beating faster and faster. I even heard his flesh stitching itself back together. I could also hear the two softer heartbeats inside.

He growled as I stepped closer, and I raised my arms. He bared his teeth at me and got lower to the ground.

It was only then that I realized that he might not know what I was, that he might think that I was just another monster.

"Hello, I don't mean you or your children any harm," I said slowly, trying to be reassuring.

I could see the confusion in his eyes, the distrust. I focused inward and triggered the change back. Saia shifted on my skin, adjusting as my wings retracted. We'd had a long talk and figured a lot of things.

Once I was back to looking a bit more human, I gave the shifter a smile. After a bit, I opened my mouth and showed fangs, letting him know for certain what I was.

"See," I said as two small shifter shapes walked up to the entrance and peeked out from behind their parent's legs. "I promise I'm a—" I paused as I was just about to say "a friend." I couldn't do that anymore. My words had weight. If I said that I was a friend, I would be obligated to act as one. I didn't know the shifter or his children.

"I'm a survivor, just like you," I said instead. "Can you shift back? So that we might talk easier?"

He looked at me, then stepped back, pushing his children inside. I didn't quite understand his fear, though he must know that he had no chance against me. If I meant him harm, there was little he could do to stop me.

Still, I didn't move as he ushered his children inside. A few minutes later, after a litany of soft growls and barks, I heard bones cracking and shifting.

Soon enough, a man walked out of the shack, holding a piece of what looked like tablecloth around his waist. He was a tall man, with skin as dark as obsidian. His eyes were brown and somehow warm, and he had a kind face.

I smiled at him. "Hello again," I started. "I'm . . ."

I paused. Which name I used was important. It occurred to me in the moment that names had meaning, they held power. The more I grew, the more I accepted this world around me as the new reality, the more I started to think of myself as Star, according to my YoKai-ni name. Marianna was a different person, but also one that held meaning in this world. The Grand Spell had shown it to everyone, along with my true name.

Estrella was an Earth version of my true name, and perhaps one that I felt closest to, despite not using it often. It was useful for when I didn't want to reveal too much.

Now, I should use the name that best reflected what I wanted to achieve. I wanted the person before me to trust me, but also to understand who I was.

"I'm Marianna Rojas," I said slowly, watching him for any signs of recognition.

The man gave me a long look, but guarded his thoughts, then he inclined his head. "I'm Oluwatobi Musa," he said in a soft tone of voice that didn't quite match the mountain of a man that he was.

"Well met, Oluwatobi," I said. "I'm glad that I noticed your plight. I was just about to turn back when I saw this oasis and the pack of beasts."

Oluwatobi deflated, as if he had finally allowed the reality of the situation to sink in. "The Mother provides," he said, then continued before I could ask anything. "I apologize, it's been a long few months. The world turned mad, and it's been a long time since I spoke with another. Especially not one, uh, like you, who can even speak Yoruba." After a beat, he added, "Master."

I grimaced. "Marianna is fine. I'm not like the vampires you hear about in stories." I tried to put him at ease, but he was clearly distressed. "You said that you haven't talked with anyone in a while? Since before the Grand Spell arrived, I assume?"

His brow furrowed. "Grand Spell?"

"The light that covered the world months ago. It changed our world. You may think of it like a god. It has transported our land to another world, merged all our continents into a single landmass. I'm not speaking Yoruba, I'm talking in my native tongue, and you are hearing it in yours."

Oluwatobi blinked, and then his eyes lit up with hope. "You know what this is? When it happened, the light came and my wife was taken, do you know what happened to her? We lived in an oasis in the desert before. I've been searching for her ever since."

His words turned frantic, almost tripping over one another.

I immediately knew what had happened to his wife. I just didn't know how to tell him.

"Your wife is likely an Exemplar," I told him. "That means that she was chosen as one of thirty representatives of our world, to be sent to other continents on the world of Kirios, or the World of Origin as the Grand Spell calls it. I was an Exemplar too. She would've spent a month on another continent, and would then be transported back here, to the place she originally left from."

His face fell. "Back to the . . . oh, I abandoned her."

I raised my hand before he could spiral. "You couldn't have known, and that is . . . I'm sorry, but Kirios is dangerous. Survival isn't guaranteed."

"I need to go back, to try to find her . . ." He glanced behind at his two children. He had probably struggled taking care of them.

"Even if she returned, she wouldn't be there anymore. She will know what happened to Earth and will probably have a plan of action. Did you see that list of top Masked names? If she was an Exemplar, she would've probably been on it. What's her name?"

Oluwatobi turned to look back at me, then he nodded. "I did," he said. "Sade. Sade Musa. I just . . . I thought that I was hallucinating, I didn't pay too much attention to it."

As many others had thought too. I was certain that she didn't enter the challenge. I would've remembered a female shifter, and her scent would've been similar to her children. I hadn't encountered it before. But him not remembering was valid. I didn't remember the one hundred names either.

"If she survived, she is back here. Did you have a home somewhere else? A place she might go to check?"

"Lagos," he said slowly. "I tried to head there, but . . . the world is mad, as if the directions have suddenly switched sides. North isn't north anymore."

I nodded. "Consequence of continental merging. I know that you want to search for your wife, but it will be a dangerous trip, especially with children." I paused, and he glanced at his kids, clearly knowing that I spoke the truth.

"I'm leading a group of more survivors across the new inland sea. We have children there. Come back with me, you can settle there. If you want to search for your wife, you can leave your children in a safe place, and have people help you."

He looked at me, clearly struggling to make a decision. "A sea? How would we cross it, I . . ."

"I'll call for a friend that can help carry you over." I smiled. "The world's changed, and we need to stick together if we are to survive. Come."

I called Saia, or rather she called her drone. It took her a bit longer to get to us, as she couldn't fly as fast as I could, but a few hours later a large silver dragon landed on the sand in front of the small shack.

Oluwatobi and his kids, Adanna and Ade, looked up at her with wide eyes. The two kids were still in their true forms, and were about as large as medium-sized dogs. I didn't know how old that would make them in human years, and I didn't pry. Oluwatobi was already clearly distressed about his wife, thinking that he abandoned her.

"This is Saia. She's my friend." I introduced her.

"Statement: Greetings."

Oluwatobi leaned back when he heard her talk, then looked at me with wide eyes.

"She'll carry you back to our town," I told him.

I let him process everything. I'd never get tired of seeing people completely flabbergasted when they met Saia.

Finally he nodded, but his expression was completely bewildered. As if he couldn't quite believe that this was all real. "Thank you," he said finally.

"Can your children shift to their human forms? It might be easier for you to ride on top of her and hold on to them that way."

"Uh." Oluwatobi looked back at the kids. "Yes, they can, but . . . we have no clothes with us."

He had already mentioned that he and his family had decided to live their lives in the wild, in their true forms. I knew that some shifters did that.

"I think that Saia can help with that," I said, then tapped my chest. "This is her too."

His confused look led to me explaining what Saia actually was. I wasn't sure if he understood it.

But, within a few minutes, the kids were back to looking like seven- or eight-year-old human children, and were wearing thin skinsuits courtesy of Saia.

Just as they were about to mount Saia, the world vanished.

Everything was replaced by a gray void filled with mist. I could still see Oluwatobi and his children next to me, but all other features of the world were replaced.

Once more, we were in the Grand Spell's realm.

The voice that was not a voice sounded, and words blazed in the air above us.

Denizens of **Terra** and **Suul'dar**, a New Challenge approaches.

The second Challenge is near! The bottom 100 Masked will be brought to a new arena for the ultimate Grand Challenge.

In three days, each of the bottom 100 will be given a choice of being taken to the Grand Challenge or staying behind. The second of five Grand Challenges.

Personal and continental rewards will be granted.

The length of the second Challenge is one real time day, and five days personal time.

The list of the bottom 100 Masked is not yet final!

Oh no. Why? This wasn't good, not at all. The bottom 100? The ones who had barely advanced their Masks? I knew who would be numbered amongst those the most.

And then a list flashed above us, with the names. I didn't recognize any of them, but their Investment was poor. The highest had two Carvings.

"Baba?" I turned as Oluwatobi's daughter spoke. She was pointing at the list.

I looked, and found her name.

This was a disaster.

Once we were back in real space, I ushered the shifters to get on Saia. Oluwatobi and the kids settled on top of her back, where she had shifted and created something akin to a saddle.

Then, we were rushing back.

I had foolishly assumed that the challenges would always be among the top 100. But now . . . The Grand Spell's goal was to uplift as many people as possible, to grant strength. According to its logic, giving an opportunity to the weak had to make sense. Yet, those who would be weakest on Earth would be children. Or those who had somehow ended up in very safe areas where they didn't need to fight, or who had no knowledge of how Masks worked.

I looked over the list while we were inside, looking for any name that I recognized and found none. Though I didn't quite know the names of all the children in our town.

But, if there were any . . . I didn't know what we would do. What kind of a challenge would this one even be?

It took us a few hours to get back. We landed in one of the squares, people already there to meet us. They knew I was coming with guests as Saia's drone had told them before leaving.

Catalina introduced herself, then quickly gathered the children and Oluwatobi, leading them to their new home. We still had unoccupied ones, and could easily take in double our current population.

I found myself in the keep, in one of the meeting rooms, with Max, Diego, Kai, and Carlito.

"You had an interesting trip, boss lady," Carlito said.

I nodded. "I'm just glad I ran into a survivor. The world feels . . . empty."

"He's staying then?" Diego asked.

I glanced at him. "His wife was an Exemplar. At least I think so. She got taken when the Grand Spell arrived. He wants to go and find her, I've offered him a safe place for his children and help in looking for her."

"You think that we can spare resources to look for her?" It was Max who asked the question.

"Yes," I answered. "Another Exemplar under our banner would be invaluable. And if we've already offered her children and husband safety, she would be more inclined to stay."

"Assuming she's still alive, and we find her," Max added. "Are you going to go and search?"

I shook my head. "No, this challenge threw a wrench in my plans. I expected to join another and speak with my allies. Now, I'm going to go and try to find them."

"The new challenge," Max started. "Thankfully, none of our kids are eligible. They've all advanced their Masks plenty. We've been helping them gain Investment and using them for more data points."

I was relieved. I didn't know what kind of decisions we could've made. "Oluwatobi's daughter is on the list. She can refuse to go, of course, but that isn't our decision to make."

The others all nodded. "Let's settle him in, then we'll talk," I added. "Now, anything new I should know?"

Diego cleared his throat. "The fishing boats have been coming back with full catches. It looks like we'll be able to feed ourselves even without rifts."

"That's good."

"And we've successfully refurbished the two sailing boats. We think that we can make use of them. Catalina also had the idea of making long oars, just in case wind isn't fully on board. And with the increase in physical strength some of our Masked have gotten, it isn't much of an issue."

"That accelerates my plans," I said.

I had found a few sailing boats in Cartagena's port, though not all had survived. The two that I dragged to town were in the best condition, and even they had to be worked on. All the electronics and metal parts had degraded, so they had to be pulled out. One of the yachts was a small luxury Catamaran yacht, with only a single sail. Obviously it was not meant to be used without a motor, but we had little choice. It was large enough that two dozen people could fit on it.

The other one was smaller than that one, with two smaller sails that were in good condition. That one could barely hold a dozen people.

My plan was to have them start heading east, along the coast, looking for more survivors, while I would head north and west, to look for Aurora.

Catalina entered the room, with Oluwatobi following behind her.

"What do you think?" I asked him.

"It is a nice town," he said softly. "Is it true that this 'Grand Spell' created it, that it was a reward from it?"

I nodded.

"I see," he said, looking around at the walls.

We still didn't have much in the way of furnishings. We'd started using the lumberyard to source wood to make it.

"Your daughter," I said, changing the topic. "If she goes—"

"She won't," Oluwatobi cut me off.

I inclined my head. "It is your family, your decision. We don't yet know what kind of a challenge it is going to be. If the other one hundred challengers end up being children, like her, then . . . she would have an advantage. She's a shifter. Stronger, faster, more capable than humans of similar age, or even some adults, especially if their Masks aren't advanced."

"I don't want her in danger. I've stressed it with her. I need her safe here while I go look for her mother."

"As I said, it is your decision."

After that, we turned the conversation to his wife, and Oluwatobi's search. It was agreed that he would go in a few days, along with a group of our fighters that could help him. It was an opportunity for them to gain Investment and advance their Masks.

After a lengthy discussion, it was agreed that they would take the smaller of our two boats, along with a few of our scouts led by Gabriela Isa and Angelo Serrano. Our two highest Investment Scouts and the two people that had escorted me to the camp what felt like years ago. I knew them to be good, solid people, and their Masks would help with Oluwatobi's search. Angelo had the Mask of Danger Seeker, and Gabriela the Mask of the Tracker Scout. With them, they would send two of their fighters who had rifles and skills that helped use them.

Most of the danger could be easily handled by Oluwatobi. Without his children to protect I doubted that there was anything on Earth able to threaten him as far as beasts were concerned.

Aside from looking for his wife, they were to look for other survivor groups. If they were small, then they would invite them to our town. If they found large groups they would try to just establish relations.

With everything agreed, we finished the meeting.

I walked through the city, looking around. People still showed me deference. It wasn't just the bowing; it was the way they stepped out of my way and waited for me to pass. The way they looked at me, as if I was their savior. And I was, I had also taken control of their lives, led them hundreds of kilometers across the land and settled them in a magically created town.

I understood their looks. Even if Father Sergio wasn't pushing his more religious belief on me, they would've still looked at me in the same manner. I'd seen it before, in the slums, when the cartel swooped down to help after misfortune. Floods, famines, sickness, it didn't matter. The cartel always helped, even at a loss. Because the cartel understood that the goodwill of the people mattered.

I was doing the same thing now. I was helping. I helped the survivors. I helped Oluwatobi. All because I wanted their gratitude, their loyalty. I wanted them to follow me, and in order to earn that I had to give.

Power could only get you so far.

The people settled well, and life seemed to have returned surprisingly quickly to some semblance of normalcy. I saw children running around, heard laughter, gossip. The harsh reality of the world around us faded away in days. The world made sense again, even if it was harder.

They had walls around them; they had food in their bellies. It was enough. And I had done that for them. It made me feel good.

Three days later we found out what the challenge was.

"A labyrinth?" I asked.

The young girl nodded her head. She had been offered the entrance to the challenge, and had refused it.

"Yes," Adanna said in a quiet voice. "It said that we had to do puzzles and navigate the labyrinth, and also something about surviving encounters."

I wish that I could've read the description myself, but it didn't sound as dangerous as the last challenge. Although, *encounters* could mean a lot of things. And if the Suul were in that challenge too . . . it would make it incredibly dangerous.

"Thank you." I smiled at the little shifter girl, then raised my eyes to her father. "When do you leave?"

"In an hour," he said. "The ship is loaded with supplies, and the wind is favorable to get us across the sea."

I nodded, having to think about the wind was not something I had anticipated, but there were people who had at least passing knowledge of how sailing worked. The fishermen were also teaching some of the kids that had simpler Masks, so that theirs might advance and change direction toward more sailing related evolutions. We would need them.

"I wish you good luck. I hope that you find your wife," I told him.

He bowed his head. "Thank you again for coming to my aid. I'm sorry for the manner I reacted initially. I . . . I've never known that vampires could change as we can, and seeing you in the sun . . ."

I waved my hand. "It's nothing. I understand. Only the oldest of my kind can shift as I do, and the sun . . . well, it is no longer our sun."

"It's a hard thing to wrap one's head around."

"That it is," I said, as he turned with a wave and left the keep with his daughter.

I turned to the others. "I'm leaving too. I need to find Aurora. She is the closest of my allies from the challenge, and her Mask could be very useful for our future."

Max scratched his neck. "I wish that you could stay. Your presence brings us a lot of peace. But . . . I understand why you have to go."

"The more powerful people we have, the safer we'll be."

That, and I needed strong people to keep the other factions at bay. There wasn't much time left.

* * *

I was ready to leave. I had my supplies neatly stored in my backpack, and my weapons and a few other things I thought I might need were stored in an improvised sack tied around Saia's back.

With her coming along, I would be going a bit slower than I could on my own, but it would be around the same in the end, as I couldn't keep up with my fastest speed for too long.

Just as I was about to head out, Kai and Carlito found me.

Both of them were fully geared, with their own backpacks over their shoulders.

"And where do you two think you're going?" I asked, I was pretty sure that they weren't part of any groups leaving the town.

"We're coming with you, boss lady." Carlito grinned.

"Oh, so you've grown wings while I wasn't looking, huh?" I smiled at him.

"Nah." He waved his hand. "Our buddy Saia is gonna carry us."

I narrowed my eyes at him. That . . . could work.

"Why?" I asked, and they got what I meant.

It was Kai that answered. "You need someone to watch your back."

I tilted my head. "Do I?"

"You're strong, but you can't pay attention to everything. You don't know what you're going to encounter out there."

That was . . . true. I didn't really have any big reason to deny them. They would slow me down, true, but not by much.

I looked at them as I was thinking. Having them around wouldn't be the worst thing. It would give me a chance to help them get stronger, but also to give me Investment for my Leader Ornament. And I had already taken them under my wing in a way. They were my closest associates in the camp. My left and right hand.

"Fine," I said finally. "Saia, if that's alright with you?"

"Feedback: They've already asked."

"Of course they did."

The Steppe

We flew along the coast for days, encountering few smaller towns or cities, but like before no survivors. With every day that passed, more and more people died. I knew that would happen. Shadow had tried to prepare me, yet I hadn't really believed it. Now, I could see it with my own eyes.

We flew during the day, taking a few detours to look for survivors further inland, and made camp at night. We cleared rifts on our way, though none we encountered were anything really challenging. The beasts we encountered were mostly bears, some mutated to have elemental affinities, though they weren't anywhere close to Invested enough for those affinities to manifest in powerful skills.

I usually made Kai and Carlito fight them in order to gain Investment, then took the blood for myself at the end. No use in wasting Investment.

Following the coast, we quickly realized that something was wrong. Panama and Mexico were missing. Where they should be, instead was a large grassland, grafted straight onto the coast of Colombia east of Panama. It meant that those lands were shifted somewhere else, which was actually the largest switched area that I had encountered so far.

The towns and cities we encountered had strange architecture, and a strange language. All of us could understand it. The Grand Spell's translation worked perfectly, but we didn't recognize the written language at all.

As we flew over, we saw a lot of horse herds running across a sea of grass. We didn't approach them, as they didn't seem dangerous. Although, I did see a herd of all white horses that rushed ahead faster than I could fly. From the distance it almost looked like they had horns.

It was our eighth day crossing the grassland when we finally encountered something interesting.

I was flying next to Saia when Carlito waved his hands, trying to get my attention. I glanced at him, and he pointed behind him, on the other side of Saia. I frowned, but beat my wings and rolled over them to the other side.

I immediately noticed what he had spotted. Two large birds were flying our way. It was quickly apparent that they were eagles, mutated so that they were almost the same size as Saia's drone.

I prepared for a fight as they came in, but then noticed that they had cloth wrapped around their legs. I frowned, realizing that perhaps the birds weren't just wild. Source mutation didn't turn all animals feral, or even more aggressive.

Some remained as they were in temperament, just physically altered.

The eagles came close, then paused, flying in line with me. I wondered if they were confused by us, a dragon carrying two humans, and a winged vampire. I doubted that they had ever encountered anything like us.

Finally, they turned away and headed back to the grassland. On a hunch, I decided to follow them. I gestured to Saia, then swerved. The eagles glided effortlessly, their keen eyes scanning the vast expanse of grassland below. We followed, keeping a respectful distance as they navigated the rolling hills of green below. After what felt like hours, a cluster of structures emerged from the horizon.

They were unlike anything I had ever seen before—circular dwellings with conical roofs, clustered together like mushrooms. Smoke curled lazily from openings at the top, a sign of life that surprised and excited me in equal measure. As we drew closer, I noticed movement: people, clad in colorful robes, tending to herds of sheep, goats, and strange beasts I didn't quite recognize. Horses grazed peacefully nearby, their coats gleaming in the afternoon sun.

People, survivors, and many of them, dozens that I could see from the air. I felt a surge of curiosity, mixed with a sprinkle of caution. Who were these people? How had they survived the chaos of the Grand Spell's arrival? I hadn't seen a lot of beasts, or even rifts, in this area. Perhaps they had it easier than the rest?

We circled the encampment once, observing from a distance. The people below noticed us, and a commotion started immediately. People mounted horses and drew bows, and a few even hefted rifles. I decided to approach, signaling to Saia to land a short distance away.

As we touched down, a ripple of alarm spread through the camp. Men and women stopped what they were doing, their eyes widening in surprise as they took in the sight of a dragon and a winged vampire—though they couldn't know what I was. The two armed humans were probably the most surprising, if they had thought us beasts coming to attack. Several men kicked their horses and headed our way, keeping their weapons at the ready.

As they drew closer, I could tell that they were of Asian descent, every single one of them, which told me that they had probably shifted from very far away.

They stopped their horses just in front of us.

"We mean no harm," I yelled, then triggered my shift to show them what I was. There were murmurs and exclamations of surprise. Then as I finished and smiled, showing fangs, they whispered the word "vampire." At least they weren't people that were so isolated they'd missed my kind coming out.

A moment of tense silence hung in the air after that. Then, an elderly man, his face weathered and lined, got down from his horse and stepped forward. He wore a long, fur-lined coat and a hat with a pointed crown. His eyes, though narrowed, held a flicker of curiosity.

"Who are you?" he asked, his voice deep and resonant. "And what brings you to our lands?"

"I am Marianna Rojas," I replied, stepping forward. "These are my companions, Carlito and Kai. We are traveling, heading north, searching for other survivors. Like you."

The elderly man nodded slowly. "I am Baatar, elder of this tribe. We are the Tsagaan Shonkhor."

Somehow, I knew the translation of the name. White Falcons. It was like a second voice speaking over the words. The Grand Spell's translation seemed to be more complicated than I thought.

"White Falcons," I said slowly as I tilted my head and glanced at the two eagles standing next to a shack in the distance with people tending to them while looking at us. "But you use eagles?"

The elder sighed, and a few of his people chuckled.

"To my eternal shame," he said with a shake of his head. "Grandfather would've beaten me senseless if he could see me now. But that is a story for another time."

He gave me a long look. "The tribe has played host to the people of the blood in the past, and you are the first people we've seen since the bright light came and the world changed. We would be honored if you would join us in the ger, and share what you may of the world beyond the Steppe."

I raised an eyebrow. I didn't know much about Asian vampire covens, but they at least had some knowledge. That was good, as they didn't seem to be afraid. Truthfully, the horror stories that humans often spoke about vampires were the outliers, the exceptions to the rule. Most vampires integrated into human communities and pulled strings behind the scenes. Making waves and going on murder sprees wasn't a smart idea.

I bowed my head. "We'd be honored."

* * *

We were led to a spacious ger, its interior warm and inviting. Thick rugs covered the earthen floor, and a fire crackled in a central hearth, casting a flickering glow on the woven tapestries that adorned the walls. We were offered bowls of steaming milk tea and plates of dried cheese and mutton. Or rather, Kai and Carlito were.

For me, the elder had offered to bleed a glass of any member of the tribe of my choosing. Apparently, it was tradition. I politely declined, showing them that I had my own. I wasn't quite ready to make a bond with these people, and I couldn't take the blood freely given without them understanding what that meant. Not unless I wanted to incur a debt.

The four of us sat next to the fire, Saia included. I'd had her separate a part of her drone to create a smaller one that could enter the tent while the rest remained outside with our supplies.

The looks on our hosts' faces when she did that was priceless. On the way to the ger, we'd learned that they were nomads, and that this was the Mongolian steppe. Inside the ger became crowded quickly, as many wanted to see and hear about the visitors.

It was obvious that they were hungry for any information about the rest of the world.

Baatar sat across from us, his eyes filled with a mixture of curiosity and apprehension. "Tell me, Marianna Rojas," he said, "your name is familiar to us." He motioned to one of the middle-aged women, who approached with a piece of paper.

I raised an eyebrow, and the woman pushed the paper at Baatar. "We've written down the names that have appeared in the great gray void, in the sky. Is the one written here yours?"

I glanced at the paper as he turned it toward me, and saw the top 100 list. I was surprised that they had the foresight to write it down.

Impressed, I nodded. "Yes, that is me."

He nodded, then gave the paper back before speaking. "Tell me, what has become of the world beyond our steppes? The two moons above us were a sign enough of change, but we would know more."

I took a deep breath, unsure of where to begin. It was difficult to explain the events of the past few months, the chaos, the destruction, the merging of worlds. But I did my best, recounting the arrival of the Grand Spell, the transformation of the Earth, the emergence of rifts and Source mutation of our world, the change of everything that we ever knew. Then I explained what Masks were and how Investment worked.

Baatar listened intently, his expression growing graver with each passing word. When I finished, a heavy silence filled the ger.

"So," he finally said, his voice heavy, "the world we knew is gone."

I nodded. "The Grand Spell has reshaped everything. The world is now a patchwork of different lands."

Baatar sighed. "We have seen the changes in the animals, the strange new creatures that roam the steppes. But we did not know the extent of the upheaval. These Masks, we believed to be the gifts of our ancestors. They've been useful. My grandson, Arban, has been given one called Eagle Tamer. It has helped immensely."

So much change, so much new danger. And they were still here, when many were not. They were exactly the kind of people that I expected to not only survive but thrive.

"We have a town, south of here, perhaps some seven hundred kilometers along the coast. It is safe, or safer, anyway."

There were barely a hundred of them here, and while they'd survived, they were also alone, and in the open.

He looked at me, his eyes filled with a deep sadness. "Thank you for the offer. But we are a simple people, Marianna Rojas. We live in harmony with the land, respecting the spirits and honoring our traditions. We do not understand these grand spells and twisted worlds. But to abandon our land is something that we'd need to discuss at length."

I nodded in understanding. I wouldn't push them, not yet.

"Your hospitality is great, especially now that the world is turned on its head. But we do need to continue our travel north."

"Stay the night and rest," Baatar said. "We'll give your people room for sleep."

I glanced at Kai and Carlito. It was already turning dark outside, and though I was sure that they could handle flying through the night, we weren't in that much of a rush. And establishing relations with these people was important.

I nodded, agreeing.

The elder looked around then motioned for a teenage boy to approach. He whispered instructions for room to be made up for guests, then turned back at me. "We've encountered a handful of these rifts, as you describe them. We've avoided them out of fear. Perhaps we might go and explore one now that we know what they are."

"Some are dangerous, but no more than everything else is now."

Baatar nodded, then exchanged looks with a few of his people, the ones that looked like hunters. "We've seen signs of a large creature at the edges of the Steppe, north, where the strange forest cuts the plane in half," he said with hard look in his eyes.

"We found dead horses, entire herds of them slaughtered. One of our scouts went missing weeks ago. We only found his horse, dead."

Death came easy in this world, especially for humans. "You didn't recognize the creature?"

"No one's seen it, and it doesn't approach the tribe," Baatar answered. "The tracks aren't anything like what we've ever seen. A few bears that don't usually live in the Steppe have made their way from the south, but this is something new."

"A beast from a rift, probably," I said.

"We've been meaning to send another group to try to look for it before it grows bolder and attacks the tribe. We haven't seen it in a few weeks. Still, it weighs on my mind. Perhaps, you could do us this favor and look for it?"

I tilted my head. "You don't know where it is exactly?"

He shook his head. "No. It is elusive, and it ranges far."

I wasn't that keen on looking for a strange creature. For all I knew it was just a cunning predator, not something too dangerous.

"I could go and take a look now," I said. There was still some light out, and I didn't need to sleep like my two companions. That, at least, would give me something to do while they slept.

"You would do that for us?" Baatar asked. He had asked, but I got the sense that he didn't really expect me to accept.

"Sure," I said. "If I don't find anything, we'll have to leave in the morning, but we'll be coming back this way eventually, and we'll probably have more time. Unless your people catch it yourselves."

Baatar inclined his head. I stood and stretched.

"I trust I can leave my people in your care?" I asked with a smile.

"Of course."

I flew out of the tribe and headed back to the coast, then north after I reached it, to where they told me to look for this creature. The wind whipped at my hair as I soared above the steppe, the setting sun painting the vast expanse of grassland in hues of orange and purple. Below, the nomadic village turned into a cluster of miniature gers, their smoke plumes rising above them as if to grasp the sky.

The freedom of flight drew me in. It was so liberating, so natural. This was who I was, who I was always meant to be. Despite everything that happened, I silently thanked my sire for choosing me, for turning me. Our past

was complicated. He had done me wrong, but this . . . I could forgive everything for this. I already did, in my heart, I realized.

I would not have been this free if another vampire had turned me.

I shook my head and turned my attention to the task at hand. I flew faster
along the coast, approaching my top speed and quickly located the area the
nomads spoke about. The Steppe had been shifted around, placed here from
across the world. The forest that was beyond it was a thick jungle, stretching
over hills and mountains.

I pushed west, along the edge of the two connected pieces of land. I
dropped down, just above the trees, and focused my senses, alert for any sign
of the creature. The grasslands of the Steppe cut off abruptly, giving way to a
dense forest, its towering trees a stark contrast to the open expanse behind me.
The air grew cooler, heavy with the scent of pine needles and damp earth.

I encountered animals, herds of horses from the Steppe, other strange creatures that I hadn't seen before but that reminded me of antelopes.

I looked for signs of fresh kills, the scent of blood. What the elder had told
me was that they had found mutilated corpses. A predator didn't generally kill
without a need to eat; they didn't leave food behind.

I saw something that caught my attention: a piece of land that was disturbed, earth gouged up and dried blood across the ground.

I landed and looked around. Whatever had happened, happened a while
ago. Weeks, maybe a month ago even. I wasn't the best tracker around; I relied
more on my senses than my knowledge, though I had been taught the basics.

I took to the air again, then used [Quick Swap Slot—Lesser
Constitution>Sharp Eye], then used the new skill. My eyesight sharpened, and
I saw more details. Tracks that led into the forest. I frowned. They were long
worn, but the tracks were of something that moved on two legs. And something that was heavy, like shifter or vampire heavy. Except that, from the shape
of the tracks, I didn't think they were human footprints.

My mind immediately went to Guo Zhang and his hybrid form. I wondered if this could be a shifter that could do the same? Probably not. The most
likely explanation was that it was something that got loose when a rift broke.

I beat my wings and got in the air again. I flew low, weaving between the
tree trunks, my eyes scanning the forest floor for any disturbance. The tracks
ended once they reached the forest. But, broken branches, trampled undergrowth, the lingering scent of blood—these were the clues I sought, the telltale
signs of a predator's passage.

The first sign I found was a scattering of bones, picked clean and bleached
white by the elements. They were the remains of a horse, its skeletal frame lying

amidst a patch of flattened ferns. The bones were old, the flesh long gone, but the lingering scent of decay remained. Something had fed here.

Further on, I discovered a trail of disturbed earth, as if something heavy had been dragged through the undergrowth. The trail led deeper into the forest, winding through a maze of tangled vines and gnarled roots.

The trail ended abruptly at the edge of a clearing. A sense of dread washed over me as I took in the scene before me. The clearing was a charnel house filled with savagery. Carcasses, both animal and human, lay scattered across the blood-soaked ground. Limbs were twisted at unnatural angles, flesh torn and mangled, bones shattered. The air was thick with the stench of death, a miasma that clung to the air and the Way itself. Symbols were carved into the ground, circular lines drawn with blood and bones stabbed into the lines at set intervals.

I landed softly on the edge of the clearing, then took in a small breath. The scent of death was old, as were the bodies, the blood. This happened more than a week ago, yet, the bodies were still here, untouched, uneaten, just decaying.

No animal had approached this. I understood. Even I wanted to run away.

I cautiously approached the nearest carcass, a horse, its flesh ripped open and its entrails spilling onto the ground. The wounds were deep, the cuts precise, as if made by the claws of incredible sharpness. There was no sign of struggle, no indication that the horse had even had a chance to defend itself.

I moved from carcass to carcass, examining the wounds, searching for any clue to the creature's identity. The kills were all similar, swift and brutal, with a focus on vital organs and major arteries. The kills were obviously not for food. Something intelligent had done this. The question was whether it was something like the kobolds in the rifts or something more.

In the center of the clearing was a large oak tree, its gnarled branches reaching toward the sky like skeletal fingers. Its surface was weathered, and the bark covered in a sheen of red substance that was familiar to me.

The base of the tree was surrounded by a ring of bones, like an offering that made me shiver. A fear that I had only experienced a couple of times before returned.

"Saia, are you detecting anything?"

"Feedback: Yes," my shirt vibrated, creating sound. "The Source-Weave in this clearing matches our encounters with the blighted beasts."

It was as I feared. This . . . ritual, or whatever it was, reminded me of what I saw in the memories of Valair Ankah, the blighted monsters and demons that had attacked one of the Vim's worlds. I didn't know what happened here, but it was not good, not good at all.

The worst part was that this happened a while ago. Whatever did it was gone. The nomads hadn't seen it in weeks. It could be God knows where by now.

I didn't want to linger any longer than necessary. It felt wrong. I took to the sky, circling the clearing one last time. There was no sign of the creature, no indication of where it had gone.

Had it been hunting people and animals for this ritual? And what was even the purpose of it? I didn't know, but for now I had to return. The night had settled in fully, the two moons shining down brightly.

I flew back toward the nomadic encampment, my mind racing with questions. I wished that I had the time to hunt it down. I knew the danger that the blight posed. But there was just so much more that I had to do. And seeing this just made me more worried about Aurora and the rest.

We weren't supposed to be dealing with the blight, with monsters. I remembered the two creatures that I fought in the pass when we were fleeing from the church. One of them was in the early stages of turning into a monster. I didn't know how then, and I didn't know how this happened here now.

I had to accelerate my plans.

Decisions That Last

I returned to the tribe and landed without anyone noticing me. It turned out that having dark blue skin and black wings made you hard to see at night.

I found my companion and a few of the tribespeople outside one of the gers.

The fire crackled merrily, casting a warm glow over the ger outer walls. Baatar, the elder of the Tsagaan Shonkhor, stroked his beard thoughtfully, his gaze flickering between his tribesmen and the two guests who sat cross-legged across from him.

Saia lounged nearby with several children running around her and climbing her neck. Watchful adults stood nearby, watching fearfully. I smiled, and shook my head.

I settled in the shadow, and listened in on their conversation, interested to hear what they were talking about without me.

"I'm glad that you survived that," Baatar said after Carlito finished speaking of something that I'd missed.

"It was crazy, old man," Carlito boasted. "Everyone tried to get out of the city, shooting everywhere, cars blocking the roads. Madness."

I gathered that he was explaining what happened in the aftermath of the Grand Spell arriving, and his escape from the city.

Then, the *old man* shook his head. "You say the world has been . . . rearranged?"

Carlito leaned back with a nonchalant air, then grinned. "Rearranged? That's one way to put it, old timer. More like tossed in a blender, hit with a fucking hurricane, and spit out the other side. Do you know that our former camp used to be in the middle of a desert? A military camp from the Middle East we think"—he nodded toward Kai—"dropped straight in the middle of

Colombia. And after what I've seen flying here, geography's taken a permanent vacation, if you ask me."

Kai, ever stoic, simply adjusted her braid. "Indeed. There are many areas that had been moved around. Such as this land here, though this piece of the Steppe appears to be larger than most that we've encountered so far."

A ripple of murmurs and confused glances passed among the assembled nomads. A young woman with inquisitive eyes voiced that collective bewilderment. "But . . . how can this be? It is mad!"

Carlito let out a bark of laughter. "Honey, God is probably having a good laugh at all this mess, we're all just along for the ride."

The elder put a hand on the young woman's shoulder. "Peace, Selenge, change always comes. We must find the wisdom that is new to be learned in this world."

"Hey," Carlito drawled, leaning forward conspiratorially. "At least you don't have to worry about any governments and nations. Everything kinda went poof in the night. You're really free now. Assuming you can survive."

A stunned silence fell over the people. I realized that they hadn't really had the chance to comprehend the new reality, the fact that all structure and order, that even their traditional way of life, all of it was gone. They had to adapt, or they would die like the rest.

"Survival of the fittest," Carlito added. "That's why you should join up with us. No one's more fit than our boss lady. I watched her tear beasts twice the size of a bear in half with just her hands. We are back to the old rules. Need to attach yourself to the biggest and baddest warlord around and hope that all others piss themselves and leave you alone."

Baatar straightened his back and looked at his tribesmen. "We shall speak on this topic, but the Steppe is all we know."

Carlito raised his arms. "Fine, fine. It's your decision anyway. I just wanted you to know that boss lady keeps her promises, and protects those that follow her."

I started getting slightly uncomfortable with listening in, so I decided to interrupt them. I beat my wings and pretended to have just landed, then walked out of the shadow and into the light of the fire.

I heard exclamations from those who didn't have the chance to see me clearly before. I shifted back, pulling my wings in, which got a lot more people going.

"I found something," I said, looking at the elder. "Can we talk in private?"

* * *

"That is . . . concerning," Baatar said, then met my eye. "You say that you think this, thing, has left?"

"I suspect it. I cannot be certain. I didn't do a thorough enough of a search for it."

"Thank you for looking at all. And for telling me this."

"What do you plan to do?"

"For now? Nothing. I'll send a few more scouts north to make sure that it isn't anywhere near. But as you've just said, there isn't much we could do. Besides, we aren't helpless. We've hunted these mutated animals for months; we've done well for ourselves."

They had, but a monster was different. I opened my mouth, then closed it. Anything that I said could be seen as diminishing their achievements, looking down on them. I didn't want that. They were capable, and I wanted them for my group. Perhaps they could deal with even a monster. People on Kirios did all the time, and I had forewarned them. They might lose people, but that was their choice.

"Perhaps you'd entertain the idea of moving more south? Closer to the southern edge of the Steppe, and the coast maybe? If you place some visible markers on the coast, you'll be easier to find, and I can have my people send boats to you. Trade maybe?"

"That is reasonable," Baatar said. "I'll speak with the rest of the tribe."

I nodded. It was the most I could do for now. I didn't want to just come in and force them to follow. I'd done it with the camp because I felt like I could do better than them. Because they had already failed. Without me, they would've been dead.

These people had survived without me. They deserved consideration. I felt like my Heart of Azure and Scarlet resonated with that decision. People were not made equal. I shouldn't treat them as such. Humans often spoke about equality, but the truth was different. I could offer the base minimal respect to everyone, but actions changed that balance, changed worth.

I excused myself and left the ger. It was getting late, and most of the tribe was asleep. I was given a place next to the fire, as I didn't need to sleep.

Saia sat near me, and I glanced at her.

"Any thoughts?" I asked in a whisper.

"Feedback: No."

"Really?"

"Feedback: Really."

"C'mon, you don't have any input?"

"Feedback: I'm designed to serve as the support for my Host. I'm here to help you do the things you want to do, not influence what you do."

"You're no fun." I showed her my tongue, which she ignored, and stood up. I walked around the tribe. The few people on watch gave me nods as I passed them by, but didn't interfere.

I walked a bit outside of the gathering of gers, to the pens where they kept their livestock. The animals were all huddled together in the center, goats and the strange cowlike animals—that I just realized could be yaks—were all gathered around the sheep, sleeping against them.

I frowned, the arrangement feeling odd to me.

"It's for the heat," a voice said from the side. I'd, of course, noticed the human approaching.

I glanced at the man holding a tall stick, a herder probably. He had a cap on his head, and wore thick furs. His eyes held a mirth to them that warmed me up to him instantly.

"Heat?" I asked.

"The sheep wool changed. It gives off heat now. Not as warm as a fire, but warm. The other animals gather around them at night for heat."

I blinked, then turned to look at the animals. Now that he mentioned it, I caught that the sheep wool was actually reddish in color and not black as I had assumed. In my defense, it was dark.

I turned back to the man and spoke. "Marianna."

"Temujin," he introduced himself.

I blinked, then narrowed my eyes. The name was familiar.

He chuckled. "Temujin was Genghis Khan's given name."

"Ah." I nodded in understanding, remembering.

"A heavy name?" I asked.

He shrugged. "Not any more than any other. It was a long time ago."

"True," I said.

"Did you know him?" he asked, and I turned to look at him with a raised eyebrow.

"Why do you ask?" I wasn't sure how to deal with people assuming that I was much older than I looked. Especially now that I'd fully matured where many of my fellow vampires had not.

"There is a story, of a woman vampire arriving at the court of Kublai Khan. She owed a debt to his grandfather, Genghis. It is said that she advised Kublai for his entire life, and even turned his son, Jingim, into a vampire. Kublai was so touched and honored that one of his line would live forever, that he then made the oath of service to the old vampire and her line. She didn't want to rule, and left the empire, but Kublai never forgot her gift. He was so grateful for her gift, so he ensured that all knew his decree, and that should Azzaya the Wise or any of her line ever return, they would have the support of the empire."

I blinked. "Huh, sorry, but that wasn't me."

"Shame," he said. "Some stories mention wings, and eyes of jade, like yours."

I looked back at the animals, thinking. It was possible that it was someone from my bloodline—the Sea. And my sire did mention that there were a few ancients like him still in Asia.

"Well, I'm glad that you didn't bring out the torches and pitchforks when you saw me," I said with a smile.

Temujin snorted. "No true Mongol ever would. Not even we who are so removed from our ancestors. Stories of vampire kind were never as horror filled and terrible as those in the west. To us, vampires were always like Azzaya the Wise, ancients that offered counsel and aid when needed. It is why we offered you our blood. It is the custom in the tribes. Vampires passing through often stopped by the tribes. At least they did in the past, before they came out and hiding became unnecessary."

That surprised me. I had grown up in the part of the world where vampires were the bogeymen, devils who turned away from God. I guess that world really was a big place.

"Do you know Azzaya?" Temujin asked as the silence stretched.

"I've never heard of a vampire with that name, but we change names often, as time passes. And . . . I'm not that old." I smiled at him.

He shook his head. "Sorry," he said. "I've just grown up on the stories of Jingim and Azzaya. It is said that Jingim still lives in China, leading the biggest coven in the world. It . . . those stories were my favorite growing up."

"No need to apologize. I understand what stories can mean to us."

He returned my smile, then bowed and left me alone.

I turned my eyes to the sky, the two moons above me. The white broken one, and the red whole. Azure and Scarlet.

I toyed with a ring on my finger, the Ring of Bloodcast. I had yet to put a skill in it, permanently at least. I used one of my shelved ones to test it out. It was powerful. It removed the cooldown from the skill in return for me paying the price in blood. It weakened me with prolonged use, but as a vampire, I regenerated. If I was actively feeding, I could use it for a while.

I'd been thinking about something for a while. My Evolve Skill trait and how it would work with my given skills, not the taken ones. What would happen to a skill that I got from a Mask if I evolved it with my other skills? Would

I lose the ability to use it without slotting it in my profiles? Or would it remain a skill that was always available to me?

I had this idea, to improve my [Blood Empowerment] skill. As it was, it made me stronger, faster, but I had a lot of skills that improved my physical condition that I could merge with it.

The issue was that such a decision was a lasting one. My other skills almost didn't matter. They were borrowed power, and I could always get more. My given skills were different.

I had so little time these days to experiment.

The moons were still high in the sky. I had the entire night to rest and play around. I returned back to Saia, next to the fire, and sat down against her side. Then I entered my soul space. It was time to farm some skills, and experiment again.

I went on a door binge, harvesting skills from beasts and humans and Suul. Like before, I didn't get many strong skills. They were too low Investment for any of them to have anything interesting. There were only two doors left in my Hallway of Doors that could hold anything truly powerful. The first was the door leading to the reaper, the beast from Ish Vimza that ambushed Shadow and me, and nearly killed him, leaving him injured.

He had said that it was in its Sixth Investment, and the fact that it ambushed us worried me. It meant that it would be hidden in the room when I entered. The situation was replicated. So it would have the chance to ambush me. I didn't think I was as strong as Shadow yet, and he missed it.

I didn't want to risk the beast managing to surprise me. The second door was that of the sikiri. It had been blighted when we fought it, driven mad by it. That had allowed us the chance to ambush it and kill it. Shadow had told me that the blight left on death, so the blood I drank was clean. But I didn't know how a normal sikiri would act, or if I could match up to it.

I knew that I could injure it, especially now with my current strength. But Shadow had done a lot in that fight. I pulled away from those two doors, not wanting to take the risk. Not yet. Perhaps once I reached my Fourth Investment I would feel more comfortable.

I walked into the central hub and stepped up to the pedestal holding my [Blood Empowerment] skill. It was an icon, not a glowing orb, like my other given skills. The skill was represented by a blood-red sculpture of myself, not terribly detailed, but enough that I could recognize myself. I picked it up, then carried it over to my Evolve Skill trait.

I placed it in the golden bowl, then went to gather the other skills. I didn't place any gemstones in them, as I didn't know how that would affect the evolution. The only one that had a gemstone was [Blood Empowerment] with a D-grade primal stone. It seemed to be boosting my physical strength somewhat, so I hoped that it wouldn't mess things up. I would've put the same in all other skills, but I just didn't have enough D-grade stones of the same affinity for it.

The first ones that I gathered were my older ones: [Lesser Stamina Recovery], [Lesser Constitution], and [Lesser Night Sight]. I hoped that they would synergize well. [Blood Empowerment] was a full body enhancement skill, so they should all work well together.

Next, I put in three of my stronger skills: [Harden Self], [Sharp Eye], and [Stone Skin]. None of them was a passive skill, but neither was [Blood Empowerment].

That left me with room for three of my newly gained skills. I'd gotten [Lesser Strength] again, this one the Suul version, then I got [Lesser Heat Resistance]—which I was very much glad for—and [Lesser Toughness].

A few of them seemed to overlap, but that shouldn't be a problem.

I put the skills in, and watched as the skills collapsed into the center. A new skill was born, another blood-red statue, but this time it had lines of different colors spreading through it.

I picked it up, and carried it over to its pedestal, then placed it down and read the new plaque.

[My Blood, Surge For Power]

Your blood surges through your body, empowering all your physical attributes for a short period.

The new skill seemed to be an upgrade, so, a success. It seemed to be similar to [Blood Empowerment], so I'd have to test it out. What I wanted to try was to see how it would work with my Bloodcast ring.

I left the soul space and stood, then left the tribe with a few words to Saia. Once I was all alone in the dark, I triggered the skill.

Immediately, I felt stronger, faster, better. My skin was covered in lines as my veins darkened, my hearing expanded, my eyesight sharpened, my smell broadened, and even the touch of air on my skin felt deeper.

I rolled my shoulders and started running, feeling my blood surging through my body and empowering me. The effect didn't last long. I felt it leave me and stumbled, then came to a stop.

The effect was barely twenty seconds long. That wasn't a short period, not for my fights that didn't last that long. But now I could see the more important part, how long the cooldown was. I started back, walking slowly. Minutes went by without it coming back, which meant that it was probably a longer cooldown.

I settled in to wait, leaning against Saia again.

"How many more people do you think survived, like they did?" I gestured at the gers around us as I whispered my question.

Saia's answer came from my shirt, with a low vibration that only I could pick up. "Feedback: Based on what we've seen so far, not many. All the major cities were overrun, the smaller ones abandoned. The projections are not good."

I grimaced. "Shadow had said that we would be reduced greatly, now and in the coming years. I feel . . . feel like it is worse for us, because of the rifts. They didn't have them. I wonder if the Grand Spell did it on purpose like that. Because our population was so much greater than that of other worlds when they were brought over."

"Feedback: Possible," Saia said. "But, such adversity is also a chance to grow. You've seen how fast people could advance their Masks."

"I have." I nodded. "It's just so sad, I guess. So many people died, and so many will die."

"Statement: It is reality. You can't change it."

"I could save more. If I march up to Baatar's ger, tell him that I'm now in charge and instruct him to move his people south, what do you think will happen? He can't really say no. No one can. That's the power I wield now."

"Statement: Power is many things. The Ke Erzi didn't have singular leaders. Each and every one of them had a voice, one that mattered. Loyalty wasn't given to people, but to causes. That is what separated them. They chose which causes to follow, curing disease, building weapons, conquering nature. Some causes were in conflict, and had to be resolved either through diplomacy or violence. But ultimately, no single Ke Erzi had the power to command others. I do not know how to navigate your mad systems of governance."

"Thank you so much," I said sarcastically.

"Statement: No problem."

I rolled my eyes. Yeah, I could command them, and I wanted to. I needed them. But . . . I also wanted for them to follow me because they wanted to.

When I came out of the challenge, I had imagined just going around and conquering, but now I realized that it was more than that. I wanted what I got from the other survivors, the faith they had in me. The looks in their eyes that said that they were grateful, that they wanted to follow me.

I knew that I was going to get it from these people too. I felt it in my bones. I only needed an opportunity to show them that I was worthy of it.

I rested for a while, pushing all errant thoughts out of my mind.

The cooldown for my new skill was twenty minutes long. Too much for me. I focused and placed it in my ring, linking the skill with it.

There, I thought to myself. *Now let's see how this works.*

Search

We left the nomads in the morning, Kai and Carlito flying on Saia's back and I with my own wings. We waved as we made our way back to the coast, then continued north.

I was worried that my sire was wrong, that the States weren't where he said they were. Or that big chunks of it were moved elsewhere.

I'd already taken too long to come looking for Aurora. It'd been just over a week since the second challenge, which had come a month after the first. And we still hadn't even found what used to be North America.

Despite that, I didn't rush us. I chose to trust that Aurora could handle herself, and looking for more survivors was important.

We didn't find any. We encountered rifts, though, which we cleared, allowing both Kai and Carlito to hit their Second Investment. I only got a single Carving, and without a skill.

It was two days after we left the nomads that we finally reached the States. I knew it because we found a coastal town with signs that hadn't corroded fully, and they told us that we were in Texas.

It was barely hours later, as we flew over the coastline, that Saia interfered.

"Input: We cannot continue further." The part of her that was my shirt said as her drone swerved and headed for the ground.

I followed.

"What is it?" I asked as soon as we landed.

"Feedback: The area ahead of us contains a significant amount of radiation."

I blinked, not expecting that answer. "Uh, radiation?"

"Feedback: That is what I said. I do not believe that my drone will be able to survive in such an area for long. I do not know how resistant human or vampire physiology is to such effects."

"Yeah," Carlito spoke up. "We ain't surviving that."

"Someone fired nukes," Kai added.

I grimaced, then my eyes widened. "Wait, is here safe?"

"Feedback: Of course. The zone is ahead of us."

"I mean, radiation is carried by the wind; it spreads. Is it going to reach here, head south to our town? How much of it is there?"

Saia's drone tilted her head. "Feedback: That is incorrect. Radiation doesn't spread in that manner. It bonds to the Source-Weave itself."

My brow furrowed. "What? That . . . that wasn't how it used to work."

"Feedback: I don't know how it worked in your Source-Weave-less world before, but from what I've detected and observed it is behaving in the same manner it would on Erzi. The radiation will corrupt the Source-Weave, destroying anything in its area of influence and creating a dead zone."

"What is a dead zone?" Kai asked.

"Feedback: A zone where Source-Weave cannot exist, where all engram constructs fall apart."

"So, a zone without magic?" Carlito asked. "Like what we had before?"

"Feedback: It will eventually become safe for living beings to enter, but in its current stage, the zone is highly volatile toward biological matter."

"We need to go around then," I said.

"Statement: It would be more prudent to do so."

"Well, let's head out then. I don't want to waste too much time. We'll head inland, look for survivors."

Kai and Carlito got on Saia's back again, and then we were back in the air, Saia leading the way as we tried to move around the radiation zone.

The more we flew, the more I realized that the radiation zone was massive. Like almost the size of the entire state of Texas. I couldn't imagine what happened to make people do that. I knew that in the opening days of the Grand Spell's arrival there wasn't a complete breakdown of all technology. It took weeks for that to happen.

But for them to do something like this . . .

I could see the death in the zone, from the few times I flew closer to try to see. Plants were withered and dead as far as eyes could see. I didn't want to risk entering the zone. I didn't know how radiation would affect me.

I didn't remember ever reading about the effects of it on vampires. For all I knew, it would kill me just as fast as it would a human. From what Saia told me, it was bad, like lethal dose in minutes type of bad.

I wasn't going anywhere near it.

It took us almost four days to reach Oklahoma in the north, or northwest actually, as the States appeared to be slightly tilted. The zone extended all along the southern parts of the next state, so we flew away from it, looking for cities and towns where there could be survivors. We found only abandoned cars on the highways with dead bodies littered everywhere. Some decomposing, others eaten clean. Oklahoma City was a ruin, shelled and bombed into a crater, but at least no one had dropped a nuke on it.

There were no survivors. Or if there were, they were hiding in the wilderness, and we didn't stay to look. I was hoping to find clear signs of life, like smoke and fires. I saw none, not even at night.

A massive horde of beasts was trampling down Route 40, which we flew above, following the road. Wolves, rats, even mutated deer, all charging as if they were part of the same herd or pack. It was strange to see predator and prey together like that, and I wondered what made animals act that way.

Two days later we were flying over Arkansas. This was where we found the first signs of army presence. An open field was littered with broken-down tanks, artillery, and corpses. The worst thing about it was that I was pretty sure there were two sides, and that they fought each other. We didn't stay for long.

Later that same day, I saw smoke in the distance for the first time since we left the nomads. I flew on ahead, hoping to find survivors.

I was too late. A large camp in the forest was destroyed, burned down to ashes. I saw remnants of tents and simple wooden buildings. I saw corpses, half eaten. Something had gone through the camp and killed them all.

It was recent too, days at most. I closed my eyes, then pushed away the guilt I felt at not getting her quicker. It wasn't my fault, and scenes like these had to be happening everywhere.

We continued on. It took us another three days to reach Alabama. There we headed back to the coast. Aurora had explained to me how to reach her town from the coast, gave me the numbers for the roads. From what I'd seen, aluminum seemed to be holding up better than most other metals. It was corroding, but it looked more like moderate rusting than completely collapsing into dust. Thankfully, the U.S. used it for most of their signs.

On the coast, we found another abandoned town, though this one's story looked to be different. The city of Mobile looked like a war zone. Craters, toppled buildings, and the dead. Piles of beasts were still rotting in places, thousands of them, with even some piles that had been burned a while ago. Dead humans too, some in half eaten states. Carrion birds were everywhere, feeding and nesting in the town. They didn't seem that interested in us as we flew over, but I saw one that looked vulturelike that had grown at least a hundred times its size. It looked more like a passenger plane than a bird.

It was lying in a large square, a massive nest beneath it.

We hurried away. I could feel its Investment from a distance. It was at least Fourth Investment. It was the first Earth animal that I had seen that had reached that far. I wondered what had happened for it to grow that much.

We followed Aurora's instructions, and reached Monroeville a few hours after. It was abandoned, as Aurora had told me it had been. I didn't see many signs of struggle, though there were some. Broken-down cars, a few corpses on the outskirts, but not the type of violence that I saw in other larger cities. I hoped that the people managed to get out, but what I saw on the way here had made my hopes dwindle.

According to Aurora, she was holing up in a shop across the street from the town's Old Courthouse Museum, a building that I easily identified from the air based on her description. The white clock tower stood out against the other buildings.

We landed in the street. Nature had reclaimed much of it. Trees had grown larger; bushes and grass had spread onto the road. But there was still a path open. The Lemon Lollie Boutique shop was clearly visible.

"That it?" Carlito asked as they dismounted.

I nodded. "It is."

I was relieved; we found it. I walked over and pushed the door open.

"Aurora?" I called. I heard no one inside, no heartbeat or anyone breathing. I took in a deep breath and smelled nothing fresh. Something had spoiled in one corner, and I walked over to find some food. That worried me. If she was here, then that would've been cleaned up. At least I hoped it would. Aurora didn't strike me as a slob.

I walked through the shop, focusing on my senses. There were faint whiffs of Aurora's scent, but it was old. Days old. She was here recently, but she hadn't been here within the last few days.

I walked back over to Kai and Carlito, who waited next to Saia outside.

"She's not here?" Kai asked.

"She was, recently. But not now."

"Could she have moved somewhere else in town?" Carlito asked. "I mean, if I had all the real estate in the world, I probably would've picked something better than a clothes shop. Just saying."

I frowned. It wasn't out of the question.

"Pick a direction and go searching, together." I gave them a long look. "I'll circle the town from the air, Saia too. Scream if you see something or you're in danger. I'll hear."

I didn't give them a chance to respond before I took off and started flying around, looking for anything out of the ordinary.

There were living things in the town, now that I looked closer. Birds flying or nesting in the trees, squirrels, mice, and rats. But not in any large numbers, or too mutated. Some of the birds had strangely colored feathers, and some of the mice were a bit faster than I expected them to be, but nothing too dangerous.

Finally, I noticed something strange, and landed. On the northern side of the town, I came upon a stretch of the road that was . . . disturbed. There were stone spikes sticking out of the asphalt, a wall of stone was raised on the side of the street, and there was a crack along a bunched section of the earth. Aurora had fought here.

I took in a breath and detected a faint scent that was familiar to me. I knelt down, then smashed my fist into the ground, ripping through the concrete. The ground shook, and the crack widened.

"Saia, could you give me something to dig with?"

My shirt flowed from my body and turned into a small shovel. I started to dig.

It didn't take me long to find what I'd detected. There was a decomposing corpse, buried. By the look of it, it couldn't have been there for more than a month.

The man was armed with a sword, and he had died by being crushed beneath the earth. Someone had attacked Aurora.

I narrowed my eyes, then took to the air, continuing my search. At the edge of town, I found another place where there was a battle. Earth was disturbed, and spikes made out of stone. Here, I found dried blood, but no bodies. I got low to the ground and sniffed, parsing the scents.

One of the blood splatters smelled familiar—it smelled like earth and stone, like Aurora. Anger rushed over me, and I let it push me forward. I started to look closer, searching for any signs that could point me in the right direction.

Trampled grass pointed the way, until I came upon a small clearing just outside of the town. There used to be a campsite here, the wood that was burned had turned to ash. Someone was here a week ago at most.

There was a big set of tracks, two of them, something rolling over the ground, a wagon perhaps, leading away from here. Footprints were everywhere.

I flew into the air, and almost headed after them, but then I remembered my companions. I turned back and found them in the city, then explained what happened.

"We going after them?" Carlito asked, looking excited.

"*I'm* going, I'm faster on my own," I added.

"Aw, man." Carlito deflated.

"I'm sure you'll have the chance to stab something soon enough. For now, I need you to stay here in case I'm wrong and Aurora comes back. Head to that boutique and wait with Saia."

"We will," Kai said. "What are you going to do if she's not . . . alive anymore?"

I paused. I didn't think that Aurora was dead. I would've found a body, or more blood. These were humans, and they were . . . assholes. If they came after her, there was some stupid reason for it. Perhaps I was wrong, and they didn't take her. Maybe she went with them. Maybe there were more groups of humans. I didn't know. So I wasn't going to rush in blindly. But if she was dead . . .

"I'll spill blood," I answered. "But . . . let me get ready for this, actually."

I entered one of the shops on the street and quickly found what I was looking for, a pair of dark sunglasses and a mask to cover my face.

"You going incognito, boss?" Carlito asked.

I nodded. "Don't want to spook people immediately," I said as I looked at Saia and the gear she was carrying. I decided against taking my weapon. It was too big for me to fly fast while carrying it.

"Can you form me a jacket or something?" I asked Saia. "Add some extra mass so that you can shift into a weapon for me?"

A small piece of her drone broke off and flowed over me, creating a tight half-jacket that accommodated my wings. I also kept my revolver and the dagger that Shadow gifted me.

With everything ready, I waved at my companions and took to the air, heading back toward the camp in the forest. Then I started following the tracks from the air.

They headed north, following the roads mostly, only getting off them in areas where they had been completely taken over by nature. The mutation of plant life wasn't equal everywhere. From what I could see, it was a lot tamer this far north. The more tropical forests of my home had become even wilder, swallowing up roads almost completely.

Here, in the U.S., one could still see and somewhat use the roads. There were cracks and breaks as a tree's roots suddenly burst through the asphalt, but not as much as it happened down south.

I flew slower so that I could keep my eyes on the tracks, but eventually I saw a change in terrain. Large mountains rose from the ground, and the eco-system changed. I'd reached another area that had been switched around. There was no more road, and the tracks led into the forest, but I could see the likely destination in the distance.

I rose higher in the air, so high that I would be just a tiny dot for anyone looking, easily mistaken for a bird. I flew forward, and over a small town on the coast of a lake in the foothills of the mountains. I didn't see much destruction in the town, and there was movement below. From this high up, I struggled to tell if it was animals or people, but I leaned toward people.

I triggered [My Blood, Surge For Power] and felt my senses sharpen, letting me see better. There were definitely people, and I saw around a dozen wagon-looking things moving through the streets of the town with tiny dots around them.

This was a group of survivors, a lot of them by the look of it. This was going to be a bit harder than I thought. I couldn't search for Aurora from the air. If she was here she was probably somewhere inside. True, she could be fine. She could've just decided to move here with other survivors. I didn't know.

The best course of action would be to just approach the people and ask. The only evidence I had of foul play was a scuffle back at Monroeville and some blood. This was a dangerous world; that could've happened for a myriad of reasons.

Choices, choices.

I turned around and flew back to my companions.

Infiltration

I returned to the town with Kai, Carlito, and Saia in tow. By the time we reached the foothills, the sun was already sinking below the horizon, painting the sky in hues of blood orange. A chilly wind whipped through the trees, carrying with it the scent of pine needles.

"You remember the plan?" I asked, my voice barely a whisper.

Kai nodded gravely. "Yes, approach, tell the truth, find out more information."

Not the whole truth, of course. They would say that they were from far south, from Colombia, and that they were sent north to search for other survivors. Make contact and share information, assess the situation. From there they would see what these people would do.

"Saia." I turned to her drone, its metallic form gleaming faintly in the twilight. "You keep yourself out of sight in the forest. Come if I call . . . or if you think I'll need you." Obviously, she could hear me anywhere, since her core was within me.

With that, we separated. Kai and Carlito shouldered their packs, supplies, and weapons. They had to make their trip believable.

The two headed into town, in the direction of the group I'd seen with a wagon. From what I assumed, they were gathering supplies, and most of the groups were then returning to a large rock rising above the lake, where a large imposing castle stood on top.

As the two gained some distance, I followed along, keeping out of sight. The darkening sky was my ally, helping mask my presence. Quickly, as I reached the town, I could see signs and writing that told me where this piece of Earth came from.

The town was called Bled, in Slovenia. Or at least it used to be. Which would make the mountains around us the Alps. A fragment of Europe then.

I moved through the backstreets, giving Kai and Carlito space and time to make contact while I explored and got a feel for the situation.

There was death in the town, broken-down cars, buildings being taken over by plant life, and blood in the streets. The city appeared to be a resort town, which made sense with its location, the lake, and the castle, named Bled Castle from what I read on the signs.

I encountered a group of humans with a wagon that had wooden wheels plated with metal—which surprised me, as it didn't seem corroded at all—drawn by what I could only describe as a demon horse, with two horns on its head like those of a ram, red eyes, and wicked teeth in its mouth. The group had around a dozen people, all armed, and they were going through the buildings, taking supplies, looting. Blankets, clothes, and some small furniture, from what I could see.

They bantered softly, but not about anything really important.

I left them behind, and hurried to catch up to the others. As I got closer to the roads leading up to the castle, I saw that the roads were barricaded with broken-down cars, and furniture, as if someone was trying to make a wall. I found Kai and Carlito in front of one such blockade that seemed to be a kind of checkpoint. I hid on a roof, crawling along the tiles and peering over the edge. A dozen people were standing near them, clearly alert as one of them talked with my people.

". . . long way from here," the man, a tall, dark-haired human, said.

"Not that long," Carlito said. "Mexico and Panama are gone. We had to cross a large Mongolian steppe to get here, but honestly, it was relatively safe. A lot safer than where we came from."

"Really? We haven't sent anyone that far south," the man said.

"Yup, even met another group of survivors, nomads." Carlito grinned at the man, trying to appear relaxed.

"You said that your group made camp in Monroeville, south of here?"

"Yeah, we're forward scouts. The rest is waiting back there. We found some signs of people living there recently, so we figured that they might've moved someplace else. So we headed this way, and here we are!"

"Oh, I heard that there was a crazy woman living there, all alone," the guard said, and my blood ran cold.

"Oh?"

"Yeah, she attacked our scouts." The man shook his head. "Even killed one of ours. It was a whole mess. Poor thing. Not everyone could handle the entire world falling apart."

"What happened to her?" Carlito asked.

"We sent a larger group to capture her. We take murder very seriously, and the count wanted to talk with her. Rumor is she has a unique Mask, and we're trying to figure out how all of that works. She'll probably be put to work somewhere until she serves out her sentence."

The man shook his head, then continued before Carlito could ask any more questions. "We need to get you up to the castle. The count will want to talk with you."

"Count? Like a noble or something?" Carlito asked.

The man inclined his head. "Yes, we're part of the Sun Kingdom. You'll see."

"Huh, don't hear that every day." Carlito looked around at the others. Now that I paid closer attention, all of them had the same motif on their clothes: a yellow sun, stitched somewhere on their ragged clothing.

"Come, we'll take you to him."

"Sure, though we can't stay for long. Our people are waiting for us."

"Of course, we'll want to talk with them too."

With that, the group split, and they started walking toward the castle. I followed. Knowing that Aurora was captured and probably imprisoned changed things. I was willing to do a lot more now.

I kept my distance, and their voices were too low for me to hear what they were talking about. I focused instead on the rest of my senses.

The castle loomed larger with every step, its stone walls rising impossibly high against the darkening sky. Torches along the road cast long, dancing shadows that allowed me to follow without being seen. There were a lot of people patrolling, most armed with swords or spears, but a few with hunting rifles. As we got to the base of the rock holding the castle, I saw large tents raised along the road and in the forest. People moved around, talking, laughing, preparing dinner from the look of it. I walked on the other side, away from them, and closer to the lake.

I kept to the shadows as they approached the castle, moving with a predator's grace. I noticed more and more commotion up in the castle. My enhanced senses were a symphony of information: the crunch of gravel underfoot, the distant murmur of voices, the rhythmic clang of a hammer against metal. I saw guards patrolling the ramparts, their silhouettes stark against the fading light. I smelled the fear and anticipation clinging to Kai and Carlito as they were led through a parking lot filled with broken-down cars and past a small campfire in the middle where a group of guards sat, and then up through a gate that led up into the castle.

I could hear a lot of people up there. Hundreds, it sounded like.

That was where I had to stop. I couldn't follow through the same way. So

I went right. Thankfully, the forest surrounded the castle. I went around the rock, then found a good spot to climb on the other side of it. I debated flying up, but didn't want anyone to notice, nor did I want to reveal that form to these people. The nomads were a carelessness on my part, which didn't turn out too bad. But these people could be foes in the future.

I climbed up the rock, my claws finding holds with ease. When I got up to the wall, I peeked over to see a large courtyard stretching in front of me. People were gathered to the side sitting on benches where dozens of tables were covered in food.

Most people seemed busy with dinner, but there were guards. I climbed higher, along the building wall and then on top to the roof. I could hear Carlito's voice, speaking somewhere deeper, and I followed it to a central building and an open window. I leaned down and listened.

"Indeed," Kai said, probably answering some question. "We have witnessed much death, much destruction."

"The same as everywhere, sadly," a soft voice said. Immediately, I frowned. I heard only three heartbeats inside—Kai, Carlito, the leader that escorted them probably, but this voice didn't match. The scent of blood hit me, then the sound of someone drinking.

No heartbeat, no sound of lungs breathing. The count was a vampire. That . . . changed things.

Once the vampire was finished drinking, he continued speaking. "Marko said you come from the south, from Colombia, yes? You have a large group of survivors?"

"We do, yes," Kai answered.

"That is great. We've heard stories from the south, from some travelers." He paused, and I heard the rustling of clothes, but was unable to see what was happening inside. Then, he continued. "That you've come all this way, must mean that you have a solid foundation, yes? A large organized group?"

"Yes," Kai answered. I'd instructed her to keep to the truth. It was easier, and it wasn't like they had much to hide. "We have a town, and we've been expanding, looking for survivors. Much like you here."

"Of course! It is only natural. I've done the same; it's how I got my new title of count! I gathered survivors here at Bled, looked for more, and eventually the Sun Kingdom found us. Now we all strive for the same goal, to survive and grow in this new world!"

"You joined them?" Carlito interjected. "I figured, with you being a vamp and all that, you would've wanted to be the one in charge."

"One thing that this world needs now is strength," the vampire count replied. "And King Proximus has that, even if he is just a human. But then again, Masks changed so much."

I blinked. That was a lot of information.

A vampire was following a human. I wondered why, I couldn't imagine a human being stronger than the count, but there was more to strength than just physical.

"Now," the count continued, "tell me more about your people! Who are your leaders? I'm very much interested in making contact. The Sun Kingdom is very keen on expanding and offering shelter to all the survivors we can find."

I narrowed my eyes. That sounded a lot like he was already thinking about absorbing us.

"Our leader is a vampire," Kai said. "Like you."

"Oh really?" the count added. "That is interesting. What is their name? Perhaps I know them, or have heard of them?"

Neither Carlito nor Kai answered immediately.

"Come now," the count said. "We're all friends here."

"We've come to make contact," Kai started, choosing her words carefully. "But we aren't the leaders of our group. We don't have the authority to divulge more than what we've said already. We really should return to our camp, inform our leaders, and set up a proper meeting. If you'll grant us leave, Master, we can reach the town by morning and have someone with more authority here by sundown tomorrow."

This was our fallback plan, in case things went south. And I could feel it veering in that direction.

"Nonsense!" The count raised his voice. "The wild is dangerous. We can't risk you dying on the way. You'll be our guests. I'll send a group that knows these woods. They'll contact your people and invite them to join us here."

I grimaced. I didn't know if this was genuine concern, or if he just wanted to have them here as bargaining chips. A way to negotiate from the place of power. It really could be genuine, but . . . They'd captured Aurora, so the way I viewed it was painted by that knowledge.

I wasn't going to let him keep them. Now, the question was did I intervene now, or wait and try to free them later.

"We apologize, Master," Kai said slowly, her voice laced with deference. "But we're under orders, I'm sure you understand."

The count chuckled, a dry, humorless sound that felt out of place in his tone of voice. There was no warmth in it at all. "Oh, I'm so sorry. I'm old, and sometimes I forget the silly notions you humans have." His voice turned glacial. "I wasn't asking. I was telling you what will happen."

And that was my cue. I wasn't going to let him speak with them like that. I grabbed the wall below me, making noise, and swung myself through the open window and into the room.

The vampire reacted immediately by straightening and taking a step back.

"No," I said. "That won't happen."

The human guard reacted instantly. He went for his gun, but my people were faster. They grabbed him and restrained him. Carlito leaned a dagger against his throat, to prevent any potential outcry.

"Well," the vampire count said, his eyes fixed on me. "I guess that we have more guests."

The room we were in was small, but opulent. Thick carpets lined the floor and decorative ones the walls. The furniture was sparse, but more because this seemed to be a receiving room of some kind. There was a large chair with a long back on one side, a sword leaned against one of its arms. It was raised on a platform, with a small table next to it. The count stood in front of that chair, holding a golden goblet filled with blood.

"You do," I said slowly as I reached up and pulled off my glasses and mask.

He was tall, with long black hair and a typical Slavic look. His eyes were pure blue, those of an Elder vampire of the Sky bloodline. He watched me warily, swirling the blood in his goblet.

"Guests usually enter through the front door," he observed, his voice smooth but laced with a subtle threat. "The manner through which you entered might make one assume that you had nefarious intentions."

I shrugged. "I had concerns, reasons to be wary of your group. Concerns that were proven right when you attempted to keep my people here against their will."

"Against their will? Not at all. I spoke the truth; they would've stayed as guests. But I guess that is not needed anymore. You would be their leader then?"

I narrowed my eyes at him, then inclined my head in confirmation.

The count didn't look afraid, merely thoughtful. He couldn't know anything about me, but my eyes revealed me as an Elder vampire, the same as him. "I thought that I knew all the Elders in the Americas," he mused. "I don't know you."

"I don't particularly care," I said, perhaps a bit more antagonistic than necessary, but I was still gauging the situation.

His eyes narrowed, a flicker of anger momentarily breaking through his carefully controlled facade. "There are rules, customs that you have already broken. Giving your name is the least you should do for barging into my home in this uncouth manner."

"Well, the world is changed," I countered. "The rules change with it. And besides, I follow no rules but my own."

"Surely we could be civil enough to introduce ourselves to each other properly?" He gave a fanged smile that held no warmth.

I thought about it, then decided that it didn't matter. "I'm Marianna Rojas."

He blinked, the tilted his head. "I've heard of you. Your name was on top of the list, and . . . de Andagoya mentioned you. Though he said that you're just a Fledgling."

I grimaced at the mention of my old Master, and I narrowed my eyes. When could he have had a chance to mention me? How did he even . . . I remembered what my sire told me. That my former Master headed north, trying to return to Europe. "He came this way?"

"He passed through a month ago with his coven. Just about the time when the first challenge arrived," the vampire said.

The urge to hunt him down, to make him pay for his betrayal . . . I pushed those thoughts aside. I had to focus on the matter at hand.

"Andagoya knows less than he thinks," I said, my voice firm.

"I can see that," the count said slowly. "I'm Cazimir Volkov, of the Carpathian Coven."

"Pleasure," I said.

"So, how may I help you?"

"I would have answers from you."

"Oh." Cazimir raised an eyebrow mechanically. "Brave to demand things in the heart of my castle, surrounded by my people."

I could hear people moving on the outside. Obviously someone had noticed my arrival. Perhaps there was another vampire in the castle. It didn't really matter. If there was one thing I was confident in, it was my strength.

I didn't really know what my sire had meant before when he said that I'll recognize my strength. Now, I knew. I could feel this vampire's **thirst**, and I knew that I was greater.

I shrugged in indifference. "You mean the people outside, preparing to charge in? They don't matter."

"Confident." Cazimir nodded. "I'm guessing that your Mask somehow advanced your maturity? Or you found something on other continents. Kirios, yes?"

My brows twitched.

"Yes." He smiled, a wooden expression that held no real emotion. "I know about . . . what were you called again? Exemplars? The way de Andagoya described your disappearance fits with you being taken. Luck shines on me today. Proximus will be glad to have another of you around."

"You seem to think that you have this all figured out," I said, my voice dangerously low.

He waved a dismissive hand. "Your eyes might reflect power, but there is more to being a vampire than that, and I can see that you are young. You don't carry yourself like someone who has lived for centuries. You don't speak like we do. You are . . . a child."

He shook his head. "Arrogance of youth, it is a shame. But I'm sure that I'll be able to beat it out of you eventually. The Sun Kingdom needs powerful people."

I couldn't help it. I laughed. A full-bodied laugh that echoed through the room, forcing me to brace my hands on my knees to keep from doubling over.

"Oh, that was good," I said once I managed to get myself under control. I raised my head and looked at the vampire. A spark of anger flashed over his face, but was quickly smothered, suppressed as all emotion was for vampires like him. "You speak of arrogance." I grinned widely at him, which I could tell unnerved him. "Yet you can't even imagine that you're the one that lacks information."

"You . . . you're in the grip of the **thirst**," Cazimir said slowly. "In the grip of your emotions. You're broken. Nadja!"

He yelled before I even had a chance to say anything. I realized that perhaps I shouldn't have pushed it that much. Vampires like him feared emotion, and those that fell under its grasp were fit only to be put down.

I forgot that.

The door behind me exploded open, and another vampire rushed in. Any chance of resolving this peacefully was over. But deep inside, I knew that this was what I had always wanted to happen. I craved this, a real test. And besides. They took Aurora. I couldn't let that slide.

I grinned and turned to meet the new threat.

Supremacy

The vampire that charged into the room was another Elder. She was tall, with dark red hair and golden eyes. She charged me, ignoring Kai and Carlito, who knew enough to jump to the side of the room against the wall, still holding the guard close and using him as a shield.

I turned to the new arrival. She wielded a small knife and was in the process of attempting to stab me. I moved faster than she expected and evaded her attack. I stepped in, grabbed her by the throat, then whirled around and chucked her through the wall, and out of the building.

I stepped, turning to mist and re-forming in front of Cazimir, who had retrieved the sword next to his chair, but hadn't managed to draw it yet. His eyes widened, and he tried to block me, but I was faster. I grabbed his head with my hand over his face, then threw him out of the hole I made with the other vampire.

I heard clicks, heard the powder igniting, gunshots fired, and I stepped aside, blurring across the room and evading. I stepped in front of the door as the surprised group of four human guards looked through the narrow doors. I reached out in a blur of movement and squeezed the barrels of their guns, ruining them. Then I kicked the first and sent them all to the ground.

I turned away from the door, then glanced at Kai and Carlito. "Take care of them." I nodded at the hallway outside.

It would be good practice for them. The hallway was narrow from what I could see, and they wouldn't be able to get surrounded. And from what I felt, the guards outside were probably not even in their First Investment.

Carlito pulled his dagger off the throat of the guard in his hands, then smacked him in the temple. He grinned as he dropped the unconscious man to the ground and dashed for the doors.

"Try not to kill anyone!" I yelled after him, then gave Kai a look. She nodded and moved to follow.

I walked over to the hole in the wall and jumped down into the courtyard. There were screams from the people that had been eating dinner on one side, a rush as they tried to get away through the small castle doors.

The two vampires had gotten on their feet and were waiting for me.

I grinned, a predatory expression that stretched across my face, fangs fully extended. "Finally," I purred, the thrill of the impending battle coursing through my veins. The **thirst** was singing. "I haven't had a real test in a while."

The woman snarled at me. "You dare trespass in our domain, upstart? And mock us?"

"Upstart?" I scoffed. "Lady, you have no idea who you're dealing with." I turned my gaze to Cazimir, who was watching the exchange with a detached expression. "As for mocking you," I continued, my voice dripping with sarcasm, "well, is the truth really mocking?"

Cazimir's expression turned into a blank mask. "Enough with the games," he said, his voice hardening as he pulled his sword out of its sheath. "Nadja."

The redheaded vampire launched herself at me again, this time with far more caution. Her movements were smooth and swift, fitting for any Elder vampire. There was no wasted movement in her attacks, no emotion, just pure, maximized skill.

I pulled Shadow's dagger from my lower back and settled in the Azure Moon Style, meeting her assault with an effortless grace, letting fear guide me as I blocked her strikes, letting her draw blood with her blade, and then retaliated. Her speed was impressive, but I was faster. My fear gave me insight, allowing me to anticipate her moves before she even made them. I parried her blows, my own strikes landing with a force that sent shockwaves through the courtyard.

Cazimir joined the fray, his sword a blur in the moonlight. He was skilled, I'd grant him that, but his attacks lacked the raw power that I possessed. I danced around their combined assault, a predator toying with its prey. It felt exhilarating. These were some of the best that my world had to offer. And I was stronger.

Then both of them stepped back, disengaging. They looked at me, and Cazimir frowned. A moment later he pulled out a vial filled with purple liquid, and Nadja followed his actions.

I frowned, and they downed the vials in an instant.

Their bodies bulged, their skin straining against the muscles beneath.

"Uh, what the—"

Cazimir charged, moving far faster than before. His sword blurred, an imprint in the Way that surprised me. Instead of a single attack, I was met with three slices that cut through my arm from three different angles.

I cursed and stepped back, but Nadja dashed forward, her body blurring, almost teleporting, as her speed soared.

I grimaced. I had gotten too engrossed in the fight and lost ground. I focused as Nadja came in, swiping with her dagger at my throat, then I released [Terror Grasp].

Her eyes widened, her body locked for a second, and I backhanded her across the courtyard, smashing her through a wall of another building. I cursed as I felt the bones in my hand groan. Her skull felt like iron.

Before I had the chance to turn around, Cazimir was there, his blade flashing dangerously close to my face. He was almost as fast as me now. Whatever he had taken boosted him. He almost felt like he could match me now, which was insane. I couldn't explain it, except to say that he was better than me. Better in how he used his body, how he moved.

"Perhaps we underestimated you," Cazimir called, his sword cutting up my shoulder. "But you are clearly inexperienced."

Nadja appeared next to me, as if she had always been there. She surprised me. I wasn't accustomed to foes getting back up when I threw them through walls. But these were Elder vampires, I had to remind myself, and they healed almost as well as I did. The moment her dagger touched my side, I twisted away, striking blindly with my own dagger at full speed. Her eyes widened, and she leaned back as my blade cut open her cheek.

I had to adapt.

[Mist Step]

I appeared behind Cazimir and attacked. He whirled, blocking, but my strength pushed him back. I danced around him, attacking as I switched to Scarlet Moon Style. Five steps after, I turned to mist again.

I wove in between the two of them, attacking with no regard for defense, letting my blood spill across the ground as I turned to mist with every fifth step, and filled the area with mist.

Then, I triggered [Mistshroud]. Hidden by the mist, I suddenly felt everything that the mist touched. I knew where the two vampires were. Cazimir stood near one of the buildings, a wall to his back.

Nadja was—she teleported. One moment she was in the center of the yard, and in the next she was in front of me. Somehow, she could detect me.

Her hand blurred with a skill and pierced my chest, straight through my heart, her arm and blade punching through until it was buried in my chest and the blade left my back.

"Got you!" Nadja whispered, her eyes gleaming with triumph.

That was it. My patience snapped. I burned my blood with my Bloodcast ring, once, then twice. Scarlet steam rose from my skin as blood inside my body evaporated, as I layered in the [My Blood, Surge For Power] skill. My strength soared. A wave of cold fury washed over me, eclipsing the thrill of the fight. I grabbed Nadja by the throat, lifting her effortlessly off the ground, her eyes widening.

A wound such as what she had inflicted would've put me down, if I was still a Fledgling. An Adult would've been crippled, but could survive a few minutes. An Elder would've survived for hours and healed from it. Me? I barely felt it.

"You shouldn't have done that," I growled, my voice low and dangerous. Her eyes bored into mine, realizing her mistake. She struggled, but my grip was unbreakable. I ripped her arm out of my chest, pulling it out of its socket in the process. My heart regenerated in five seconds flat. I grinned at her, then I took a step next to the cliff.

"You . . . you wouldn't dare . . ." she stammered, her voice choked.

I smirked, a cruel twist of my lips. "Oh, wouldn't I? Have a nice swim."

I chucked her off the mountain, sending her hurtling through the air and straight into the lake below. Her scream wasn't of fear, but rage. I laughed.

I turned back to Cazimir, who hadn't moved from his position. He had obviously heard everything, but the mist was thick around us. He couldn't see.

I moved, each step sure and refined, I danced.

[**Scarlet Moon Style**; Dance of the Shifting Mist]

The mist whirled, following my will. Cazimir jerked as it condensed around him, as it pushed through his nostrils and into his lungs. He coughed, then clawed at his throat. I dropped [Mistshroud] and let my control go. The mist slowly dissipated as I dashed over to Cazimir. With a swift strike, I cut his sword arm, removing it at the wrist and making him drop his weapon.

Then, as he was confused, I grabbed with both arms and raised him up before smashing him against the ground, cracking the stone and shaking the mountain. Somewhere behind me, something cracked and collapsed, but I wasn't paying much attention.

I stomped on his chest, pressing down with all of my weight. He grunted, his eyes staring up at me.

"Who are you?" he whispered.

I pulled on the **thirst**, and I shifted. Wings grew out of my back, and my skin turned blue.

"I am *The Star That Dances in Blood Beneath the Light of the Broken Moon.* I am the blood of Asza, the blood of Ji."

His eyes widened. He looked down at my foot, ready to crush his ribcage to paste. He gulped audibly, then nodded. "That . . . answers some questions. Uh . . . Master."

I raised an eyebrow, then leaned down and whispered into his ear. "Well, now it is my turn for questions, and answers. You've captured a woman by the name of Aurora, blond hair, quirky, can move the earth."

Cazimir blinked, his eyes growing confused. "I . . . how did you—"

"Know?" I interrupted. "Well, you see, she's my friend, and she is why I'm here."

I could see him struggling to absorb that information, his brow furrowed in concentration. He opened his mouth to speak, but then we were interrupted.

"Stop!" a loud voice called. The stomping of feet followed and then the shuffle of guns being pointed my way. "Release the count, or we'll shoot."

I turned my head, moving a wing out of the way so that I could see. On the other side of the courtyard stood a group of humans with weapons pointed in my direction.

I raised an eyebrow, and noticed a glint of something silver in the sky above. Then, a blaze of orange flames came down from above, gouging a line in between me and the humans. They screamed in fear, stumbled backward from the heat.

And then Saia's large form dropped onto the molten stone with a thud.

"Now you make it work? Really?" I asked her.

Saia's head turned in my direction.

"Feedback: My repair of the engram was actually ahead of my projections."

I nearly growled, but then shook my head and turned to look at the bewildered vampire beneath my feet.

"Now, how about you show me where my friend is, and then we can talk about the future?"

He nodded rapidly, and I stepped back, releasing him.

I looked around at the destroyed yard and hummed to myself. For my first conquest, this wasn't bad, not bad at all.

Aurora was being held in one of the rooms in the central building. I stood next to her bed as a nervous human fed her an antidote for the sleeping concoction that they had been using to keep her asleep, because . . . well, a Mask that can shape stone in a castle made out of stone. It was probably a smart thing they did.

Cazimir had been very helpful, almost subservient since he saw me shift and since he heard who my sire was. I caught him staring at me with wide eyes when he thought I wasn't looking. Thankfully, the people here were all loyal to him, and once he submitted they did too. Nadja had made her way up the mountain, soaking wet, and was glaring at me from far away. Cazimir talked with her briefly, telling her that our fight was over.

Kai and Carlito had bashed a few heads, gotten a few cuts and one gunshot wound, but they were fine. Carlito was already laughing with the guards he had stabbed to all hell, so I guess I didn't have to worry too much.

Though, I was told that there were some people loyal to this King Proximus down in the town. But I could deal with that later.

For now, Aurora was more important.

She woke slowly, blinking rapidly.

"That's my teddy," she mumbled as she hugged a pillow and tried to turn back to sleep.

I rolled my eyes and walked over. I pulled the covers from her, then shook her, perhaps just a little bit too rough. "Rise and shine, sleeping beauty!"

She jerked, then sat up in an instant, her eyes alert and her arm raised as if to throw a punch. She looked up at me and paused.

"Mari?"

"You couldn't stay out of trouble, could you?" I grinned at her.

She looked from me to the other people in the room then back. Finally, she sighed. "Ugh, I can't believe you saved me. I'm going to have to suffer through the humiliation of hearing all about it constantly, aren't I?"

My grin widened, turned more predatory. "I mean, probably."

She groaned and threw herself back onto the bed. "Kill me now."

I laughed and felt lighter. I found my friend, and she was safe, I beat up a couple of vampires and took over their castle and probably people. Things were looking up. There even was a kingdom and a king for me to look forward to beating into submission.

My little empire was about to start to grow.

Epilogue - It Ends, It Begins

Andrew Carter sat in the chilly laboratory in what used to be a dungeon, deep beneath Hohenwerfen Castle. He started at his alembic as he distilled the strange liquid he'd been given. Apparently, it was a reward from one of the rifts, and when used it killed the person drinking it.

Now, it was Andrew's job to figure out why. His [Document Trait] skill had told him that its properties had something to do with the Source. His hypothesis was that the draught was intended for Mage-related Masks, as a way to replenish a resource they spent to use Source-related skills.

But he wasn't certain.

A loud groaning noise alerted him to a visitor. Andrew didn't turn around. Footsteps approached him, then stopped a few steps behind him. Andrew's hand twitched toward his drawer and the vial sitting there. After a moment, he sighed and pulled back. He turned, jumped off the stool he was sitting on, mindful of the chain tied to his ankle, and glared at his visitor.

"What do you want?" Andrew asked with a tired voice.

"Is that any way to speak to your king?"

Andrew just continued to glare without answering. The tall, blond figure that looked like he was sculpted by God's hand just sighed.

"Must you act like this every time, Andrew?" the king asked, his tone level and regal, his posture perfect. His clothes were immaculate, and his hair was pulled back behind his ears and framed by the crown on his head.

"Why don't you try being chained up in a dungeon, and forced to work with barely any rest, and see how you'll act then, Proximus?"

His visitor just shook his head. "I thought you understood. We are all answering to a greater calling. You, as an Exemplar, should understand it more than any other. We must unite the land and people, stand against the danger on its way."

"I don't need to hear your speeches, Proximus. I'm not one of your zealots or a poor soul searching for a light in this dark world. Please spare me the theatrics."

Proximus's entire demeanor changed. His eyes darkened, and his entire aura turned foreboding.

"If that is what you wish, Andrew, I can make things harder for you."

Andrew had to bite his tongue to prevent himself from speaking.

Proximus kept his intense gaze on Andrew the whole time, just waiting for a word. Finally, he nodded.

"We need another batch of Dusk."

Andrew grimaced. "I just delivered one this morning."

"We are sending more groups out to search for survivors, and we have two new rift hunter squads. I also just received a letter from Cazimir. His people need a refill."

"You know how difficult it is," Andrew started. "I can't keep doing this. You want me to make you Dusk, and you also want me to experiment and make new things. I'm stretched too thin."

"We are all sacrificing for the greater good. You have two days."

Andrew struggled not to say anything. He already knew what the result would be.

Proximus looked at him for a few more seconds, then nodded and turned around, leaving him all alone.

Andrew sighed and slumped onto his stool. He felt exhausted, and not just from being overworked, but because of Proximus's presence. His Mask was oppressive. It forced people to listen, to follow.

He turned back to his table, then pulled his drawer out. The vial filled with golden liquid taunted him. If only he had the courage to use it.

He pushed the drawer closed and turned his attention back to his work.

In Asha Kai-ni, in the land of always mist, the strongest Oni-yi clans had come together to discuss the upcoming expeditions. Portals would open across their continent, in unknown locations. Portals that would lead to new lands, new resources, new challenges.

The gathered clans discussed how they would divide the portals, and who they would send. Each portal could only handle a certain amount of power passing through it. And the more Invested a person was, the more of that power they spent when they passed through.

A single portal might be able to handle three hundred First Investment Masked going through, or just a hundred Second Investment. The precise numbers changed from Expansion Interval to Interval, but all knew that distributing that power was important.

"A single Fifth Investment Warrior of our Clan will be enough to protect one entire expedition," a burly Oni-yi said, his voice booming through the tent.

Another Oni-yi, Bellows of Clan Roiling Mist, cleared his throat. "I do not doubt the might of Clan Red Fist, Anger, but a Fifth Investment Masked will mean a lot less support people going through."

"And so what?" Anger of the Red Fist questioned. "We know that this new world possesses powerful beings that can shapeshift into animals like the Elven druids, but without the need for their totems. We need a powerful presence of our own. Even the other continent has their own champions, the Simmering River Clan reported that the Suul have powerful members, these Speakers of the Ancients."

The knowledge gained from the Terran and Suul Exemplar was confusing, but many present at this meeting had witnessed the shifters' power, respected it even. The Suul were more a mystery, but they would send an expedition there as well. The more land they could gain, the more they could grow their clans.

"Bah," another voice announced itself. The oldest of them present, The Mighty Rock of the Mist Upon Which the Tide Breaks, waved his hand in a dismissive gesture.

"Stop worrying about who and how many we'll send. And start worrying about how we'll get all the portals on Asha Kai-ni for our people."

"With respect, old one, but who would dare steal from the clans? The Kitsu-oi?" Anger asked then laughed, prompting a few other Oni-yi to laugh with him.

"The Kitsu-oi have been moving lately, but it is not them I worry about. It is the Southern Kingdoms. They've been quiet for too long. This could be an opportunity for them to strike."

The Oni-yi present grimaced. The Southern Kingdoms were their greatest shame. The land of YoKai-ni, held by outsiders and traitors. The kingdoms where Elves and Dwarves lived on a land stolen centuries ago through invasion. The YoKai-ni who lived among them, abandoning their true heritage in the pursuit of coexistence, were the worst kind of traitors.

"They wouldn't dare," Anger said.

"Perhaps," Mighty said. "But we should be vigilant."

At that, all of them nodded.

Their discussion turned back to the distribution of power for the portals.

None of them noticed a tiny little drawn creature crawling across the ground, its body painted with a brush and colored in the bleak hues of the ground.

On a mountain, three valleys away, a Kitsu-oi sat and listened from atop her sitting pillow as she held a canvas and a brush.

The Cruel Mist That Lurks in the Deep Shadows of Old Tree Beneath the Light of the Broken Moon chuckled at the Oni-yi plots. They were such simple creatures, Stealing a portal from them would be hardly a challenge.

The presence of The Mighty Rock of the Mist Upon Which the Tide Breaks was problematic, though she had a few paintings that could fool even the old bastard.

Regardless, it was going to be the most fun she'd had in ages. She couldn't wait to meet her new daughter.

In the center of the cratered and irradiated wasteland that used to be called Texas, something pushed on the fabric of the world that connected reality to the Way itself. A flicker of red pulsed through the world, and then a tear opened up.

A realm filled with all the colors in existence spilled through, an echo of the Way. The colors were imbalanced, harsher colors glowed brighter, with red being the predominant one.

The display of color lasted for only a short period, before something stepped through. It was a tall being, walking on two legs, with two arms, and two black wings on its back. Its skin was deep blue, its hair like midnight. Emerald eyes glowed out of their sockets, then flashed to red as deep as the blazing heart of rage. It turned its eyes to the two moons shining above.

"Ah . . ." It sighed. "The turning comes again. I've waited for so long . . . Will I see you again at last? Pandemonium beckons us all. Perhaps you'll make the right choice this time."

The being looked around, then picked a direction and started walking, it was not in a rush. It would reach where it needed to be. The True Way demanded it.

On Ish Vimza, in the deepest parts of the jungle, in the core of what had once been the great Vim Empire, a detection net recorded the breach of the fabric of the world, detected a familiar presence.

A protocol was triggered, and the single living occupant of the bunker was woken up.

The mechanical triggers turned, and the being entombed in the suit of machinery and metal death woke up.

"Brother," a mechanical voice spoke from within the monstrosity of metal, breaking the silence that had lasted for an age beyond counting. From within the vessel, a being of flesh almost fully withered and broken by age and time opened its eyes. Emerald light shone through the gap in the vessel, and it moved. Its mind moved metal limbs, filling the room with the sound of pistons and gears. The flesh hurt, and suspended in its harness, hooked up to hundreds of wires and tubes, the being pushed through the agony of its existence. "Time comes." It spoke as it stood, information downloaded directly into its mind.

"Ten, ten, ten," it repeated, mind lost in the memories. "Failure. Six. Khanum. Six. Forgive us."

It lumbered down the corridors that had long since collapsed, tearing a new path through, blowing apart the mountain it was buried under by bending the Source to its will, a Mask permanently bonded to its ruined face.

Hours later, it burst from beneath the ground, and stepped into the light cast by the moons above, its silver form dirty and marred with an age worth of marks, each earned in combat, repaired over and over again.

The being tried to connect to the satellite above but found nothing there to respond. "Failure. Failure."

It started walking, following the only signal it had access to. "Brother, Sadness, The First Turning Comes."

"I—I . . . I come, Mother," it said as it walked through the blighted lands of the inner ring of Ish Vimza, its direction turned straight for the newest continent on Kirios.

"Sacrifice awaits on Terra. Home that is not Home."

About the Author

Ivan Kal is the author of Vae Victis, an apocalypse LitRPG series originally released on Royal Road. He has been writing for over a decade and, in addition to producing his web serial, has published more than thirty books on Amazon. His other interests include martial arts, computers, and gaming. Visit his website at www.ivan-kal.com.

Podium